Rise of the Lost

FALL OF KINGS

RIELY O'SULLIVAN

 FriesenPress

One Printers Way
Altona, MB R0G 0B0
Canada

www.friesenpress.com

ISBN
978-1-03-912175-1 (Hardcover)
978-1-03-912174-4 (Paperback)
978-1-03-912176-8 (eBook)

1. FICTION, FANTASY, ACTION & ADVENTURE

Distributed to the trade by The Ingram Book Company

Rise of the Lost

FALL OF KINGS

The Blood of Brothers

S ome would call them scars, but to Ivan, they are memories—
memories of pain. They are reminders of the slow and scorching heat that boiled the blood under his skin. It could have been
three days, maybe even a week; Ivan had lost count. The sun would
not peer through the thick veil of mist too often, and when it did, it
only intensified the pain. Thus, each man began to fear the sun, to
fear its yellow face that weaved its light through the labyrinth of mist
and fog that hid them in the mountains. They were prisoners. They
were all prisoners. Ivan and his crew had hit land roughly a month
ago, but it didn't take long till their arrival in this strange and alien
land was noticed. Their captors were strange, their ears were pointed
upwards, and their faces were sallow and angular. Thankfully, they
resembled something at least humanoid, for there was much in this
eerie land that could not be explained: strange shapes and creatures
that brutally contradicted any formal notion of normality that they
had all once possessed. It was an old land, full of pain and sorrow.
Ivan and his crew could see it in their captors' eyes as if their torture

were somehow personal. It was the land of Medearia . . . and nothing could have prepared them for a place like this.

The sun climbed high into the sky, reaching its zenith, and its light began to pierce the armour of the cloud that protected the Pools. Ivan could barely stay awake. The torment was simply too much. The pulsing burns from the water shot searing pain at each point in his body. The old burns were now bathed in a fresh coat of pus from the oncoming infection. Underneath the leaking facade of pus was nothing more than bare, sunken flesh that had grown numb from the monotony of pain. Each of the dozen men had been tied to a cross that shot out from the middle of the boiling pools, and if the water didn't kill them over time, the fumes certainly would. However, the toxic air that choked them until they fell into the scorching depths of the water seemed like a merciful death. But *they* kept them alive. Each day a few dozen of them in full armour would walk down from the mountains to lower each wooden cross till the men were down to their necks, and those who were lucky passed out from shock. But alas, there were those who held onto consciousness through it all, and their screams filled each crack and crevice of the mountain pass with a shivering terror, like a ghastly wail of a wolf on a frozen winter night. The creatures would arrive at any moment, and Ivan and his crew would then be forced to endure the same torture as the day before, but Ivan no longer feared the water; he instead simply accepted it now. He then felt the tug, the tension of the pulleys at work, and he knew they had come, he knew there would be new scars.

"No! Please, I beg of you, stop it!" screamed Robert, who had seen no more than sixteen summers, nothing more than a child. Ivan looked over at the boy. He was a mess: his skin was red and swollen, and his burns were somewhat worse than the others'. They could barely recognize the poor boy now. His hair had fallen out, and his scalp looked nearly inhuman as only a few strands of hair now shot out from his skull, for his flesh was now too burnt for anything to grow. "Please, LET ME GO! I—I'll tell you anything, anything, you hear me?" yelled Robert, but it was in vain. There was no answer. "Oh mother, help me," said the boy as he wept, "save me from this cruelty . . . I . . . I want my mother!" Ivan wanted to tell the boy she was coming and that she would be there for him soon enough, but he couldn't. He knew there was no hope left for them, and his lips were too cracked and dehydrated to move. Robert's toes began to slowly plunge into the boiling water, and thus the bone-chilling cries began: a shriek so innocent and horrid it brought tears to Ivan's eyes. "Mother! OH GOD, MOTHER!" It was then that the child's cries curled into a shriek that could not be identified as words, only the pure product of pain.

The Pools now were thick boiling soups of burnt and rotten flesh, and what once was crystal clear water now had turned into a thick broth, red with blood. The stench of death and disease was heavy in the air. Ivan reached out his hand as if in one last feeble attempt to comfort the boy, but Robert still writhed violently until the ropes that bound him to the cross began to rip and tear at his already wounded skin.

"Please, someone help! I WANT TO GO HOME! I WANT TO GO H—" Before the young boy could finish his plea, his head stooped forward and hung over his chest as his hands grasped his heart. He had died. The pain had been too much.

Ivan waited in the long silence before his plunge, and in his lethargic state, he looked at the boy's body; he gazed into the child's baby blue eyes that sat there, staring into the hateful void of the world. As Ivan stared at Robert's lifeless body that hung there far away from home, far from the benevolent grip of his mother's arms, something broke inside of him. How could any creature do this to another? It mattered little now, for he now began his descent into the cauldron of death, and he could feel the red hue of the water glare back at him with eyes of malice: a boiling red liquid that was the child of pain and was born through the deaths of his brothers.

Ivan awoke with a scream. As he rose, he rolled onto his side, forgetting about his burns; it had been more than a nightmare—it was a memory. The tall trees of the woods swayed to and fro to the evening breeze. The melodious wind ran through the underbrush, sending a chill through the air. Sitting all the way up, he then shuffled his body closer to the fire to warm himself from the bitter cold of the night.

"What's the matter?" asked Baldwyn from across the fire.

"Nothing. It was nothing but a dream," said Ivan.

"What about?"

"If I told you in detail you would regret wanting to know."

"Try me."

"It was of the Pools and of Robert," said Ivan, and there was a long, awkward pause. Baldwyn fiddled with his grey beard as if contemplating a thought or memory he hadn't wanted to ponder over, and yet he did. He thought of the scars that painted his body in deformed flesh, scars that he would carry as a reminder for the rest of his life. The reminder that had been branded into his mind by fire—they should have never set foot on the shores of Medearia.

"Poor boy," said Baldwyn, "seventeen, was he?"

"Sixteen," replied Ivan, "and we led him to his death." Both men then sat silent, smoking their pipes in sorrow, smelling the aroma of burnt pine and cedar, listening to the breath of the wind wheezing in their ears and the crackling snaps of the fire's embers. The moon smiled up above, and its light fell upon the forest like rain. Their burnt and rugged flesh lay hidden by their cloaks, yet even then the wind ran a chill upon their wounds, and both men winced.

"We're still being hunted, Ivan. They've undoubtedly been gaining on us since our escape from those wretched mountains. We should set out again to the boat before dawn," said Baldwyn.

"Agreed. Although, that is assuming the boat is still there. Face it, my friend, there is little hope of us ever making it home."

"There never was. But this is what we signed up for when we chose to follow you, friend. If we do nothing, we will die. Our bodies will never be buried on home soil, which I'm fine with. My wife would most likely piss on my grave the moment she got the chance," said Baldwyn with a laugh. "Lighten up there, lad! Nothing, in my mind at least, could be worse than dying with a piss-poor frown on your face. Let's have a drink before we hunker back down again, shall we?"

"Fine. Vodka?"

"Nothing but." At that, a shy smile crept onto Ivan's face that could be seen through his long, dark hair, and Baldwyn chuckled and passed the bottle. "First swig's yours." Ivan leaned back with the bottle, taking only a couple of gulps before passing it back over. "Burns, doesn't it?"

"It does, but it gets the job done, at least," said Ivan. Both men then snickered before retiring back to the cover of their thin sheets to shield them from the night.

Ivan awoke just before dawn to see Baldwyn up and ready.

"Stay here," said Baldwyn. "I'm going to get a look ahead to see if the boat is still there. I'll be back before midday." Ivan found himself too tired to argue, and slowly drifted back to sleep.

When Ivan awoke, a grey gloom gripped the air, and he could feel the rain coming. Pine trees stood erect all about him, yet he could only see so far as a body of fog had fallen low onto the forest floor. The morning environment was all too eerie for Ivan's liking. The unshakeable notion of being watched haunted his every thought, and every minute movement was done with the consciousness of the possibility of an arrow through the throat. The smouldering vestiges of embers from the night's fire still burned ever so slightly, and the stench of warm charcoal greeted Ivan's senses as he sat up. Old and withered pine needles stuck themselves to the blanket that Ivan had cocooned himself in, and as quickly as he had awoken, he set off to pack his belongings. Once what little they had was packed away, he stooped low and began a surreptitious walk into the woods. The impenetrable fog made it nearly impossible to identify his surroundings. The terrifying and unbreakable paranoia of eyes watching him was constant in Ivan's mind. The sun was difficult to find through the fog, but midday could not be far off, and he could expect Baldwyn to return at any moment.

Only a hundred meters ahead, the plateau on which he stood dropped into a valley that led to the sea, and Ivan slowly crept and made his way to the cliff. It was silent, too silent for his liking. As he came closer and closer to the cliff's edge, the fog began to fade and shift with the distant gales from the south. The green valley below took form before him, and not too far over the sea of green forest, the ocean spread its blue arms along the edges of the horizon. A streak of lighting then painted the sky and was followed by a tumultuous roar of thunder. The clouds above him then darkened, and rain began to drip down from the heavens, slowly getting heavier and heavier. But behind him, the thick body of fog was still present. Ivan turned towards it, and it smiled back. Suddenly, there was a crack of a branch that broke the silence, and then there was a scream. And then there was nothing. Ivan rushed back into the jaws of the woods, and as he did so, he began to feel as if his mind was spinning in a perpetual dance with a hidden foe.

"Baldwyn," said Ivan in a hoarse whisper. There was no response . . . only blood. Scarlet droplets of bodily fluids dripped onto Ivan's forehead, and he looked above in horror, but there was nothing, only a dense sheet of white that seemed as if it was alive. Ivan still gazed upwards to the sky and after some time in the realm of pernicious silence, the fog was broken, and the body of Baldwyn came hurling down from a nearby tree. He had been hung by his neck. Ivan fell back in terror as the lifeless eyes of his friend greeted him. However, each limb was missing, and red heaps of muscles and tendons hung out from his wounds, and a wide pool of blood rested beneath him. Ivan could not speak. He could only run. Sprinting through the underbrush like a wild banshee, Ivan ran through the maze of woods that bathed in an ocean of fog and mist in search of any path that could lead him to the sea. He often stopped, second-guessing his way and turning to another, yet all the time the malicious laughter of an ominous threat that could not be seen could be heard above as if mocking his every step. A wide organic path hugged against the cliff's edge, weaving to and fro in a broken pattern until it reached the valley, and to the north of Ivan, a towering waterfall vomited its liquid down into the valley's heart. Ivan knew if he could follow the river, he would make it back. Three men, Gerald, Earl, and Martin had been left behind on the boat on the day of their arrival, and Ivan prayed, prayed to any gods who were kind enough to listen that they had survived and had kept the ship free from the enemy's grip, but the chances were slim. Onwards Ivan ran down the path that glided slowly down into the arms of the valley. He oftentimes lost his footing on the various screes and rolled until he could grab a hold of something firm. The path grew steep and narrow, and its edges became loose, as if it would take a mere wrong step for the whole cliff edge to tumble down. Ivan slowed his pace. He stopped, listening for any pursuer. But then it came to him—he could hear nothing, not a sound, not even the faintest of movement in the forest above. These creatures had stalked their every footstep since their escape from the Pools, and for some unimaginable reason, they would not strike, not yet, not until they had played with their food until they were satisfied. They would not kill until they knew that *it* had suffered. And indeed, every man that had followed Ivan on this foolish expedition east had suffered beyond their previous idea of the definition of the term. They now knew what true pain and despair looked like. It looked like Robert's eyes as his heartbeat slowed and stagnated until it was lifeless; it felt like the boiling pools of death that smouldered and scorched the skin until their flesh bubbled underneath. Ivan bent over and caught his breath. As he turned to start his flight again, he stepped forward, expecting the firm texture of the rock beneath him to hold his step, but the ground did not stay true, and it did not hold. The edge of the path crumbled, taking Ivan with him. He fell. His body writhed in the air like some lifeless doll being tortured by its owner, and soon the inclined edge of the rock wall met with his feeble legs. Ivan heard a snap that rang through his entire body as his limbs condensed against the surface of the cliff. He rolled and tumbled in a perpetual spin as he plummeted to the valley. He saw the world as nothing but a blur in his descent as if it was nothing but a wet painting that some child had smeared his hand across. Suddenly an unsettling sensation clapped against his skull, and then all was dark.

Ivan awoke beside the river, and his legs were broken. The adrenaline that surged through his body numbed the pain, yet still the dull pulsing feeling of shattered limbs coursed through his very veins. His head lay softly on a pillow of moss, and before Ivan came to his senses, he lay there, listening to the soft moaning of the river and the constant chirps and songs of birds. He tried to move his body, but a paroxysm of pain jolted through his nerves, and the cold and cruel realization of his immobility throttled his mind. He would die. He knew it. There was no chance of making it to the ship in his current condition, and it seemed as if the fears of dying here, away from the love of one's mother, forgotten by the rest of the world, would become a heartless reality. And instead of fighting to grasp the last fleeing strand of life, Ivan accepted to look upon the face of death . . . and he allowed his eyes to close.

But then he felt it. He could feel the cool touch of steel against his throat. He opened one eye to see an arrow pointing towards him, and a fiendish creature staring into his dying eyes with its yellow irises. The creature would not move, nor did any evident sign of emotion slip through its slender lips. It gazed into the man's eyes with a disciplined and solemn focus, and it was then that Ivan felt another thud on his head, and a thick black rag veiled his vision.

Ivan awoke once more with toxic fumes biting at his lungs. He didn't have to see it—he could already smell it, he could smell the foul air, and he could feel the heat cooking his skin. He was back again at the Pools, alone in the desolation of terror that they offered. His hands were once again bound to the cross that was erected in the middle of the water, and before him, the bodies of his friends and brothers in arms tumbled and rolled in the boiling cauldron of death, falling beneath the water's surface only to emerge again. Surrounding the Pools were the creatures, their yellow eyes studying his naked body, too haughty and pompous to blink, yet their gaze was that of hatred. They watched in silence. Tears filled the crevices of Ivan's eyes, and his head sank low in despair. He had failed. The grand escape had come to ruin. He would never leave this wretched place; he knew it deep down in his heart. But even as Ivan wept, he knew he would not rest until he was free, free from their loathing grip. He would not stop until Ederia was nigh. Until he was once again . . . *home.*

A Portrait of a King

The mountain pass was frigid that morning. Cool droplets of dew rested upon the blades of grass like tears of a glacier. Cornelius wrapped himself tightly in his cloak, and the black ends of the wolf hide that curled around his neck protected him from the frozen dawn. In his hand, he held a vase that carried three violet flowers—they were for her, they were for Iris. Cornelius, the king of Ederia, marched forth on the path, and as he turned the corner into a small meadow that overlooked the city, he began to see others that had already made the great climb up the Wyvern Mountains. The meadow rested just below the two peaks of the mountain, and those who the king had allowed to come stood there in silence with their heads pointed towards the ground, yet all faced the casket that had been laid before the cliff's edge beside an oak tree. The tree itself was ancient and served as the warden of those who had passed. Iris lay in the casket, and as Cornelius approached, the pale and lifeless face of his beloved wife poisoned his heart. What once had been a face so beautiful and full of love had become as white as a lost lily flower in a black pond. She had been a crimson rose that had been caressed by the wrath of death and thus turned white with sorrow.

Cornelius's hands trembled as his fingers cuddled against her cheekbone. He almost hoped that in this last long moment of silence, her eyes would open, and her lips would curl into a cute smile as they had always done. But it was in vain. She was dead. There was no expression, and no hint of love in her eyes, and she was cold, so very cold. Cornelius almost felt as if he had been enchanted by some northern spell of bitterness that chilled his body to the very marrow in his bones. A tear fell from his eyes, a tear that clashed against the perfect skin of his wife, like a child nudging at the dead body of its mother in one last attempt to feel her love again. Yet still, all was in vain.

The wind sang a song of melancholy as if it too felt the pain Cornelius bore within. And its tune whistled through the twin peaks of the mountains, swaying the grass of the field. All then watched as their king laid the flowers in the hands of their queen, shaping and maneuvering each finger until they clasped the flowers perfectly. Cornelius rubbed his eyes and wiped them clean of tears. He was a king, the king of Ederia, and no king, nor man for that matter, could be caught shedding tears.

"May you tread softly under the waves as you sink into the sea. My time of judgment is almost upon me," whispered Cornelius. Stepping back, he found himself reluctant to leave knowing he would never see her face again. But it was too late. The casket began its descent into the ground that gaped wide like a dark, gluttonous mouth with teeth of rock and veins of roots. Cornelius held an unfathomable amount of power just in his voice, and for some reason, he could not find it in him to speak, to tell them to halt and let him gaze at her beautiful eyes once more. He could not; he knew she was no more. And thus, the greatest fear of Cornelius Helladawn took a hold of him, like a cruel taste of reality: he would soon forget what she looked like. He would lose the memory of her face, the sweet and soft bridge of her cheeks, the tenderness of her lips, the feeling of running his fingers through her raven-coloured hair, and the sound of her voice seeping into his mind like honey on a summer afternoon. Cornelius then mustered his strength, and a sternness came to his tone. "Where are my sons?" asked the king.

"They are here," said Julias from the crowd, and by his side stood two boys no older than ten. Both wept and dug their faces into Julias's cloak, attempting to hide their tears. Cornelius squatted down.

"Come closer!" said Cornelius. The boys, almost frightened, obeyed and went to their father. Cornelius placed his palms on the backs of their heads and embraced them. "Do not cry, Cassius, and do not weep, Vidicus," said the king with a sigh. "We men do not cry. We love and we hate, these are true. But you, the princes of House Helladawn, do not weep. It is not your mother's wish to bless us with sadness with her passing. We shall begin the journey back to Ekmere, and I will teach you boys what being a prince truly means."

✳

Cornelius looked over the sprawling city of Ekmere. The smoky-white houses of stone and dark rooftops dotted the twin peninsulas of western Casthedia, and the port was congested with many ships that boasted their red silk sails. "The Jewel of the West," it was called by many—the largest city of men in the known world. Thither the roots of the city made their way for miles upon miles, embracing the edge of the sea and onward unto the shielding shadow of the Wyvern Peaks, where hamlets took residence. To the north, small creeks ran through the hamlets as if they were the veins of the mountain. As the sun rose, creeks, rivers, and oceans began to twinkle as it climbed into the sky. The early songs of the birds could be heard from far away treetops, smells of lilac and frigid morning dew emanated from the royal gardens, and the shapeless grey void of the valley took form as the sun spread its arms of euphoria, cloaking the valley in soft golden light. As the sun began its ascendance to its peak upon the sky, Cornelius retired into his quarters for breakfast. In attendance were his two sons. All was silent as Cornelius, the king of Ederia, took his seat. Cassius and his brother, Vidicus, gazed down over the long, silk-covered table into the eyes of their father. His face was sallow and somewhat angular, and he possessed a stern frown that was seemingly sewn into his face and typified his power as king. The sun gradually lifted itself into full view and could be seen through the windows; its heat emanated and was amplified as the ire of its light caressed Cassius's left cheek, causing him great discomfort. A deep silence filled the room, apart from the sounds of cutlery banging against plates, and the slow, wet sounds of mouths chewing their food. It would have been a jovial day had the passing of their mother not soaked the spirits of the family in grief. Instead, sorrow and sadness made their presences known, along with an infinite notion of loneliness. A strange alienation came with their father's title, King Cornelius Helladawn, and with that title came the responsibilities of a ruler. Alas, familiarization with one's children wasn't of utmost concern when ruling a kingdom. Thus, indeed, they had their father, but the two brothers could not have been more alone. Their father cleared his throat, wiped his mouth, and placed down his cutlery. The boys straightened their postures and pushed their chairs further under the table, ready to listen to the inevitable pontification. But their father uttered no words. He instead rose from his seat. He was a tall man with black hair that fell nearly to his shoulders and was swept behind his ears. His stature was haughty and demanded an immense amount of respect, but at times a drop of warm love could be perceived in his eyes. He approached, taking only a few steps until stopping halfway across the room. Stiffening his posture and putting his arms behind him, he spoke. "I have something of great importance to show you." His voice was calm yet vital. The boys were somewhat hesitant in halting their breakfast;

Vidicus had barely touched his food—he had taken their mother's death much harder than Cassius had, and he grew ever so silent at times, rarely speaking at all. Cornelius turned to the doorway and exited the room, passing by two guards. The boys followed reluctantly, walking down the hall while staring back at the two guards. Their presence was sublime. Mother and father had always told the boys that any man in the royal keep would gladly give their life for them. It may have been true, however the multitude of men plated in a facade of full steel sets of armour still gave off an eerie feeling. Cassius had once heard from his cousin that visited them from the south that there were no men under the armour at all, and they were mere hollowed spirits sworn to protect the kingdom. The idea was quickly shut down by his father, but a part of Cassius still longed to believe in such silly fantasies.

As the king walked down the hall, the boys followed, along with the two guards. Cassius caught Vidicus staring stupidly at the towering red banners of House Helladawn that hung on the walls: a golden dragon standing on its hind legs, breathing a body of orange flame. The company walked down a spiralling set of stairs. Vidicus winced as the bitter coldness of the stone ran up his foot; Cassius, however, walked with great confidence, jumping two stairs at a time and rushing to his father's side. Each step echoed and was juxtaposed against the silence. Once the company reached the bottom of the stairs, the confined hallways and narrow spaces ceased, and a door opened into a great hall. Reaching nearly a hundred feet at its pinnacle, it was upheld by numerous pillars that were carved in ancient and forgotten techniques, thus they captured one's eyes in their smooth perfection and alluring cream hues. Brilliant drapes of a seductive red colour hung from where no man could ever reach. The fabric, depicting ancient didactic lore of the Casthedian people, hung low and high for all eyes to see. Long and wide was this glorious hall, and to the end stood a gate of old varnished ebony oak. The floor was polished and serene, in a cream colour matching the pillars. But standing in bodacious pride over everything on its dais, pitying the world in its excellence, there stood the throne. The floor surrounding it was similar in hue to the rest of the great hall, however etched into it were a series of intricate golden carvings in a language few could decipher. Their beauty was indubitable, as if they were the embers of dragon fire. The company walked across the hall, and once again silence gripped the air. Cassius looked down, trying to make out his reflection in the polished stone. Meanwhile, Vidicus lagged behind; the guards stopped as he did. As Cassius strutted like a child, peering into his hazy reflection, Vidicus's attention was drawn to the throne, and he stopped to bask in the sight of it. He was a small, fragile child being stolen by the awe of a giant, caught in its web. The throne's allure was immense and was something few could put into words. It was as if it was calling towards those who fell under its wrath, tempting them to give in to their deepest desires, or seducing them into falling into its trap. It was a notion so tangible it could be felt in the very air. And that was when he saw her—his mother. It was as if she had never died, for right before his eyes she stood, silent, and adorned with her usual smile that had always reminded Vidicus that he'd be okay, that he'd be safe. He looked over to the others, wondering if they had seen what he'd seen, but they seemed oblivious, and when he looked back to where she stood she was gone, and the foul smell of rotting flesh was now heavy in the air. The miasma broke him from his trance as he noticed his brother and father exiting through a corridor that led to the Hall of Arts, and he then trotted over in a hurry and reunited with the company.

The Hall of Arts was tall, yet not nearly as enormous as the throne room, and its beauty mostly came from the subjects of the art itself. There was a vast variety of objects ranging from paintings of long-deceased renowned artists to masterfully crafted statues of the old gods and goddesses that once roamed this land. Few now believed in the old religions, for science and factual ideologies had become the norm and there was simply no room for foolish beliefs in times like this. There were ancient artifacts rumoured to hold old and foreign magic, however any suggestion of their magical power being real was complete nonsense. All of Ederia knew magic was an ability feigned by the old scholars, but the works of art had been in the possession of House Helladawn for nearly two centuries. There were weapons that the finest swordsman history produced had held, with virgin edges so fine and pure a mere glance could seemingly cut. But there was one piece that was held in high regard above all else. Centred at the end of the hall, between the two doorways, was a wooden stand with a box on top. Cornelius drew out a key as he approached the stand. The boys had not seen such a key before; it was silver and had worn through the ages. Unlocking the box, the king drew out a glass ball larger than his hand. Few had had the privilege of seeing such glasswork, even in the royal keep, but the true attraction lay inside. There was a metal rose, and it was far from ordinary.

"I am aware you two are wondering the meaning behind all of this," said the king. The two brothers nodded their heads, and their father gave a slight smile as he gazed upon the rose. "What do you see when you look at this rose?"

"It's made out of metal," proclaimed Cassius.

"Indeed," said the king, "it is metal. Can you guess the type of metal this is?" Cassius's eyes darted up as he began to delve into deep thought, mouthing the names of all the metals he knew— which wasn't many.

"Silver?" asked Cassius.

"Dragonite," corrected the King. "Long before we Casthedians ruled Ederia, even long before our people even set foot on these shores, dragons ruled over the first men of Ederia. Long and cruel was their reign; men, women, and children sought protection where they could, but there is little harmony to be found when faced with the malice of fire. The first men of Ederia were nearly driven to extinction, however, my sons, when great peril is nigh, thus conjures the need for bravery. Eventually, the brave arose from the trenches of fear and began their hunt of the dragons. Multiple wars ensued. They were bloody, and they were long. From the ancient lore, we have gathered that the dragon king, Vulldarkhan, was slain over six hundred years ago, in the year 684 AC." The king's sons struggled to keep their attention on the spontaneous history lesson, while their father was lost in the rose until he looked back at his children, catching their attention once more. "To conclude, the first men of Ederia learned how to manipulate dragon scales into metals of immense strength—and worth. But its real worth comes from the lesson it is about to teach you. When I look upon this rose, sure I see an artistic piece of immeasurable worth, but I prefer to see its true nature. It represents a balance," said the king, while his sons looked at him with great confusion. "It possesses great beauty, yet also the ability to do harm. It is poised and it is amicable, however, if the need arises, its thorns can draw blood. Can you guess as to what this metaphor may represent?" The question was mainly directed towards Cassius, the first son, but there was no response, only the uncouth demeanour of a child.

"A king," interjected Vidicus. His father's eyes darted towards his second born son with great surprise and the slightest hint of amusement.

"A good king," said Cornelius. "There will come a day, Vidicus, when you shall become a great lord of Ederia, and Cassius, you shall be its new king. One must learn the importance of balance if he is to do so. Your preparation for such roles begins today. Grieve your mother as you will, for I shall do the same. Do not expect any form of feminine generosity from me. I shall be hard on the both of you, and at times cruel, but know this: it is for the sake of making you children into men. In my heart resides love for both of you, for you are my sons and the future of the name Helladawn." The brothers smiled at the slightest amiability from their father, and a shy grin grew on the king's lips like a rising sun peeking over the horizon, however the grin was lost as a swift change in the king's mood overcame the atmosphere. "It is nearly midday," said the king. "Vidicus, make your way to the fencing grounds. Sir Hadrian shall be there waiting for your arrival—I would like to speak to your brother alone." Vidicus did not move immediately, staring into his father's demanding eyes only to be overtaken by their dictating wrath. Vidicus turned reluctantly, biting his inner lip and clenching his fists out of the anger of being left out from his father's primary attention, and made his way to the fencing grounds. Vidicus had never enjoyed being the second-born child; indeed, the title granted to him came with power, but fate always seemed to hold his future in the shadow of his brother's candle.

Then he smelt it once more: rotten flesh. He ignored it at first, but as he walked across the throne room, he began to feel as if his back was being watched and that something was most certainly behind him. His pace slowed. He wanted to look behind him but was afraid that if he did, he wouldn't like what he'd see. As he walked, he could almost hear footsteps stalking him from behind, and when he stopped, they stopped. Slowly, he turned around, and his body began to shiver . . . but nothing was there. Not a soul. Yet now the smell of death was even stronger . . . and in the corner of his eye, he could see the towering shadow of *something* or *someone* behind him. He could feel the sickly aura of a body looming over him, watching him, and it took Vidicus a few seconds to realize that he could not breathe. His heart thumped beneath his chest, causing his ribs to seemingly expand in unnatural ways. Before he gained the courage to look for himself, *it* placed its hand on his shoulder. Vidicus turned his head to get a glance, but when he did, he saw what could never have been expected or even explained: it was his mother again. The smell of death was gone and replaced with her usual lovely fragrance that Vidicus always associated with feelings of love and belonging. Iris smiled, causing her son's eyes to be soaked in tears, and without thinking, the boy embraced her, feeling her love once again.

"My lord Vidicus, are you all right?"

The boy opened his eyes to see that his face was pressed up against a cold steel wall, and when his eyes looked upwards, he saw was no more than one of the guards. He distanced himself, nearly falling backwards in the process. It hadn't been her. She was never even there. And then the bitter reminder came to him: she was still locked away inside the earth, and she would remain so until the last grains of time slipped away into the unknown. Vidicus relaxed his breathing and tried to believe what he'd seen was no more than an illusion . . . but it had felt so very real, and the smell of it and the sight of his mother were things that he'd never be able to forget.

✳

Cornelius led Cassius down a spiralling staircase, torch in hand. The subtle clinking of metal from the trailing guardsmen grew silent as father and son walked further down into the darkness. The ancient crypts of the fallen kings of Casthedia were nigh. The flame of the torch danced to and fro against the black void, illuminating very little apart from a small strip down the centre of the stairs. Unlit torches were found as the two circled downwards, and the king lit them as they passed. The company walked in silence for quite some time. The air was thick and heavy, as if the whispers of the dead filled the black air with tales of a forgotten time. The king halted and lit another torch, and as he did so a vast crypt took form in the dark void in front of them: large rectangular tombs of stone were set in rows that made up the catacombs. Statues of gargoyles made themselves the pillars that supported the ceiling; their tongues and teeth seemingly leaped forward in malicious intent towards Cassius, and the child drew back in fear. Each tomb was covered in a briar of spider webs. Cornelius appeared to be searching for something, twisting his body side to side in a desperate search. As he did so the light from the torch shot low, illuminating the variety of small and enormous arachnids; some had burrowed themselves deep within their homes, and others were teetering and dancing across the silk boughs. Their eyes shone in the darkness like distant stars in the night sky, watching the king and his son walk amongst the labyrinth of tombs. Far away, at the end of the crypts, there was a tall figure, and the two seemed to be heading towards it. Once upon it, the king stopped. It was a statue of a man. He held a sword in both hands and was pointing it downwards, seemingly resting upon its hilt. However, there was little sign of rest in his stance, for he stood in solemn pride. He had long hair with the top tied back behind his head, and his face was grim and almost melancholic, as if he was contemplating a poignant memory that filled him with grief.

"Do you know who you stand in the presence of, my son?" asked the king.

"No," replied Cassius.

"He is King Henselt Helladawn—my father," said Cornelius, and sorrow now began to grow within him. "An honourable warrior and a good man, but a poor king. He was reckless and drew to conclusions with haste, forgetting reasoning. But alas, he was still true in heart. He cared for his people, as a king should, however he lacked the intellect to see what he had done to his kingdom by subjecting them to countless wars. Thus, he was killed before I grew to be a man, forcing me to adopt the throne at a young age. I now hold the continent of Ederia in the palm of my hand. I have corrected my father's wrongdoings, as every son should, and one day my face shall be carved in stone and left to the silence of these eerie halls, and I shall be put to rest by the cold grip of death. I can only hope that you should make an even better king than myself so I may do so in peace." Cornelius gave a sigh as his son basked under the eyes of his grandfather.

"Why am I to be king, father?" asked Cassius. Cornelius was altogether surprised by the words and gave a moment of thought before he spoke.

"You will have to show me, Cassius."

His father's words echoed in his mind, and Cassius wondered if he would ever be ready to be a king.

The Lost Princess

Sathelia floated softly over the crystal face of the river as it guided her through the woods. The birds sang their soft songs from the boughs of the trees, and the elvish princess listened to each word as she drifted under the arches of nature. Vibrant green moss hugged the banks of the river and the sweet fragrance of magic hung in the air. Beautiful light emanated from the water, which was cyan in hue, and it shone up through the branches and was filtered by the forest canopy. Great stags and songbirds waited at the riverbank to watch the girl drift by, and as she did so the stags bowed their heads and the birds whistled with delight. It was forest so green and thick with life one could not fill themselves with all of its euphoria in a single lifetime. In her hand, the princess held a silver harp. She played a poignant tune, full of sorrow yet with a touch of happiness. As the princess played her harp her face depicted the melancholy of the past, and soon after she began to sing. Her voice was like starlight that had been sewn into words, and it cast a beguiling spell over the forest. However, her tongue was strange, as if it was in a language only remembered in ancient times, and thus only a few knew it. But the trees understood it, as did each rock and field of moss. Each living mammal that scurried beneath the towering forest roof now stopped to listen to the girl's tale. The forest was hot and humid, and a visible green veil draped itself over the air, and now turtles and frogs joined Sathelia as she journeyed through the kingdom of nature.

Each turtle poked their head above the water to peer at the princess. Her hair was black as the eternal abyss of the sea, her delicate face was pale in complexion but with a drop of sweet pink, and her eyes were a deep violet, like rare amethyst crystals embedded into an even more scarce beauty. The stream now slowly curled around to the right. The small river now widened to thrice its size, and in the middle there was a small island. Such an island was the princess's destination, and it was a mere dozen arms' length in diameter, but at its edges various foliage, vines, and roots began to climb and spiral towards the middle, where the body of a tree loomed high above. It had made an organic shelter underneath. At one side of the shelter, the roots split, creating a small entrance where one could duck under and into the tree. Soon Sathelia drifted to the mossy shore of the island. The boat gently pressed against the shoreline, and the elvish tune ceased. She stepped out. Her soft, bare feet sank into the cool sand, and she could feel each grain running through the spaces of her toes. The brisk water of the ground came up to tickle against the naked flesh of her feet. She smiled, inhaling the crisp air of the spring afternoon, and she closed her eyes in satisfaction. Sathelia walked forward, and with only a few paces, the small shoreline of sand was gone, and she now walked upon a soft blanket of moss.

The tree shot up before her eyes. White daisies sprouted from its green facade. She entered the shelter. The underside of the oak tree had made a small room, and in the far left corner there lay a small bed. Its frame consisted of slender roots intertwined together to form a level plane. Just ahead of the princess there was a small mirror that hung from the knuckle of a root that shot out ever so slightly. Altogether, the area strongly resembled a bedroom, but the air in such a place was doused with the fragrances of the forest. The elf then studied the allure of her face in the mirror, posing as if to increase her perfection. But such a task would prove impossible, for such beauty could not be improved upon. And with a rush of glee, Sathelia fell back onto her bed and shut her eyes. The world was now nothing but darkness, and the cries of the wild and the sounds of nature slowly began to fade as she drifted into slumber.

✳

Sathelia awoke to the soft nudging of a snout just below her knee. A tall and proud stag stood over the princess as she lay in her bed, as if to guard her against any threat that crawled in the all-consuming darkness of the night. Long veins of light ran through the stag's antlers, illuminating the room, and the luminescent crown emanated a deep ocean blue colour. Sathelia writhed in her bed, stuck between dreams and reality, and there then came another nudge, this time a little harder.

"Ruedenhiem? Is it you that awakens me from my sleep?" The stag leaned in towards her and lowered his head to the level of Sathelia's shoulder, and his towering antlers were the only source of light in the darkness. Sathelia embraced her companion and placed the palm of her hand atop the stag's head. Then a sudden feeling of communication surged through their physical connection, as if the stag was somehow speaking to her without making a sound. And with the connection, information was conveyed to the princess.

"Father wishes to speak to me? At this time?" asked Sathelia. It had not been long since she had begun her slumber. It was five hours past noon when she had buried herself into the soft seclusion of her sheets, and it could not have been past midnight by now as the darkness had only begun to take its grip of shadow across the land. "Well, if my father wishes to marry me to that fool of a prince, Hellthearan, you may send him my bitter regards yourself!" yelled the princess in the night. But the stag did not sway. Instead, his black eyes merely blinked and gazed upon the girl, eyes that were so dark they were like deep pools of ink from which no surreptitious thoughts could be withheld; they were all-seeing and all-knowing. "I am sorry, Ruedenhiem. You are a great friend of mine, and I know you have travelled far to reach me. But what could be so important at this hour? The moon still rests upon its throne of darkness in the sky. Can it not wait until morning?" The stag made no sound, not even the faintest of whispers, yet a form of words was conveyed, not through any verbal means but through that of the mind, and Sathelia understood what was being said. "There is news of my mother, you say?" At this news, a grave and fey mood fell upon the princess, and with a soft caress of her body she conjured a white dress that began to take form upon the curvature of her body and then climbed over her breasts, and she was thus fully clothed in a beautiful white dress that shone in the darkness. "We must ride with haste!" said Sathelia, and the princess mounted the stag and rode off into the night, crossing the river and into the sea of shadows within the forest.

The wind blew in her face. Ruedenhiem, the Great Stag of the North, rode with such haste as to put any valiant steed to shame. His crown of light streamed through the darkness as if it was a rebellious star, fleeing from the grips of the heavens and the touch of darkness. The stag trampled over the forest floor, leaping over any obstacle that stood in his way, and soon the density of the woods receded, and a deep grassy meadow awaited them. Sathelia broke through the borders of the forest and charged into the long meadow, and she rode across the overseeing spine of the valley. The pale moon watched the fey princess as she rode across the meadow with a devilish desire, and its paleness emanated and illuminated the world in a grey light. A gale rose from the north and struck Sathelia from behind, and she winced, trying not to cower from the wrath of the night. On the horizon, Elsibard, the great city of the high elves, slept in silence. The air was cold and full of strife, conjuring a hateful chill into the princess's warm heart, and she buried her face into the thick fur of her steed. Much of the long ride then faded into a blur, and all that could be remembered was a vast painting of stars and the pallid face of the moon above them, watching over his kingdom of starlight. The grass of the meadow faded, and another body of forest sprawled itself before them, boasting evil upon its face. But the stag's light prevailed, and it guided them through the night.

Ruedenhiem leaped with pure grace and elegance. His troth was solemn, and it would be met. And thus, before long, the walls of Elsibard stood above them and the two raced through the gates like phantoms racing through the night. And as the city slept, Sathelia weaved through it, making her way to the palace, and once she drew nigh, guardsmen attempted to question her and ask her to proclaim who rode so carefree at this hour, but she did not halt. Suddenly the palace gates rushed up before them, and Ruedenhiem came to a sudden stop. Sathelia jolted forward on the back of her steed.

"We have arrived, and in good time, my friend. A thousand thanks I shall bless upon your humble soul, as you have done well, but the journey is not over. I must hasten and find father." The princess caressed her steed's head with her soft cheek, and she gave him a kiss on his forehead and entered the palace. A pale light shone through the windows, and the glorious hall of elvish lords was plagued by frozen darkness. The moonlight peered into the hall, dancing atop the chandeliers, and an inexorable sadness made its home within the palace. Something drew nigh. Sathelia scurried across the blue carpet that was laid across the throne room and she cried for a guard to meet her. As she did so, two came rushing from the Hall of Vitality, however a grave expression was sewn onto each of their faces.

"Hearken! Wherever is my father?" cried Sathelia. The two guardsmen looked at each other, and their words failed them at first.

"My lady Sathelia, your father awaits you in the Hall of Vitality, but—" Before they could finish, the princess stormed off in a flurry of speed. Waiting in a small room at the end of the hall was her father, Estideel, king of the high elves of Medearia. His expression was simply gone, as if his very capability for emotion was stolen from him by the sight of what was laid before his eyes. Her father and three other elves were gathered around a bier, but Sathelia could not see what they saw. She approached.

"Father, have you any news of—" But her inquiries were cut short by the dread that was brought to her by what lay on the table: thereupon the bier was what was left of a white silk dress, soaked in blood, and a knife that was wet with a rich mahogany red. It was a dress of her mother's. Before Sathelia could utter a word, she fell to the ground and wept. She then felt the gentle touch of her father's hand on the back of her neck, but even he was lost within a storm of sorrow. Estideel then crouched down to his daughter, wiped the tears from her tender cheek, and embraced her. His body felt frail and timid, as it was the first time in the life of Estideel in which his strong will and powerful frame failed him, and Sathelia could feel the age of his body, a body withered by half a millennium. His heart had broken as well at the hearing of the message, a message his daughter would not have the misfortune of hearing from anyone but him.

"They found her clothes in the southern swamplands, and they were drenched in the blood such as you see before you. She is presumed dead," said Estideel. But as he said such, great strife and sorrow fell upon him, and his mind nearly crumbled underneath it. Sathelia released herself from her father's arms and stood up, gazing upon the dress. It reeked with the stench of death. Hellthearan, who she likely would be forced to marry, stood next to her, and he clasped her hand with his.

"Release me from your grasp! Do not touch me!" cried Sathelia, jumping away from the prince to the side of her father, seeking protection in a time of pain.

The king put his hand on his daughter's shoulder and then, with great struggle, he spoke. "Speak, Wraithenor, before I am too drunk with melancholy to listen."

Wraithenor then spoke from the opposite side of the bier. "My men and I searched the mires for days unknown until we came across this dress, along with the knife."

"You mean to say you have come without proof of the death of my mother?" said Sathelia, and her tone was bitter.

"My lady, few are capable of surviving the cruelty of the swamps. It is an evil land filled with malice, and many fell and foul beasts prowl its innards," said Wraithenor.

"Yet there is no assurance of her death. Could it be too soon to presume us bereft of my mother, your queen?" asked Sathelia.

"Your mother was sick, my daughter. You know this. Long had she proclaimed about ending her life, and before my eyes, I can piece together that my wife has done such," said Estideel.

"Have you no desire to be sure, father?" asked the princess, whose eyes were livid.

"Do not let hope guide you to a path of further sorrow, my love," said the king. "I know deep within my heart that she struck herself with that blade, and she has thus passed into the land of the Ecaval." The voice of Estideel sank low and hopeless, and he lowered his head and let despair take him.

"No," proclaimed Sathelia, "I shall not settle for mere assumptions of her death. I shall search the mires myself!" And before anyone could stop her, the princess stormed off, racing to the throne room, wiping the cold tears away from her eyes as she ran.

"Sathelia!" cried her father. "Come back to me! I shall not lose you as well!" Estideel raced after his daughter with what strength he had left, strength that had only been conjured by the innate responsibility as a father to protect his child, his little girl. But Sathelia was swift and ran too quickly for Estideel to catch her, and she flung open the palace doors with an inorganic wind that had come from her fingertips.

"Come, Ruedenhiem! It seems we must ride where they are too craven to tread!" said the princess. Her valiant friend came to her at once, and Sathelia rode off under the smile of the moonlight.

✳

The night had reached its pinnacle and Ruedenhiem soared through the gaining shadow like a blue arrow of light, like a proud tree too stubborn to submit to the power of the hurricane. Sathelia's tears had ceased, and she was blessed with an armour of fearlessness and a cunning desire to smite the grip of woe that had taken her. What would have taken any horse till morning to reach, Ruedenhiem would make it to the mires long before dawn could shine its way into the world. Hard he rode, without rest and without tiring, as if he was possessed by an oath too strong to break. The monotonous sound of him galloping through the dark shredded the air. Through crevice and canyon, the stag galloped onwards, teetering on narrow cliff edges and down into quiet grasslands that were encircled by sudden and stark mountain ranges that were cloaked in a sublime gloom. Three hours had passed since midnight, and the mires were now in sight. They released a foul miasma into the air, and it was thick with the tang of the dead; Sathelia found herself almost struggling for the next breath as she and her companion trotted through the woods that led to the mires. Suddenly, the shadow of the woods waned, and the endless grey void of the swamps grew more prevalent as the trees became scarcer, and with a sudden and stark change, the trees halted and splayed out before the elf and her steed were the southern mires of Medearia. Long and grey it was, like a sea of misfortune and death that basked under the stars. Mosquitoes flew in large clouds over the pungent face of the sticky and wet moss, and the dark waters were menacing to look upon. They appeared thick, as if they consisted of decomposing flesh. Alien cries of unknown creatures sang their unearthly songs. Each cry was long and drawn out and altogether . . . unnatural. Sathelia was no longer in the Woods of Cassemor. This land held no benevolent magic, nay, it was odious and foul.

Where should I even begin to look for her? Alas, I haven't a clue as to where the trail begins. Dammit! I should have been more prepared! Well . . . I cannot turn back now, thought Sathelia. Ruedenhiem slowly walked amongst the mire, taking great care as to where he placed his hooves for it could only take one false step to be lost to the unknown depths of the pools. Even the proud blue light of his antlers seemed to falter in a spell of turmoil. A black veil of vexation was hung over the princess, and her sight was hindered. Suddenly a sound was heard, and something stirred behind them. Sathelia turned to see what it was, but nothing was there, only the dubious smile of the mire. Even Ruedenhiem seemed to be feeling the fear of something watching him.

"This is too eerie for my liking, Ruedenhiem. But we cannot turn back! I know you are afraid, but as am I," said Sathelia, and her steed seemed to grow confident with the words of his lady. A few furlongs they had walked like this, all the while Sathelia's eyes running back and forth, searching for any sign of her mother's presence. But nothing could be seen save for the yellow eyes of creatures in the deadly gloom. And soon any hope of finding her mother failed inside Sathelia's heart, and the quiet throes of failure crept closer and closer towards her mind. It was a hopeless night. But then something Sathelia had not expected happened. Ruedenhiem jerked his neck to the ground, almost throwing his princess off of his back, but he had caught a scent—and it was strong and familiar. "Have you found something?" asked Sathelia, struggling to hold back her vehemence. But her companion made no reply for he was focused on the trail, and quickly what once was a slow walk began to hasten into a trot. The princess inhaled deeply through her nose. "I smell it too—perfume!" proclaimed Sathelia. Then the stag weaved through the pools, and up ahead a large mere came into view through a shroud of fog. They entered the large white body of the fog, and the sky was lost to the impenetrable mist. It was thick, and Sathelia could only see a few yards in front of her, and each step Ruedenhiem took separated the white air like a drop of rain into a lake making many ripples. The stag then stopped, as they had reached the large mere. The water was calm and serene, motionless, as if it was anticipating its prey, ready to pounce at any given moment. Sathelia would not blink for her eyes were fixated on the water. She wanted to yell for her mother, but something held her back, for there was an undeniable unscrupulous notion that hung about the water's edges. Sathelia now felt as if she stood at the very edge of a gaping mouth that was ready to bite down upon her neck.

"Sathelia," hissed a voice from the water.

"Why have you come? I seek solitude from you and your father in death and yet you bother me even in the afterlife!" said another voice from behind her. It was a voice so fell and evil that it drove Sathelia to a fear that had been unknown ere this moment. She felt cold, so very cold, and alone. Far away there seemed to be laughter, as if a child ran gaily through the swamps. She could not move. Suddenly she began to see the forms of wraiths glide just above the water's surface, circling slowly towards her. She tried to speak but her words failed her, as did her courage, and even Ruedenhiem began to falter in his stance, backing up from the bank of the lake. The whispers prevailed, and each voice chilled the princess to her very bones. They could be no less than the incarnation of malice, and Sathelia covered her ears, trying to block out the evil that was being poured into her mind. But as she did so, a wraith that looked as if she was a maiden of terror rushed them like a rogue gale, brushing up against the chest of Ruedenhiem, and the great stag rose to his hind legs, giving out a cry of dismay and launching the princess off of his back and onto the slimy surface of the bog.

As Sathelia arose, her friend was nowhere to be seen, hidden by the fog. Ruedenhiem, the Great Stag of the North, was gone. Sathelia wanted to weep, and she began to foresee her own death.

Could this be the end of my tale? Is this the doom that took my mother and shall soon take me? It would seem so, thought the princess as all hope and happiness retreated from her body and left but a hollow shell in its stead. Her face grew wan and pallid, as if an immense burden now rested upon her shoulders, dragging her down to the surface of the cruel land. Not too far away she could now see a dark figure being juxtaposed against the white cloak of the fog, and it appeared as if an elf—not a wraith or fiend, but an elf—looked at the princess as she stood frozen with terror. As Sathelia caught sight of it, she began to run towards it. "Wait! Do not leave me! I am lost and alone! Mother, is that you? Mother! Why do you run?" But there was no answering call. The princess leaped over the pools that dotted themselves around the vast bog, and she could now see the figure had stopped and she was gaining on its position. But as she came to where she thought the elf would be standing, the figure faded back into the fog, and there was nothing there.

"Daughter," said a voice from behind her, and Sathelia turned frightfully to face what she had just heard. As she turned, she was greeted by the sight of her mother, who stood in a white silk dress, and in her hand she held a knife that was cutting her wrists. The scarlet blood dripped down the length of her forearm and seeped into her garments, and a cruel smile of malice was on her face. The princess's eyes rolled back in fear, and she collapsed under the wrath of the demon that stood before her. As she fell the ground gave way, and her body slipped through a series of thickets and fell into a deep and dark pit. The princess suffered a blow to her eye and her vision was obstructed as she hit the ground. Her very life began to finally flee from her as the world morphed into darkness.

The Escape

The moonlight flooded through the iron bars and into Ivan's cell. He was awake. The perpetual sound of the ocean crashing against the rocky shores below made it so that sleep was rarely an option. It was right there. So close. Freedom. Each cell in Brazgul Prison was faced toward the sea so that one side, apart from eight solid iron bars, was open, and the scent of the sea was free to drift in as it pleased. His hand stretched out through the bars, reaching towards freedom, feeling the cool air on his skin. It was acts like this that were reminders of how close freedom was, but also just how unattainable such a dream would be.

After his escape from the Pools, he was quickly relocated after being captured. He spent his time drifting from prison to prison, fighting other inmates along the way. The scars left from the Pools' water had healed but left everything, apart from his face, grotesquely deformed. The warden made sure that he was kept malnourished, even more so than the other prisoners, so that when fights *did* break out, he was beaten to a pulp. At times, guards even let fights break out; elves didn't need much of an excuse to hurt him, and his scars bled easily. Thus, when the beatings did take place, the floor of his cell quickly turned red with blood, and Ivan slept in puddles of his own pain.

He had spent time in the Pits of Utherious, where slaves were forced to fight for their freedom. And so, he was forced to adapt, to learn the art of swordsmanship, and he did so exquisitely. He could not be beaten. They dared not send their champions to fight him over fear of having them bested by a human. When he did fight, the elves made sure no one attended the matches—publicly showing off a human was foolish and bound to cause an uproar, so they quickly moved him to Brazgul Prison where he'd be isolated from the mainland. It was on an island that belonged to the sea elves, and amongst the guards there was pride of that prison; no one ever escaped, and they intended to keep it that way.

In solitude, his senses were heightened. He learned to listen to every word. Every clandestine whisper that was ever uttered eventually came to his ears. Prisoners talked, and so he heard rumours of elvish spies living deep in the heart of Ederia, sending information back over to Medearia. He also heard talk of a war between the two continents on the horizon. When guards heard prisoners speak of such things they beat them and sent them somewhere that Ivan never wished to go. Were the spies and the preparations of war correlated? It was quite likely. Espionage was an intelligent tactic, one that could shift the tides of war with ease. Normally such news would interest him, but Ederia was not his home now; his cell was his home.

His eyesight became better and better from adjusting to the darkness of the night and from studying the horizon in the direction where he knew Ederia was. He could taste the sea now, even formulate his surroundings without looking, knowing that his other senses could simulate his world for him. He was a weapon. A deadly force that was left waiting, pondering vengeance until it consumed every desire he had, all except one. He hadn't thought of his mother much since the day she died; life had simply taken him down the river of fate too quickly for him to look back. But now, in a place as terrible as this, he had time . . . and he spent it thinking of her. When he was little, he'd tell his ma and his pa that they'd all be royalty one day, and he'd make sure of it. But now they were gone. Dead. And Ivan's innocent dream of being a king one day became a nightmare that would not leave him be. It was impossible, he knew it; that was simply not how Ederia worked. The Helladawns would be the kings of their empire until someone powerful enough to do so disrupted their rule. Even still, he blamed the name Helladawn for the death of his family. After all, the men who killed his mother rode with the dragon banner of their house over their armour. They were supposed to be wardens of peace. Just another lie spoken from a cruel world.

The cold touch of salt water awoke him from sleep, making him shiver. Ivan opened his eyes. It was morning, and the sky was grey as the clouds slept closer to the land. There was no real point in being awake anymore, not even a point in being alive. If he had the materials, he would have surely killed himself by now, although it was getting to the point where he'd entertain the idea of smashing his skull against the walls. Who knows, maybe his brains would paint a pretty picture for the guards to see. Truth be told, he doubted he had the strength to generate enough force to smash his brains out. And so, he once again leaned back, letting the rusted edges of the bars dig into his skin as he tried to sleep the day away.

*

There was a muffled shriek in the night. Swords were drawn only to fall to the ground and clang against the stone. Ivan awoke and put his ear against the cell door, listening to the sound of death. What was happening? There were more screams, but from who he did not know. Then, the smell came: burnt flesh. He knew it well.

The sounds of footsteps.

Closer.

Closer.

The smell of blood and charred skin.

Closer.

Closer.

Silence. Ivan waited. His heart pumped beneath his chest as the reign of silence ensued, and the thrill of the moment filled him with euphoric adrenaline. There was a knock on the door. Whoever had dealt the cards of death that night now stood just beyond the domain of his misery. Ivan backed into the far corner, readying himself for whoever would enter. But no one did. Instead, he heard the door be unlocked . . . He was being freed . . . but by who?

"Who is there?" asked Ivan, his voice broken and faint. There was no reply, and so he crept towards the door, still wary, for there was an untrustworthy amount of serendipity to all this. "Hello?" Again, silence. He pushed the door forward . . . and it opened. His path became clear, and any suspicion was dispelled. He had to escape. And he had to do it *now*. When he stepped outside of his cell, it felt as if his very existence had purpose again; he now had something to live for. The guards were dead. All of them. Some were burnt, but others looked as if their bodies had simply imploded, and their innards had been sucked away. To the left, down the hallway, stood an elf in grey. His face was hidden in darkness and veiled by a cloak, but the glow from his fiery eyes shot through the shadows with ease. Had he done all of this alone? The elf turned and began to walk. Ivan followed. "Hey! What's this all about? Where are we going?"

"*You* are going home," it said calmly, turning towards him and shooting Ivan down with its gaze.

"Home?"

"Yes. Ederia."

"I don't understand."

"Do you understand how to sail a boat?"

". . . Yes."

"Good. You shall need one. There is a ship waiting for you on the shore. Come! More guards shall be here soon." Ivan refused to ask any more questions; they would only be wasting time, and that was not something they had an abundance of.

The elf was fast, so much so that Ivan could barely keep up with his pace. They ran down the hallway, avoiding the fallen bodies, and down through a spiralling set of stairs. As they descended, Ivan lost sight of his rescuer, and as he entered the first floor of the prison, a body of flames ran through the air, being summoned from the hand of the mysterious elf. Three guards writhed in pain as their skin was seared beneath their armour. One elf who was lucky enough to avoid the flames brought his sword down towards the rescuer's neck only to have his knee bent sideways. The guard's leg collapsed in on itself, and Ivan could hear the rolling sound of ligaments and the crunch of splintered bones. But there was no time to linger. The hooded elf picked up a sheathed sabre from the warden of the prison and tossed it to Ivan. He caught the blade: it was light, lighter than any sword he'd wielded before. The edges of the sheath were gilded, and the primary colour was black. He couldn't wait to see how it cut.

The running continued until they made their way to the main gate, hearing the bitter howls of inmates who watched in envy as a human was led away and they were left to wither and die. Seagulls called out from the beach. The guards in the courtyard had been dealt with, stinking of death and fear. Ivan would be lying if he said he wasn't taking pleasure from seeing dead elves. After all, it was they who taught him what *true* misery felt like. They entered a small cove that was hidden from view a few hundred meters away from the prison walls. A small vessel awaited them. Ivan did not hesitate in the slightest. He climbed aboard but waited for his saviour to follow . . . He did no such thing. He watched, standing on the shore as a wave of mist came for them all. Still, his face was hidden beneath his hood, but he seemed trustworthy—he had saved Ivan's life, after all.

"Are you coming?" asked Ivan. There was a long pause between them.

". . . Your journey is not mine to take. Go. Return to Ederia, and your fate shall fall beneath your feet." Ivan had no reason to argue. The idea seemed nearly unreal. He would be coming home. Finally, he was free. Ivan readied himself and let the sails loose to catch the evening breeze. As the ship sailed away, Vandulin, the Sage of the West, watched from the shore, and withdrew his hood, letting his long, grey hair fall to his shoulders. His fiery eyes smouldered in the darkness, illuminating the surrounding gloom. He smiled, knowing his plan was in motion.

The Council

It had been eight years since the death of his mother, and Cassius drifted between consciousness and sleep while the whore's fingers ran themselves through his long, golden hair.

"You haven't fallen asleep on me, have you, my prince?" Cassius smiled as he fully awoke, greeted by the body of a woman next to his. He shifted over on his bed to the nightstand to his right and poured a goblet of wine. Turning himself around, he looked upon the woman: her face was somewhat beautiful, apart from her yellow and overdrawn teeth, but her body was to the prince's liking. He leaned in and pressed his finger against her cheek and slowly caressed down onto her breasts and then down onto her thighs. The girl giggled in excitement; she had seldom felt the touch of royalty. Indeed, many men from the royal courts scurried down here after dark while their wives fed their babes, but any whore would dream of sharing the night with a prince. The woman rolled on top. Her hands latched themselves to his chest and made their way down between his legs.

She attempted to laugh but gave a snort instead as her long brunette hair fell into the prince's eyes and mouth.

"Sorry, m'lord," said the girl with great awkwardness and the demeanour of a mere peasant on the lap of a proud lion. Cassius's attention drew elsewhere, cogitating some deep and unknown thoughts. Seeing that she had lost her customer's focus and lustful desire, she lunged forward with eagerness to please the prince, like a dog sitting for its master. As she pressed her plump lips against his, Cassius jerked away. She scoffed in embarrassment and nearly came to tears. The prince's face grew red with annoyance, and his cold blue eyes pierced her freckled face.

"You may take your leave," said the prince. Failing to hide her tears, the girl covered her eyes and sobbed, throwing herself away from the prince and standing next to the bed. The cries were pitiful and were muffled by her hands yet remained painful to the ear, and the tempestuous woman cowered, lowering her gaze to hide from the prince's wrath.

"Forgive me, m'lord. Shall I bring you more wine?"

"I am curious as to why you still fill this room with your boorish miasma—make your leave before I lose my patience!"

"Yes, m'lord!" The girl took to putting her clothes on with haste and had only gathered them all from the corners of the room when the prince interjected.

"Out with you," he said.

"Yes, m—" The whore's speech was cut short by a wave of fear. Her throat clenched, and she grew hot, allowing no word to be uttered. She exited under a veil of shame and embarrassment.

"Sir Hadrian!" shouted Cassius. "Bring in the next one. Oh! Along with more wine, if you are able, my good knight!" The next woman came in, wine in hand. She was dark of skin and was evidently from the south—most likely from the province of Ruzadia. She was clothed in robes that were rich and fragrant and were of a deep violet hue. Her lips were perfect, plump and tender, and the seductive shine of her golden eyes stalked the prince like a cat stalks her prey in the night. Cassius's blood boiled in the dreadful longing for her touch, and the anticipation was nearly too much to bear. She was ideal for the taste of royalty. The sun pierced through the windows, making the very air boil. She approached with confidence and fervency; she would indeed satisfy Cassius's voracious, lustful appetite. But her seductive approach was broken by the opening of a door. Vidicus entered.

"I see you have not strayed from your usual habits, brother," said Vidicus.

"Never, my dear and beloved Vidicus! I remain a firm believer in getting to know my people!" said Cassius. Vidicus studied the state of the room and was split between disgust and shame. Vidicus had grown into a man of tall stature and was like his father in numerous ways: his hair was jet black and long, and his face was pale and wise, possessing a grin that hung heavy with composure. Vidicus then reached into his purse and withdrew a single gold coin and gave it to the woman. "You may attend your other customers, my lady. You shall not find any use from the boar that rests upon the bed," said Vidicus. The southern beauty then strutted away with a grin on her face.

"Now look what you have done, my brother! You have ever so rudely interrupted my morning routine! I now fail to see myself leaving this brothel all day, and that is of no fault of my own, mind you."

"Your mind grows ill with the stench of wine, Cassius."

"All the better for sharpening it, I say."

"Your idea of sharpness falls short of most, for even the words you utter are soaked in liquor."

"I'd rather find myself wet with blissful ignorance than to remain a dry dullard such as yourself," said Cassius.

Vidicus grew tired and impatient with the drunken mannerisms of his brother. This was not the first time he'd been forced to watch his brother soil the family name in liquor and whores. He would watch no longer.

"Nay, I say. For you have no notion of the time of day. Morning has since passed nigh two hours ago, and you are late for the council meeting." Cassius groaned and rolled over, hating the thought of being strapped in a cramped doublet and attending the royal council. "You shall not free yourself from your duties as a prince. And to think you shall soon be crowned king!" said Vidicus, growling with disdain.

"Watch the slither of your tongue, brother!" Cassius snapped away from his lightheartedness and drunken delusion and sat up from where he rested with a wave of fury. "You think of yourself as my better, and thus you rest upon the lap of our father. I too know the ways of courtesy but happen to abandon its laws by my own will. I refuse to be a tool of royal expectancies." The eyes of the two brothers met each other with a tangible stream of ire, and the room grew hot at the presence of an undeniable intensity. Vidicus was the first to speak.

"I shan't bicker with you here, brother, as we are expected elsewhere, but this talk is far from over. We should discuss our differences another time, for I should like to illuminate your faults while you glare at them with sober eyes." And at that Cassius swallowed his flared pride and agreed. The two made their way out of the brothel and began their journey back to the keep on horseback. Alongside them were a dozen guards sent as escorts. Each guard wore the flaming red tabard of House Helladawn over their steel plate armour, and atop their heads they wore great helms. However, no escort was held in equal regard as Sir Hadrian Blackwood. He was an older man that had seen more than sixty winters, and he once taught the brothers all he knew of the arts of swordsmanship—which was quite much given his notoriety. There was once a time, long ago, in which the old man was feared across Ederia as the deadliest knight in the Casthedian Empire. "The Dragon of the North," they called him. Alas, that was long ago in the Vazareth Wars, and he now dedicated his life to protecting the lineage of the Helladawn family. The two brothers rode alongside each other in the dirty crevices of the palm of Ekmere. Men, women, and children were coated in a fresh facade of mud and poverty, and it took the brothers half an hour of riding before they were able to reach a relatively decent area of the city. Yet still, the dubious eyes of begrudged peasants stared them down as folk thronged into the outdoors to get a look at the royal company passing by. By the time they had reached the markets, the city had sprung into life. Hundreds flooded the streets. Merchants advertised their elixirs, shouting amongst the crowds. Spices were sold and foods were eaten, giving rise to a tasteful smell in the air. However, the crowd was soon divided as they kept their distance from the passing royal party. Finally, after an hour of riding, Cassius and Vidicus had reached the keep's walls. There was a stark and sudden discrepancy in the allure of the architecture: mud roads morphed into cobblestone paths, thatched roofs turned into dark shingles, and the rock walls and arches were now made of finely crafted brick. They then came to an archway that opened to a wide staircase that climbed upwards and eventually through the two walls that semi-circled around the keep.

As Cassius and his brother made their way through the defending walls of the keep, the stairs began an aggressive climb until the entire city was sprawled out before their eyes, and as the brothers and their escorts made the great climb, the keep began to peer into view. It stood tall and proud, as if it was a bright star gifted by the heavens above to the land of man. After the company had travelled many furlongs there stood the gate to the keep. Once mere seconds had passed, the towering wooden doors slowly began to open, and they climbed even further upon the widespread stairs. Far away to the east, the sudden pinnacles of the Wyvern Mountains slid into view, only caressing the belly of the towering clouds, and they were cloaked in the hazy blue arms of the horizon. As the gate opened, a vast courtyard formed in front of them. Splitting open the vibrant green grass were sidewalks so pure and bright, it was as if one had spilt milk upon their faces. The path they were on divided into three: the right and left paths each led to a series of gardens and fountains where the rich would love and drink wine under the moonlight, while the middle path—which was their way to take—led them straight to the keep's wooden doors of varnished ebony oak. The keep itself was white with dark blue shingles atop its peaks, and it began with a long hall with bastions in each corner with buttresses to support them. Beside it there were homes and towers that rested low, hugging the sheer edges of the mountainside. There the majority of the nobles made their residence, away from the peasant squabbles and the pungent tang of the poor. They escaped into the clouds where they were kept safe by vigilant walls. Behind the hall, there was an even larger tower that could only be reached by bridge. So high was this tower that it nearly fled completely from view. It acted as a laboratory for a select few, and a place where deep thoughts could be conjured by the king, where the only hindrances were the morning winds and the odd bird. The end of the keep was driven to the very edge of a mountain as if it were a foe of the city, hanging to the cliffside by the grip of its ancient stone.

The air was cool in the courtyard, and the sweet fragrance of the neighbouring flowers hung heavy in their senses. All was silent apart from the chirping of small songbirds in their laurels, the monotonous sounds of horse hooves tapping against the walkway, and the infinite sound of the fountains singing their melodies. Before the company could reach the door, it had already opened, as if the keep eagerly waited for their arrival. A group of men in blue robes exited from the door to meet them. It was there that the brothers and their guardians dismounted, and the men in robes guided their horses to the stables. As the brothers and their companions entered the great hall, Aaron Froy, a small and slender man in a white and golden doublet, strutted towards them: his arms were bent behind the arch of his back, and he walked with a pace of immense power and prestige. His face was small and fragile, with short hazel hair that was pushed to the right side of his scalp. It had wisps of grey within its roots. He had a well-kept beard that shot out primarily from his chin and was trimmed lower on his cheekbones.

"My princes!" said the man. "The royal council has been waiting for your arrival for quite some time. We are glad you have come before it is too late."

"Pardon our late arrival, Master Aaron Froy. How long has the council been in session?" asked Vidicus.

"We have yet to start, my lord," said Aaron.

"Ere now I have been met by a series of misfortunes, and it is good to see something has gone my way at last," replied Vidicus. Aaron looked at Cassius as if to signal a conversation, but the prince made no effort to converse. Instead, he hung his head low in a storm of apathy and the longing to be elsewhere. Cassius always found himself displacing royal accords and responsibilities with goblets of wine and fine women. The call of the crown was nigh, and soon Cassius would be crowned king of Ederia, however the idea of it was distant to him, and he never found himself apt to the call of power; he was nothing like his father after all, and aside from the hair, he most resembled his mother. His face was well sculpted, and his long, blond hair hung just short of his shoulders.

The brothers then made their separate ways. Vidicus headed to the council room while Cassius retired to his private quarters to be dressed in the appropriate attire. In his quarters sat a red doublet, neatly folded and ready to be worn. Cassius made no attempt to wear the lavish garment and instead found a dull grey tunic for his apparel. A large mirror sat in the far right corner of the room, and the prince made his way towards it. Cassius may have thought himself a man, but staring back at him in the mirror was only a child of eighteen summers, lithe and golden under the light of the sun.

Am I truly ready to be king? Can I send men into battle to meet the malice that I jest about from afar, knowing I have sent them to a thoughtless demise? Could I delve into the quagmire of politics or carry on the mantle of might that has been passed down by my forefathers? Nay, without doubt, I am no king, thought Cassius. And with such thoughts, he reached into his satchel, which lay on the dresser, and withdrew a waterskin that was filled with wine. The prince washed away his questions and doubts that casted a spell of self-hatred on him. Once the last drop of wine had quenched his thirst, he was ready for the council.

✳

"Master Cassius? Are you ready for the meeting?" asked Sir Hadrian from outside the door. There was no reply. "My Prince, are you there? Shall I come in?" The prince was still silent, and thus the old knight entered the quarters. Cassius lay sprawled out against the floor with his neck propped up against the bed frame. "Master Cassius, you have drunken yourself ill again! Here, take some of my water," said Sir Hadrian. The prince accepted the knight's waterskin, and his lips mumbled something too imperceptible to perceive. "My prince, I would rather not summon the might of your father in times such as these, as I promised him you would attend this meeting—and any other future meetings, for that matter."

"Y-your eyes . . . deceive you, old man," said Cassius with great struggle, as if his life had been lost within the bottle . . . And it had. "I shall attend the council! Shall we revel and converse with the rats that scurry under my father's feet, my knight?" The old man had now come to the foot of a daunting dilemma: satisfy the desires of the prince and keep true to the king's demand, or further soil the emblem of the royal family. Sir Hadrian tucked his arms under the prince's armpits and hoisted the boy to his feet. Cassius swayed to and fro until he finally came to feigned sobriety. The prince and the old knight then crossed the hall and—with difficulty—ascended a short flight of stairs till they came to the entrance of the council room. Waiting there stood Vidicus, Aaron Froy, and a multitude of other politicians, respected lords, and generals, most of whom glared at one another with unscrupulous intent and haughty spirits. As Cassius came into view, he could feel their animosity hit him as he walked towards them—he had, after all, made them wait nearly four hours.

"I see you are here at last, Prince Cassius," said an elderly man from afar. "There is much to discuss!" The voice was scornful in its tone.

"Julias! It has been long since I have been a subject of your teachings. So long, in fact, since you and I have spoken, I had begun to believe you rested beneath the earth—caged by a coffin!" said Cassius in reply to the older man's greeting.

"Fortunately for myself, I am doing quite well!" said the old man with a laugh. Cassius gave a smile in mockery. The crowd came to an unnerving silence. All conversations between the council members ceased as their attention was fully drawn to the prince's evident drunkenness. Not a whisper of the air, nay, not even the breath of the earth could be felt or heard. They knew what was afoot, for it was not the first time their prince had greeted them in this manner. Cassius's eyes darted across the room under a spell of panic.

The older man was not shaken or daunted by Cassius's uncouth remarks—for his will and pride were potent but were held at bay by a solemn heart. Julias Titus was his name, and he spoke back to Cassius, "Indeed, my prince, I am old, very old! But before the inexorable touch of time catches me, I shall sit and ponder over the great deeds I have done. I hope, in much time, you may do the same when your passing is nigh; however, hope is hollow when facing the truth, and so I ask you, my prince, shall you do the same?"

"How dare you speak to your king like this!" cried Cassius.

"But you are no king," said a voice from behind. It was a voice so powerful and sonorous that it stole the eyes of all that glared and mocked Cassius with haste. It was the true king. Cornelius walked through the crowd. Not once did he give his son the honour of his attention. He then opened the council room doors, and each lord and master hurried behind their king's lead. All except for one. Vidicus glared with pity at his brother for a moment before heading into the room. His sombre eyes felt like storms of sadness to the heart of Cassius. Vidicus then joined the council before his brother, refusing to wait for him to finish sulking under his stupidity. Before the doors could close, Cassius slipped in. The council was ready to begin.

The door opened into a large room, and at its centre stood a long oval table. On its oak surface rested a large map of Ederia and various carved wooden pieces that represented militia or local lords and dukes. The council members then took their seats around the table; the king sat at the far end by the window, in a large chair whose backrest rose above its sitter's head.

"I have called this meeting for more than the mere local squabble of peasants and rumoured information, but alas, we must start with such things," said the king. The council erupted in a series of whispers as they prepared the monthly report. Cassius rested in his seat and attempted to drown out the monotonous babble of politics and did so quite effectively until he noticed the man in black in the corner. He did not sit. Instead, Cassius found him leaning against the wall—a stance seldom found in the royal palace—and the prince could tell he was a strange man, indeed. He was cloaked in black with a hood that draped over the top half of his face, and all the prince could make out was a presence of brunet stubble. He smoked a long pipe and stood listening to each word that was being said with great enthusiasm and attention, pondering each topic of discussion within his mind. And to Cassius's surprise, he found himself terribly attentive to the room, listening to each council member—not because he was interested in the topic at hand. No. Rather, he listened to see what was running through the mysterious man's mind. Quite some time passed of constant conversation and questions asked and then answered after much controversy and discourse.

"And now for the true reason I have brought you all here today: what news have you brought to me from the east?" asked the king.

"The gathering of hateful surfs to the east, as you all know, has been unified by the Duke of Sacadia, Gareth Mordred. But due to the province of Sacadia's open rebellion, Prag and Berentheer have now joined them," said Julias. There was a wave of shock and almost terror that gripped the room, but the king held steady and persisted in his calm nature.

A dark-skinned man with long dreads then stood up from his seat and said, "I see no reason for us to cower at the notion of the eastern rebellion. So what if the east rebels? Duke Gareth is a mere stag under the claws of the dragon. He shall have the wrath of the crown fall upon him, and he shall break under its weight, and the eastern provinces shall bow before you, my king!"

"However, Master Kastilldor," said Aaron, "you forget that other provinces may join in this revolt, and even Sacadia itself still stands as a worthy adversary to Hellandor. Bruxstan grows weak without its monarch, and thus we may presume it shall fall if Gareth decides to lead his armies west."

"You seem to be forgetting the rest of Ederia." Kastilldor laughed.

"Rumour has already begun to spread that Etheel may yet join the rebellion, and Ruzadia and Vazareth are thousands of leagues away, so we shall not receive any immediate forces from the south," said Aaron.

Julias then stirred in his seat and said, "Alas, our immediate sortie to the uprising shall be from Hellandor, Tallonthor, Thellenor, and Sullthearia, and in due time, the southern forces shall arrive. Thus, we are the favoured victors indeed, but this is no time to meet such insubordinate actions to the crown with lightheartedness." The council then grew silent in hesitation. All played the deadly game of guessing the thoughts of their king, fighting for his approval and affection. Once the air grew still in the room, Cornelius found himself being the subject of all eyes as they loomed ominously from the far side of the table.

"No drop of doubt stains my thoughts," said the king. "Bruxstan grows weak, and we have been foolish not to realize the weakness that grows in the heart of Ederia." But the king then paused as if he was stuck between thoughts, teetering before a decisive action. "I hereby declare Vidicus as Duke of Bruxstan. My son, I believe you shall rejuvenate the power in the heart of Ederia." Vidicus was overcome with joy but also dread at the news. He attempted to speak, but no words could complement the web of emotions his heart was stringing from within.

"But, well, father, are you certain of such actions?" asked Vidicus.

"Do not let your happiness or fear cloak your judgement, my son. If I were not sure, I would not have spoken. Come a fortnight you shall pass thither beyond the Wyvern Peaks and pass the Gates of Pelendeer, and in the north of Bruxstan you will find the city of Luxtheil already awaits your arrival."

"Father! I shall lead with honour! And I will not fail you." The topics of the council now fled from Vidicus's thoughts for nothing could break the gratitude he was now swayed by. No longer was he the lord of his brother's pitiful shroud, he stood upon a small seat of power to call his own.

"If I may, my fellow lords! What of my coronation as king that draws nigh to the present?" asked Cassius, once again attempting to own the room. The room ceased in the discussion as the prince's remarks broke the flow of the council. Each member paused and withheld their contemptuous thoughts towards Cassius. And indeed, the young prince felt as if he could guess the contempt they held towards him. Cassius, the future king and the soon to be sovereign of the land, felt as if he was a pawn, a soldier in the battle of kings.

Do they truly loathe the coming of my reign this much? thought Cassius, and the boy now rested with a boorish glare upon his face that protruded with questions over the council—as if the very touch of his eyes was meant to belittle anyone who met their gaze. "No one?" The liquor had begun to fade, and his wit came back to him. "Humorous, isn't it, my lords, how easily you love to forget where the true power shall lie in the coming days."

"My prince, if we have offended you, you are owed our dearest apologies," said Kastilldor as he and the rest of the council bowed their heads in obedience to the prince.

"No boy shall hold my kingdom," said the king. "Indeed, my son, you shall become king once you have learned how to be a man, and you have evidently yet to do so."

"Nonsense, father!" proclaimed Cassius, springing to his feet with fumes of ferocity that hewed the room with a fell swoop of silence. "It seems you cannot part with the power the crown has bestowed upon you!" Cassius hunched forward over the table like a hound that was sick with rage, and all his composure was quickly abandoned as he lost what little patience he had for events such as these.

"You will sit down now," said the king in a voice so terrifying and quiet that fear began to seep into the very marrow of the prince's bones. The cold eyes of the king almost controlled Cassius's mind, compelling him into doing their bidding. Before Cassius knew it, his head had cooled, and he was once again sitting. The tension in his father's face was retracted, and he now retired back into composure. "Have no fear, my son. A royal banquet is expected; there you might just be able to practise your couth and kingly pride." The tension then drew back from the room like a wave retreating into its slumber within the ocean.

"My king, if I may, there seems to be an eerie man watching over us," said Aaron.

"An eerie man he might be, Master Aaron, but he happens to be the subject of our final discussion, one I have kept from you all for quite some time." Cornelius gave the mysterious man that stood in the corner a nod, and he then escaped from where he had watched the council from afar and took the centre stage. The smoke from his pipe floated gently in the air, filling the room with the pungent aroma of sweet tobacco. Once he stood by the king's side, he flung his hood back to reveal his identity. His long, dark hair was swept back, and his face was worn and wise yet held an admirable amount of wit and sharpness. Beneath his black cloak was a leather jerkin, and at his side was a deadly sabre; the sheath was black and gold and had to have held a great amount of worth.

"You'll have to excuse me, m'lords, I haven't the same experience in the royal tongue as you all do, so I shan't pretend otherwise," said the man. His voice was hoarse, as if his breath had felt the touch from the air of the darkest depths of the world. "For a time uncounted, our king has kept secret a plan of his, and I am what you call his instrument for such a plan."

"My liege, what is this plan he alludes to, and who is this vagabond that has forgotten to name himself, along with his purpose?" asked Julias.

"Be patient, my friend. He shall explain all in time, so hearken his words," said the king.

The eerie man now paced along the council floor and did so in silence for but a moment until speaking. "Long has Ederia been our cage. Too long. I have delved through ancient lore that was once thought lost, and I have roamed through mountains and tunnels; cracks and crevices, to find what was needed. But I shall not speak of the dark places I have journeyed to bring you this information." And with saying such the man flung a heavy pile of ancient manuscripts from his satchel onto the table: they were old and yellow in hue and had visibly begun to crumble over time. "Have no fear, my good lords. I am kind enough to tell you of its contents myself. From it, I have learned such: far to the east lies a land untouched by man for hundreds of years. Medearia is its name."

"Foolery! My king, do not listen to this jester! All who are wise in the history of the world know there is nothing beyond the eastern sea. Infinite evil waters lie to the east, borne of hatred and malice. No ship has ever returned," said Kastilldor, and a song of hushed whispers in agreeance from his fellow council brothers came soon after Kastilldor spoke.

"If my name will give you ease, I shall give it. Ivan is what most call me. If you are going to ask me if I know the existence of this place to be certain—I do, for I have been there before."

"My king, if this land truly exists, then why must we go in times as perilous as now? And the money we would have to spend on such an expedition would prove detrimental in the war effort," said Aaron.

"In war, do we not need resources? Timber for walls and siege engines? If we are able to expand our territory to alien shores, we would have the east encircled," said the king.

"But can we not merely harvest resources from the land we inhabit or sail north and around to the eastern shores?" asked Aaron. But the king gave no explanation. An uncharacteristic mood had come upon him. Seldom had he ever failed to articulate his motives, and thus one thing was clear to the council—there was something he had yet to tell them.

"I shall hear no more questions and doubt from you all. My mind is absolute. Vidicus, soon you shall make way to Luxtheil, and I shall go myself to meet this uprising. Six thousand I will take to march east, and I shall speak with Lord Samuel Herven of Thellenor and Lord Caspern Crude of Tallonthor to gain insight as to how many men they can muster; anything greater than four thousand shall suffice. But as for you, Ivan, I declare you the leader of such an expedition. I shall supply you with men of valiant arms and a small number of my soldiers," said the king.

"No offence, my liege, but I have already chosen the men that are to join my company," said Ivan.

"Well, if you believe you will do better with smaller numbers, it shall be so," said the king. "How long shall it take you and your men to prepare for such a journey?" asked Cornelius.

"No more than a month's time," replied Ivan. It was then that the decision to sail east was made, but there was something afoot. The council had not seen their king act in such a manner: impulsive and rash, ignoring logic. It was clear that the king had hidden something from them, but what it was, none could tell. But it was there the meeting met its ending. Each lord began to exit and make their way back to their quarters until it was only Cornelius and his sons that remained. Cassius attempted to sit up from his chair, but his hand was caught by a swift force—a force so strong and full of hate, it caused the young prince to wince. It was his father. His face was grim and dark and had coiled up in a snarl the boy had not seen before.

"If I find you walking into this again smelling of whores' perfume and reeking of liquor and piss, I shall drag you out by your golden hair and away from us all so we may not have the displeasure of looking upon you," said Cornelius. With his father's cold words, Cassius's heart sank into a forlorn pit , and still the eyes of the king smote through his proud facade and into his soul, scraping it with an unpleasant touch. And all that Cassius could find in the lonely trenches of his mind was that he was failing not only his brother, his father, and even his mother . . . but also himself.

Goblets, Tales, and Gardens

A letter lay upon the pillow of Cassius's bed, and he knew exactly what it was: an invitation to the royal banquet. Each lord in the keep had waited long for such an event, and rumours began to spread that there would be dancing. Lords, nobles, local dukes, and their ladies would come from all over Ederia to take part in the banquet. Cassius ran his finger along the edges of the letter: golden ink was intricately weaved on the borders, and the paper smelled of cinnamon. No peasant and surf, or even a middling man and woman for that matter, could ever dream of being invited to such a grand and rich spectacle. There were to be oceans of food and sweets, and beautiful decor, along with the romantic meetings of betrothed and the tense encounters of politicians and suave knights. Cassius knew it was to be a night he would not forget in any foreseeable future. Wine and rare cheese would rest in his gut until he could horde no more. It had been three days since the calling of the council, and

Ivan spent much of his preparation in the company of the king in the high tower across the bridge. Of what they spoke none could tell. Not even rumours dared to spread of such a thing.

The sun had just touched its peak upon the sky, and the warm spring day was ready to be challenged, and yet the young prince could not tear himself from the maddening questions he possessed.

Who really is this Ivan, and what is his business with father? thought Cassius. He could not find it within himself to breach through his bedroom doors and look upon the yellow face of the sun just yet. Instead, he pondered atop the silk sheets of his bed, thinking, and guessing the motives of the strange man that they had met in the council. And through much time and thought, Cassius found himself fascinated. Even Ivan's look was somewhat intriguing to him; there hadn't been any man within the city that he knew of that possessed a sword like his. The blade was long and lithe, and it was sharp on only one side. The tip of it was curled towards the wielder.

The prince guessed it was most likely from the south as he had heard tales of their foreign culture. So long ago was Cassius's journey to the south throughout Vazareth and Ruzadia that he hadn't even the vaguest recollection of what it was like. But from what he had been told, the people were dark-skinned—in a similar tone to Kastilldor—and they inhabited landscapes that ranged from long and seared dunes to a profusion of tropical woodlands. But as the prince was in the midst of lifting his mind from the strange man, the last powerful paroxysm of inquiry struck his mind, and Cassius could bear it no longer. He had to know. He could not lift his vexation without knowing. There wasn't a single lord who slept in the royal keep that would not ponder the very same questions as they dozed into sleep. The solicitous nature of the prince could not be cast away—it would not—and so he would have to satisfy his appetite for answers. Cassius leaped from his bed, dressing in a black tunic and leather pants, but this time, he rummaged through the back corners of his dresser and pulled out two long and withered cloaks, one of which was red and the other was black. Cassius draped the red cloak over himself and raced out the door, however in his right hand he still held the black cloak.

To his surprise, Sir Hadrian was nowhere to be seen. In his stead, there were two guards whose faces were hidden underneath their helms. He would have to lose them if he was going to make it anywhere near the tower. Without a glance, Cassius passed the guards and ran down the spiralling steps that led to the hall that was left of the throne room. The guards followed as expected. But the young prince raced down the stairs at an unexpected speed. The guards saw this and quickened their steps. Cassius raced downwards in an almost perpetual turn, but soon he reached the bottom and scurried down the hall towards the southern gate.

"Master Cassius! Why do you run with such speed?" asked one of the guards, and his voice echoed down the circular walls of stone and leaped into the hall—but their calls were in vain. The prince was far too swift for the men in their armour, and he turned a sharp corner and halted. His breaths were deep and in numbers, but he had not stopped to suck in air for long. He withdrew his red cloak and put on the black one that he had kept in hand, and he tugged the hood over the top half of his face, masking his identity. The guards arrived at the place where Cassius had stopped, but there was no prince in sight. A man in black walked towards them, and as he turned away towards the southern gate, the guards lifted their visors and spoke.

"Master Ivan, is it you that walks these halls?" said one of the guards. The cloaked man did not reply with words, instead, he gave an amiable wave and exited the keep. Cassius exited the gate and fled through the southern gardens with haste. Laurels were planted on each side of the path, and Cassius kept to the left, shielding himself from the sun as he ran in the shadow that rested underneath the green giants. The arch of the bridge began to peer into sight. As he ran across the yawing stone surface, he looked over its edge, but all

Cassius could make out was a distant and undetailed painting of green that portrayed the surface of the fields that were behind the city. Wisps of fog floated beneath the belly of the keep, and they drifted with the commands of the wind. Just how many feet he had stood above the ground Cassius could not guess, but he knew if he fell, in time he would appear as if he was a mere insect, plummeting to his death with a cloak of fire around him. Or so he guessed. At times, the clouds sagged low enough to a point where the bridge ran over them, and it would seem as if he was dancing along a surface of soft silk—the terrain of the heavens. Cassius did not look for long before heading back towards the tower, and it emanated an intimidating notion as if it was an omen of power. The scholars of the city had said the tower had been built long before the foundations of Ekmere were ever seeded, but something about it told Cassius it was even older. Its stone contrasted that of any other in the keep; it appeared ancient and somewhat rougher, eroded by centuries of gales thrashing its walls like hungry invaders. It loomed above the prince, dwarfing him with its presence. At its feet, there was a staircase that led to a small wooden door. However, no guards stood by at watch, something Cassius truly had not expected, for a time was seldom found when the king had abandoned his protectors.

As if he was a sly cat slipping through the crack in the door, Cassius departed into the confinement of the tower's borders. It was dark save for a series of torchers that were spaced out along the right side of the wall that circled upwards in a spiral to the tower's peak. Each step crept upwards with a deep hunger to ascend, and it wasn't long until Cassius had arrived at the first floor. The room was lighted strictly from the illumination of the torches that hung over the stairway, and it was dark and grey. The air was thick, and Cassius couldn't shake the feeling that the air seemed to hold still, so still that every inhale and exhale seemed to trouble space and cause a hurricane of dust. It appeared as if no man had breathed this air for centuries, for those who lived in the royal keep knew that the king spent much of his time at the tower's peak, like an eagle upon his perch watching over his city. Hugging the sides of the walls were bookshelves holding various tomes and ancient literature. Cassius could not let the air of this room fill his lungs any longer, and he turned and headed back up the stairs. He passed a variety of rooms similar to the first, however the prince did not halt this time. Instead, he carried on the long and dark climb of the tower. It wasn't until Cassius had passed dozens upon dozens of levels that he came to a room that was quite tidy and well kept; he presumed that this place and the floor above were where the king would spend his time. Although, he hadn't an idea just how close he was to the top floor. But his legs ached, and he grew weary of the merciless climb, and his feet could bear his weight no longer; each step was a challenge and a fight renewed again and again with each stride forward. He could feel his joints pop and tighten in ways they truly were not meant to. Yet he prevailed. Grinding his teeth with but a shred of a wince, he marched onwards. "I must be drawing near to the tower's pinnacle," whispered Cassius to himself over his deep breaths. At the centre of the room was a long wooden table, and opened books were strewn atop of its face. Behind the table, pinned to the wall, was a map of a place Cassius could not recognize. He stood over the table of books, but the language was alien to him, nothing more than futile and meaningless swirls of the quill. But to the right of the books was a feather and an inkwell that stood over a long sheet of paper whose tail draped over the front side of the table. It was messy, as if it was the rough works of an artist. Droplets of ink were splattered across the paper's edges and the writing was divided between the foreign symbols he had seen earlier to the left and that of the common tongue to the right, as if it was an attempt to translate the language.

But Cassius's moment of silence was then broken by the sound of voices. They were muffled at first, but then he heard the booming voice of someone roaring in the room above.

"The death must be swift and careful if we are to avoid any suspicion; this is to prevent a war, not cause one!" said the voice.

"It'll take time, time to gain his trust, but it shall be done," replied another voice. As Cassius heard the voices an instantaneous feeling of fear and regret fell upon him.

I must leave . . . and quickly. I have no business up here! thought Cassius. And as panic rose within him, Cassius twirled towards the stairs, knocking over the inkwell in the process, and the glass shattered. True fear now gripped the prince with its cold hands as the sound of the glass breaking filled the room. The voices above ceased and were replaced with footsteps. Not too far up the stairs, Cassius heard a door swing open, and the footsteps grew louder and echoed throughout the tower. There was no time to clean the mess nor make it out of the tower—he would have to hide, and quickly, for the foreboding echoes of footsteps slapping against the stone were racing towards the prince like a wolf gaining upon its fleeing prey. Cassius now found his body moving without thoughts to dictate it, and thus his legs carried him backwards, pressing him against a wall to the far side of a bookshelf. It was a poor excuse for a hiding spot, and the men from the floor above would surely find him. Cassius found that the idea of him being caught and scolded was no less than a certainty now, and he pressed himself to the wall with immense force. It was no more than a pitiful attempt, cowering in the face of inexorability. His jaw clenched, and he began to tremble. The monotonous tapping of boots on stone grew maddening, and the waiting was deadly; Cassius almost wished they would finally be upon him so the anticipation would subside. He then pressed his hands against the wall even harder to stop the shaking, but as he did so, he noticed something.

The surface of the wall seemed to almost dip and rise again in a straight line that ran from five feet from the floor to the bottom. He traced the line with his finger up, down, and across—but it was too late. The men ran under the archway and into the room, and Cassius pushed back with one last pitiful attempt, and the wall that he had rested against broke free and flipped. Cassius went with the turn. He had kept his eyes closed out of fear, and yet now as he opened them he stood in an entirely different room. The voices were once again muffled, but he could hear them more clearly now.

"Inkwells do not shatter by their own will! There was to be no one anywhere near this tower, let alone in it! Could it be that they have already arrived, and it is they that crawl in the darkness of the city? Find him and be quick about it, Ivan," said the voice, and at that point, it was clear it was the king speaking. His voice sounded strange to Cassius, almost fearful, as there was something out of his control, a dark threat that he could feel yet not quite see.

"It is a possibility that would be deadly to ignore, my king, for they are masters in the arts of deception. They may appear to be your closest allies until they slip a dagger between your ribs. Sleep with an eye open, do not roam in solitude, and keep only those you truly trust by your side. There are those in Ederia who are loyal to them yet appear to follow you, and it is difficult to unmask their true beliefs. Yet you speak to one who is more than able to do so. I shall deal with this rat," said Ivan. Cassius then heard no reply from his father, as if he was now lost in the nightmare of Ivan's words. Now nothing could be heard, not even the faintest of footsteps against the cool stone of the tower, nor could Cassius's attention bear resisting the abnormality of the room that lay before him. The end of it was curved as it seemed to hug the edge of the circular tower, and it was quite similar to the previous area: books and dozens of loose manuscripts that smelled of the tang of ancient times were scattered across the room on each and every available surface, however to the right side a fireplace moaned and crackled in the corner. Its embers were slowly dying, but they still popped and shone in their path to death. The smell of burnt cedar filled the room with a smoky aroma, and it was clear that someone had been in here not too long ago. A sword hung on a mantlepiece over the fire, but it was strange and foreign in appearance. Cassius had not seen such craftsmanship before, even in the Hall of Arts. It was somewhat thick, yet it was long and curved and had a short line of red fabric hung from the bottom of its hilt. Everything alluded to it being Sarakotan steel, however the same obscure dialect was engraved on the blade. More questions and inquiries had now been planted in Cassius's mind than before, but something new now arose, and it was a brutal and pernicious fear, the fear of the unknown. He could stay here no longer. But before the young prince could flee, the powerful urge to prove what he had found overtook him, and Cassius found himself reaching and grabbing for each loose paper he could find, hoping that one of them would give him at least some explanation as to what was going on. Each paper either crumbled or tore as Cassius hurried to shove the papers down into his satchel. The secret room held a second entrance, an entrance which one was able to enter by ladder, and fortunately for the prince, it was quite visible and unhidden. But as Cassius opened the hatch, he could hear the rage and the panic of his father. The ladder ran down a small unlit tunnel, and thus all was dark and still, and the words of the king echoed throughout Cassius's mind: *"The death must be swift and careful."* And the only questions that filled Cassius's mind as he slowly descended the ladder through the darkness were who was to be killed, and just who was trying to kill his father?

Time had waned further than Cassius had expected. It was already past midday when he began his flight back to the palace, and he was now just passing over the gaping bridge. A sudden pall veiled the sunlight, and the prince's path was darkened as a result. His pace slacked as his stamina dwindled, and he turned a sharp left corner into the gardens where he saw Vidicus sitting on a bench at a stone table by a fountain. Vidicus looked over at his brother and was surprised and frightened at what he saw.

"Brother? Your skin appears to be red and hot. Where have you been running off to?" asked Vidicus. But his brother's expression was grave and fey, as if a whirlwind of terror plagued his thoughts.

"Are we alone, brother?" asked Cassius.

"Well, not exactly. Sir Hadrian sits just on the other side of the laurels. Why do you ask?" Cassius paused in an attempt to poise himself and calm his breathing, and soon his complexion returned to him.

"Then I shall tell you but the basics, for the details, well, I would not dare utter any here," said Cassius.

"Then sit yourself down and enlighten me. I have wine and cheese and tender meat to soothe your thirst and hunger."

"I could not imagine a world in which I could deny such an offer," said Cassius, sitting across from his brother at the other end of the table. Before speaking, he gathered and prepared his meal, wrapping the aged cheddar in a thin sheet of roasted ham, and he then devoured his delicacy and followed it with wine to wash down the meal.

"This Ivan fellow," said Cassius. "I could not help myself, you see. I had an unshakeable desire to learn what his motives are and what exactly he and father have been up to of late within the tower, and I believe I have gained an insight that may prove ill if I am to speak of it to the wrong individual. Fortunately Sir Hadrian I trust, but there are others in this keep who are undoubtedly untrustworthy with such information."

"I presume you are wise to hold your tongue then, brother," said Vidicus, looking around the gardens for any possible eavesdroppers. "But no rats crawl among us. Only Sir Hadrian and you and myself. Now, what troubles you?" asked Vidicus whilst eating his meal. Before speaking, Cassius took another gulp of his wine and wiped his mouth before opening it, but as he did, a ghastly tone took him.

"I have reason to believe father has tasked this strange man with the assassination of someone. I do not know his or her identity as of right now, yet it fills me with unease. But what I heard next did more so: it appears as if father expects an attempt on his life as well." Vidicus's eyes widened in shock, and he almost choked on his food; his brother's words soaked him in unforeseen anguish. But he calmed his mind before speaking as his usual demeanour returned to him.

"Indeed, what you say troubles me also, but Cassius, you are aware that we are at war, are you not? It could very well be an assassination on the Duke of Sacadia or some other opposing figure—which is certainly nothing to trouble your mind over. But what truly is bothersome is if there is a threat within our walls. That is troubling news, yet it is also presumptuous, for we do not know these things to be true," said Vidicus.

"I know, brother, yet there was something quite peculiar about the tower itself: there were rooms filled with manuscripts of a language I could not read, and a map I could not recognize. And there was a hidden room I came upon just below the tower's pinnacle, and so I cannot help but feel there are nefarious things afoot, and it all started when that Ivan fellow came."

"If I may, I must say that your knowledge of geography doesn't exactly meet the standard of most. So, I am not surprised you didn't recognize the map, as you barely can make out southern Ederia," said Vidicus with a laugh. "A mere jest, brother, for I shall not wish to find myself being drawn and quartered once you are king."

"That will be the first thing I do." Cassius laughed. "I could speak of that tower for what would seem like an eternity, but I shouldn't for the sake of both of our sanities. Instead, tell me, what are your thoughts on father naming you the Duke of Bruxstan?" Vidicus once again found himself at a loss for words at the idea of his new title, Vidicus Helladawn, Duke of Bruxstan, and he could only ponder the question, attempting to find the best-suited answer.

"As for the moment, I truly do not know," said Vidicus, staring into the ruby-coloured pool of wine within his goblet. "Of course, I am grateful, yet I am also terrified, I suppose."

"You're terrified?" asked Cassius. "The great Prince Vidicus is afraid? I find that hard to imagine."

"And you are not?"

"I do not fear to be king," said Cassius. "I suppose I am afraid that I am not fit to be one. And I think you and I both know who the true king is of the two of us."

"Cassius, you flatter me too much. You are not as useless as you may think . . . and I think we both know what the true menace here is."

"And what would that be?" Cassius's brother made no immediate reply. Instead, he poured Cassius's goblet with wine and presented it to him. As Cassius grasped the silver goblet with the strength of his fingers, it would not move for his brother held onto its foot.

"This," said Vidicus. "This is the hiding menace that drains you day by day. I will not stand by anymore and watch my brother, whom I love, drink until his true self is no more. You will make a poor king if you carry on with your current passions: drinking with whores and wasting your money away. Sure, it is no crime, but your honour dwindles with each expense. Is this the king you wish to be?" Cassius sat silent for quite some time, listening to the soft chirps of the birds, smelling the organic perfumes of the garden, and watching the sun as it uncloaked itself of the clouds and illuminated the world. Cassius thought of the words his brother had spoken. Who was this king he meant to be? He then whispered to himself so softly that only he could hear his words.

"What type of man do I wish to be?" asked Cassius to himself, staring into the goblet at the ocean of red inside that glared back at him with its bloody eyes.

"Promise me, Cassius, that this shall be your last drink before your coronation. And no more shall you drink in such ways as you do now if you truly wish to please father; he will think better of you, I know it. He has been bitter towards you, but it is solely due to your actions, and I think he will show his love again once you clean yourself up." Cassius was still silent, lost in thought. "Cassius!" said Vidicus. Cassius's attention was caught, and his brother quickly reeled it into him. "You must promise me." Cassius hesitated before he spoke to truly cogitate the meaning of what he would say.

". . . I promise, brother. Not a drop shall touch my lips," said Cassius, and as he spoke, he poured the wine onto the floor until the goblet was empty. After Cassius did so, the two brothers found themselves under a spell of interaction, and they spoke of merry things until the sun slowly climbed down from the sky and down onto the far-off horizon of the western sea. Such laughter and genuine conversation the two boys hadn't had since they were children, and it was only when the sun had all but faded that they arose from their seats, and they retired back to their quarters. As they walked between the laurels, the blue hue of the sky gave way to a darkening grey, and the brother's backs were lit with the pale light of the moon. They, along with Sir Hadrian, slipped away into the keep, but as they did so, a figure cloaked in black appeared in the darkness of where the two princes had spoken. Ivan had been watching, and he had been listening. By the time Cassius and Vidicus had entered the halls of the keep, none were awake. All was silent. The eyes of the moon peered through the windows above, and it wasn't long until the brothers reached a crossroad and each of them made their way to their rooms. Sir Hadrian guided each boy to their chambers but did so to Cassius last, and the young prince and his loyal knight climbed the stairs to his room; Cassius's steps swayed and wavered as if he was a mere child too tired to stay awake and walk along with the strides of men. He collapsed onto his bed and huddled under his warm sheets. The knight then looked at the boy with a smile before turning to take his leave. "Sir Hadrian!" said Cassius with all of the remaining energy he could muster.

"Yes, my lord?" asked Hadrian, turning to the boy. The knight's dark blue eyes glinted in the moonlight, and his amicable face filled

Cassius with feelings of security—the assurance that the long night and the fears within his mind could not harm him.

"Will you make sure father is all right?" asked Cassius. And at this, Hadrian smiled and re-entered the room. He stood over Cassius and withdrew a necklace from a satchel that he kept at his side. A black string was threaded through a golden loop that held an emerald that almost seemed to light up the room with sparkles of bright green. Hadrian looked at it one last time, and at this, his stoic eyes wavered and became poignant. However, as he adorned the prince with the necklace, his sombre eyes were lost.

"Never shall you find your family under any harm if I am to guard it. Even when my sword-hand has all but broken, I will be the shield that protects your family name. If age finally catches up to me and my heart stops, I shall find a way to beat it again. I shall be the lonely watchtower whose eyes do not wane, even once they are white with blindness. Thus, do not fear, my prince. You, your brother, and your father shall be safe. I gave your mother that promise, and I intend on keeping it. This stone has a name, you know. It is called *En Estar*. It is said to be old, very old, and although I know little about it, it is said that it guides its bearer to their destiny," said Hadrian.

"I cannot accept a gift such as this," said Cassius.

"You can and you must. Do not let the fear that has been bred by what you think you learned today control you. For now, you must sleep," replied the knight, and before Cassius could say anymore, Hadrian left and tiptoed down the stairs. Rest could not have come to the prince any easier now as his vision faltered, and slowly his eyes began to shut until he could bear consciousness no longer and he fell into a slumber. Time drove onwards as midnight dwindled, and the dark beginnings of the morning were upon them. But the peace of the night was then destroyed. A haunting shriek came from the gardens, a deadly and bone-chilling cry that echoed briefly across the sky of shadow until it was swiftly muffled. Cassius awoke to the ominous wale, and he knew that death was about.

The Banquet of Ekmere

A long smear of fresh blood stained the stone floor. The disturb-
ing warm scent of iron was pungent as Ivan dragged the lifeless
body into the secret chamber. Ivan squatted down and hoisted the
body of Kastilldor onto a table. The chamber that Cassius had happened on by accident prior to now had been cleared, and a small
bier stood in the middle where Kastilldor was stripped of his robes,
revealing two red holes where a dagger had pierced his flesh. His
throat had been cut as well, and even now blood arose from the slit
and bubbled as it seeped out and dripped onto the bier. He had been
alive not long ago, yet the stench of death had already begun to creep
into the air. Cornelius looked upon the body with a heartless face.

"I trust you were not seen," said Cornelius.

"No, m'lord. He struggled, like a pig unready for the coming
slaughter, but none could hear him in the dead of night," said Ivan.

"I shall hold you to that," said the king. "Does he bear the mark?"

Ivan tilted the body onto its side, revealing a strange black mark just below his neck, and as the king looked upon the mark, his heart sank.

"The Mark of Medearia, a mark only seen after death," said Ivan.

"So, it is true," said Cornelius, and his voice dropped low and was full of dread, as if he could now see the threat that he had foreseen. "Dubious eyes have been watching and certainly waiting, for how long I cannot say, but I shall answer the call of his lord with no less an answer." Suddenly, the door to the main chamber swung open. Cornelius gave but a glance and Ivan understood; he covered the body with his cloak to hide it while the king stepped out to face the intruder. But he was too late. Sir Hadrian stood in the doorway, and all that the knight could see was Ivan hunched over the body of Kastilldor. Instincts and shock took over his limbs, and the old man reached for his blade, but his draw was halted by the hand of the king. "Calm yourself, my friend, all is well," said Cornelius. Sir Hadrian exhaled slowly, calming himself as he approached the body.

"Who is this?" he asked.

"Your good friend Kastilldor, from the looks," said Ivan.

"What? How has he died?" roared Sir Hadrian. "My liege, what has happened?"

"I cut his throat no more than an hour ago," said Ivan. The old knight's face grew red as he boiled with rage.

"You what?" asked Sir Hadrian, drawing his sword out of pure passion and hate, forgetting his knightly morals.

"Pipe down, old man. It seems your friend wasn't exactly who he said he was."

"Why, you—"

"Silence! Both of you," said the king with a hissed whisper. "Sheath your sword!" Sir Hadrian broke out of his spell of abrupt rage and came to reason. "He is no enemy. I shall explain all soon enough, but for now, you must know that there are those in this keep who are not who they say they are," said Cornelius.

"What do you speak of, my king?"

"You're asking a lot of questions, old man," said Ivan.

"Be quiet! I am speaking to our king, not to the likes of a murderer!"

"Your sword shall not touch this man! I did not intend on having you find out this way, but it seems I now have no choice," said Cornelius

"I am still not certain as to what I have found, my liege."

"Ivan and I shall explain all, but not here. Follow me," said the king. It had been years since Sir Hadrian had found himself taken away from his monotonous daily routine of unbroken harmony. The adrenaline that surged through his veins filled him with shock, yet also with sweet memories of battles fought long ago. He had forgotten the euphoria that was conjured through the primordial instinct to fight. Cornelius then led them to the final floor of the tower—the peak. Upwards they marched until they came to a thick iron door. They entered to find a small fire burning in the middle, and the roof was split with circling arches that acted as windows. Around the fire was a stone table where the three men then sat. The night had yet to wane, and the sky was painted with the light of the moon. The black void of the world was juxtaposed against the stars. Once all had sat down, it became quite apparent as to why the king and Ivan spent much time up here: the pinnacle was lonely, yet was also quite peaceful, in a sense that they could be hidden from the rest of the world, and their only arbiters were the sun and the moon. Cornelius would often make the climb up the tower to simply escape from the never-ending madness of court ordeals and the dilemmas of politics. Once he had arrived at the top, he would sit and cloak himself in a blanket to shield himself from the morning breeze, pour some tea, and read a book before watching the sunrise. It was times such as these when Cornelius had the pleasure of forgetting the immense weight of the responsibilities of ruling an empire, and he could simply enjoy the things in life that made him happy. He could be nothing more than a man. He was no longer the king, no longer a bearer of a title that forced others to feign admiration and loyalty to him, but instead, he was Cornelius Helladawn: a connoisseur of literature with the love for tea at dawn first, and the ruler of Ederia and the Casthedian Empire second.

"Four summers ago," said Cornelius, "I retired to my quarters to sleep the night away when I saw a man standing before the hearth. The man seemed to pay no attention to me, he would only stare into the embers of the fire before he introduced himself. 'Ivan is my name,' he said. As to why I called no guard I cannot tell, but for reasons I can't comprehend I listened to him. He told me he'd be willing to sell me information about a coming threat. I thought I'd bite, so I listened. He then showed me the manuscripts that he displayed to the council. Of course, I thought them to be rubbish, so I half-heartedly told him to prove that such land exists as nothing more than a jest before finally calling the guards. For three years the memory of our encounter escaped from my mind, until a year ago when he returned, and had somehow snuck his way into my chambers again saying he had come with proof," said Cornelius before tossing an old and worn piece of paper onto the table. "Such proof now lies before your eyes: my father's words before death." Sir Hadrian looked at the writing avidly. He could not speak, for any words would be far too plaintive for a man of his pride—it was without any doubt King Henselt Helladawn's hand.

1256, Jansire 14th

I cannot shake their eyes. They are all-watching. All-knowing. I believe I may be driven to pure madness from what I have learned. Ever since the Battle of Dunhollow, he has come to me each night in my dreams—nay, they are not dreams, for they are nightmares that are the creation of a demon's cruelty. Each dream is quite similar, full of terror: I find myself each time in the woods, and night has fallen. I can hear the howling of wolves behind me, and they grow louder and louder until I find myself now running for my life. It is cold, so very cold. No bow do I have, or axe, only my bare hands, and I am crawling through the thickets and the frozen mud like an animal until I come to a clearing where something always awaits me. It is a man . . . yet different. His ears are pointed, his hair is grey, and he stands nearly half a foot above me in height. At first, I could not speak—only watch. And thus, the first few nights I did just so, I watched and studied this creature. His eyes were grey as well, and full of age. Each time I found myself gazing into them, it was like peering into a bottomless, dark pit that has seen centuries unfold before it. At first, the dreams were harmless, and it wasn't until the third night in which I could finally muster the strength to speak. "Who are you?" I asked, but he did not reply right away. Instead, he began to study me, looking me up and down, circling me just as a wolf does its prey.

"Treat this as but a warning," he said. I tried to reply, but my voice failed me, as if I was speaking with my head underwater. "For hundreds of years we have watched, and we have waited. For hundreds of years we have remembered, thinking of the time when Ederia and Medearia were one. When humanity was at its knees, we elves lifted you all from the trenches of despair. But alas, how quickly you forgot. My memories of peace and harmony alongside your kind are all but gone and have been replaced with the memories of shackles, the searing pain of a whip ripping my flesh to pieces as it digs its way to my bones, chipping away at them until they have eroded. I remember watching my son die as your kind slashed at his wrists like madmen until he stood over an ocean of blood, and my daughter could cry no more . . . Yet through it all, I still wish for the days of old when there was peace between us. However, King Henselt Helladawn, know that our eyes caress your every step with a breed of hatred you do not know. I warn thee, if humanity does not stray from their ways of hate, a foul demise awaits us all, and there are those who shall show you the wonders of true pain," said the creature. And it then would say no more. It walked away and slipped out of sight into the darkness, but then I heard them. The wolves were upon me. I could see their snarls of hate and the pure instinctual lust to feed. Foam dripped from their mouths as their tongues stirred it around in their cauldron *of teeth. It only took one to attack before all others followed: their fangs ripped and tore at my flesh, spilling open my guts. They flossed their teeth with my intestines. I wish . . . I wish I could tell you I was numb to the pain, but it felt real, so very real. It was unbearable until it became so monotonous and infinite that the only things I could feel were the dull pulse of my heart and my blood slowly seeping out. And then I woke up. I haven't any idea how long these nightmares have gripped my mind. A month? A year? A century? I do not know. But it is the same dream each time. It begins with my life and ends with my death. Who are these creatures who speak of things I know not of?*

1256, Jansire 28th
I have begun to lose trust in the men around me. Just last night I swear I heard hushed voices that I did not recognize outside my chamber doors, and I find that I cannot rid myself of the creature's words. "Our eyes caress your every step with a breed of hatred you do not know." It's decided, I shall double—nay, triple the guard. I fear to exit the keep now for fear of never again returning.

1256, Mirthorn 17th
My hair has begun to fall out, and I've begun to hear whispers in my walls at night; it is the voice of a little girl speaking in a strange tongue. The nightmares have changed: there are more of them, more of those creatures, yet still the grey-haired one speaks to me. I have become so used to the pain of fangs ripping at my body that I no longer care or fear them. I know now that my death at night is inevitable. I know not what they want from me. Is it to make amends for the faults of my forefathers? Yet they speak of a genocide carried out by humanity that no lore or tomes suggest ever happened. I think I am beginning to truly go mad.

1256, Mirthorn 19th
The dreams have stopped. I think I may yet find peace, and no words can come close to being able to convey my happiness. I shall be able to

see my son again, to trust and love others, to walk among the orchids and the roses once again in peace. I admit I am quite embarrassed by all this. "King Henselt Iron Hammer is afraid of nightmares like a child fears the dark." That is what they shall say. Alas, I shall live with such, and yet I shall also rejoice, for my perpetual and never-ending terror has finally ended!

1256, Mirthorn 20th

Mutiny! There has been a coup in the very keep! They are after me. The servants and spies of these foreign creatures have slain my guards. I do not have much time left. I have sent my son away, and I have been told reinforcements are to arrive soon. We have sealed off the West Wing, but our doors shall not hold for long; there is a strange and evil magic in the creatures' nature. They appear as men and women yet act as if they are something far more cruel, full of malice that gives them strength. We have enough provisions in the West Wing to hold out for a fortnight, thus hunger is no fear of mine. Instead, I fear that this now proves that my dreams were filled with a horrid truth, and if they break our defences, none shall be left alive.

1256, Mirthorn 30th

The doors are mere splinters now. I can hear the fighting erupt from my chambers, and I have half a mind to unfurl myself into battle, war hammer in hand, but for the very first time in memory, I am simply too afraid. I can hear the voices of friends curl into shrieks of pain from the throes of death, and the halls of my family have been painted red with blood by them. But all is now silent, and I write as the ordeal rages about me. All is silent.

1256, Mirthorn 30th

I hear footsteps. They are coming! I have armed myself in one last attempt to fight and die with honour, but I shall not feign my courage, for I would run if I could, and I dare say any man would do the same.

The stench of blood draws nigh, and the foreboding notion of my coming doom is upon me. I am to die now. I know it. The wolves are inexorable.

"My father's last words and thoughts before his death," said Cornelius, now looking deep into the flames before him with eyes that appeared sick with sorrow. All was still and all were speechless around the fire. The flame flickered and danced, spreading a long shadow overtop the king's face.

Then, Sir Hadrian finally said, "As much as your father's words fill me with unease, they also fill me with questions."

"Then allow me to answer them," Ivan said. "It is thought that beyond Ederia, there is nothing, and any who dares to sail off its shores takes the risk of being lost to the infinite sea. *That* is a myth. There are other lands that lie beyond the sea, and I have seen them and the horrors that they hold with my own eyes. You have heard of the Massacre of Folka Island?"

"Of course."

"Good. Then you know that prior to the deaths of the scholars that did their research on the island, they discovered a Sarakotan ship offshore that had sunk in the shallows."

"Everyone in Ederia knows this story."

"History is full of lies and inaccurate recollections," replied Ivan, seeming somewhat bitter. "The ship was not Sarakotan . . . it was built in Medearia. Kept safe within a pocket of air was a chest. What was inside? Many things. Books, journals, illustrations, gold, but that is also where I found King Henselt's diary, one that had been confiscated by his killers so that what occurred stayed an utter secret. I am under the assumption that this ship belonged to the spies that killed King Henselt."

"Just how do you know such things?" asked Sir Hadrian.

"He," said Cornelius, "was one of those scholars on Folka Island . . . and the only one to escape with his life."

"There was something even more incredible found in that chest: a talisman. We brought it back, studied it. Then, in the dead of night, we heard the *whispers*. They were faint at first but grew stronger over time until we could understand them."

"The talisman . . . spoke to you?" Sir Hadrian could not help but laugh to himself slightly.

"Yes. It did. But it did more than speak, it taught. We learned about Medearia and its existence, we took notes, catalogued everything it said. It taught us all that, long ago, we humans and the various races of Medearia once lived alongside one another in peace. But that peace was short-lived and ultimately broke. We enslaved and systematically killed the elves and the other races of Medearia that called our land home. Blood and hatred ran free in those days . . . I don't know how they were freed, but when they were, they covered their tracks and fled back to Medearia. But it was then that the talisman began to speak to me specifically, and only when the others were asleep. It told me Medearia must be discovered once again, and quickly, before it was too late. When I awoke from my slumber that night, the school was in flames. The others were dead. I gathered the information we had recorded from the talisman before the flames could take it, and I fled . . . But I did as I was told. I found Medearia . . . and I was shown first-hand the type of malice that lives there.

"From my time as a prisoner there, I learned that as we have been oblivious to their existence, they have never failed to keep an eye on us. They have kept informants buried everywhere, keeping their king informed on everything that occurs here."

"And Kastilldor, a man I have known for years, was such a spy?" asked Sir Hadrian.

"Yes. An Eye of Medearia."

"How did you know?"

"I studied his behaviour during the council meeting. I guess you could say I became suspicious. I followed him, raided his quarters, and found this," said Ivan, raising a talisman and resting it on top of the table. "It is similar to the one I found all those years ago in the chest. It seems that through talismans like this, they can communicate to their superiors and relay important information. He was likely going to tell his king about our journey to Medearia."

"And just who is this king you speak of?" asked Sir Hadrian.

"King Estideel is his name," said Ivan. "He is the king of the *Ard Ciel*, or in our tongue, the *high elves*. It was one of them who plagued your liege's father with midnight terrors. I don't know anyone who possesses the power to communicate through dreams, so I cannot name this individual, but their king, I have heard much of him. He is not one to make idle threats. I roamed his lands for years before I managed to escape back to Ederia, and I know the creatures who King Henselt speaks of well," said Ivan.

"So, there were no witnesses left alive to tell the truth of King Henselt's death," said Sir Hadrian to himself.

"Exactly."

"One thing still doesn't add up," Sir Hadrian pointed out.

"There is much that doesn't," replied Ivan.

"Why would they want us to rediscover their land, but at the same time, they murder our kings and loathe our very existence?"

"Good. You're smarter than you look, old man. The truth is I don't know. There is *much* I still don't know. But there seem to be two different intentions: one is malicious, the other is benign. The elf I spoke to through the talisman seemed eager for me to sail east. It could be that there are two different individuals dealing out orders. It might be that some spies are loyal to one and not the other."

"Two different kings?" asked the knight.

"No. There is only one king that rules Medearia, but still, there might be a power struggle occurring. It's impossible to know for sure," said Ivan.

"I cannot help but ask you now, my liege: what are your true plans for this King Estideel?" asked Sir Hadrian.

"He will die, and that is final," said Cornelius. "If these savages believe they can murder the great kings of Ederia without feeling the quakes of vengeance, they truly are mistaken. The death of my father will not go unpunished, for it is also a threat, and they have been foolish enough to suggest they are preparing for an invasion. Ivan has told me that they prepare for war. Thus, the way I see it, we have no choice but to act swiftly in the matter. It is of utmost importance that the true nature of your journey, Ivan, is kept secret."

"Understood." Ivan then withdrew from his satchel a capsule that held a sample of wolfsbane—a poison. "This is how I'll do it. All I'll need is to have him in my sights, and I'll figure out a way to make him suffer from there."

"I trust you know what you're doing then . . . and that you will not fail me. You are to leave tomorrow, before sunrise. There you shall be hidden in the gloom of the night and will make way to the port of Hartshire, a small village to the northwest that should allow your voyage to Sarakota to go unnoticed. Once in Sarakota, there will be a ship that awaits you to the north in Hagami Bay. Once aboard, your voyage shall begin by travelling through the Mortem Sea and then sailing further east until the shores of Medearia are in sight," said Cornelius.

"I shall gather my supplies then, my lord," said Sir Hadrian.

"I don't mean to offend, old man, but this journey is one that requires speed; we will not have time to wait for you as you trail behind," said Ivan. Sir Hadrian felt the knife of offence pierce him and his pride, but before he could rebut, Ivan's claims were supported by Cornelius.

"You have no need to prove your worth to me," said Cornelius, "for I already know of its great value, but you belong at the side of my sons while I am away."

"Of course, my king, I shall not refuse such an honour. But I have ridden by your side for every battle to come, and I have fought for the glory of Casthedia against every foe who has risen against you.

My years remaining are numbered, it is true. But that is why I ask of you to allow me this last long ride out to war," said Sir Hadrian.

"I will not throw away and leave myself bereft of my most loyal knight and long-time friend. You shall safeguard the future of my house while I am gone. A greater honour I cannot give."

"Then it will be done, my lord."

"Good," said Cornelius. "Now we must call this council to an end and dispose of the body of Kastilldor." It was then that the council ended, and Sir Hadrian and Ivan descended from the tower, carrying Kastilldor. As if the journey by normal measures wasn't difficult enough, the descent was hardened by a lifeless load that swayed and leaned in an unpredictable nature. By the time Ivan and Sir Hadrian had reached the bottom floor, their skin had grown hot and wet with a fresh facade of sweat that boiled under their leather apparel. None now knew of the fate of the body of Kastilldor, for it took part in the great plummet from the bridge to the southern fields of Ekmere, and as Ivan and Sir Hadrian hoisted the naked body out the window, they could track his lifeless flesh for only seconds before it grew too small for any human eye to see and was then lost in the dark fall. Ivan leaned his body over the edge, watching the land rise up and down with a sinister coat of mist that hugged the surface.

"It is alarming, isn't it?" asked Ivan.

"What is?" replied Sir Hadrian.

"That all around us could be the eyes and ears of those who are spies of the East, ready to slip a dagger into each one of our hearts. They could be our closest friend, our beloved . . . or even you," said Ivan, looking into the old man's eyes.

"And how can I know you are not one of these 'high elves' you speak of?" asked Sir Hadrian.

"Perhaps I am."

"Perhaps you are. But if you are, you would have killed me already, so I know you are no spy. Yet still, I do not know who you truly are, nor do I trust you," said Sir Hadrian.

"Not many do. Maybe there will come a day when I can tell you the tales of how I discovered the lands to the east, but today is not that day. These are dangerous times, and one does not flap his or her tongue without a worry of a knife at their throat," said Ivan. Sir Hadrian turned to take his leave, but his hand was caught. Ivan had latched onto the knight's forearm like a vulture snapping a hare with its talons, and he held a short blade to Sir Hadrian's wrist.

"Speak a word of what you have learned to anyone, and you shall meet a similar fate to your friend." Ivan's words were dark, and tangible deadliness emanated from him. The old knight would not flinch, not even blink. There the two men stood. Motionless in their stand-off, waiting for the other to make the first move. Sir Hadrian, although old, was still a man to be feared with a sword, yet he was undoubtedly at a disadvantage. Ivan could slit his wrist in a matter of seconds, and the old knight knew he would soon die if he made an attack of his own. But before any man could act, the sun rose from the east and began to illuminate the dark land in which they stood. Ivan smiled and twirled the dagger before sheathing it, and the two men then turned and took their separate ways.

His mother and father never liked it when he poured honey in his tea, and back then their words were to be followed without question. But Cornelius was king. He bowed to no one. And yet, as he sat atop the tower, watching the sunrise and drinking his tea, he thought of them and their warnings about his childish cravings. He needed to calm his nerves, and it was moments such as this where such a thing could be achieved. He sipped, letting the heat of his drink cook his cheeks before sitting forward in his chair. The ancient pages of his father's writings sat on the table still, reminding him of his fears and about the severity of the situation. There was no point in lying to himself. He was afraid. The ignorance of Ederia would be his downfall. Of course, even the implication of other lands beyond theirs was deemed idiotic, but he was no fool. It was certainly possible. The

Casthedians had, after all, sailed over to Ederia from their homeland before the seas managed to take it below. He hadn't mentioned it before, but he had taken time to read pieces of the literature that Ivan had brought with him. To the king's pleasant surprise, studying the history of Medearia proved intriguing. Although he still knew quite little, he could already tell its history dated back much further than Ederia's. There were books that were from the sixth century, speaking of races he'd thought to be pure fantasy. Sections of the text covered the multiple sub-species of elves that lived primarily in the western regions. Further to the east, however, the land and the species that inhabited it began to change drastically. Unfortunately, he did not have the time to delve deep into those chapters just now, but the fact remained true that his curiosity of Medearia—his new-found enemy—had grown.

One singular thought was on his mind now as the sun's body came into full visibility over the mountain. It was of Cassius. He loved him. But one could, at times, dislike what they love, could they not? With so many emotions intertwined within the relationship between a father and his son, it was easy for things to turn sour. But what was he to do with him? If he became king, there would be constant advising needed, but even then, Cassius was not obligated to listen to his advisors. It was entirely possible that he'd abandon the position altogether, and Cornelius would find his son unconscious in the city's streets, bottle in hand. He could not let that happen. So, the question remained: why did Cassius drink? To his shame and astonishment, the king could not find an answer . . . but still, he longed for one.

Am I to blame? Is it me that has failed Cassius? And Vidicus, have I let him down as well? thought the king, and at that, he placed his tea down on the table and stood up, looking over his city. In his hands he held a violet-coloured flower, and Cornelius gently caressed its petals. The king's mind was elsewhere, and he turned his gaze towards the sky, thinking of his wife. *Have I failed in turning our boys into men, Iris? I miss you … more than anything. Surely, you'd know the answers to these questions … I am lost without you.* Suddenly, his touch grew too strong, and one of the flower's petals broke free and fell. Cornelius then watched as the wind carried it away.

✳

The early morning was then flooded with guests arriving to attend the royal banquet. Men and women of all colours and races stormed the walls of the keep, adorned in bright and beautiful attire that had been crafted by the most renowned tailors in the land. Everyone was driven by the powerful desire to roam the ancient halls of Ekmere, to see the ruby chandeliers glitter in the sunlight, or walk along the silk paths of the gardens, and each spectacle filled them with awe and an unspeakable feeling of wonder. Of course, they were nobles themselves, yet every castle paled in comparison to the architectural brilliance of the city in which they had arrived. It almost appeared as if the city itself had been shaped by the hands of a god. Rich meats and wine and other rare sweets were brought into the keep by horse and carriage. Each vacant room was given up to the guests. In total there were to be one hundred and thirty, although it seemed the true number could have been thrice as many, for even the palace seemed to grow dense with the presence of bodies filling the halls up with the aroma of sweat that had been masked by perfume. During the hysteria of guests arriving, Vidicus was there to greet each of them, conversing with other lords and admiring the beauty of their maidens' apparel. Even the Duchess of Ruzadia, Philomena Evergrado, had journeyed far from the south to meet the young princes of Casthedia. Her beauty was spread by the wings of words by the people of Ederia, yet even the tales of her allure fell short of what they beheld. In all the various greetings of politicians, dukes, and duchesses, Cassius, the future king of Ederia, was nowhere to be found. Indeed, many wondered where their inevitable sovereign was, however most inquiries were stagnated through perpetual greetings and, of course, the presence of the king himself, Cornelius. Hundreds of bodies shifted through the palace halls as the eyes of guardsmen searched each pair of eyes, however no knight or guard was as fearful of such a scene as Sir Hadrian, who knew more than he liked about the ominous situation and the danger the king was in. Poised was such a threat, hidden to all, yet its presence was undeniable.

The old knight watched everyone as he stood at the side of Vidicus. Suddenly, the sharp ring of a bell bit at the ears of each guest, signalling the beginning of the banquet, and with the ringing of the bell, the mass of the crowd huddled slowly towards the ballroom's doors like guided cattle being herded into a pen. The ballroom floor was covered with a long red carpet to typify the colours of House Helladawn, and it was a large, open space filled with candlelight and hints of the aroma of smoked cedar. The air was so brisk and clean it was as if it had been harvested from the northern winds that lived atop the lonely pinnacles of the world. As the room began to fill with guests, cliques and circles of private conversations formed naturally. Rumours were spread of marriages and the deaths of distant relatives, and the sounds of surreptitious speech and laughter between pompous figures filled the air. But the room was quickly silenced as the king and his entourage entered the premise, slicing through the horde of bodies and dividing the room as he and his knights strutted to the opposite end. It was there that they stopped, and the king spoke to his guests.

"My fellow lords and ladies, knights and councilmen. Your presence in my halls soothes the very air and eases my mind in times as perilous as these. But I have not gathered you all here to speak of the terror of war! No. Tonight shall be a night to rejoice and to fill our heavy hearts with gaiety and laughter before the long night. Come morning, we march to war. And thus, the vestige of joviality from this night shall follow you and brighten your path through the dark times to come. But fear not! Look not to the future of war, but to the goblets of wine you hold in your hands and to the barrels of mead that shall soothe any sorrow you possess," said Cornelius. And after the king spoke there was a roar of approval, along with clapping. To the right side of Cornelius stood a rather small man who was dressed in a tight blue doublet, and he held a small bronze bell that he rang to gather the attention of the guests.

"The royal dances will now proceed," he said in a bland and lifeless tone, but even so, couples readied themselves to dance as the young men and women around them mustered their courage to ask one another for a dance out of the pure will of adolescent lust. And as this occurred, an orchestra entered the room through two small doors. In their hands they held drums, harps, flutes, and a copious variety of brilliant musical instruments that were engraved to the finest degree. At the forefront of the orchestra was the conductor, who led the group to the dais to the right of where the king stood. It was there that they played sweet and melodious tunes with but a drop of sadness in their tone, and as the beautiful sounds spun around the room, the talking of the guests ceased, and the dancing began. Maidens spun, and their dresses twirled and twinkled like starlight in the night, like rubies and diamonds exchanging glances of light that glimmered off each other's bewitching faces. The joy was so pure and innocent as smiles and genuine love coated each and every person. The bodies of each man and woman stuck to each other through ties of sexual desire, and each waist moved in perfect synchronization to its partner. Aside from lovers' rituals, others who weren't lucky enough to receive a dance crowded around the food and drinks, and amidst all of this, Cornelius looked upon all, watching his people with delight as a lion does to his pride. However, it did not take long until the king himself stepped down from the dais, and as he did so many nobles and dukes approached, squeezing through and dodging the dancing couples as they weaved through the crowd until Cornelius stood before them. Indeed, the night began merrily and as according to plan, and thus all found joy under the crystal chandeliers of the palace; all except for three men. Sir Hadrian stood by the corner of the room with his eyes fixated upon his king, watching every move of every guest, meanwhile Ivan made no presence, for he was to depart soon on the perilous journey eastward, and Cornelius found himself proud for his people yet as ever alone. The old king had not danced nor felt the lovely touch of a woman since the passing of his beloved, a woman so kind and benevolent as to tame the bitter fire of Cornelius's heart. It was Iris. Yet none would utter such as the grief that Cornelius held in his heart was all too great, and any mention of her brought the rains of melancholy down upon the king's heart, releasing a feeling of sorrow and bitterness into Cornelius that none dared disturb.

But at times, Cornelius would rise early in the morning and walk amongst the flowers as he and Iris had once done. It was there that he would then pick a flower and journey to the top of his lonely perch and prepare a meal for two, and it was there and only there that the king would express his grief.

"My king! It is good to see you on a night as joyous as this," said Aaron as he and Julias came to meet the king. "It has come to my ears that the duchies have gathered their armies and are prepared to march east. All they do now is wait for their king," said Aaron

"Then they shall do so for but a while longer. Come two days' time, the armies of Hellandor shall march, and the golden dragon banner shall be raised for battle."

"We look forward to your victory, my lord," said Julias, and both men nodded with respect.

"Forgive me, but I do not wish to speak of war on a night like this," said Cornelius, walking between the two men and taking his leave.

After hours that seemed mere moments, the dances had ended. No more did any skirts cloaked in scarlet diamonds spin around the floor; it was time for the royal meal. Long tables were wheeled out, and a silk tablecloth was thrown on top. Once the tables were set, long lines of chefs carrying exotic and grand foods atop silver platters entered the room, and the savoury smells of roasted pork and sugar-sweet pies roared into the air like a stormy rogue wave in the deadly moonlit seas. A roasted pig was placed at the centre of the table. Warm liquified lard oozed down from its baked pores, painting an appetizingly wet and glorious coating of flavoured juices around the flesh, meat so tender it could almost fall from the bone by just a glance. It did not take long until the guest's plates were filled with food to soothe their appetites. Lithe and petite ladies moved with delicacy, too hesitant to sink their teeth into their meal out of fear of seeming uncouth, or as some would put it, "unwomanly."

Before Cornelius could stab the hunk of flesh that stared back at him with his fork, the doors opened, and a man hurled himself forward through them, stumbling as he made his entrance. It was Cassius. He had resorted to the bottle again. The prince mumbled to himself as he struggled to walk straight, and as the prince's strides became more unstable, more guests looked up from their meals to see their future king.

But no eyes watched with a greater ire than those of Cornelius, watching his son walk down towards him as a hawk does its feeble prey. The king's mouth curled into a malicious frown, but no feeling was stronger than the paroxysm of pity that his heart bathed in and the feeling of failure—a failure as a father. Vidicus could not watch because he knew his brother had broken his promise. As Cassius walked past his brother, he put a hand on his shoulder and gave a crooked smile, a smile shattered by wine and mead, but Vidicus still could not bring himself to look into Cassius's eyes. Cassius, although slow in stride, came now to his father, and it was only then that the young prince took notice of the utter silence. It would have filled him with terror if not for the alcohol that ran through his body, pumping his heart with inebriated courage that silenced all reasonable thoughts. Cornelius sat there, silent, and in his brooding silence, flames flickered in his eyes, like two canary coals burning with a composed hatred. Yet the malice of the king was kept at bay, for the last vestige of love for his son was still proud and present in a storm of thorns that infected his heart, thorns that were dipped in the poisonous pools of pity. Cassius opened his mouth to speak, but no words would fall out. Instead, Cassius went for what he thought was his: the crown. The prize jewel of the entire Casthedian Empire, the symbol of power that would one day belong to him was now being spun around Cassius's finger like a trinket that some peasant had picked up from the market for a few silver pieces. Cassius took it from his father and placed it on his head. The young prince twirled with delight, mumbling some fictitious and imperceptible drunken language. The king calmly stood up. Without turning his body towards Cassius, Cornelius looked over his shoulder towards his son.

"You asked me, long ago, why you were to be king, and I told you that you must show me *why*. Tell me, son, is this your grand attempt to show me the type of king you are to be?" asked Cornelius.

Cassius stopped dancing and spinning and now looked towards his father, as well as the hundreds of guests that watched his intoxicated performance. The frightful hum of laughter and snickers rang like a drum in Cassius's ears. Something had happened that he wasn't quite aware of. Cassius looked around, searching to and fro in search of what could have caused the uproar of laughter, but before he could see it, he felt it: the warm dampness of his tight pants, the feeling of an odoriferous liquid seeping from between his legs down to his feet. He was pissing himself. He chuckled and then stumbled. He was too drunk and stupid to be embarrassed. The king turned towards him and approached. To Cassius's surprise, he could feel the fear of his father be conjured into his mind, and his heart began to race as the king drew even closer. Cornelius stared into the eyes of the prince, the eyes of his son, and he was so close Cassius could feel his father's breath tremor with rage, yet still, such rage was kept tight on a leash of royal courtesy. Cornelius sniffed the air, breathing the fumes of urine, and smiled with pity. "You are no king, and you are no son of mine."

The Swallow's First Flight

Cassius awoke to the feeling of cold stone against his cheek. His mouth gaped open clumsily as saliva slowly dripped out from his gums. He stirred, and in doing so, the stone floor brushed against his front teeth. He winced and sat up. As he did so, Cassius could feel the blood in his body shift from his head to his limbs, making him dizzy. His body ached, and the headache was unforgiving as it throbbed, running pain down his neck. Cassius remembered little of the days that followed the banquet, for he had spent nearly every hour in the gutters of drunkenness. He thought hard, pondering the passage of each second that had followed his father's words: "You are no son of mine." Unknown to Cassius, it had been three days since the banquet, days in which the prince confined himself to the walls of his room. Cassius's hands were pale and sick in colour and shook uncontrollably—he needed the morning drink, to feel the burning sensation of vodka down his throat to soothe the effects of withdrawal. Sitting up from his bed, Cassius stepped forward, tripping over loose papers, empty goblets, and shattered glass. The prince's quarters reeked with the bitter stench of wine, and flies scurried back and forth from each sticky pool of spilled liquor, sucking and feeding on the remnants of the night's spoils. Cassius pulled his shirt up and off from his body like a snake shedding its skin to reveal a sick and slender figure. Cassius's ribs protruded from his sallow body. It was then that the sweating began. The prince grew hot, and his skin was accompanied by a fresh layer of feverish sweat. He needed the drink, and he needed it soon. Cassius tore his room apart, searching for any signs of fresh liquor to soothe the pain. He threw himself down on his hands and knees, scouring the ground that lay buried in a heaping mess of clothes and tobacco ash.

"Where the fuck is it!" said Cassius as he panted in abrupt hysteria. "I know you're hiding from these lips, you little shit." But his search was halted. The hinges rang and the door swung open.

"Am I interrupting something?" asked Vidicus.

"As a matter of fact, YES. You are, brother," said Cassius as he returned to his grand search for a morning buzz.

"I guess your words are hallowed," said Vidicus with a sigh.

"The fuck you on about now?" asked Cassius. In response, he received a pitiful laugh.

"You don't remember, do you? Who am I kidding, of course you don't. When was the last time you left this room?" Seeing that he could not relieve himself of his brother with ease, Cassius turned and stood up and faced Vidicus. "Ugh, look at yourself, Cassius. You could use a shave and without any doubt a bath, I can smell—"

"What the fuck are you doing in here, Vidicus?"

"I'm—no—*we're* worried about you, Cassius. You don't sleep, you barely eat, and by appearance, all you seem to do is waste your days locked away in here with a week's supply of wine. You do not look well, brother. Please, Cassius, allow me to help you."

"Where is father?"

"Well, he's quite busy at the moment. He readies himself for the journey east for war."

"I see," said Cassius. "He cares naught for me and my state, only of himself."

"Please, brother, you couldn't possibly be so ignorant!" said Vidicus. Cassius was silent for a moment as if sizing his brother up, looking at him up and down.

"You FUCKER! Give it to me! You've had it this whole time, haven't you?"

"What? What are you talking about," said Vidicus, backing off while pulling his right hand behind his back. But before he could realize it, Cassius went for his throat, like a viper snapping a mouse in between its fangs. Pushing Vidicus against the wall, Cassius reached for his brother's right hand. In it, Vidicus held the missing bottle. Cassius latched onto his brother's wrist and tore his prize away from the grasp of the enemy. Vidicus's hands tightened themselves around Cassius's neck, and he then threw his brother off, and Cassius stumbled, falling to the ground and smashing his head against the opposite wall. Both brothers breathed heavily. It had been a short scuffle, yet one that had been filled with emotion and nerves, nerves that drained their stamina as the fight went on. "If you become king," said Vidicus while bent over like a tired hound after a hunt, "we will all be doomed." Vidicus rested his case and made his way out of the room, leaving his brother to bask in the pungent disorder of his own creation. Cassius covered the blow to his head with his hand, and he could feel his warm blood drip and hang on to the edges of his fingers. He looked at his hand and gazed into the deep red stain he now bore, and the image of blood was engraved in his mind.

The throbbing in Cassius's head increased. Any thread of light that made its way into the room felt as if it was a needle slowly sinking into his eyes. He crawled into the nearest corner, and the sickening pain of his head began to spread down into his neck again. The acidic taste of bile began to flood his esophagus along with the awful taste of the previous night's drinks. The broth of his stomach's corrosive fluid rose like a volcano, and Cassius threw up all of what he had previously eaten and drank. His vomit bit and chewed at his gums and teeth like they had been bathed in a pool of poisonous fluid. Cassius suddenly felt his vision blur, and the prince dozed off into an unexpected sleep.

The world was red, bathed in an ocean of ruby. The moon's face was full and smiled upon Ekmere with a bloody grin, and the air was frigid, almost frozen, and it was still, almost crystallized in place. Cassius was running through the gardens, looking up at the red sky in horror and awe. He stopped where he and his brother had shared their meal not long ago. There was no one there, save for a goblet of wine that had been spilled over onto the floor. Cassius approached only to find that it wasn't wine. It was far too thick and warm. It was blood. Cassius looked at it for but a second longer before making his way to the palace doors. As he wandered this strange world, he could hear a voice that almost seemed as if it was calling to him, but it was far too faint to make out its message. As he leaned into the doors, opening them, the voice became louder, and it was now that it almost seemed like a child singing to himself. Cassius ran down the hall into the throne room, and it too was soaked in a dubious facade of red. But it was empty and quiet. Cassius felt forlorn in the great hall. He stared at the throne that rose before him, yet all he could feel was the agony of nothing, nothing but the touch of a winter storm on his skin, and the deep pain of an icy blade slowly plunging into his heart. Cassius trembled. The child's voice became more and more clear—it was coming from the Hall of Arts. Cassius listened momentarily and began to walk towards the voice.

"H-hello? Is there anyone there?" asked Cassius. No reply, only the song, and as the prince got closer, he could make out some of the words.

Long live the king, long live the king.

The love, the regret, and the crest upon thy chest.
The falling dragon passing through the sky.
Long live the king, long live the king.
The journey had ended!
The fallen moan.
What a wonder to hold a beating heart of stone . . .

Its tune was that of a coarse whisper, like a snake in the dark of night telling tales of the plains of serpents. Cassius made his way to the hall's entrance and entered reluctantly. A child stood near the end with his back turned to him, and he was holding something, something of great interest to him. Before Cassius could open his mouth, the song stopped. "Do you want to see?" asked the child. Cassius recognized the voice immediately.

"V-Vidicus?"

"Who else would it be, silly?" The child turned to reveal the young face of Vidicus, however each eye had been torn out, and blood trickled down from where his eyes had been. Cassius could not move. He was powerless against the rapid and untamed storm of terror that hung in the air, encircling him, cornering Cassius until each limb was frozen in place. He wept, and as Cassius did so, droplets of blood dripped down from his eyes.

"W-what the fuck is happening? Where am I?"

"Isn't it beautiful, brother?" replied Vidicus, raising the box he held in his hands, and Cassius fell backwards onto the ground.

"Get . . . get away from me!" said Cassius as his brother approached, and when he did so, the two bloody holes where his eyes had once been were beginning to pulse, revealing the red innards of his brain. Vidicus resumed his song as he crept closer and closer, and Cassius found himself almost subconsciously crawling away. He had to get away! It was too much! Cassius became dizzy, swaying from side to side as if he had been enchanted by the powers of fear.

The blood, the blood, dripping from the sky!

Twirl! Twirl!

Prepare to die . . .

Vidicus opened the box, and in it was the head of Cassius staring into the crimson-bathed world with two pale white eyes. Cassius let out a wail of fear and crawled back towards the throne room before managing to make it back to his feet again. Cassius ran wildly through the halls like a white rabbit fleeing from the fangs of a wolf. Blood oozed and seeped from each crack and corner in the walls, and red droplets came plummeting from the ceiling, pecking the cheeks of the prince as he came back to the throne room that was now buried in a sea of snow. Cornelius knelt at the far end near the doors. His back was turned, and in his hands he held a woman. Her hair was raven coloured, and she seemed deprived of life.

"Father?" asked Cassius, running forwards through the snow that had been polka-dotted with circles of blood. "Father? Where are we? What is this place?" Again, no answer. "Fine! Ignore me like always!" There was no reply from Cornelius, only silence. "You know, I don't see why I even bother anymore. You act as if you're too high and mighty to speak to your very own son . . . Well? Anything? Damn you, old man!" Cornelius turned, and the woman in his hands was Iris. Cassius ran towards his mother as Cornelius lay her down on the sheet of snow.

"Cassius," said his father, "my time of judgment is upon me, as is yours. It is time for you to show me what you think you are worthy of being."

Suddenly, the bloody rain began to pour as if the gates of hell had let their juices seep into the realm of the living. Soon everything bathed in the scarlet mess of the divine, and all the time the deafening screams of Vidicus rang in Cassius's ears, making him cover them as he winced. The screams did not stop. The river of blood would not end. It would not end.

Cassius seemingly woke in a field of mist. A woman clothed in white slept beside him. However, she was strange in appearance: her ears were pointed and long, yet she was still beautiful. As Cassius came to his senses, he noticed the girl.

"Um, hello?" Cassius asked. Yet she was fast asleep. Cassius nudged her, but even still she did not move. Finally, he rolled her over, so she was facing him. She was beautiful! Cassius had never seen a woman like this in all his life—if the term "woman" was even the correct way to describe her. Cassius reached to nudge her once more, but as he did so, her eyes opened, eyes like shards of fiery amethyst blinding his sight. The ground then morphed and curved inwards, defying the laws of existence that had previously been drawn out by reality. The world bent in obscure ways, stretching, creating colours that were once incomprehensible to the human eye. Cassius fell through the earth into a black void where the presence of physical matter was not absolute or altogether certain. He plummeted through the warped tunnel where time became a mere artistic thought. Stars and swirls of light spun around uncontrollably, faster, and faster until they were but a constant image, a flaw of existence. But then the world began to fade into white until all around Cassius there was but a pale canvas, ready for life to be painted. Cassius could feel the edges of his mind begin to crack and shatter. He turned, although even the notion of direction was not a strictly defined thought, and as Cassius turned, he saw a man with long grey hair. His ears were pointed too, and as was the case with the woman. Cassius felt as if he was not entirely human at all. On each side of the figure were three wolves, all of whom were turned away from the prince. They seemed distant, however simultaneously seemed to be sliding closer through the very fabric of this foreign plane they inhabited. They grew closer and closer until Cassius realized that he had been walking towards them this whole time, as if some unexplainable force drove them together. Cassius was no more than an arm's-length distance when *it* began to speak.

"I have long awaited this meeting, Prince Cassius Helladawn," said the man. Cassius attempted to reply, but his voice felt drowned, as if he was swimming underwater. "We prepare for war in Medearia, a war that is not needed. We have watched you grow, Cassius, and we believe you can stop the bloodshed before it is too late. I see the Tree. It is far away, beyond the Plains of Shadow, and beyond the lost realm of Arealia. We must cure the Tree, Cassius, if we are to prevail. Do not ask any questions because our time is short. But know this—your judgment is nigh upon the horizon. You know well the decision you must make; you must now only make it. Hearken my words, human. Find the girl. Find her . . . Find Medearia." The grey-haired man turned, revealing his sombre grey eyes that took hold of Cassius in a grip that felt as if the very arms of time held him in their grasp. He looked into the creature's eyes and felt as if he could read the history of the world just by looking into them.

Reality bent again. The air seemed to slowly turn into a light blue as mountains and cities spread themselves out before Cassius's feet. The idea of time and space came back to him as he realized he was now falling. Faster and faster, he fell to the earth like a meteor that has come from a distant and strange place. Soon Cassius could make out the buildings of Ekmere and the palace walls, but still he fell with greater speed. He fell through rock and wall, wood and marble, until suddenly, Cassius found himself in the corner again, in a room that smelled of liquor and of shame.

"Prince Cassius? Cassius? Wake up." Sir Hadrian knelt over the prince, checking his pulse. "Cassius—" The prince awoke in utter shock, looking forward as if attempting to see a place that just wasn't there.

"H-Hadrian? Are you there?"

"Yes, of course. I am here, my prince," said Sir Hadrian. The knight held the boy, comforting him as best he could. But Cassius's hand darted towards Sir Hadrian's knife. Cassius shrugged the old man away and ran for the door. Sir Hadrian took after the young man with a surprising pace, and as he came to the long hallway, he could see Cassius running towards the gate that led to the tower. "Prince Cassius, come back at once!" But the cries did not hinder Cassius in his flight, and soon enough the prince hurled himself through the doors and into the light of dusk. Yet still, Sir Hadrian kept close behind him. Pounding his feet upon the stone paths, Cassius ran like a broken spirit that roamed the plains of purgatory. The prince ran until he stood at the midway point of the bridge. There Cassius stepped up and onto the edge of the bridge, and as Sir Hadrian drew closer, he saw that the boy was in tears. "Cassius! Please, step down from there," said Sir Hadrian.

"Y-you don't understand! None of you fucking get it." Cassius wiped the tears from his eyes, thinking of jumping, hoping that death would provide the happiness that life promised.

"I do not. And I won't pretend to, my liege."

"Cut the courtesy from your tongue! The only reason you speak to me with respect is that you must, not because you'd like to. So do us both a favour and just back away," said Cassius, pointing the knife towards the knight. Sir Hadrian raised his hands in the air.

"I am no threat. Please, I beg of you—let us talk; tell me what I don't understand," said Sir Hadrian. Cassius looked down towards the fields below that stood miles away. It was a much farther drop than he had once thought. "Tell me, Cassius, what has happened?"

"You all condemn me. You hate me, I know it! But I do not blame you . . . I guess . . . I guess I've begun to condemn myself. Damn it all! Hadrian, if I am no king, then just who in the fuck am I?" Sir Hadrian stepped closer only to be held at bay by the tip of a knife.

"Sure, you are a prince, and sure, that *does* mean you will be king. But you are also *Cassius*. You are still that sweet little boy that once glared into his reflection on the marble floors as you walked alongside your father—who *does* love you. But to be honest, you can have all the titles in the world and still be sad. You, Cassius, *you* decide whether or not you wish to be happy. You decide who and what you wish to be. Forget about being a prince! Forget about being king!

99

Focus on who you, Cassius Helladawn, could be." As the boy listened to the knight's words, a drop of love and tenderness touched his pain, but as he readied himself to step down towards Sir Hadrian and into safety, a gust of wind rolled through the keep, knocking Cassius back towards the edge. He fell. Sir Hadrian leaped forward, clutching the boy's torso before he could fall, and he then lifted him up and over the parapet. Cassius looked into the eyes of the knight, almost in disbelief of what had happened. No words were needed, only actions. The prince embraced Sir Hadrian with deep and genuine love. He was grateful, and Sir Hadrian gave a smile of relief.

"I . . . I am sorry!" Cassius then began to cry into Hadrian's leather jerkin.

"Shh. You don't need to apologize to me, my boy. Come now, let us head back to your chambers." And the two did just so. Once they arrived in Cassius's room, they sat in silence, hiding away from each other's gaze, only contemplating the events that had unfolded.

"Sir Hadrian," said Cassius after some time.

"Yes?" answered the knight.

"Have you, well . . ." Cassius paused, gulping, before continuing. "I had a dream this morning, a horrible dream." Sir Hadrian's ears perked, and he began to listen attentively to what the boy had to say. "I saw many things that filled me with terror, things I wish I could just un-see. But I cannot. I saw—I saw this man—and a woman! But they were strange. They looked different from you and me. The man spoke to me with wolves at his side. I was frightened, Sir Hadrian, and I could not speak. But *he* spoke to me."

"What did *he* say, Cassius? You must tell me!" said Sir Hadrian, immediately thinking back to King Henselt's diaries.

"I don't know! It all happened so fast! All that I can remember is that he told me that my time of judgment is now upon me, or something like that. But he also said I can stop the bloodshed that is to come. I don't know what it means. He said so much more but it's all so damn hazy."

"Do not worry, my boy. You have said nearly enough. But do you remember what he looked like?"

"He, well, he was tall, quite tall. His hair was grey, I think. But there's one thing that I simply can't shake from my mind—his eyes! They were old, very old and full of sadness, I could tell." Sir Hadrian's heart sank, and his jaw opened.

"This is a dangerous being you have spoken to, my young prince, or at least your description leads me into believing so." Sir Hadrian stood up and walked over to the window that overlooked the gardens. The old man brooded and pondered as Cassius did the same.

"I am leaving," said Cassius as if stealing the words out from Sir Hadrian's mouth.

"No, Cassius. *We're* leaving. I have reason to believe these dreams are no mere fantasy, and your life may be at risk. But what has ignited your urge to leave?"

"The reason why I will not speak of yet, I can only tell you that I feel I must go."

"Go where exactly?"

Cassius paused, raising his head, and finally looking at the old knight. "To Medearia."

Sir Hadrian appeared utterly perplexed by the prince's claims.

"Out of the question entirely! I'm sorry, Cassius, but it is my duty to protect you, and going on some quest to a land that we do not know even exists is just, well, it's insanity!" said Sir Hadrian, looking quite red, as if his temper nearly boiled at the thought of the prince's intentions.

"Not an ounce of what you just said was false, and yet, I must still go."

"We will make our way south to Vuldhear, where you will meet your cousin. And Cassius, we will not stray from our path in the slightest, do you understand? We leave in a week," said Sir Hadrian. Cassius then fell silent. The knight patted the boy on the shoulder and then left. Cassius was now alone, alone to ripen his thoughts and emotions until they bore the fruits of ideas. His eyes glared into the mirror, and he did not like what he saw. He saw a boy with the potential to be a man, a prince who truly wasn't ready to follow the tracks of his destiny. No, not yet. He saw a boy whose happiness had been drained by self-loathing and hidden insecurities that none would ever guess even existed. But most importantly—he did not see himself. But who was *he* exactly? He came closer to the mirror, looking deep into the pitiful reflection before him.

"So, if it is the time of judgment, and a time for decisions, then let it be that my mind is made up . . . I'll show them . . . I'll show all of them that I'm more than just some worthless drunk," whispered Cassius. But it was then that he remembered the papers he had stolen from the towers.

Maybe they would give me a clue as to where Ivan and his company have gone, thought Cassius. He then managed to collect each stranded piece of paper that was scattered around the room and organized them until they seemed in order. Most of what was there had been written in a different language, save for three pieces. The details of the voyage east were explained only slightly, and Cassius finally thought he began to make some sense of what was truly going on. The journey was to begin with Ivan setting off with his men to the port of Hartshire.

> *You are to make way to Hartshire, and it is there you shall find a ship awaiting you that will take you to Sarakota.*
> *-Cornelius Helladawn*

Cassius had only a vague idea of where Hartshire was, but it would have to do. The thought of leaving frightened him, but also enticed him and filled him with a guilty joy. It was like staring up at night into the blackness of the sky. The starry sky was beautiful, yes, but also daunting and a constant reminder of how small one was in a place simply too large for their comprehension.

✳

Night had fallen upon Ekmere, and the world was unusually quiet under the watchful eye of the moon. Cassius buried his clothes into his bag frantically, searching for the most valuable of clothes and possessions: a pipe and smoking tobacco of course, water skins, a walking stick. Copious amounts of food, along with pans. Cassius knew he would almost certainly forget something—most likely multiple things. But he'd have to pack light.

I wonder just how far this Medearia is? thought Cassius. *Probably a lot further than I could ever expect.* He roamed his quarters in the darkness; the only light came from a small candle that he carried around to illuminate his surroundings. Cassius paused every now and then momentarily to listen to the guards that stood outside his door. Nothing, nothing yet. No sign of the guards stirring out of suspicion. Even still, he had to be quiet. Cassius crept across the stone floors of the room like a cat strutting and fretting to the melodies of the night when few beings lie awake. He reached into his chest and took out a broadsword. He had hardly ever had to use it, and even then, it had been years since he had done any sort of training with Sir Hadrian. Yet he would need it nonetheless. The scabbard was of red and gold leather with a ruby gem closest to the hilt on each side. Finally, he grabbed his red cloak and strapped his bag on his shoulders, and very slowly, Cassius unlocked the small glass door of his window. He dropped the bag first, and there was a small thud. Cassius's heart stopped as he listened to see if any noticed the sound. Still, there was nothing. However, now came the true challenge of squeezing himself through the door, and of course, landing in one piece. He would start with his hands. Cassius dangled his torso out into the gardens through the door, and the cool, brisk midnight breeze ran through his nose. *I could make it, maybe,* thought Cassius. As he wiggled his body through the window like a worm crawling through the dirt, he could tell he had begun to make noise.

"Prince Cassius, is that you?" asked a guard from outside the chamber doors. Cassius paused. His heart had stopped.

"Ah yes, Sir Dane! Just—just having a rough sleep, that's all. Nothing to fret about."

"Should I fetch some new pillows and sheets for you, m'lord?"

"NO! No. I will be fine, thank you!"

"You sure, m'lord? It's really not a big kerfuffle at all. I mean, it'd take me . . . why I'd say only a few minutes to get down there and back."

"Sir Dane, all I need right now is a good rest, yet you seem to love interfering with it, don't you?" Sir Dane gasped, shocked by his stupidity and stubbornness.

"My lord, my apologies! How stupid of me, right? I suppose it must be these late shifts that be getting to me head of late."

"I'm simply doused in sympathy, Sir Dane," said Cassius.

"Really? Well, that's rather understanding of you, m'lord," said Sir Dane.

"No! Not really! Now shut up and let me sleep, please and thank you!"

"You're quite welcome, my prince!" Cassius rubbed his eyes in frustration. It surprised him how a complete oaf such as Sir Dane had ever become a knight. Probably for drinking unheard of amounts of beer and thus being the first guard to be too fat for his armour. He was kind-hearted, yes, there was no denying that, but he also happened to be a bit dull in the head.

By now all had become quiet, and Cassius was able to breathe once again. He slid inch by inch until most of his body had slipped through and his legs followed. He fell about eight feet into a mound of dirt. He was out. He was free. Yet now it was time to flee.

Cassius stuck to the shadows, clinging to the palace walls as if fearing the moonlight. His heart raced, pumping in his chest in a relentless attempt to simply burst through his body. He looked at his hands; he was shaking uncontrollably. Cassius could hardly believe what he was doing, it was as if some power dictated his own will, and his body and mind simply followed. This was it. It was time Cassius paved his own path, did what he truly wished to do in an attempt to find out what and who he really was without any titles of royalty. An outside entrance to the Hall of Kings was around the corner on the north side of the palace, and as he came to it, it began to rain, and a torch just outside the entrance gave Cassius some comfort in the lonely and frigid night. Before entering, he raised his hands to the weak flame. Slowly his palms and wrists began to thaw; he had begun to soak far faster than he had expected, and the cloak offered little resistance against the rain. After warming himself up, he grabbed the torch and headed inside and down the stairs that led to the catacombs. The cold air was still and felt untouched. The constant drip of water falling and crashing against the limestone felt almost melodious, and each drip echoed in the cool chasms of the earth. Cassius slowly walked down the stairs, lighting more and more torches as he approached the resting place of the kings. Once the prince had reached the bottom, the sound of rain had ceased, and the great hall where the lords of Ederia slept lay before him. Memories of being a boy flooded back to him, and he halted, thinking of the days in which his father would walk him and Vidicus down here where they would play with various kinds of bugs. For some reason, it had felt warmer back then. In fact, all things had seemed better back then. Long ago before his mother had died, and when his father was less grim and heartless—they were all truly happy back then. But now such memories felt like hazy dreams, foolish dreams of an almost-forgotten time.

Cassius's eyes watered, but he did not weep. Once he had finished basking in poignancy, Cassius took one step forward and looked up. *Today, I forge my own path and my own destiny. I will see the far reaches of the world perhaps, and maybe, just maybe, I'll reach my journey's end, and I will return not only to my father but to my people, and show them what kind of king I am,* thought Cassius. Then, the prince set off, fleeing into the darkness and down a secret passage that led down into the fields below Ekmere. He was gone. He was free. He was reborn.

The Mortem Sea

The inn at the port of Hartshire was quite lively for a Sunday morning. Sweaty drunken men swayed to and fro, singing broken sailors' songs and arm-wrestling atop the bar that was encased in a sticky facade of old mead and flies. Boisterous laughter roared all about Ivan and his two companions as they sat in silence in the corner of the inn. Their hoods covered their faces as they smoked their long pipes. Azrad and Connell sat at the opposite end of the table to Ivan. They had been his companions before, and he trusted each of them with his life.

"We shouldn't be here, Ivan," whispered Azrad. Ivan took his time to respond, blowing clouds of smoke into the air.

"Take it easy. Remember, we're trying to blend in here. Besides, the ship has already docked in port. It won't be long until it's ready to sail," said Ivan.

"I know. It's just this place, too many people, I guess. Puts me on edge."

"Well, we'd be smart to stay on edge here, just at least try to fit the part. Remember, we're not mercenaries anymore; we're to go as spice traders. A good disguise should make our journey east go relatively unnoticed," said Ivan. Suddenly Azrad felt a hand smack him across the back of his head. Behind him stood a large man with his arms crossed in an effort to intimidate the men sitting down.

"You there! Browny!" said the man. Azrad poked his head up, looking at the greasy giant that stood before him. The man's bodily odour spread across the room and made any who got too close wince in response.

"Sorry, bud. Don't think I know you," said Azrad, returning back to his pipe and drink. The man stepped closer, clenching his fists.

"You misunderstand, *friend*. We don't want your fucking kind here," said the man, spitting into Azrad's drink. Connell stood up slowly, staring into the eyes of the offender with brutality in his eyes as he clutched the leather handle of his claymore. Connell towered over even this man, and all that was needed to de-escalate the situation was a mere glance at Connell's wide frame. Azrad had paid little attention to the man and simply smoked his pipe with a grin upon his face.

"You're gonna buy my friend another drink, or I'm gonna tear you the fuck in two," said Connell. The man then gulped and would not utter another word. Instead, he went off to do as he was told.

"Fucking locals," said Azrad. "Thanks, big boy. I think I've seen enough of the north already." Connell sat back down and gulped at his ale. The yellow liquid seeped through his thick beard and then dripped down onto his chest.

A short woman then entered the inn. She was Sarakotan by her looks; her hair was black and tied back into a bun that lay under a straw hat, and she wore a white and blue kimono. She immediately stuck out in the boorish cluster of males and as she entered. A sweet cherry perfume floated into the air, mixing with the pungent smell of masculinity. Most fell silent, looking at her with sour frowns on their lips. The Sarakotan lady walked through the crowd with confidence in each stride. Still, all was silent, and all eyes were upon her. She went to the bar.

"I am looking for some spice," said the lady, breaking the awkward silence, and the innkeeper chuckled.

"What do you think I look like, some merchant?"

"Do you really wish to know what I think you look like?" asked the woman. The innkeeper made no response. "That's what I thought. I believe you are already aware of how disgusting you appear to *any* woman. Now . . . of course, I did not bring myself into this shit hole to look for you. No," said the woman with a laugh, "I am looking for three men. They work in the spice business, mind you. So, are you going to tell me where I can find them, or are you going to keep staring at me like it's the first time you've seen a pretty girl with your own eyes?"

"Calm your tits, lassie, I was only having a bit of a jest. They're over there in the corner," said the innkeeper. The woman approached Ivan and his companions, and as she approached, Azrad gripped the knife he kept on the side of his boot.

"Stand down, Azrad. She's the one who's going to get us to Sarakota in one piece," said Ivan.

"Everything is ready," said the woman.

"Thank you," said Ivan. "I suppose I should introduce you three. The two assholes across from me are Azrad and Connell, and the lovely lady before you is Yuikiri—I would try your best not to piss her off."

As Ivan spoke, Azrad caught a glimpse of a beautiful black and silver sword at her side that had been hidden underneath her robes; it was curved, and on each end of the scabbard there were small inscriptions written in the Sarakotan language.

"Well, let us not delay then. The sooner we leave the mainland the better, I'd say," said Azrad.

As the four of them got up and headed for the exit of the inn, Connell brushed up against a man in a red cloak. Their shoulders hit one another, but Connell was far larger and sent the smaller man nearly to the ground. He didn't have time to look back, and so the man in red was lost to the crowd. As they walked out into the muddy streets of Hartshire, the innkeeper and the man that had disturbed Azrad and his companions earlier stood outside waiting for them, along with three other men that had been inside the inn.

"There they are!" said one of the men in a twisted and rough voice.

"There's that brown-skinned fuck and that Sarakotan bitch I was telling you boys about," said the innkeeper as he smiled with his yellow teeth.

"Listen, we ain't got no issue with you true northerners," came another, pointing towards Ivan and Connell, "but it's these outlanders that don't belong here. Go back where you came from, or there will be trouble!" Yuikiri stared down each man. Their brutish tones of voice did not affect the likes of her.

"Step aside," said Yuikiri with a calm and composed demeanour.

"Is this bitch fucking blind?" asked one of the men to the other. As Ivan and his companions stood still, Yuikiri walked right towards the threatening men, paying little attention to them, as if they weren't even there. As she approached, the innkeeper grabbed her by the shoulder and tried to swing her towards him . . . yet with blinding speed, his arm was broken in two places. The innkeeper screamed. The rest of his men looked at her, perplexed by what had just occurred. Her touch had been graceful yet precise, and it had appeared as if she had merely tapped his arm twice. However, the results were undeniable: the innkeeper rolled in a puddle of his own rage and pain. Yuikiri unsheathed her sword, and a sparkle of light twinkled on its tip. As she entered a lethal stance, the brutes before her shuffled backwards in fear. Yuikiri raised the blade up parallel to her gaze while slowly turning to face each attacker.

"Fuck this," said one of the men, spitting in her direction and dragging the innkeeper away with him. Yuikiri sheathed her sword and continued down the path towards the docks.

"That happens often?" asked Ivan.

"I've gotten used to it," replied Yuikiri. The four then said no more until they made it to the ship. It was quite large and had a rather foreign look to it. The crew was all Sarakotan in ethnicity save for a few men who hailed from other regions of Ederia. Yuikiri then took the three of them to the captain's quarters, where she sat down behind her desk and put her blade down on the table as she pulled out a fan from her drawer. "Terribly humid weather it has been of late, I tell you," said Yuikiri, taking off her hat. Ivan and the others did not reply. "Listen. We are not going to Sarakota. Instead, we are sailing straight through the Mortem Sea and into the east."

"What? This isn't exactly what we had discussed," said Ivan.

"Sarakota grows dangerous, and ever so strange as the months go by. It would be wiser to sail straight to your destination, a destination you have yet to tell me?"

"That is something I cannot do," said Ivan. "Not yet. I shall wait until we have passed beyond the Mortem Sea, but for now, I shall tell you that it is a place that I would like few people to know about. The same goes for this journey itself."

"Understood," said Yuikiri. "Come. Let me show you to your beds, and you can meet my brother."

Yuikiri then led them down under into the interior of the ship. The tangy smell of salt and aged seaweed filled the inside of the hull. The interior was crafted with wood, which had been soaked and eroded by years of sea voyages. Each wall felt more like a sponge that sucked up the miasmic air and slowly exhaled it. As the four walked down the main hall, seamen poked their heads out of their cramped quarters to look at the newcomers. Ivan investigated one as he passed, and he could tell he would already feel claustrophobic. A man in a red cloak sat crouched on his bed with his hood drawn over his face, and there was something rather familiar about him that Ivan could not quite describe. He halted, stopping his two companions. But before he could say anything to the cloaked man, Yuikiri broke his concentration. "My brother, Hiroki, is just inside here." They entered. It seemed this room had been much better kept, and the door was made of iron and had an emblem carved into its face. As they entered, a man sat on his knees in silence at the far end. This room did not have the stench of rugged salt and rum. No. This room smelt of cherries, peaches, and orchids, and the flowers grew in urns in the far corners. The melodious hum of chimes drifted softly into their ears.

"Before you say anything," said Yuikiri, "Hiroki has taken a vow of silence, given to him by the monks of Fu Island. It is a punishment for his actions." Ivan looked at the man as he meditated, paying no attention to his visitors.

"What has he done?" asked Azrad.

"We . . . we do not speak of that. All you should know is that it tainted his honour, and in our culture, honour is above all," said Yuikiri. Hiroki then stood up, and his sister told him the names of the company as he shook their hands. The eyes of Hiroki were cold; Ivan and his men could tell they had seen death too many times. His hair was charcoal black and was tied behind his head. Yet, the right side of his hair had turned grey, as if he had been touched by the frigid fingers of death. "I can see you are wondering about the grey patch on his hair. Do not worry, he does not mind. It is part of his punishment as well. It was given to him also by the grandmaster monks of Fu Island. The Okami Breath, it is called," said Yuikiri. Hiroki shook their hands, giving a slight bow with each greeting, before returning to the place where he had sat. "Would you like to see your rooms?" Ivan and his two companions still fixed their eyes upon the silenced man yet followed their guide towards their rooms that were behind yet another iron door. Each room was much nicer than those they had seen before. Ivan had a room to himself, and

Azrad and Connell shared a room that was luckily quite spacious with bunks in the corner.

"I think we both know who's on the bottom," said Azrad with a laugh as he climbed onto the top bed after putting down his bags. Connell groaned out of disappointment, but he had grown used to such things, and as he lay down, the entire frame began to creak and bend.

✳

The journey to Hartshire had gone far smoother than Cassius could have predicted. However, the greatest challenge was convincing the captain to let him onto the ship; she was quite stubborn and strong-willed, yet she finally gave way once she had a few gold coins and gems in her fingers. Cassius only hoped that on the ship he would find Ivan in a jovial mood, and that he would be willing to allow him into the company, but he hadn't the slightest clue as to what he would say to him once they met. He had seen them in the inn and the companions that he was with, and in fact, one of them had nearly knocked him to the floor as their paths crossed. Cassius stood up, mumbling to himself. His hands still shook, and he craved the touch of liquor on his tongue, but he could not fall into his desires. If he did, Cassius knew he would have failed in what he sought out to do.

It would be so easy to get one bottle to myself or even but a drop on my lips; anything to take the shakes and the headaches away, thought Cassius. He would have to subject himself willingly to a pain of his own creation, and Cassius knew deep down that if he faltered at all in his goal, there would be no turning back. He would soon drink himself to death if he could.

He rubbed his eyes and his temples. The constant grind of the headaches seemed as if it would never end, and his mind felt lost or foggy—he had troubles forming any long string of linear thoughts in his mind. The prince knew it would be a long voyage ahead, and he soon sat down in his bed of straw. The odour of sea salt that had been embedded into the floorboards and the lifestyle of the poor were not things the prince had ever experienced. No roadside brothel could have prepared him for this. And as Cassius tried to kill the time, he found himself tumbling and writhing in his bed out of discomfort. *I could really use the pillows Sir Dane offered right about now,* he thought. Soon Cassius, to his surprise, found himself drifting into sleep, only to re-awaken every few hours or so to the startling stench of the open sea.

✳

Ivan spent most of his days aboard the ship in the solitude of his room. Yet Azrad and Connell soon became quite accustomed to life at sea, learning the art of sailing by speaking to the crew, and soon enough they were on terms with each and every crew member. They'd often drink and play games of dice and cards with them at night; Ivan could hear the tumultuous roars of the men from down the hall, and when Connell and Azrad would stumble back to their quarters, Ivan could smell the fresh scent of broken barnacle flesh on their boots. Yuikiri would come and speak to him every other day or so, yet each discussion was quite brief, and all this time her brother spent in deep meditation. And when Ivan would walk by amidst his ritual, he could sense deep sadness and regret within Hiroki's cold, dark eyes. He couldn't decide on whether or not he felt he was lonely or simply stuck in the deep meres of remorse. From what Ivan and the others had observed, most of what Hiroki would do, aside from meditation, was sit and drink tea as he painted and read in a corner.

Five days into their journey north, the ship finally turned east into the entrance of the Mortem Sea. Ivan had heard evil things about the northern seas. They were frigid and nearly frozen, and icebergs towered overhead while their glacier roots dove deep into the frozen waters. But the tales of the northern seas were what sprinkled grains of terror into the dreams of each man aboard the ship. A few of the sailors had shared their personal stories over a hushed candlelit table in the hours before midnight. They spoke of wraiths that glided over the ocean's surface, looking for souls to ravage to soothe their appetite for the living. Ivan thought all of this to be nothing but rubbish, and he still did, yet even still the dreams of maidens drifting over the water, singing the songs of the dead in the darkness of the pale moon, kept him awake at night. However, it took three days for them to cross the heart of the Mortem Sea, and nothing eerie or nefarious occurred.

The evening clouds were illuminated by the pale light of the stars. Ivan tried to listen to the soft moaning of the wind but could hear nothing, not even a breath. It was calm. His body was wrapped in various animal furs and hides. Azrad and Connell had already gone to bed, and it was here on the top deck where Ivan could free his mind. He thought of times long ago, he thought of the Pools, and he pondered the list of names of friends he had lost there. And the memories of pain and scars flooded back to him. He would avenge every one of them, he knew it to be true, and the more blood the better. He would make King Estideel pay for his actions. But there was more. *Far more.* Deep from within, he always had a hunger for power, and a part of him, at times, flirted with the unrealistic idea of being king one day. Of course, it was unlikely, and yet the idea prevailed and before long he wondered, if he could ever gain such power, how would he do it?

If I were to ever sit on that throne in Ekmere, I'd need an army, of course, to get me there. But that might not be as difficult as it seems. Afterall, Estideel is already looking to invade . . . He has an army, but how would I gain control? I only have Azrad and Connell with me, and if I were to ever act upon these ideas of power, I'd have to let them in on the plan. But I could trust them, I know it. What am I thinking about? This could never work; gaining the power to dictate an army in land like

Medearia would be impossible . . . However, the impossible is always far more intriguing than the possible, thought Ivan, and what started off as a foolish and unrealistic idea of himself having power . . . actually began to take hold of him, and the difficulty of it was enticing. After only a few minutes, Ivan went back inside and fell asleep in his bed, yet what had been faint memories of evil times and aspirations of power still gripped his every thought. He awoke many times in the night, tossing and turning . . . There was something evil afoot that made its lair in his mind and on the crystalline face of the ocean. *Could it be done? Could I ever be king?*

※

The room shook. Thunder cracked like a whip. The cool air whistled through the ship's cabin. Cassius awoke to his belongings being hurled to and fro, and the burning coldness of the ocean crashing against his face. A storm had fallen upon them. A cruel storm, full of winter malice. Cassius stood up only to be flattened by the brute strength of the wild gales. There was a hole in the nearby room to Cassius that was spreading further and further, getting wider as the seconds passed, seconds that felt like an eternity in a frozen doom. Water flooded like a perpetual river into the ship. The ocean was cold. It was a type of cold Cassius hadn't known before. It was the coldness of death, the coldness of a black and hateful sea. It was the coldness of terror upon his skin that jolted him awake in the night, and Cassius would have been grateful for it doing so if the instinctual rush of adrenaline hadn't surged through his veins, forcing him to move without thought or proper direction. He had to survive.

The water began to rise as the ship sank. Cassius grabbed onto anything he could in a pitiful attempt to stay upright. The halls of the cabin were flooded to Cassius's waist, and he found himself in a fearful horde of sailors attempting to save themselves. But the water rose and rose, and he could feel his body grow numb as his skin turned pale and blue. He shivered as he pushed his body through the crowd. They would not budge.

Am I about to die? I . . . I am. It was all a joke. My life was nothing but an artistic painting of failures and wrongdoings, thought Cassius. He could feel the ship bend in the throes of destruction, and there was a snap, and then another. The frame was beginning to fold, and as Cassius pushed at the fleeing bodies, the ship snapped in two. Suddenly the world was blue and marine. What had been the interior of a ship moments ago was now mere scattered splinters in a dark ocean. The prince slowly sunk, plunging deeper and deeper into darkness. He could not feel the cold anymore; in fact, all was peaceful and quiet under the water's surface. Cassius, for a moment, even felt happiness. He was not Cassius anymore, and he was certainly no prince on a foolish quest for self-discovery. Instead, he was a soul. A naked soul in the calm moments before its passing. But then he remembered. He remembered his name, his goal, and why he felt he must achieve greatness. And most of all, he remembered why he could not fail, for he would rather die in the aquatic spaces of the sea than live a life without finding a true purpose. His movement returned to him and even the small embers of fire within began to smoulder and stir. He was alive. He swam upwards towards the surface, and with his newfound strength the feeling the icy water came back. His lungs felt as if they were being squeezed harder and harder, and the surface was still far above. The moonlight shone through the water, and it was all Cassius could see in the darkness, and still the cold grip of the sea strangled his lungs until all his air had been spent. He wouldn't make it. His body began to shut down regardless of his desire. He wanted to keep going, to keep fighting. His heart stayed true, but his body was failing him. And then Cassius took his long last breath, and two bubbles floated thither towards the moonlight.

❋

The waves towered over Sir Hadrian, but his ship held strong. The old knight had taken the king's personal vessel, and it glided through the waves like a needle slipping into flesh. Sir Hadrian focused his gaze onto the moonlit horizon, unfazed and unhindered by the blinding splashes of the sea on his face. He was focused on his troth to do what he sought out to do. He had tracked down the prince since Cassius had fled from Ekmere. Lighting illuminated long threads of the dark sky, and in the distance, he could see a ship split in two and slowly sinking into the depths of the ocean.

"Starboard side! Five hundred meters!" yelled one of the men from down below. The ship rolled over a wave only to speed down another, and again this monotonous routine persisted until they reached the wreck. The storm's eye was upon them, and the waves settled momentarily as Sir Hadrian ran down onto the main deck and looked over the ship's edge. His heart stopped. The red cloak of Cassius was draped over a large piece of the wreckage, and as if the old knight had lost his sanity, Sir Hadrian stripped down and dove into the water. His body pierced the frozen sea and sunk deep into the ocean, where many bodies floated lifelessly in the aquatic void. Their skin was pale, almost blue. The water was cold, and it bit at the knight's flesh, but he kept swimming deeper and deeper until he found a shadow swimming up towards him. However, it slowed as it came upon him. Sir Hadrian took hold of the body. It was Cassius. Without hesitation, he pulled him up to the surface with the strength granted to him by his own solemn will. Yet even then the knight struggled as he reached the surface, and it became nearly impossible to stay above the water. But it was then that Sir Hadrian took hold of a large piece of wreckage from the ship's hull and held onto it, placing Cassius on top. Sir Hadrian was tired and confused and knew that the effects of hypothermia were beginning to take him. He hadn't any clue how long Cassius had been submerged for, but he did know his chances of survival were slim, very slim. His strength waned, and slowly he began to drift back into the sea until a lifeboat came into view. He wanted to scream, but his voice failed him, all that would come out was a faint whisper that was accompanied by a frigid breath. Instead, he flailed his arms in the air. He did anything, anything to make himself noticeable. The boat held four people and hidden from Sir Hadrian's view was a woman who was laying down and a man who was bent over her. The two others held lanterns, and their gazes were bent towards him, searching for any survivors.

The world seemed awfully peaceful to Sir Hadrian, yet unlike Cassius, he knew what was afoot. He *knew* he was dying, and that this sweet and seductive phase was simply the pleasant path down towards death. He would not walk this path. No. Not if his heart still beat within him. And yet, his vision faded away softly, and the world went dark.

Gales whirled around the lifeboat, and Hiroki bent over his sister as she winced in pain. Blood poured out from her stomach where a thin piece of wood had pierced her body. She held back tears, but she was afraid, afraid of death, and she did not care who knew it. Yuikiri looked up into the cold eyes of her brother and smiled because, for the first time in years, she could see them begin to thaw and melt like a snowy meadow falling under the spell of the spring's sun. She caressed his cheek and spoke, but her words were too faint to hear, and Hiroki listened even closer as he put pressure on the wound.

"I . . . I am going to die here, brother. Do not fret," she said with a smile, "the light is there waiting for me, and one day it'll be there for you as well." Hiroki was too stubborn to let her go. Every stubborn instinct he possessed, and every grain of his hearts desire wanted to save her, yet beneath it all he knew it would be in vain for she grew pale now, so pale that it felt as if she had been kissed by the moon and laid to rest under its light. "Hiroki," she said softly, "I forgive you . . . I forgive you for the death of our mother, and I always did. Goodbye, big brother. We will walk again amidst the cherry blossoms one day, when your time comes. I can see her. I can see my mother, and she is smiling at us. Have no fear, and let your words be free under the spell of a newfound spring," she said as she let out one last tear before her breath slipped away into the northern air. Hiroki whispered something that not a soul could hear into the ear of his sister, and he looked upon the fresh coat of his sister's blood that lay upon his hands; the dark hue looked back at him with sadness. He wiped his hands clean and shut the eyes of his sister as he let out a single tear. Her eyes were shut, and they would never again reopen.

"I see one! There's one over here! I see Sir Hadrian!" said one of the men who held out a lantern. The boat floated over to an old man who had taken refuge at the side of a piece of the wreck that held another man on top. It took both men to haul out each body from the water. Only one was still conscious. They quickly wrapped them both in blankets and checked their pulses; they were alive, barely. Their moments of peace were nearly over. The eye of the storm was beginning to pass, and its strongest winds would soon be upon them.

"We need to get back to the ship and quickly. Wind's picking up again!" said one of the men, and they quickly rowed their boat back to the king's ship; its red sails fluttered in the growing rage of the gales. Sir Hadrian felt tired and drowsy, and he had trouble maintaining his focus, yet his eyes were fixed upon the prince, begging to any god above that would listen that they would bless this young boy with life and greater vitality. The water from the waves tickled at their cheeks and grew more ferocious as the time passed, until each wave began to grow again into rolling hills that carried the small boat up and down. It was then that the lighting cracked, and the ship slid into view—what was left, that is. A small glacier had split its hull down the middle, and it too began to sink. Hope fled from them now at a pace too quick for any heart to follow as the wind around them swirled and danced, sending them into the pits of despair.

"Trevor," said one of the men, "if we don't head back to land soon, we'll find a grave for each of us at the bottom of the sea. That is, if we don't freeze to death beforehand." It was then that each capable man, even Hiroki, took up an oar, and they fled south towards land, fleeing from the growing storm that brewed in a cauldron of hate. Cassius's heartbeat was slow and weak, and every now and then one of the men would drop their oar to check on him and Sir Hadrian. If luck would be on their side just once, they could make it.

※

The rain picked up even more as their journey south went on, and it soon became a challenge to even see ahead or hear the calls from their peers, for thunder laughed and mocked their attempt to survive, yet still, onwards they rowed through the night without rest and with the embers of hope steaming through their bodies. It kept them going. It would have to. But even if they made it to land, the danger was far from over, for a blizzard ran through the northern regions of Ederia. It was an endless wasteland of snow and ice, mountain, and rock, however life still prevailed there, and it was this life that worried them the most aside from the cold.

After nearly three hours in a relentless battle against the sea, luck proved to be on their side as the fingers of Ederia stretched out before them through the thick pall that surrounded them. At this sight, they rowed even harder with every ounce of what was left of their strength. Water crashed against the icy cliffs that loomed above, but further south, they found a small cove that led to a suitable shore where they could hide from the bitter night. As the boat ran up against the bank, a gust of snow brushed against their backs and down to touch their spines. They leapt off, panting and clutching the ground in disbelief that they had survived. But the fight was far from over. A frozen trough ran down into the sea, coming out of a short rock wall that stood covered in a facade of ice. The survivors dragged their boat over until they were under the cliff, flipped it over, and hid from the cold underneath the boat. It was cramped and each man huddled together for warmth. All except for Hiroki, who hugged the lifeless body of Yuikiri to keep warm. But her body was cold, and thus it was a cruel reminder of her death. There they were: five men trying to survive, trying to outlast the torture of the storm that seemed as if it would not end.

A Father's Love

The meeting in the war tent had reached an end, and each general and knight took their leave at the permission of the king. Cornelius hunched over the map that lay across the table, looking at each wooden figurine that represented each military force. He sighed. It had been a long day of strategic discussion, and they finally decided to move a large portion of their forces to the front lines. Their forces were running through every rebel outpost and camp with ease. They had yet to meet the full resistance of the enemy, but Cornelius was confident beyond measure that they would succeed in the coming battle that would take place. The king rubbed the circles beneath his eyes—it had been far too long since he had allowed himself a bit of rest. He needed it.

I am king, after all, thought Cornelius. *I should be able to rest when I know I deserve such.* He then exited the war tent, and two guards followed him as he did. Apart from him and his generals, the majority of the army slept in the valley below, and in the darkness, the screams of dying men could be heard. Although, most were hardly men, only young boys who were too naive and ignorant to the realities of war to truly understand the peril they had run so readily towards. The torches of the army's camp below flickered like candles in the night, feeling the tremors of battle within the air. Hundreds of tents ran down the hill that oversaw the valley, and even in the dead of night, couriers and generals hurried all around the king, eager to attend to their tasks. There was a deadly tension in the air, but the men that camped upon the hill were veterans, ones that had seen the horrors of battle and were numb to the fear of it by now.

In the centre of it all was the king's personal tent. It was far larger than any others that surrounded it, and its linden-wood floors were covered with various animal hides save for three pathways that allowed one to walk around its interior with ease. As Cornelius entered, both guards stood watch, allowing the king to thrive in his solitude. He poured himself a cup of tea and wandered over to his library, which held many books. He pulled out an old tale. *The Thief and the Moon*, it was called, but as he pulled it out another fell off and landed on the floor. Cornelius picked it up and was quite happy at what he saw. *The Fables of Yore* was its title. He and his wife, Iris, had read it to Cassius and Vidicus when they were children. *I wonder if they would still remember it*, thought Cornelius, and to his surprise, he began to read it. Before sitting down, the king found some violets that reminded him ever so sweetly of his wife and placed them in a vase on the table. He began sipping his tea as he opened the book to its first story. *The Tale of the Lost Cub*, it was called. Cornelius sighed at the grace of poignant memories, of times that seemed so far away, back when things were quite simply good. *This had been little Cassy's favourite*, thought the king. He laughed. He hadn't called Cassius by his nickname since his mother passed, and he found himself missing it. Cornelius flipped through the pages, reading only the lines that he recalled reading to his boys so vividly, and he looked at the old pictures of heroes and villains that Cassius and Vidicus had either aspired to be or hated. He flipped back to the table of contents, searching for what had been Vidicus's favourite, but he could not remember. It could have been any of them or none for all he knew. He was ashamed. And then the fact came to him like a frozen spike through his heart: he had failed to show Vidicus love, and instead gave it only to his brother, but when Cassius showed that he may make a poor king, he abandoned him and presented his love only to Vidicus. He had failed to treat them as equals. *Why . . . why does Cassius drink?* he thought. *Maybe he does not drink for the mere purpose of pleasure. Instead, maybe he drinks to drown out the melancholy he may feel. But what could make this child so . . . sad? He has had everything he could ever want. He is destined to be the most powerful man in Ederia,* thought Cornelius. But then the answer came to him plainly and blunt. It was obvious, and he was frankly embarrassed that he had not seen it before. Cassius did not drink because he despised his father, he drank because he loved him, and as much as he tried, he would never receive the same love back.

Cornelius dropped the book and looked ahead, almost in tears. Suddenly, he felt he had to fix this before it was too late. He didn't know the last time he had expressed his love for his sons, and they were all that was left of what held together his broken heart. *I shall write to them both!* thought the king with a smile on his face as he prepared his inkwell and papers.

To my dearest sons.

I sit here in my tent pondering some memories as I flip through some of your favourite books from when you were children, and it has, well, I suppose, reminded me of something I have forgotten. I have forgotten you both. I know this may seem quite sudden and strange, but I see no other way of mending the mistakes I have found in my duty as your father. I have been a good king, I know this, but I have failed you both as a father and as a mentor. It may have seemed as if I shunned you as a child, Vidicus, and maybe I did. Maybe I was so focused on Cassius and preparing him for his future that I forgot about you. Now I know I have made you the Duke of Bruxstan, but if I am to be truly honest, I only rewarded you in an effort to hopefully encourage your brother to improve his ways, so that maybe he could see what happened when he followed my teachings. I was wrong for that, and you may hate me under that smile of yours; that's what I always loved about you, that no matter the situation, you tried your best to be respectful and polite. However, my son, I do not deserve your respect. I know this. You are not your brother, and you are not a king—you cannot change these things. But you needn't, for you are something equally as precious: you are a treasured son of mine, not some loathed second pick, and I love you just as equally.

Cassius . . . perhaps you may never open this letter, but it matters not. I have been bitter towards you, even hateful at times. It is only occurring to me now, though, that I do not despise you for not being who I wished you to be. I despise myself. I don't know why I do; I just do. It could be that I blame myself for your current issues. I have treated you of late like, well, a problem that needs fixing, however I always assumed that this was a problem that would be best solved on its own. How foolish and utterly hypocritical of me to say. Why? You see, I have always believed that one should be responsible for the problems he or she creates. For the past eight years, I have looked at you as either a prince or a burden, but never for who you really are as an individual, and thus it seems as if I forgot who you are because I was simply too focused on who I thought you should be. When I return from the war, I shall speak to you personally, Cassius, but not as a king, as a father, and I hope you and I can begin to understand one another. And I am sorry for what I said to you at the banquet. It could not be further from the truth. You are my son . . . and I am proud to be able to say so.

I know you shall bring honour to our family, Vidicus. At your new position of power, you will be a major chess piece in the game that is to unfold, I just know it. As to you Cassius, I look forward to the day when I can look into the eyes of my son again, for the next time I see you, I shall place the crown upon your head.

I love you both, and even now, I can feel your mother sitting next to me, and she is smiling; she always had the prettiest smile. Take care, both of you, and I look forward to our next meeting.

Love, Father.

Cornelius put the pen down, looking at his writing. He hoped that this could somehow rekindle his relationship with his sons, and a genuine and true smile took to his lips. He would write another the same as he had written the first one; one letter for each boy. Once he had finished the second copy, he folded the papers into two separate envelopes and sealed them. He finished his tea and felt proud of what he had decided to do.

"Godfried!" said Cornelius, asking for his courier.

"Yes, my lord?"

"I have two letters for you. Send one to each of my sons," said Cornelius. And the courier set off, and the king was glad he had decided to take some rest.

Blood on Ice

There were no flowers to place at the side of Yuikiri. It was a land far too frozen and bitter for the likes of her; she deserved better. Hiroki had been awake since dawn preparing the funeral, and his steps were weighed down by sorrow as he walked around the cove, gathering any shells or branches that represented any beauty. The others had gotten a small fire going and huddled against the cliff's walls. Cassius and Sir Hadrian had begun to strengthen, however both still struggled to form any words; instead, they resorted to coarse whispers that were drowned out by the cool air. Trevor and his brother, Colton, had been the two men who dragged out the prince and the knight from the water, and they boiled water for tea as Hiroki knelt by the boat at the shoreline, staring into the horizon. Yuikiri lay in the boat atop small bundles of sticks and kindling, and her hair hung loose. She was beautiful, even in death. Hiroki whispered a prayer in his own tongue; he had broken his vow of silence, yet his sister's forgiveness seemed to almost justify his heresy.

Colton looked over at Hiroki with sombre eyes, eyes that understood his pain. He took out one of the longer branches from the fire, which held onto the flame, and walked down to the shoreline with it. Hiroki heard him coming and turned his head. Colton could say nothing for he was smitten by the fixed gaze of Hiroki's eyes, and he felt that he could only move again once Hiroki turned away to face his sister.

"It is time," said Hiroki, and Colton was almost shocked at hearing his voice, and he obeyed its wishes. He dropped the smouldering stick into the pile of kindling. The two covered it just enough for the fire to breathe and then blew on it, and the red flame began to flicker and smoke. By now Trevor had stood up and walked down to the shoreline to see what was occurring. The flames grew quickly, as if they were fueled by the sorrow in the air, and Cassius and Sir Hadrian looked upon the others on the shoreline. Hiroki placed his sister's sword firmly in her grasp and stepped away from the boat. The three of them pushed it away from the bank after they had all said a few words, and Yuikiri drifted softly in the northern wind towards the unknown horizon.

Later, towards midday, the company sat around the fire and began to eat a small portion of their food that Trevor and Colton had scavenged before they fled to the boat. Fortunately, each lifeboat carried a small amount of food and supplies, enough to last a few days. All were silent, as if they were waiting for the other to speak, for them to take the lead.

"Well," said Trevor, "If it brightens anyone's day up, we're farther south than I had originally thought, so that at least increases our chances of surviving up here." There was a long, awkward silence after he spoke, and he opened his mouth once more as if to speak again, but his confidence dwindled quickly, and he looked back down towards the fire. Yet even in his weakened state, Sir Hadrian loosened his blankets and animal hides from around him and slid out of his cocoon.

"We're about a week's march north from Bruxstan, maybe even a little less, but for now, we are well sheltered from the wind, and it would be best for us to stay put until—" Sir Hadrian paused, looking over at Cassius, "—my *friend* and I have gathered our strength."

"Agreed," said Colton. "But what are we going to do about food? And there are surely other survivors that made their way onto the shoreline as well."

"That is true. Some of us will have to go out to search for food and supplies, but hearken my words when I tell you this: do not be far from camp when the moon rises and the land darkens . . . there are enough corpses that litter these parts," said Sir Hadrian.

"Then my brother and I can head out in search of food and other survivors at noon, and Hiroki can stay and tend to you both until you are strong enough to head out on your own," said Trevor.

The company agreed, and after they finished up their meal, Trevor and Colton packed each of their bags with only the essentials and took two old hatchets for weapons. Sir Hadrian gave them words of warning about the northern regions of Ederia, for the two were sailors and hadn't much experience in the desolate tundra of ice they inhabited.

By noon, the two brothers had left, leaving Cassius and Sir Hadrian to the company of Hiroki, and the three continued to sit by a fire.

"Tell me, what is your friend's name there, and what is a knight like yourself doing this far north?" asked Hiroki, putting his book down and looking at Sir Hadrian with his ghostly eyes.

"His name is Brandon, and he is the son of a baron that has tasked me with protecting him while he sets out to the war in the east," said Sir Hadrian

"Ah, I see. Well, the boy will surely live, and I look forward to speaking to him when he does," said Hiroki with an expressionless and cold face and with eyes that did not falter in their gaze, yet neither did the old knight's. Hiroki suspected something, and Sir

Hadrian knew it. "I heard the sailors call you a name that I am well aware of. You are the notorious Dragon of the North, are you not, Sir Hadrian?"

"Yes," he said with a laugh. "That is what they used to call me."

"This must be a very important and wealthy baron for him to have someone of the likes of yourself safeguarding him," said Hiroki, pulling a stick from the fire and waving it in the air before going back to his book, and the old knight returned to his pipe and taking care of the prince while he slept.

✳

The wind had calmed, and the morning sun had begun to settle upon the land. Ivan crawled slowly through the entrance of the ice cave until his torso wormed out into the world. Azrad and Connell still slept at the bottom of the cave where the ceiling was higher, and Ivan took this time to familiarize himself with his surroundings. The cave was completely man-made and was submerged within a deep blanket of snow that rested against the feet of a short cliff. To their right and down into the valley was the bay upon which they had washed ashore, and even still Ivan could see the miniature slivers of the ship's wreckage on the horizon. He knew the north well, and he knew it was possible to journey south into Bruxstan and continue their journey east, although this meant they would need to head deep into the heart of the ongoing war, deep into conflict and blood-shed. Ivan did not like the idea of it, but it was the only way.

He turned and began to climb the backside of the hill that oversaw their cave, and once atop its shoulders, Ivan could further make out the land. He could see the arm of Ederia spread northwest before him, thus he knew that they were luckily farther south than he had thought. The land was an unforgiving tundra of frost and brutal winds; it was a desolation of northern spells and chills, and few life forms could thrive in a region such as this. Yet all danger paled in comparison to the looming threat of nightfall; there could be no survival, for death awaited almost all things in the blackness of the night once the moon smiled and bared its teeth in the frost-infested ruins.

Fortunately for Ivan, he was well prepared, and as a gust of wind brushed and encircled him, he was not fazed. Instead, his eyes were fixed on the horizon, and he could see a large group of men and even women coming towards them at an alarming speed. Ivan looked closer. They were still quite far away, therefore little could be seen, but it appeared as if much of the party rode atop sleds that were run by dogs or tamed wolves. If not for the shipwreck and the possibility of coming survivors, Ivan would have fled, for only bandits and dangerous folk inhabited these parts. Food was scarce, and nature made its way with the minds of humanity, pitting them against one another in a game for survival.

Ivan rushed down the sloping spine of the hill and down to the mouth of the cave.

"Get up! Both of You! And keep your weapons close at hand," said Ivan. Azrad and Connell slowly came to their senses and crawled out of the entrance, weapons in hand.

"What is it?" asked Azrad.

"Thirty or so men coming down from the north in sleds. They could mean us harm, and I would certainly know so if not for the possibility of them being survivors of the wreck. They seem to be riding sleds, so outrunning them isn't an option."

"What type of shipwreck survivors have sleds and dogs waiting for them at the shore?" Ivan made no reply. Instead, he and Connell began to climb the hill, gaining the higher ground. Once the three of them had reached the pinnacle, their pursuers had come closer into view, yet no weapons could be seen, and a smaller party trailed behind them on skis. Connell readied his claymore but did not unsheathe the great blade yet, and Azrad loaded a bolt onto his crossbow. All the while Ivan looked at and studied the group; he could see two men leading it, and each manned their own sled. The group then halted about half a furlong away from the hill, and the two leaders dismounted their sleds and raised their arms in the air.

"Hello! We come with no ill intentions! We are survivors of the shipwreck! My name is Trevor, and this is my brother Colton; we have been sent to gather any remaining survivors! Neither I nor my brother are armed, and we wish to speak to you!" Ivan and his companions exchanged looks of doubt amongst each other.

"They're lying," said Connell.

"Oh, I know they are, but I still wish to speak to their leaders and ask them a few questions. If they act up, we take them as hostages and take those sleds of theirs," said Ivan.

Once all three agreed, they waved the brothers up, and soon enough after the climb, Trevor and Colton stood before the company.

"Are you survivors as well?" asked Colton.

"Yes, yes we are," said Ivan. "And you say you are also?"

"We are, yes. My brother and I washed ashore with three others, and we have camped just a little south from here," said Trevor.

"You seem to have a bit more than just three others with you," said Azrad, pointing down towards the crowd below.

"They are also survivors that we have gathered up, and luckily we found a family in the hills over yonder that was willing to lend us their sleds."

"Did they now?" wondered Ivan with a grin on his face.

"What do you say? Will you join us? Our chances of survival up here are far greater when we are in numbers." Neither Ivan nor any of his companions made a reply, and the three of them turned to each other to discuss what they would do.

"I don't trust him," whispered Connell.

"I don't either," said Azrad

"And I agree with you both. We will keep a close eye on each of them, but we do need food, and their camp is on our way south," replied Ivan. "And when we set out again, we take their sleds—I'm sure they'll be serving us far better anyways."

The three then turned towards the brothers and nodded in agreement to their proposition.

"Perfect," said Trevor, "we will set out immediately, and you three can ride with us in the sleds."

The Company of Ekmere then made their way down to the sleds, where they greeted the majority of the other survivors, however, they didn't have much of the look of sailors; their faces were brittle and cloaked in scars, and Azrad and Connell hadn't recalled this many women being on the ship. Something was amiss, and thus they carefully watched every move they made.

After a long three-hour ride in utter silence, aside from the breath of the wind at their ears, they finally came to the cove where Sir Hadrian and the others were taking refuge. It had passed midday, a veil of clouds shrouded the sky, and the white winter realm grew even colder with the absence of the sun. Trevor and Colton stood over the cliff, looking down at the others.

"Any luck?" asked Sir Hadrian.

"You could say so," replied Colton, looking back at the survivors behind him, and the crowd crept closer to the cliff's edge, revealing their numbers. Sir Hadrian was shocked, but he was left speechless save for a small laugh at the sight of one man who glared back at him with equal surprise. Ivan and the knight stared each other down, and both were perplexed and silenced momentarily by disbelief.

"You certainly are a persistent old fuck," said Ivan, and Sir Hadrian merely laughed, almost choking on the cold air. "Well, to say the least, I definitely have a few questions to ask you, old man, but I'd prefer to ask them by the fire."

"We may have to have plenty more than one fire. You seem to have brought far more companions with you than I had thought. They don't slow you down, do they?" asked Sir Hadrian with a drop of disdain on his tongue, remembering Ivan's former comments about him being a burden on his journey. But Ivan made no response, and he instead made his way down with the rest of the survivors and into the cove where fires and camps were then built. Once all had been set up and each person comforted himself or herself in their new surroundings, Ivan and his companions joined Sir Hadrian by the fire. But one person stood out to Ivan, and it made things *far* more interesting. He recognized the face of Cassius immediately, and a smile of intrigue crept upon his lips, but he said nothing. Cassius was now awake, yet had not come fully to his senses, but even then, he knew the face of the man before him. The air within his lungs fled from him, and in the frigid desolation, it grew ever so hot, as if the wrath of the sun peered through the lairs of clouds and watched the greetings of these men with a childish delight. Cassius said nothing. Both knew that neither of them was supposed to be there, and they only exchanged quick and rushed glances, but they were glances that held a copious supply of meaning and emotion.

"And who might you be?" asked Ivan with a feigned enthusiasm towards the prince.

"Brandon is my name," replied Cassius.

"Would you mind if I sat down and warmed myself by your fire?"

"Not at all," said Sir Hadrian, shifting over towards Cassius to make room. Ivan looked at Hiroki for a second before noticing the man was making no effort to greet him, and he then rifled through his belongings in search of any scraps of food he could scavenge. There was nothing, nothing but the vestiges of supplies that had been soaked and later frozen over in the night. He looked around the fire and could almost feel the awkward air fill his body.

Cassius looked over at the man as he chewed and gnawed at a piece of cooked meat before ripping a small strip off and passing it over to Ivan.

"Thanks."

"Don't mention it."

The day dragged on, and soon enough the new arrivals settled in. Azrad and Connell joined Ivan and the others by the fire, and once all were introduced, silence took them. They had much to discuss and many questions that needed answers, but all had a subconscious understanding that all should be discussed at night and without this many eyes upon them. And thus, they waited. They sat in a mute circle around the weak flames, listening to the melodious crackle of embers and charcoal from brittle wood and the maddening monotony of the wind's whistles and tunes that ran through every ravine, mountain, and canyon. Even the remote icicles that hung on the boughs of distant trees shivered in the unforgiving chill. Cassius wondered how anything survived up here, and just how *they* were going to survive up here, for that matter.

This journey of mine has gone to ruin already. It seems I am pretty good at failing, thought Cassius, and he sighed at the realization of his failure and tried to doze off into sleep again, but he found he couldn't because there was one question that grappled his thoughts: how was he going to reach Medearia now?

They had no boat.

No supplies.

Little hope.

And a prince who did not quite know just what the fuck he had gotten himself into. However, he had Sir Hadrian by his side, and that thought comforted him. He also had Ivan, who seemed quite experienced in these situations, and he had supposedly made the journey before. So, hope, like the fire before him, was weak, yes, but still very much alive.

Once all had adjusted to the annoyingly ever-present notion of boredom that came with survival, the day seemed to progress quicker, and soon small sparkles of light began to peek through the darkening blue sky. It was then that Cassius finally found himself capable of sleeping. He dreamt of beautiful colours that floated across the sky, painting the darkness in a river of light and spontaneous allure. His body began to levitate upwards towards the sky, and the multicoloured bridge of beauty that spread across the night sky like veins of the sun came closer and closer until Cassius found himself sleeping atop the structure. He rose from his bed, feeling surprisingly well rested. He looked down and could see small dots of orange flames from the camp. In the distance stood a figure. He had grey hair and beside him stood two wolves. Cassius recognized this *thing* from his last dream, but he had not put much importance on it. It was only a dream, wasn't it?

The being turned towards the prince and raised its hand; a long pale finger pointed towards him. Cassius felt his heart pump with fear and the instinctual onset of adrenaline took its natural course through his body. He turned and ran, but no matter how fast he ran, no matter how hard he pushed his legs, he seemed to almost be going in the opposite direction, towards the creature as if he was being dragged towards it. He turned to see just how far away he was. There was nothing there. He looked forward again, and there he stood. The creature took the palm of its hand and placed it on Cassius's forehead, and it spoke a strange tongue that the prince again could not understand. Cassius's eyes rolled back into his head, revealing the jelly-white sclera of his eyeballs. Images flooded his mind: he saw blood, despair, torture. He saw fear, but most of all, he saw fire; flames that engulfed all, scorching bodies to a crisp until he couldn't make out exactly what they were. There were severed limbs, abandoned children, and ruined towns and villages. Then the world shifted, and he could see Ekmere engulfed in flames and innocent civilians crying out, begging for their lives to continue, but whatever force caused this, it would not listen, and death took them all. And it was then that Cassius saw it. He saw a tree shrivelled in a black and unnatural skin. It was sick. It was lifeless.

And then it was no more.

The images stopped, and Cassius could see the creature before him, but now it was knelt by his side.

"So, young Cassius, what did you see?" it asked.

Tears began to fill Cassius's eyes without any warning, and he felt obligated to answer the question solely by the significance of what he had just seen and the fear that it had given him.

"I—I," Cassius stuttered and found it too difficult to speak. The grey-haired being stroked the prince's throat with the tips of his fingers (they felt quite soft and forgiving, which surprised Cassius). But he then found himself able to speak again. "I saw . . . fear . . . I saw . . . *suffering*."

"Yes. And what then?"

Cassius's eyes did not look upon the creature before him. Instead, they focused ahead of him, gaping wide open without blinking, as if hands had torn off his eyelids, and the light beneath him burned them.

"I saw a tree. Yes . . . yes, a tree," said Cassius in an almost dull and lifeless tone.

"What did this tree look like?" But it wasn't really a question, for the creature knew all too well what the boy had seen.

"Dark. Dark and sick. It was dead, nothing more and nothing less, simply dead . . . lifeless."

The creature looked down, thinking to himself. It cursed something foul in its own language before standing back up and turning away. "We don't have much time left . . . The balance is breaking. There is no light without the dark, nor is there dark without the light . . . and I cannot balance it on my own. We need your help, Cassius."

"Who are you? What are you? What . . . what is this place?" asked Cassius, now having time to think and realize the abnormality around him.

"There is much I cannot tell you, not yet that is, if we are to prevent the doom that awaits us. I have been called many names, but you will know my true title soon enough. The next time you and I speak, it will be face to face. You will be desperate and in pain, but fear not, for you shall prevail. Find Sathelia, and your fate will then fall beneath your feet." The creature then placed his palm on the prince's forehead once more, and the world turned to darkness.

"Brandon," whispered Sir Hadrian with a nudge on the prince's shoulder, and Cassius awoke. His eyes were fatigued, as if he had just awoken from a deep slumber.

"What is it?"

"It is time for us all to speak to one another. Come, there is much to explain."

Cassius widened his eyes, fully soaking in the night sky, and above him were dazzling lights that stretched along the face of darkness in the sky, lights of blue, green, purple, and red. They were startlingly similar to what he had seen in his dream. Sir Hadrian saw the boy staring into the sky, and he could see that he was evidently bewitched by its beauty.

The knight laughed. "They are called the aurora borealis. Beautiful, aren't they?"

"That's definitely an understatement, to say the least," said Cassius.

Aside from Hiroki, who slept the night away, the prince and Sir Hadrian were all that were left at their campsite. The rest had already made their way to the meeting place. Each fire had been put out, and it appeared as if all who took refuge in the cove were now fast asleep. Cassius followed Sir Hadrian, yet still, he felt tired, and his bones seemed heavy; Cassius was more like a pile of flesh wandering through the night than an actual sentient being that could conjure thoughts and emotions. He followed the knight with little thought as to where they were going. He had one objective: stay awake and follow the leader. They walked up a stony path that zigzagged its way until it reached the top lip of the cliff. In the distance, they could see a small circle of men hidden in cloaks and furs, with torches in their hands to illuminate their surroundings. Sir Hadrian did his best to guide the prince through the darkness until they arrived.

"You took your time," said Ivan.

"Then don't waste any more of it," replied Sir Hadrian.

"There's no polite way of putting it, at least none that is coming to mind, so what the fuck are you two doing out here?" asked Ivan.

"I think Cassius could best explain this," said Sir Hadrian.

The prince yawned. He still didn't know exactly why he was out here in the cold, and he could feel the air rip and tear at the inner walls of his lungs. But what he did know was that all eyes were now on him, eyes that said, *Well? Answer!* They intimidated him, even Sir Hadrian at this point.

What am I really doing here? thought Cassius. *This has all been a disaster, a disaster choreographed by a fool!*

"Go on, Cassius, tell them of your dream. But I'd also like to know just why in Ederia would you go down this path?" asked Sir Hadrian, and his voice gave Cassius the confidence he needed, but he could see that Ivan and his companions' faces appeared distraught and worried when the knight mentioned his dreams.

"Well, I guess—"

"Oh, spit it the fuck out, will ya?" shouted Azrad.

"Quiet, let him speak," said Ivan.

"I wish to join you on your journey to Medearia," said the prince, and everyone's eyes seemed to widen and be taken by the spell of shock that blurted out simultaneous to Cassius's words.

"I'm sorry, you what?"

"Hush, quiet down, Azrad. We can discuss your participation in this journey later, Cassius, but first, you will tell me of these dreams," said Ivan.

"It began with a nightmare and nothing more, but then things changed. I saw a man—no, not a man. He is something else entirely. Its hair is grey, and it is tall, and around him stood many wolves."

Ivan stepped closer with fire in his eyes. "What did *he* say to you?"

"He told me I must find Medearia, then I must find a girl, and then finally, I must find the tree," said Cassius and as he spoke, his eyes began to water. Ivan looked plainly at him but was almost confused. He bit his lower lip, concentrating, contemplating what he had just heard.

"It doesn't make sense," whispered Ivan to himself as he paced to and fro. "Why would he need you or even speak to you of such things," said Ivan, now mumbling to himself in deep thought.

"You told me you do not know this creature," said Sir Hadrian.

"Who is he?" asked Cassius, but no one would reply.

"I do not know him personally, but I do know of him, and I know the things he has done. As do you, Blackwood."

"What are you both talking about? Answer me!" yelled Cassius.

"Shh, keep your voice down," hissed Ivan. "This *thing* once spoke to your grandfather when your father was a mere boy. This *thing* is responsible for the death of your grandfather."

"Now you know why I insisted on taking you away from Ekmere, but this is far from what I intended," said Sir Hadrian.

"But he does not seem as if he wishes to hurt me?"

"That is what frightens me," said Ivan.

"But why would he wish to hurt me, and who is he? And what is he?"

"He is an enemy. One of many who inhabit Medearia. From what I've gathered, long ago, the races of men and what we once called elves united to defeat a common enemy. But once this was over, we did what we do best—we began to hate. With our hatred towards that which is different from us, we began to have disdain for the elves, and in time they became our slaves. We quickly killed them off, eradicating them from Ederia entirely as if they were a disease. And in order to survive, they fled back to their homeland of Medearia and tried their best to cover their tracks by destroying any historical evidence of their existence. They would have stayed hidden if it weren't for a voyage gone wrong by me and my crew eight years ago. It was there that we drifted east and soon found ourselves being pulled towards a strange land. I will speak no more of that journey, but for now, all you must know is that *war* is brewing in Medearia, a war to end all of humankind. They seek revenge for what we have done."

"This doesn't make any sense," said Cassius, trying to speak, but his mind felt twisted and utterly betrayed.

"Look, I don't know why *he* has spoken to you, but the matter in which he does is puzzling to me. As far as I know, he has never spoken with benevolence with any human before," said Ivan.

"Cassius, this nonsense of heading east stops this instance! It's absurd!"

"Quit acting like my father, old man!" said Cassius, and Sir Hadrian backed off as if the words of the prince had hurt him.

"Do you know what your father would do to me if anything happened to you?"

"I'd rather not think of it," said Cassius.

Sir Hadrian readied himself for a response that would hopefully change the prince's mind, but his focus was caught by something else. Far away in the cold gloom of the night, three torches glowed in the snowy surrounding, and then more and more appeared until there were nearly two dozen. They were coming from the entrance to the cove.

"Hello there!" said Azrad.

There was no reply. They only crept closer and closer, and the only sound that could be heard was the relentless whooshing of the winter wind biting at their ears. Sir Hadrian's eyes immediately noticed something about their stride, as did Ivan and his companions: it was no walk of greetings and good fortune. No. It was the walk of a hunter stalking its prey.

"Cassius," said Sir Hadrian, "get behind me now."

"Why."

"Do as I say."

The group that had joined them and camped with them in the cove now circled around them, drawing in closer and closer, and the company of five began to condense into a small circle that faced the creeping stalkers.

"What's happening? Why won't they speak to us? Hello! What is it you need?"

"Quiet, Cassius," growled Sir Hadrian.

Suddenly Trevor and Colton pulled through the centre of the crowd.

"So, it is the great Prince Cassius Helladawn of Ekmere, the future king of Ederia and warden of Hellandor. It is truly a pleasure to finally meet you, little prince. But I must say, you're a little far away from home, aren't you?" said Trevor, pulling out a rusty hatchet from behind him. His brother came to his side, exiting the masking veil of the snow.

"Remember your own words, old man? 'Do not be far from camp when the moon rises and the land darkens.' Sound familiar, Blackwood? I hate to be the bearer of bitter news, but there are going to be a few more corpses added to the night's collection—*five,* to be exact," said Colton. Sir Hadrian was the first to unsheathe his sword, and the beautiful blade looked as perfect as the day it was forged; each jewel shone under the cool evening moonlight.

"Who sent you?" shouted Sir Hadrian, looking dead into the hearts of each foe.

"Oh, I think you know who . . . in fact, you were just on your way to meet our Lord of Medearia. Shame you'll never meet him," said Trevor. Each man now drew their weapon, even Cassius, although he barely remembered how to use it, and even then, he had never had to actually use it on another human; he doubted he could even really kill someone. All he had to do was look the part, he thought. Despite being outnumbered, he felt safe; he had Sir Hadrian by his side, one of the greatest swordsmen in history, or at least that was what the tales said. And if Ivan's blade and confidence said anything about him it was that he too was one to be feared, along with Azrad and Connell. Cassius could feel his heartbeat through his chest, pumping blood through his arteries and lifting his rib cage up and down.

One man leaped towards the prince, raising his arm and swinging it down for a fatal blow to the neck, and Cassius, frozen in terror, watched as Azrad shot a bolt through the attacker's throat. And as if that had been the conductor's opening swing of his hands, the sweet song of violence ensued and was accompanied by the barbaric cries of men yearning for blood. The attackers charged, and Cassius closed his eyes. He was afraid. He was not ready for something like this. He caught no more than glimpses of men charging them and soon falling with a spray of blood in the air. Cassius could feel the rush of air from Azrad's crossbow fly by his ear and the sound of swords piercing flesh, cracking bones, and spilling open pools of fresh blood like spilt milk on easy summer mornings. Panting, sweat, and untamed hysteria ran about. Two men ran towards Ivan. He sidestepped, drawing in one at a time and catching his blade with theirs and then pirouetting to the left to meet the other foe, and meet him he did. Ivan's sabre slipped into the man's skull like a needle, and Cassius could hear the grotesque sound of Connell's claymore crunching down at the shoulder blade of the woman that stood behind Ivan.

Yet still, more attackers flooded in. There were too many. Far too many. When Cassius opened his eyes again, he could see a faint image of a strange object coming towards them with speed. And before he could make out what it was in the dead of night, he could hear it. He could hear the grunting and snarls of sled dogs, and it seemed to suck away his imagination of safety. But then something happened that Cassius did not foresee. Three small objects came flying out of the sled, each with a lit fuse at the end, and they landed just ahead of Cassius. There was nothing . . . and then there was indeed something.

Fire. Fire and sparks spun away from the objects, producing a deafening sound that seemed to distract the enemy, and the sled rushed over towards the company.

"Get in!" said the voice from the sled, and they obeyed without hesitation, hopping onto the sled and strapping themselves onto anything they could hold onto. Cassius slid under the bundle of blankets in the front to hide from the pursuing terror. The mysterious man whipped the backs of the dogs, and the sled sped off into the night, but the attackers fled back towards their own sleds. Death had not given up that night, not yet. Their saviour unveiled his frozen hood, revealing the face of Hiroki.

The Whitefrost Tribe

They fled through the long night, and even when the dawn came they kept on, even further for three days and three nights of constant flight to the Fields of Ukron. Through the sublime moonlight and the cruel mornings, they fled their pursuers with little rest. After the first day they had lost sight of the enemy, and this indeed brightened their spirits but also disturbed them. It was strange and uncharacteristic. Ivan did not like it, no one did for that matter. But on the fourth morning, the dogs could take no more punishment, and they were forced to halt momentarily. Sir Hadrian studied the horizon behind them, ready to see the black image of their foes juxtaposed against the blue sky. He was nervous, and he didn't like the idea of stopping for too long. Cassius lay down on the rolls of blankets, trying to get some sleep as Azrad and Connell searched their bags for the last remaining remnants of smoking tobacco, but they were soon disappointed to see nothing that was suitable for their pipes. Meanwhile, Hiroki sat in silence atop the shoulder of the eastern mountain, listening to the wind and its tales of times that had been long forgotten, breathing in the cool magic of the morning, and he too looked for any sign of the enemy. But there was nothing.

"Good morning," said Ivan as he walked up behind the Sarakotan. Hiroki had heard nothing, not even the smallest indication of the informal greeting between the soles of Ivan's feet and the icy surface of the snow. Nothing. He was good. He was a killer, and Hiroki knew how to recognize them.

"It is a good morning," replied Hiroki, and Ivan stood behind him in silence for a moment to take in the beauty of his surroundings and warm his naked hands against the sunlight. Ivan tried to be cool, to be casual and natural, but Hiroki knew what he was doing, and Ivan caught onto the scent that Hiroki knew his intentions. Ivan was watching him, studying his actions to predict whether he would turn on them as well. He did not trust the Sarakotan, not yet. But he had trusted his sister, and he knew Yuikiri was one to stick by her word. "We will not escape them," said Hiroki. "They are planning something, but just whoever *they* are, I do not know . . . but you do, don't you?"

"Yeah."

"Interesting."

"What's so interesting?" asked Ivan.

"The fact that two Casthedian sailors turned on you and gathered bandits to hunt you down. What for, I wonder? What could you possess that is so precious?"

"They're certainly not your common group of bandits. If I were to guess, I'd say they are from one of the tribes that reside in this land."

"You didn't answer my question."

"You certainly are the inquisitive type, aren't you?"

"Only when I must be," said Hiroki. "But I guess these are things you will not tell me."

"Correct."

"Is it for the same reason that you would not tell my sister where you are going?"

"Yes," said Ivan, and Hiroki seemed content with his answer and resumed looking at the mountains that peered back at him through a body of clouds.

"I have a friend, a blacksmith. He is Sarakotan as well. We can make it there in seven days' time," said Hiroki.

"Where is he?"

"On the border of Bruxstan and Sacadia."

"He's a little far from home, is he not?"

"Fell in love with a woman. He couldn't leave her after that. Olsa is her name."

"What about the smith?"

"Taku. They can feed you and prepare you for whatever your journey is, and I will leave you then once you set off," said Hiroki.

"You have my thanks, again. We are in your debt."

"Thank me not with shallow words but with an answer instead. How do you plan on escaping from those who pursue us? We cannot run for much longer," said Hiroki.

"Let's say that I am owed a favour, and I have come here to call upon them. Also to study your character."

"Did your study go well?"

"It certainly did," said Ivan, and Hiroki got up and left him there atop the mountain. Ivan withdrew a horn from his bag and blew thrice before pausing to listen for any returning call. He could hear his own call echo through the land, but there was no answer. Something was up. *Something* eerie ran with the wind. And then he heard something he should have expected long ago: war drums, malevolent cries that were lustful for battle. Ivan ran over to the side of the cliff that was furthest away from where they camped and saw a large pack of wild men racing towards him atop skis and sleds that were run by wolves and winter leopards, all armoured for battle. They were prepared this time, in fact, further prepared than they needed to be to hunt down six weary travellers. Ivan knew there would be no escaping if the help he had signalled never came, and it looked as if it wouldn't. *Things are about to get dicey,* thought Ivan as he smiled in the face of doom.

He turned and ran down the snow-ridden slope of the mountain. His cloak under his fur jacket swung off his head and flailed in the wind, and Ivan ran with an enticing flame of violence that beguiled his step. He liked it—nay, he loved it. Ivan only felt alive when his life was on the line, and he truly was alive now as he made his way back to the sled, waving his arms in the air, trying to signal to the others about the coming attack, but it was then that he noticed a second enemy sled racing down the western mountainside towards them with an army of its own.

Each army consisted of bow-welding bandits on skis. Hiroki ran to gather the dogs as the others packed their things, but the frantic aroma of fear made it difficult to even think straight. Hiroki found himself reaching for his sword, but he was distraught to feel that there was nothing there to greet his palm; he had not gripped the handle of a blade in years. The enemy was gaining on them at an unnatural pace, and their cries of war could be heard more clearly by the second.

"Quickly!" roared Ivan as he climbed on top of the sled, and he was soon followed by the others.

"*Yah!*" shouted Connell, and his booming voice commanded the dogs to run, and run they did. But there was little chance of fleeing from their pursuers without tainting their weapons with blood once more. The sled kicked up a wake of snow that stuck to their cheeks. Azrad pulled out his crossbow and readied it to be fired. It was a fight that they could not run from. They were no more than a hundred meters away now, and that number was decreasing by the second.

"I haven't got enough bolts!" yelled Azrad.

"Then make them count," said Connell.

The two sleds slid in parallel to the company's, and bowmen reached for their quivers and drew back their strings, ready to fire, ready to unleash their cold, rusty iron arrows into the hearts of their foes.

"Get down!" said Connell as he veered the sled over to the back side of the one on their left, brushing up against it momentarily, and in that moment, swords clashed and sparks flew, but no blood was spilt. The bandits unleashed a short volley through the air and most arrows landed just short of them, but one lucky arrow slipped past the thigh of Cassius, cutting him open only minorly. But the boy winced in agony and gave out a short cry of pain. Azrad retaliated and released a bolt from his crossbow that spiked through the skull of one of the enemy drivers, but the sled kept on, and more and more of the bandits began to draw back their bowstrings. Seeing this, Connell fled further east, away from the enemy. However, more bandits began to pour down from the sloping spine of the mountain, and they too wore skis. Their run was timed perfectly, meaning that the company would soon be trapped between the sleds and the stampeding army of bandits to the east, and the Company of Ekmere would be torn apart by blades and arrows. Cassius felt as he was being forced by some entity to watch as his fate unfolded, and the notion of the inevitable pain of a death that was soon to come felt worse than death itself, like a late summer flower forced to watch as the winter draws closer and closer and its friend's petals begin to fall, winter taking each of them to their grave.

"Azrad! Aim for the hounds and cats!" said Ivan, and the Ruzadian man shot three bolts away towards the sled dogs and leopards. He could see and hear the pain of each of them as his bolts ruined their beautiful coats of fur. It did not feel right bringing death to an animal who was oblivious as to why it deserved it, but it had to be done. As each one tumbled down, the one behind tripped over it, and the entire sled abruptly jolted to the right, crashing, and crushing those who rode upon it. Only one was left now. But now their own sled dogs were being targeted, and the ski men drew nigh with malice in their cruel hearts and an unexplainable animus with their very presence. Each man hung to the edges of the sled like pirates of the frozen seas, feeling the air touch their skin, and every now and then, clumps of ice flew up into the air, blinding the company for a few seconds until they regained their vision.

Another pack of wild men came racing down the western front. This time they rode atop large rams, reindeer, and even the most famed white, armoured bears that resided in the most inhospitable places of the north. The company would meet their demise head-on and with pride as the two tidal waves of doom came crashing upon them. Cassius could hear the snorts and grunts of the mammals that came for him with swordsmen that rode on their backs, roaring malice that twisted and turned in a hurricane of hate.

"Ready yourselves! Draw your swords!" yelled Sir Hadrian with glory in his tone as he placed his body in front of Cassius. Even now as death was near, he still lived to protect, and he still valued those he held dear with greater regard than his own life.

If only my father were like this, thought Cassius.

Twenty meters.

Fifteen.

Ten.

Five.

Each man gave one last scream, for they wished to be remembered as one brave enough to look at their coming death without fear. Cassius closed his eyes. He was not one of them. He was not fearless, nor was he even a man. He was a child that was foolish enough to think he could make a change.

Cassius expected the blow to be quick, but he felt nothing. Was he already dead? No. He was very much alive still, but he had expected to hear the sounds of his companion's deaths around him. But he heard nothing from them. He opened his eyes to see that the two armies were now fighting each other, and he and his companions were simply stuck in between them.

Ivan's help had come at last: an opposing northern tribe that was at war with the one that pursued the company. Ivan assumed that the brothers, Trevor and Colton, were indeed Eyes of Medearia, and they had somehow convinced one of the tribes to help them kill the company off. A man that was separated from the battle that ensued around them rode over to the company's sled that was now halted. He rode atop a massive white bear that towered over everyone, and he wore a facade of plated silver armour. Cassius gulped. The man seemed to pay little attention to the battle that engulfed all in a blanket of madness, and he pointed his spear towards the company.

"Where is the one who bears the Horn of Ethway?" Ivan withdrew the horn that he had used to call upon the army. "So, you have returned after all these years, Ivan. Come, we will speak later. Let us make way for the caves," said the man, and as he spoke Cassius could see that nearly all the enemy's soldiers had been run down and slaughtered. They were no match for the other tribe, and the snow around them was painted in red. Each step they took on the snow stained their boots. Cassius could smell the foul stench of death that reeked of raw intestines and other human innards, but he looked at the others, and he could see that he was the only one that paid any attention towards it. They were used to such things. But Cassius couldn't see how anyone could get used to something like this. Even still, those who had not died yet lingered and cried in pain, and Cassius wanted to help but soon saw that their limbs had been torn off and strewn across the snow. He saw a woman, which surprised him, and her stomach seemed to push out, signifying that she was with child. A man walked up to her and stuck the end of his spear through her belly; the child died instantly, but the woman screamed until all Cassius could hear or think about was her howls in the throes of agony.

"Cassius," said Sir Hadrian, "look away," and the knight let the prince pass him as he watched his new allies butcher the woman that would have been a proud mother in a few months' time. She was the enemy, sure, but only because two men had paid their tribe's leaders to hunt them down; they had no personal hatred towards them, they only wanted food and a few coins to get by the winter, just like everyone else.

And so, with their newfound allies, the company followed them south, taking the turn around the bend of the eastern mountain and down into a deep canyon where they found a series of ice caves that led into the guts of the earth. Each cave was rough and wild at the mouth, but as they progressed onwards, they could see that the ice and snow began to fade and transitioned into bare rock and soil. As they followed the tunnel, they came to a large opening in the earth that held a small city that lived under a glacier roof. When the summer came, the glacier would melt, pouring down what they treated as rain, and it would fill the city streets with streams of the purest water. It was small compared to the cities above, but there were markets where herbs and exotic spices were traded, places to eat and drink, and even underground hot springs where men and women lay naked in the warm baths that filled regions of the cave with thick steam that was quite refreshing when compared to the frigid air above ground. It was far from the great architecture of Ekmere, but huts and wooden shacks felt like a drop of paradise to Cassius and the others.

The opening where they now stood was met with a thin set of stairs that went down into the city, and it was there that the man—who appeared to be the leader of this tribe—introduced himself.

"Your friend Ivan is aware of this place and who I am, but I can see that the rest of you are not. This is the city of Dayhenigh, the second city of the Whitefrost Tribe. I am called Maktai; I am the chief of this village."

"We are honoured to be your guests," said Sir Hadrian.

"I can see you all could use some rest. I will show you where you can stay and store your things, and then, if you so choose, you may restore your spirits at the hot springs," said Maktai, and then he—not any servant, but he, Maktai, the village chief—took his own time to guide the company around the streets of his village. He showed them the best places to eat and even his favourite spots to sit and rest away from the draining monotony of society. Finally, he showed them all where they could stay, which were five caves that were carved into the foot of a hill that led to the lodge that held the village elders. To Cassius's surprise, each cave was rather nice and was spacious enough for him and his belongings. Connell and Azrad, on the other hand, were forced to share a cave, and the two spent their first few hours of the afternoon arguing and bickering about whose space belonged to who, like an old married couple who had been together for far too long.

Once Cassius had placed his things and settled in, he finally began to feel the weight of the past few days begin to weigh on him. He hadn't imagined before that he would be so far from home and that neither father nor Vidicus would know his whereabouts, and this act of rebelling was thrilling. He felt less like a prince and more like himself then he had in years, and he was proud of what he had accomplished so far. But still, he was unconfident in his path and his journey, like walking in a field of mist where one can only see so far ahead. Sure, he knew what was behind him, but the path ahead was hazy and unclear, and during his time of cogitation, Cassius remembered *him.*

The dreams.

The wolves.

The fire and the blood.

. . . The hate.

But most of all, he remembered the Tree and the face of the two creatures he had seen. *What had Ivan called them again?* thought Cassius. *Was it elves? What a strange word. I am surprised I have never heard it before though, not even in school. And this genocide that Ivan also spoke of, why was it hidden for so long? And why have we always been taught that there is nothing but empty seas beyond Ederia?*

Cassius planned on asking Ivan in the evening when everyone had gotten their bearings, but until then, he was left to ponder. It made sense to him that there were other lands out there, after all, the Casthedians had ventured over to Ederia after the land of Celladia sank into the sea. He also had overheard Ivan speak of the Eyes of Medearia, and he wondered what they were all about, but for now, he settled with his own answer, and that was that they watched over humankind in case if they ever decided to rediscover Medearia. Maybe that was why those men were after them? He did not know. But thinking back on their encounter with them, Cassius felt ashamed. He had showed little to no bravery or strength, and this was something that he thought all kings should be capable of.

He stood up from his bed and unsheathed his sword. It felt heavy. He swung it around a few times to get the feel of it. He laughed. If anyone ever chose to fight him, Cassius hoped that they would see the beauty of his sword and assume it signified that he was one to be feared, although that couldn't have been further from the truth. He swung it thrice more, trying to remember Sir Hadrian's lessons from when he was a child, thinking of what stance to take and how to move correctly. He turned and pivoted towards the cave's opening and was startled to see Sir Hadrian leaning on the outer lip of the cave.

"Have you decided to resume your training, my prince?"

"Well, to be honest, maybe a little," said Cassius.

"In that case, we may start tomorrow, but for now, take this advice: do not fret about being brave enough. You don't have to obsess over proving yourself, Cassius. Simply do your best without any thought of people's opinions of you, and you will soon notice that they begin to respect you for who you are. So do not train with your sword to be better than those around you, train to be better than you were the day before. Also, your stance could be a little wider and your grip a little looser," said Sir Hadrian, and this made the prince smile. But it was then that the knight gave a quick and surreptitious glance around the room for any sign of liquor. There was nothing. Not a single bottle, and Sir Hadrian began to notice a change in the boy. He seemed younger and full of joy, but also older and more composed in thought. Although there were times in which the immaturity that came with his age flared up, that was to be expected. "Well then," said Sir Hadrian with a smile, "I was simply checking in. Do you wish to eat with us tonight? We are all having a fire by the hot springs."

"I'd enjoy that, Hadrian. I will see you tonight," said Cassius, and he sheathed his sword as the old man turned and walked away.

When night came, the moon's light filtered through the glacier ceiling and illuminated the village below in a silky white hue. Cassius walked through the streets alongside Sir Hadrian, and it didn't take them long to reach where the others had made a small fire. Ivan, Azrad, and Connell were sitting down, telling stories and drinking every time they heard a part in the tale that excited them. Cassius sat down, and as he sat, a whip of fire shot into the air with a crack, and the others greeted him with a cold mug of beer.

"It tastes like shit, but it'll do the job," said Azrad with his arm outstretched, handing the mug over to the prince. Cassius stared at it almost as if it was some unknown object that emanated an unexplainable awe too immense for words to convey. "You gonna take it or just keep staring at it?" Cassius wanted it. He truly did . . . but he could not give in. Sir Hadrian watched the boy and wondered what choice he would make. What type of man would he become? Would he follow his words or go back on them?

"Maybe another time," said Cassius.

"Suit yourself then."

"To each his own," added Connell.

"We were gonna play a drinking game. Wanna go grab Hiroki?" asked Azrad.

"Where is he?"

"Over down there," said Connell, pointing over to the far side of the hot springs that stretched out into the dark abyss of the cave. Cassius then stood up and walked down towards where Hiroki sat beside one of the pools. His eyes were closed, and he looked to be at peace. Cassius felt hesitant to disturb him.

"What brings you here, my lord?"

"Excuse me?" Cassius was somewhat startled by the instantaneousness of the Sarakotan's words.

"You don't need to hide it anymore. I know who you are, Cassius."

"Well then . . . um . . . I just wanted to let you know that the others are wanting to play some sort of drinking game. Are you in?"

"Drinking," said Hiroki, turning towards the boy almost with a look of disgust on his face, as if the very word made him sick. "No. I do not drink, my lord, but I will come and watch."

"You know, you don't have to call me lord if you don't feel like it. I don't mind."

"As you wish. A force of habit, I suppose," said Hiroki, and he stood up with grace and great care in his movement and followed Cassius back to the fire.

"There's my fellow ethic brother!" yelled Azrad, and Cassius could tell that the liquor was beginning to get to him. "Come! We're telling stories. I just told Blackwood here about the time I fucked these two women. One was from Vazareth and the other from Thellenor. They ended up tying me to the bed. Now, in my humble defence, I'm all for nefarious kinks, so I thought I was set for quite the pleasant evening. That was until I realized they had tied me up so their husbands, who I suppose I owed money to, could beat me to a purple pulp. And beat me they did. There I was, cock and tongue hanging loose in my punch-drunk state. They let me go after they were satisfied and, of course, after they had robbed me of my money.

"But, in the end, it was I who had the last laugh. I fucked the two of them once more. They left their husbands and came to me. It was then that they asked to wed, and I agreed, but only until they had spent all their money on cheap wedding dresses. After that, I left them. Haven't seen them since."

"Amateur," said Sir Hadrian, and the others laughed tumultuously.

"Well then, enlighten me on the women you have mingled with in your time," said Azrad.

"Maybe when you're older," replied Sir Hadrian.

"What about you, Hiroki?" asked Connell. "Any stories to tell?"

"Probably nothing you'd find interesting," said Hiroki.

"Oh, come on! Have some fun," said Azrad.

Hiroki thought to himself for a moment. He had many exciting tales to tell, but he never enjoyed speaking in front of people, so he never told them. But then he thought of something, a tale. A sad one.

"Do you wish to know why I bear the Okami Breath on my hair?"

"Yes," said the others.

"Do you wish to know why I took an oath of silence and why I have been forbidden to carry my sword?"

"Yes!" said the others.

"When I first met you, Cassius, you did not share your identity with me, but I do not blame you—you didn't trust me, but now it's my turn to trust you all. I have not been entirely truthful about who I am either." The others listened closely with unwavering attention. "My name is not Hiroki. My true name is Mitsunari Miyamoto . . ."

Every jaw, aside from Cassius's, fell to the floor. The others looked at the prince and were amazed at his naivety about the situation. He should have been perplexed, starstruck, bewildered, but he simply did not know the significance of that name—not yet, that is.

"But it was said that you died at Fushin Castle, defending Lord Shinzu," said Sir Hadrian.

"Do you know what happened to Lord Shinzu?" asked Mitsunari.

"Of course," said Sir Hadrian, but as he spoke, he began to catch onto what Mitsunari was alluding to. "He died while you defended him."

"Precisely. I am one of the Saranorn, so letting those who I have sworn to protect die is the same as death for me."

"So, you felt ashamed of your failure?" asked Ivan.

"Yes," said Mitsunari, and his words were soaked in the waters of regret. It was clear that the memory of that long and terrible night brought him great pain.

"Cassius, do you really not know who this man is?" asked Azrad.

"Well, I now know his name."

"That's only half of it. Mitsunari Miyamoto is one of the greatest of the Saranorn," said Azrad, and he appeared to show great enthusiasm and reverence to the man, as he spoke like he was a child looking up to his idol, and he was now looking at Mitsunari instead of Cassius.

"Who exactly are the Saranorn? I've only heard of them, long ago, but I've never learned what they actually are," said Cassius.

"Are you being serious?" asked Azrad. Cassius felt even more naive now and altogether unintelligent. Who knew one could learn so little while being locked away in a palace their whole life with the wisest of scholars to teach them daily? "They are the greatest warriors in Sarakota, peacekeepers and protectors of their way of life. I tell you, they sure didn't teach you much back in Ekmere."

"Well, if I had known just who exactly was in our midst, I'd have been more willing to trust you earlier. Why would you change your name?" asked Ivan.

"On the mainland, they still show respect to my name, but in Sarakota, I am condemned for my failure . . . I . . . even tried to take my own life, but I saw that as taking the easiest route out, and so I changed my name. That is why I have sworn away my sword and was punished with the Okami Breath."

"What about your vow of silence? It seems that it has been broken."

"Lord Shinzu was not the only one I let down that day. My mother was killed in the attack as well. Yuikiri condemned me for my failure for many years but rarely expressed it. But as she died . . . she offered forgiveness . . . and her last wish was to see me happy once more, speaking with pride as I once did, and the wishes of one's family go beyond any vow of silence . . ."

Mitsunari lost himself to the pain of his story and would continue no more, and everyone fell silent for a time until Ivan raised his head.

"Tell us, Cassius, why have you really set out on this journey?" asked Ivan. Cassius looked down at his feet, thinking of something smart to say, something to impress them, something to make him seem like a man . . . more of a king. But there was nothing. Instead, the only thing that could come to him was the underwhelming truth.

"Because I need my father to know that I can be what he wants, that I can be the king he wants me to be. Before this, I would drink and squabble with whores until the sun went down and the moon rose, and even then, my daily habits continued. I didn't like who I was turning into, but I guess that simply made me sadder, and so I drank more to drown my sadness. But after some time, those around me began to condemn me, even my father," said Cassius, and he began to feel that he was speaking to more than just those around him. He was speaking to himself and unveiling the wounds that were left unhealed in his heart. "Soon enough, my father began to ignore me. It was as if he had forgotten who I was. I was a stranger to him, and he was one to me. Vidicus, my brother, was always more 'king material,' and so I think I grew jealous of him.

"And deep down, even though he shows love for me, I know he condemns me as well. He wants to be king; he wants power but is too humble to admit it. This is why I have come all this way. I need to be more than what I am now. I need to be the man who I know I can become."

"Then I cannot deny your fate from meeting you," said Ivan. "There is something bigger at work here, something that goes beyond our control. I think you are destined to come with us. What do you think, Sir Hadrian? Do you still wish to take the prince home?"

Sir Hadrian took his time to think before speaking. "It is my duty to protect him from any danger . . . but not to protect him from his destiny. If Ivan allows me to join, I will follow you, Cassius, until my bones wither to dust." Cassius's eyes lit up, and the light of the fire illuminated the joy in his face.

"And you, Mitsunari, if you choose to join us on our journey, you have my permission," said Ivan.

"You'll have to tell me where you're going."

"East. To Medearia."

"I would be honoured to walk by you all, but I have never heard of any lands beyond the Great Sea. Are you sure that this place exists?" asked Mitsunari.

"Very sure . . . I have been there before."

"Then it is settled. Henceforth, the Company of Ekmere is completed," said Sir Hadrian, and those who drank rose their cups and rejoiced, for there was a newfound vitality and life that came upon all of them, and they began to believe that their journey's goal would be fulfilled. *However,* only four men knew what the true objective was: King Estideel's head on a pike. But that information was too valuable to spread, and it could not be told . . . not yet.

Journey to the Battlefield

The steam from the pools seeped into Cassius's nose as he sunk deeper, feeling the gentle grip of the warm water around his neck. Azrad sat across from him with Connell and Mitsunari, and they discussed things between themselves, however Cassius paid little attention to the topic. He was instead more focused on the graceful caress of the water on his skin and the three women to the right of them in a separate pool. Suddenly, something aroused Cassius's interest. "Where is Ivan?" asked Cassius, and there was a short spell of silence that surprised the prince.

"Well, you see, he's never taken much interest in water. That is, ever since . . . Well, I'm sure he can tell you himself," said Azrad.

"Ever since the elves imprisoned me and my crew," said Ivan from behind. His voice was cold and cruel, as if he was contemplating a time that he wished to forget. But this was something that just could not be forgotten. Ivan stripped down and stepped down into the hot spring, but he halted as soon as his feet were submerged. There he was: a body of burnt and seared flesh being paraded for everyone to see. Cassius found himself staring, and the sight almost startled him. The three women from the far pool walked past, looking at Ivan with fear and disgust in their eyes. Ivan felt ashamed. He knew now that it had been a mistake to come here, and that after all these long years, the brand of Medearia still rendered him a monstrosity to others. All eyes were on him, and they sunk their sights into him like needles oozing in the fluids of disgust.

Finally, after some time, Ivan found the strength to sink down into the pool, but he could not do so without thinking of the mountain pass, of Richard crying for his mother's caress, of the throbbing burns and puss that flowed from each wound . . . and the eyes. The alluring yellow eyes of his captors. They were full of hate. They liked what they did. "Ah, fuck them. They can glare all they want, I don't care," said Ivan, but his words were hollow—he *did* care. Each time he looked down into the water's surface, what was a beautiful blue would morph into the same thick, bloody red broth of human corpses that boiled and bubbled. Eyes and various limbs and flesh that rolled off the bone would rise to the surface. They were the parts of his friends, and they were the only family he'd ever known, and they were all dead now.

Ivan's vision shocked him, and he let out a scream of horror and lifted himself out of the pool, and before anyone could say a thing, he had already gathered his clothes and left.

✳

Maktai led the company down into the more remote regions of Dayhenigh until they reached the mouth of a series of tunnels that led to the Fields of Ukron. Their mounts had already been prepared for them.

"You may take the ice bears," said Maktai. Cassius approached the large beast and placed his hand on its thick white fur. It shook and grunted, and Cassius jerked back, but as he did so, he could hear the boisterous laugh of Maktai from behind. "This is Ragnar. He will be your mount. I hear you are heading south into Bruxstan and Sacadia; this will be a deadly path with the war raging there," said Maktai.

"It is our only path," said Ivan.

"Then we should gather the bears' armour. They will take you to the border between Bruxstan and Sacadia. There they must leave you and come home, but a finer companion you cannot find." Cassius now grew more confident when around Ragnar and began to pet his snout. "It is important to know, young prince, that you do not ride an ice bear, you merely are being carried. He shall choose his path, but you can trust that his actions will be in your best interest."

"I see," said Cassius, now fascinated by the great and mighty animal that stood with pride as if it was very much aware of its enormity and intimidating presence.

Once each bear had their armour strapped on, Maktai said his farewell to the company and gave them one word of direction to guide them through the long tunnels that would hopefully take them into the heart of Bruxstan. Ice hugged the ceiling of the tunnel, but at its base, it was rocky and wet, and the terrain continued like this for most of the path, a path illuminated by faint torchlight. Each step echoed, and a soft breeze filtered the air. Ivan led the group, followed by Sir Hadrian, Cassius, Azrad, and Connell in behind to watch the rear. It would take three days to reach the tunnel's end, but with the ice bears this number would be largely reduced; Ivan guessed they'd reach it by midday tomorrow, but only if they went on through the night, and it was the night that worried him, but he could not place why. It was the air, he felt. It felt alive, as if it was the breath of a sleeping giant, still yet in motion, warm and yet quite cool.

It wasn't until when evening struck that Ivan voiced his thoughts. "We should stay on guard tonight. There's something eerie about these tunnels," said Ivan, and the others agreed. They too felt the same strange notion, a feeling of being watched by lidless eyes, eyes with no need for rest, purely designed to watch and study. Even the bears began to feel uneasy. Cassius could feel Ragnar's heart begin to race whenever a strong gust of wind rushed in towards them, and it smelt like death. Thus, slowly the air began to feel poisoned and unnatural to inhale.

"I—I need air," said Azrad, but no one would reply. They were all too focused on their own breathing. Ivan hadn't any clue what time it was now, which was strange; he could almost always guess the time of day, but things down here felt hazy and unclear. Cassius felt a small drop of dew drip onto his forehead. It was warm.

Strange, thought Cassius. That was until the liquid began to seep down between his eye and his nose and he could see it was not dew at all—it was blood. He wiped it off in a hurry but it was only to be replaced with two more droplets of blood.

"What the—"

Sir Hadrian looked back at Cassius and then to the ceiling that was now dirt instead of ice, earth soaked in blood.

"There's something unnatural about this place," said Connell. "Something ain't right here—"

"Shh, listen," said Ivan. And listen they did, but nothing could be heard at first. Save for the soft moaning of the wind and the groans of the earth, they heard nothing, that is, until the faint cries of men could be heard above. It was the slow melody of violence.

"A battle rages above," said Sir Hadrian. "Strange, I did not think the war would come this far north."

"It is said in the south that once the battlefield has been silenced, and the dead are left to linger, wraiths descend down from the moon to steal the wandering souls," said Azrad with a grin on his face, and

Cassius, who rode ahead of him, knew this story was only an attempt to make him feel more uneasy.

"Enough of the folktales, Azrad. When we reach the surface, we must be cautious—there are worse things that scour the dead," said Ivan.

It was then that the company travelled in silence for many hours, letting the ice bears carry them onwards through the night. After the first hour, the cries of war ceased, and all that could be heard were shallow breaths from each of them. Given his age, Sir Hadrian found it particularly difficult to carry on, and he began to waver. He was old, and he was beginning to feel it. The skirmish up north had taken him by surprise, and he had not noticed it then, but the fact that it had been the first time he had seen battle in many years dawned upon him as his vision faltered. No longer was he the famed Dragon of the North, the Red Knight of the Casthedia; no longer was he the capable young man he once was in his youth. Time seemed to be his greatest foe now, and he was unsure if he could best it.

After three hours, a warm breeze drifted towards them, and the bears halted, sniffing the air. They were close to the surface.

"Do you hear anything?" asked Connell.

"Nay. Not a sound," replied Ivan, and thus they carried on with haste, with a hunger for sunlight and air. The tunnel began to twist and turn, yet simultaneously increasing the incline of the path, and they took one last sharp turn before they saw it: a burning white flame that opened wide before them.

They had reached the surface.

Ivan was the first to exit the tunnel. The dull light of the morning blinded his vision.

He winced, squinting his eyes, but once he adjusted to the environment, he began to see just exactly what it consisted of. Mountains of decomposed bodies lay all around as far as the eye could see; there had to be thousands of them, and many were cloaked with arrows in their backs and sword wounds that had drained their body's blood and spilled their guts out onto the grass. It was a smell so odoriferous that they wished to be back in the tunnel immediately, the smell of death, the tang of rotten human flesh and bone, and the miasmic vapours that came from bodies that were now the new nests and burrows of maggots and flies. The sky was dark. No sun could be seen in the sky that morning, only the grey palls that signified the coming rain. Suddenly, thunder cracked like a whip upon a naked back, and it began to downpour. The rain caused the blood to flow downhill, and it wasn't long until the company, led by the bears, began to walk down a river of blood and death. Cassius could barely see the grass. He had not seen this much death before. He felt hot, claustrophobic almost. He had to escape the horror before him. He wanted to leave, to go home and hide beneath his sheets. Cassius then looked over at the remnants of a Casthedian soldier, and he wondered if he had known that man, wondered if he had any children, any wife that was now widowed. He had half of his face still intact, yet the other half was hollowed with his brain split and ripped in half beside the empty part of his skull.

Cassius leaned over the side of Ragnar and vomited over the body. He wanted to seem strong under the light of death . . . but this, unknown to Cassius, was something that no man, no matter how brave, could look upon without disgust and sadness.

"Cassius! Do not look down," said Sir Hadrian, and his bear slowed its pace so that he fell back to the side of the prince.

"There's . . . so much death," said Cassius, trying to hold back tears, and he felt somewhat embarrassed. they all seemed so used to things like this.

"Cassius, no man or woman is strong enough to look upon this without fear. If you are numb to your emotions, that is a problem within itself," said Sir Hadrian.

Cassius could think of no response, instead, he stared forward in shock, only thinking of darker thoughts, thoughts of pain and suffering. Each man then threw his hood over his head, protecting himself against the onslaught of rain and thunder that plagued the skies, and they started off down southeast towards Sacadia.

The company had travelled through dark oceans and frozen desolations, and soon enough they would arrive on the eastern front of Ederia. Beyond that was a place where questions would be answered, and certainly, blood would be shed.

※

Taku's hands rummaged through the soaked clothes of the fallen. He stood crouched underneath a half-sunken roof of a farmer's house that was unfortunate enough to have been caught in the battle. Taku had hoped that the family had made it out; they were nice. He had met them once before, but he found the body of their child, Priscilla, slouched up against the fireplace.

Taku looked at her body.

A damn shame to live in a world as meaninglessly cruel as this one, thought Taku. He felt bad, no, downright horrible for what he was doing, but times were tough with the war about, and the Casthedian army drew closer by the day, and more and more refugees fled east and south to try and escape, meaning that the borders would be difficult to cross. But he could not leave. The forge could be rebuilt, sure, and the livestock could go with them, but the gardens would stay, and much of their food came from it, and to Olsa, well, Taku always knew that if she had not married him, she'd have married her pumpkins or tomatoes or something else. If she could, that is.

And so, he travelled west, away from his farm and family to scavenge the dead. It made him feel more and more like a peasant and less like the forge master of Sarakota, but that wasn't his life anymore. He loved Olsa, and she loved him, and his kids, Callum and Astrid, were far greater gifts to him than what Lord Shinzu could have offered. Yet, every now and then, he missed speaking with his lord; he had been a good leader and an even better man. Sometimes he wondered what Sarakota was like now, how it had changed, and just how Lord Ishiki ruled the land now, or if his friends remembered him at all. Mitsunari would remember, that much was certain.

His hand felt the round and smooth texture of an apple in the inside pocket of a young man who must have bled out from his wounds. It wasn't much, but it was something. He stored it in his bag with the rest. If he could, Taku would also search for any steel he could melt down and use, but most blades of the Sacadians and Praganese were forged with material that was inferior to what he would use in his blades. It had been long, though, since he had ever forged a weapon. There had just been no time since the kids were born, and they were now eight years old. However, the passion for forging still burned within him.

The crows had arrived before him, and flocks of them swooped down to feed from the decomposing bodies. Taku had seen all he could in the farmer's house; he had seen all he could bear. He now walked along the sea of bodies where every now and then a small mountain of the dead would rise, and all that Taku could see were bones, maggots, and unidentifiable pieces of the human bodies squished together. He was no warrior. He had seen battle and spilt blood before, but he seldom had seen anything like this. The smell was something he had not imagined. He had known it would be bad, but not this bad.

The terrain ahead began to slope upwards, forming a small hill, and at its ridge, he could see lightning reach out across the sky and soon the clamorous sound of thunder rumbled far away. He crouched down once again, hoping for something good, something more than the shitty remnants of some other peasant's delights. But as usual, there was nothing. It was a dark day, and to Taku, the whole world seemed to be dyed in blackness and a sombreness that he could smell in the rain, feel in the earth, and see in his misfortune. This had been a wasted journey.

Taku then froze.

He heard something.

Laughing? thought Taku. *No, grunting. Yes. Something big, something large—an animal? Yes.*

He darted towards the beginning of the hill, hoping that the steep incline of the ground could hide him. It seemed that the noise was coming from up there, and it was slowly coming down.

He slid out a small knife from his pouch as he hid amongst the bodies. The smell was utterly revolting. He wanted to vomit, but he needed to keep calm; there weren't many benevolent folks or beasts who prowled the dead. He happened to be one of the very few who were kind at heart, in his mind.

What had been solely grunting from an animal before was now joined by soft whispers. *Cutthroats? Soldiers? Either way, they're bad news,* thought Taku. The forge master held his breath again, and the only thing his eyes could look at was the motionless mouth of a small boy that lay dead, but also served as his cover. He had been eighteen and delusional enough to believe that he could make a change in the war by enlisting. He'd only found out how wrong he was now as his dead eyes stared into the fearful heart of Taku, mouth wide open with flies buzzing to and fro, sucking on what little liquid was left on his tongue.

Taku found himself lost in thought for far too long, and when his focus came back to the voices . . . he heard nothing. They were gone. He waited for a while, trying to listen further, but the only sound he heard was his heart pumping blood through his body.

Lub. Lub, dub.

He exhaled slowly, but his breath was matched with the chilling touch of steel at the back of his neck.

They were upon him.

"Don't move a fucking muscle," said Azrad. "Put your bag and knife on the ground and kick it over here. Then I want those hands in there, and you're gonna take three nice and long steps forward."

Taku shook uncontrollably. He wanted to cry, but he knew he must stay strong in the face of death as all men must do when the great arbiters of the sky brought forth their judgement upon them. His eyes watered. He tried to speak, but he stuttered, forming nothing that could be identified as words of the common tongue. Ivan and the others were still mounted atop their bears, and each of them leaned over to get a better look at the man. He was old, but not too old; maybe in his forties, from what Cassius thought, but he needed a better look at his face if he was to be sure. His hair was dark and long with silver strands, and he possessed a well-kept amount of facial hair that was mostly on his chin and upper lip. Most of his face, however, was covered by the large brim of his straw hat. It kept Cassius wondering just who they had found; it wasn't often that one found a Sarakotan in the middle of Ederia.

"Turn him around," said Ivan. "Take that hat off of him." Azrad did as he was told and turned the man around without his hat.

"Taku! Is that you?" The forge master recognized the voice of his friend immediately, but he could not believe that he was hearing it.

"M-Mitsunari?" Taku was still in shock over the face and voice of the man that he saw before him. It was certainly the face of Mitsunari, but still, he believed his mind betrayed him.

"Yes, it is me. What are you doing so far away from home?"

Taku gulped, reclaiming his voice and confidence as the conversation progressed. "I could say the same thing to you."

"Lower your crossbow," said Mitsunari. "This is the smith I spoke to you about, Ivan." But he too was taken back by the serendipity that had come upon them. Azrad lowered his weapon and walked back to the group, but still facing Taku, who began to feel as if he may just live. Certainly, if this was *the* Mitsunari he had known and grown up with so long ago, in a time that seemed more like a dream now. "It is your choice, Ivan, but this is a man I would trust with my life. He can give us shelter from the rain," said Mitsunari, looking over at his friend with questioning eyes.

"Yes! Yes, of course! I would be happy to give you all shelter—and food! Lots of food!"

The company looked at each other, and it seemed as if they all knew what the other thought.

"How far?" asked Ivan.

"We'd reach my farm by the evening, on those mounts, at least," said Taku, and without words, Ivan signalled for him to mount up with Mitsunari, and he did as he was told. Taku felt his heartbeat slow until it rested at its normal pace. He had lived. He owed Mitsunari, his dear friend, once again.

The Madness of Vidicus

The steps echoed, and the long halls of Luxtheil Palace were ever so silent save for the footsteps of Vidicus. The northern snows were upon him, and he had only now begun to feel used to the loneliness of these eerie and dark halls. At first, they frightened him, but now he was their warden, their lord, and the taste of power awakened him; he had grown far too used to his mundane life at Ekmere. Vidicus grew to like this place. He liked the silence that came with the strong winds of the night. The city's people were far below in the belly of the valley, freezing as the storm withered their spirits into dust. Aside from his servants, Vidicus had spent the past few weeks in sweet and savoury solitude. No longer did he have to deal with his brother's mistakes or suck up to his father; he felt like his own lord now, his own king. In fact, he was surprised at how little he had thought of his family since he had arrived at the gates of Luxtheil. He felt like his true self now, not confined to speak and act as others thought he should, but to live and act as he pleased.

Vidicus sat alone in his study, listening to the whispering winds that swirled outside his window. He looked outside into the deep blizzard while fiddling with a brass globe in his hand, a globe of Ederia. Suddenly he heard the hinges to the door operate and it slowly swung open with great care and politeness.

"Lord Vidicus," said Casperad, one of the servants. "We have received a letter from the king."

Vidicus looked at the man, and Casperad seemed almost frightened; his lord appeared rather ill of late. He did not sleep nor eat much anymore since he'd arrived here.

"Well, well, well, how wonderful. I wonder just how my father is faring in the effort against the rebellion; he's getting old for things like this. Come! Bring the letter to me," said Vidicus. Casperad approached and placed the letter on the table. It had his official stamp, thus it was the king's letter without question. Vidicus traced his fingers along with the envelope's corners. "Leave me be," he said, and Casperad followed his lord's command.

Vidicus rubbed his eyes.

He was tired, but his mind felt sharp, sharper than usual, but it did not feel entirely his. He had been having strange thoughts of late, thoughts and powerful paroxysms of unfocused envy and hate. He felt nothing like the man he was at Ekmere, the polite and obedient second son, destined for nothing but second place—the scraps of Cassius.

Still, the letter sat there unopened.

Vidicus thought of Cassius, about what new whorehouse he had hunkered away in.

He probably doesn't know what day it is anymore, or even who exactly he is, thought Vidicus. He rubbed his eyes once more, and he could feel the strong hands of sleep and deep slumber tug and pull at his mind, stretching thoughts into abnormal ideas that one would not think of when feeling well slept. He feared the night but also was delighted at its coming, and when dusk came, the strange thoughts grew and boiled in his mind . . . It was all thanks to *her*.

He rubbed his eyes again, and this time, fell asleep and rested his head on his desk, and the cold wind sang its melodious lullaby, putting him deeper into the darkness.

When Vidicus awoke it was still dark out. And he awoke to the soft touch of her hand on his shoulder. She walked behind him, touching him where she knew she could gather his attention, feeling him with just the right amount of force and gentleness to awaken him into the night with a silly euphoria in him.

"Must we do this now?" asked Vidicus.

"I know you, Viddy," laughed Iris. "You'll want it any time of the day."

"Don't call me that."

"Oh? And why's that?" asked Iris, leaning into him, exposing her breasts in an attempt to seduce him.

"Because that's what my *real* mother used to call me. I don't know what you are or why you come to me," said Vidicus. Iris bit her lips and shot him with a submissive stare of her emerald eyes and made a soft sound that she knew would make him in the mood.

"So, I'm not real enough for you, am I?"

"I—I don't even know what's real anymore! You are a demon that plagues my thoughts! Leave me be, fiend!"

Iris purred and then chuckled as she circled him around his desk. "You are right, my lovely prince—I am a part of you, just as you are a part of me. What troubles you, Viddy? Do you not love me, your mother?"

"*You're not my mother,*" said Vidicus, and his voice was weak as tears flooded his eyes.

"Do you not love stroking and then pulling my hair? Do you not yearn for the touch of me on your pale skin? I can be a whore if you wish . . . I can be and do whatever you please, boy," said Iris, grabbing

Vidicus by his groin and suddenly changing faces into someone else entirely, someone he did not know. A prostitute, he presumed. Vidicus stood up from his chair and leaped backwards.

"This—" Vidicus tried to speak, but words were failing him now. He wanted her. He did, but he didn't exactly know what *she* was. She visited him each night, but in the mornings he had only a vague memory of her, but he could notice a change in his demeanour: it was darker and more malevolent. "You! You are not real! You're just some witch or spirit who haunts these eerie halls, driving me mad with each coming of dusk!"

"I see we are feeling feisty tonight!" said the woman, changing back to the face and body of his mother. She bit her lips again and tugged at her black dress, pulling it farther up towards her hips, revealing more and more skin.

She took a step forward.

And then another, like a predator staring down its prey, knowing it has already succeeded in catching its dinner and thus simply basking in its success. She was close to Vidicus now. So very close. She touched his chest and exhaled slowly onto him. Vidicus loved the smell of her, the taste of her lips on his. Her hand slowly crept down between his legs and tickled him ever so slightly, only to stop when she knew Vidicus wanted more.

"Do you want to undress me?" asked Iris. Vidicus was breathing heavily, and he could feel his throat burn and his eyes water. He needed to get out, but he wanted to stay. She was beautiful, just like his real mother had once been, with hair as black as the night, eyes as beautiful as green diamonds, and skin so fair and a dress so black that her entire image was like a painting of the night sky, with the stars and moon contrasted against a black canvas.

She was getting impatient. She wanted the feeling, the feeling of him inside her, and she bit at his neck like a poorly behaved cat. "Come on, don't you want it?" whispered Iris, pushing her groin into his and taking off his clothes. Vidicus thought for a moment, but he didn't need to think . . . he already knew he was lost, so very lost within his own darkness that consumed his mind.

"Yes. Yes, I do!" said Vidicus, and as if an entirely different man had replaced his heart, he turned the woman around and ripped her black dress off her from behind, revealing her naked body that made his blood boil with sexual power and lustful ideas.

She flipped around to face him. Vidicus looked into her eyes, and she curled her legs around him, trapping him inside of her. She had a smile on her face, a dubious and nefarious grin that Vidicus loved so dearly. She was evil, and he adored it.

"Hmmm, yes. You like this, don't you?"

"Yes."

"You want me forever?"

"Yes!"

"You miss your mother, do you not?"

"Yes!"

"She is right here, my young prince, right before your eyes! If you want her, come find her in the darkness," said Iris with a sexual moan that made Vidicus want to do anything, anything for her.

"I will follow you!"

"Good then," said Iris, flipping Vidicus over with terrifying strength, and she then took her hand to his throat while riding him for her pleasure. "Listen carefully, boy. You know you want it. You want the throne and the power that it shall bestow upon you. You keep it hidden beneath your gentle face, but hate them, you hate all of them! Do you not, little boy?"

"I do! I want it!" said Vidicus, noticing that her grip was tightening around his throat, and her voice seemed to grow deeper and older, but he didn't care. He was addicted to her touch, her sweat, her breath, and the intensity of the sweet and rough sex.

"Then let me show you how to get it!"

"Show me! Show me everything! I want to know! Show me!"

Iris kissed him on his mouth once more before stopping, and her groin and hips halted in their thrusting. Her expression went dead as the grave . . . There was something new about her, something far more evil in her eyes than there had been before.

"Kill your father. Take his golden crown and wear it as yours," said Iris, and Vidicus stopped.

"You want me to do what? No! That's blasphemy!"

Iris went to speak, and as she did her skin melted off and sank in, showing protruding bones and her skeletal body, and what was left of her skin was rotten and yellow. Vidicus fell to the ground in fear, pressing his back up against the wall.

"Whatever is the matter, my prince?" asked the creature, and Vidicus could see her tongue move behind her fangs and skull. Before he could yell for the guards, she was upon him, lifting him up into the air by his neck. "You fool. Your mother is dead, boy. I am the darkness in your thoughts! I am Vidicus Helladawn just as much as you are. I am the spirit and the physical embodiment of your surreptitious thoughts that you are too cowardly to listen to."

She opened her mouth, and her tongue stretched to lick and cuddle Vidicus's face, and he shrieked, cried, kicked, but her grip was far too strong. Could she be right? Was any of this even happening? Vidicus did not know, but what he could see was a bright light from within her. He could see it in her mouth and eyes, shining from within, hypnotizing him into a trance.

Vidicus went limp, hanging by her grip. He was still conscious, but barely. He was unable to speak. Instead, he listened to the creature's words. *"Take it! Take it! Take it as yours! The throne, the land, everything. All you must claim beforehand is your father's head. He never loved you. Never!"* The woman laughed. "You are an afterthought, an insignificant leaf in the wind that your father sent away in order to rid himself of you. But you will not let him live with such a deed. No.

"Take his life. Take your brother's. Kill anyone who shall stand in your way."

Vidicus could not reply, and he could feel the light from within her blind him and sing him to sleep, and what exactly she was Vidicus could not tell, not for sure. However, deep down he knew what and just who she was—she was him. She was every dark thought he had, every desire, every ounce of malice within all beings. She was powerful, and Vidicus had only gotten a taste of it.

When he awoke, he was back at his desk with the wind blowing behind him as usual. It was as if nothing had changed. Not a thing. The note from his father still sat on the tabletop, the same brass sphere of Ederia looked at him as he awoke from a deep sleep. The door opened and out came Casperad.

"Good morning, my lord. You look well," said Casperad. Vidicus hadn't heard him at all, as his mind was far away and shattered into pieces.

"Was . . . was there a woman here last night?" asked Vidicus.

"No, my lord. The palace was quite empty apart from myself and the guards. Believe me, if there was someone new in here, we'd have seen them."

Vidicus made no reply, and Casperad once again made his leave.

He looked at the letter from his father.

A fire raged within him. A fire of envy and of hate. There was a darkness in his heart that he could feel had been awakened. Thus, Vidicus looked upon the letter, and he knew what he would do.

Blood on Each Hand

The smell of the battlefield had diminished long ago, and the company, led by Taku's directions, had passed the border into Sacadia no more than an hour ago. The pungent odours of death had been replaced with the wet and moist aromas of damp moss and soaked cedar and ferns. Cassius quite liked it; it was something about the cool and crystalline air that felt good on his lungs. At times he found himself taking deep breaths in an effort to fill his body with the natural pureness of his surroundings.

The bears had left them at the border, and they walked now on a dirt path that weaved its way through the woods. "It's not far now, just around the corner. Please, I apologize for my daughter's manners beforehand. She can be rather, well . . . blunt in her opinions of others, which is quite typical for an eight-year-old, I suppose," said Taku. They took a bend around a small ravine where a river lay, singing the tales of the mountains above, and Taku's farm, along with a small hamlet, slid into view. It wasn't large, however, its garden was vast, and friendly smoke rose from its chimney. "Come!

My wife and I can prepare dinner while you warm yourselves by the fire."

Cassius looked down the mud road that ran through the village. There were six houses with thatched roofs on each side. Some wary folks watched with unfriendly eyes from their doors. Some houses had been burnt down, and Cassius could see the marks on the rooftops where flames had once run wild.

"What happened here?" whispered Cassius to Sir Hadrian.

". . . It is not uncommon for soldiers to raid nearby villages for gold, food . . . and other things. Raids like that can oftentimes turn violent. They'll surely be wary of any outsiders, so stay close."

They entered through the garden and came to the front door, where he and the others left their belongings under the overhang of the roof. "Come in, come in. My apologies for the mess," said Taku, and the company flooded his house. Olsa and the children rushed out to see the mysterious newcomers who appeared out of nowhere, soaked to the bone and chilled to their souls.

"Taku, what are you doing inviting strangers into our home? There's a war about! Are these refugees?" asked Olsa.

"Friends. Most new but one older," said Taku, looking over at Mitsunari; he had never told her much about his old life on Sarakota and who he'd once called friends.

"*Amazing! Grand!* But just what in Ederia are they doing in my house, eyeballing my children like they're about to gobble one of em up?"

"My dear, they needed food and shelter, and who am I to turn down a heartful soul?"

"You're me husband, and I'd expect you to make good decisions. They could be a band of cutthroats, for all I know," said Olsa. Taku looked back at the others, seeming somewhat embarrassed. "Oh well, I suppose one night shan't be such a bother. I'll make you your beds and all. Taku, go and get the kettle on, and then I'll get supper going; we're having bangers and mash tonight with salmon from the port, cause why not, right? Gluttony is a privilege, not a sin, I say," said Olsa, and she showed the men to the guest rooms. As Connell walked past the children, their eyes widened with wonder.

"How'd you get so big, eh? You's a monster who eats little kids like me or something? That how you get so big?" asked the little girl, Astrid, but she was hardly frightened.

"Yeah. You got a toothpick anywhere? I think I've got a fingernail stuck in between my teeth," replied Connell, attempting to make a joke.

"Nope. You're gonna have to use your fingers," said Astrid.

"What a shame. Thanks anyways, little one," said Connell with a smile. Astrid and her brother, Callum, then ran off down the hall to show the travellers to their rooms. There were only two, and they were quite cramped, but it was far better than sleeping under another tree and feeling the sharp droplets of the morning rain crash against the pores of their skin, chilling them as they tried to get a single iota of sleep to aid them through the day. However, being inside, the sound of the rain was quite calming. Once they had brought their things inside and into their rooms, Ivan and the others sat by the fire and sipped on tea and smoked their pipes, brooding in silence and smelling the fresh aromas of herbs and spices that marinated tonight's meal.

"Boy, come here, if you don't mind," said Olsa. Cassius stopped what he was doing and looked over to the kitchen.

"Me?"

"Yes, you."

Cassius sat up and entered the kitchen.

"How old is you?"

"Eighteen."

"Little young to be travelling with a crowd this rough, aren't we?" Cassius paused for a moment, pretending to be distracted by the herbs she was mincing on the cutting board.

"Well, it was either I set off with this crew or waste my life away as a meaningless peasant," said Cassius, finally.

"You? Peasant? You haven't got the look. No. You look like royalty to me if I've ever seen it. I guess that's where me fault lies—haven't seen royal blood, haven't even been to the capital, Ekmere. Been spending me entire life cooking and cleaning on this farm, and then I met Taku. Pile of bones he was then, let me tell you, so I fed him up. Been treating him like a prince ever since," said Olsa. Cassius laughed, although he wasn't quite sure if he had faked it or not. "Now be a darling and start peeling the potatoes, would ya?"

"Excuse me?" Cassius was quite puzzled by her demand. It hadn't occurred to him before, but he was far from used to being ordered around, especially by common folk, and he could tell his royal pride was still present within him.

"Peel the potatoes with the knife there and put them in the pot on the fire when you're ready. I'll get the sausages going. But make sure you salt the water first, won't ya?"

"Um, yeah. Yeah, I got it," said Cassius. Now he *knew* he was lying to himself; he had never had to peel a potato before in his life.

While Cassius did this, Taku told the others about the war and who was winning and where the next battle was likely to take place. The company took great interest in his tale, and they would need to if they were to avoid any conflict between Casthedia and the rebels.

"It will not take long for the war to get here. King Cornelius continues to drive further east, so it won't be long until Sacadia is taken. Once that happens the rebellion is pretty much no more," said Taku.

"Do you have a side?" asked Sir Hadrian

"Not really. Life was tough here before the rebellion, but the war has made it worse and made the memory of Casthedian rule far more pleasant. I only hope that our farm will stay intact by the end of all this, and my wife and I and the children won't become refugees like the rest of them."

"The king has no interest in burning down villages that he helped build and protect not long ago, however his soldiers are something else. They are unpredictable, and war brings out cruelty in the kindest of hearts. I would be careful if I were you," said Sir Hadrian.

"Agreed," said Taku. "Now, my old friend Mitsunari, what has brought you to lands such as these with men such as these?"

"They sailed with my sister, and I've had few places to be since the death of Lord Shinzu and the disgrace that it brought to my name. So, I travelled with Yuikiri, and that is how I met these folks."

"Your sister, how is she doing?"

". . . Dead," said Mitsunari, looking into the flames of the fire. Taku said nothing. He could think of no words that could console him for none existed in this tongue, and so he said a few words in Sarakotan and Mitsunari gave him a nod of respect.

"I am sorry to hear such a terrible thing. So, where are you going to head in the morning?"

"Further east," said Ivan, "and then once we reach the nearest port, we plan to set up a trading post for spices and furs."

"You're well armed for spice merchants," said Taku.

"It's a dangerous road from Hellandor to Sacadia," said Ivan.

"That it is. But I saw that you, Mitsunari, were not armed when we met at the battlefield. I still have *it* if you are wondering," said Taku.

"And you may keep it. I have abandoned the way of the sword."

"Well, I respect your decision, but as your friend said, these are dangerous times to be about. Let me at least show you the forge."

"You still make swords?" asked Mitsunari.

"Not really, no. Don't have the time. But one day I'd love to feel the warming embrace of the coals on my skin again and work with Sarakotan metal as we did years ago."

"Those were good times," said Mitsunari, and his voice was poignant and soft.

"Your sword, Kazemaru, I have kept in good condition."

"Thank you, but if I grip the blade once more, I fear I shall only bring further dishonour to the Miyamoto clan."

"Then I shall speak no more of it. I think you will all be glad to know that I have been saving a bottle of rice wine for a night such as this. Will you drink with me?" asked Taku, but he knew the others would not decline, thus the question was mainly directed towards Mitsunari.

"Two cups. Maybe three," said Mitsunari with a smile, the others had never seen him smile until now. It was strange, almost unnatural. "May the moon not judge me harshly for what I am about to do."

Suddenly, Olsa entered the living room with the kids close at her heels. "Your little journey to the forge will have to wait. Supper is ready! Your work is finished, Cassius. Go and relax now. I'm old, but I am not in the agony of dotage, I tell ya."

It was then that they sat down and enjoyed their first real dinner since they had begun their journey. Cassius looked around. Those who had once seemed like strangers who intimidated him were now something more—he saw a family. He listened to the merry laughs that rang around the table like a song whose words consisted of joyful chuckles instead of words. Tales were told and Olsa, after a few cups of wine, insisted on letting everyone in on her secret to cooking. No one had asked, but she simply felt obligated to share in the secrets of her passion. It was strange. Cassius felt something when he was with her. She was rough around the edges and sharp in her tongue, indeed, but still, he felt the same feeling he had once felt when he was with his mother. It had been far too long since he had had that feeling. It was somewhat warm, and it made him feel young again, as if he lay in a field of beautiful summer flowers that would always keep him safe and protected. He missed her. And this seemed to be almost the first time he had thought about her in what felt like years. He wondered if Vidicus thought about her still, and just how his brother was doing with his new position of power. He would do well. He was Vidicus, after all. He was not born to be a king, but he had always wanted to be one—this Cassius knew but never voiced to anyone. But, in his mind, he believed that being the lord of Bruxstan would soothe his brother's need for power.

After supper was finished, Cassius could tell that sleep began to seduce him, and he would not resist for much longer. Thus as the adults spoke in length, he made his way into his bed and drifted into sleep, thinking about his mother and father and brother, remembering the times in which they would walk in the gardens, and it was there that his mother would let loose her voice and sing to them. Cassius yearned for times like that to find him once again. But they were lost.

Who would have thought that you, Prince Cassius, King of the Bottle, would find himself deep into enemy territory, and on a journey in which he would travel to a land where few men have stepped before? This is still quite hard to believe. A month ago, I spent nearly the entire day at the brothel and drinking to cheap whores, but now I wake with the dawn and walk with the wind. I wonder what the dreams mean. Who is the grey-haired elf? I think that's what Ivan called them. I try to ignore his words and focus on my own journey, but I can't help but think that there is more that lies before me, more than I can see. My path is hidden. I feel as if, at times, I walk with both eyes open, but I couldn't be more blind to what is really happening. My answers lie in Medearia. I know it. Who was the woman that the grey elf mentioned? Was it Sathelia? Yes. That was it. I saw her lying down in the fields in my dream. She was beautiful, she was—but it was then that Cassius could not hold back the forces of sleep any longer, and he dozed off into the night.

The house was empty, save for Olsa and the kids. He had slept in. The sun shone through the window, warming his groggy face. He sat up and yawned. Water, he needed water. Cassius walked over to the kitchen and smiled at Olsa and the kids.

"Good morning, dear. I hope you slept well—you certainly look it. The others, well, they went to the forge. I pity them, they'll be late for breakfast, and I ain't about to let it get cold now. Come on, dear, sit yourself down at the table." Callum and Astrid were there waiting for him, and they smiled and snickered, whispering to each other, and laughing once they heard what the other had said.

"What's so funny," asked Cassius.

"Nothing," said Callum with a wide grin on his face, showing his teeth and the food that clung to them.

Cassius went back to his business and dug into his breakfast, but the laughing ensued; the two devils were relentless in their mockery. Cassius stopped and looked up at them, putting a silly smile on and making his sights go cross-eyed to force even more laughter upon them. It worked, so very well. Callum and Astrid leaned back in their chairs with laughter in their bellies. "Look—look at his face, Astrid," yelled Callum, pointing his bacon-greased finger towards Cassius.

"You gonna tell me what's so funny now?" asked Cassius, and as he interrogated the two demons of mischief, Olsa poured him a warm cup of coffee to wash down his food. "Thank you," said Cassius, and he then turned his attention back to the kids.

"Well . . . it's your hair!" said Astrid. Cassius ran his hand through his hair and realized he had been struck with a terrible case of bedhead. He laughed and fixed it immediately.

"Well, where I come from, they'd be ashamed of me for not having my hair freshly groomed. I tell you, it feels kind of nice," said Cassius.

"Astrid made you a little something. Ya know, so you can remember us when you leave," said Olsa from the kitchen. There was a pause in the conversation. Astrid looked over at her mother, and Cassius could tell she was a bit embarrassed now that she had been put on the spot. "Well go on, ya little munchkin, show him what ya made," said Olsa. Astrid fiddled with her gift from under the table and twisted back and forth to cope with her childish anxiety.

"Here you go," said Astrid, handing over a circlet of yellow flowers that she had picked from the garden. Cassius placed it gently on his forehead and smiled with gratitude. "Momma told us it brings good luck to those who wear it—so don't you go taking it off now!"

"I could never! It is beautiful, Astrid. Thank you, thank you very much," said Cassius, and he could see his thanks brought joy to her little heart of honey. He truly was grateful, and he hoped that the next time he wore his father's crown that it would feel this good and this honouring.

Suddenly, he heard the sound of hoofs from outside, jokes and laughter being tossed to and fro between men. He did not recognize their voices.

"Have no fear. I'll get the door, see who's out there making all the ruckus," said Olsa, and she opened the door and saw what she could see.

Taku led them up the cobblestone path that led away from the farm. The surrounding bushes and trees had been kept tidy, and thus what was natural forest seemed to become a garden. A waterfall could be heard not so far away, and its mist floated through the trees and into their nostrils, hydrating their senses. Pools and mires looked like small villages for the smaller inhabitants of the woods, and as they marched down the slender path, the forge rose before them. It was little more than a shack in the woods with a forge inside along with a shrine to pray to, but it was all that was needed to capture the harmonious tunes and feelings of nature.

"Cold as ever," said Taku, looking over at the forge.

"I see you still pray to the gods," said Sir Hadrian.

"Not gods—spirits. They can be found all over the world, but you will know when you see one because it is something that moves your soul," said Taku.

"It is an old Sarakotan religion," said Mitsunari.

"Do you have any examples of your work?" asked Azrad. "I'd be interested to see just how good you Sarakotans really are—"

"The best. I only have one piece that I have hung onto over the years; that would be Kazemaru, Mitsunari's sword. If I have his permission, I would be honoured to show you my work, however keep in mind that it has seen much action. Although I did, long ago, take some time to sharpen it and revitalize the blade," said Taku."

Mitsunari gave a nod, and Taku led them into the forge. It was quite spacious, more than what the exterior would suggest, and in the back, next to the shrine, there was a black box with golden hinges. They approached it, and as they did so, Mitsunari quickened his strides. He may not have shown it, but he too was eager to see Kazemaru again after so many years away from it. "Would you like to do the honours?" Taku asked.

"No," replied Mitsunari.

"Very well then." It was then that Taku opened the chest. Inside lay Kazemaru.

Ivan could sense it. They all could. A spirit slept inside the sword. It was ominous, yearning for blood and malevolent deeds. It was dark, and it brooded in the shadows, yet it was fair and just in its presence. In utter awe were the others, but not Mitsunari. He stepped forward towards his old friend, but with hesitation, as if he approached something he wanted yet could not have. He knelt down and rested before it.

"It's . . . beautiful," said Azrad.

"Thank you," said Taku and Mitsunari simultaneously, and thus followed a long stretch of silence where the company looked around the forge. Ivan stepped outside, and something seemed to be troubling him.

"Do you hear that?" asked Ivan. The others were silent and only looked at him with confusion. "There's that . . . that smell again—" Suddenly, without another word, Ivan stormed off back to the village, and Azrad and Connell followed his lead.

"What has gotten into them?" asked Taku.

"Nothing good," said Sir Hadrian. "Follow me."

While the others raced after Ivan, Mitsunari was still lost in thought, staring into the dark eyes of Kazemaru. He thought of his old home in the palace, where men and women would bow to him out of respect instead of protocol, and all of that respect was lost the moment he failed to uphold his oath of protecting Lord Shinzu. He was once a mountain, but now he was rubble, a shard of glass that belonged to his former reflection. He was nobody, not to others but to himself.

But then he heard it. He heard the cries, the desperate, delusional calls for help in the throes of death and passing. He could smell it, and it was a smell that brought shivers to his skin and froze his tears before they could fall. The farm was being attacked. He could not sit back and let the others handle it, for he did not know if they could. Too much was unknown, and what was certain was that if he went down empty-handed to meet a foe too great for the likes of his companions, he would surely die, along with the others. However, if he charged in, Kazemaru in hand, he would break every oath he had ever taken. First was his failure to protect his lord, and then letting Yuikiri die and breaking his oath of silence, and he could not break another.

And yet he could not let them die. He could not fail another again by watching as their blood was spilt while he knew it could have been avoided. No. Mitsunari Miyamoto would not stand by and fail again. Mitsunari Miyamoto would paint in red once more and Kazemaru would be his brush of choice. His life was one that was defined by honour, and he would have it no other way, but he would also not be consumed by it if it meant watching those he loved die. Hiroki knelt in silence, but when he stood up, he was truly once again Mitsunari Miyamoto.

Ivan ran through the underbrush, ignoring the continuous slaps of branches on his cheeks. Azrad, Connell, Taku, and Sir Hadrian followed him, and as they drew near to the farm, they could smell the burning incense of wood, but also something more. They could smell flesh . . . burnt flesh. They ran harder down the path and back onto the flats where the farm stood in flames.

"NO!" roared Taku. The others stopped, but the Sarakotan ran blindly towards the front entrance. That was when they saw the blacksmith fall. An arrow slipped right through his throat. In disbelief, Taku placed his hands around the arrow and could feel the warm liquid that he knew was blood but did not want to admit it. He felt it, and his throat bubbled, and he choked and fell to the ground, and in his dying moments, he saw them: Olsa, Callum, and little Astrid hung on a tree branch. Their bodies were scorched and burnt to a crisp. The love of his life and his baby children were no more than cooked meat, left for the crows. He looked at what was left of their faces. He wanted to hear their soft voices in his ear, but all he could hear were flames laughing at him and looking upon its three victims with pride in what it had done.

He wanted to scream, but his wails were silenced by the arrow in his throat that drained him of blood . . . and then he was dead.

Ivan was the first to see them, and then the others caught up and lost themselves in shock of what had occurred. Other villagers who had protested were burnt as well, while some were strewn across the street in their own blood.

"Stop," said Ivan. "It is an ambush! Take cover."

"Those fuckers will pay for this," said Azrad, and too much rage boiled inside Connell for him to make any coherent and sensible comment.

"Then we shall make them, but we must be smart about, it for we do not know what lies beyond the bushes," said Sir Hadrian. They drew their weapons and listened, but even Ivan, who had the sharpest senses out of all of them, could not hear a thing.

"These are not bandits," said Ivan as he squatted behind a barrel of hay. "Medearia's Eyes I reckon. Fuck! I knew we were being too careless."

Sir Hadrian then realized that Cassius could not be seen, and any sort of methodical thinking fled from him. Indeed, he was sworn to protect him, but he loved that boy like he was his own, and he would do anything to keep him from harm, whether he was ordered to or not.

"Connell!" shouted Sir Hadrian with fury in his tongue that frightened even the likes of him. "You take the right while I take the left, but move up with the cover to hide behind. Azrad, you keep a distance and use your crossbow. Ivan, follow my lead," said the old knight, and Ivan followed his orders with reluctance and only did so given their dire circumstances. The knight sprang forward, making a dash towards the north side and cutting through the garden. He made it into the front entrance and entered the wild blaze in search of the prince. Nothing could be seen aside from the growing flames that lived and breathed as if they were alive. The heat encased him in a facade of sweat.

He turned towards where he'd come in, only to see an entire Casthedian patrol waiting in the field for him. They sailed the red banners of House Helladawn, and yet one man, whom he assumed was their leader, held Cassius by his neck with the prince's arms bound and a knife to his throat. The others had been caught and were held as hostages with arrows pointed at their heads.

The old knight stepped out of the flames. Ashes cloaked his path. He looked over at Taku and his family and then back to Cassius and the others, and he realized that this moment here was the very moment where he must face death head-on, without hesitation and without delay. Their lives were on the line, but Cassius was most vital to him. He would have to be intelligent about his actions. One wrong move or a single stride executed too quickly could make them nervous and ultimately result in the death of each of them.

"You would be wise to put that knife down, boy," said Sir Hadrian.

"And you, old man, would be wise to take a big old fucking step back," said the captain of the patrol, who held Cassius. Sir Hadrian looked at the prince; he could see that he was screaming through his gag that silenced his voice.

"If only you knew who the fuck you were speaking to," said Azrad with a laugh, and the soldier behind him whacked him on the back of his neck, putting him to the ground.

"As you can see, we're the king's men. You know what that means?" asked the captain with a pitiful amount of pride in his voice. "Don't worry, old man, I know your ears probably don't work all too well so I'll tell ya. Being the king's men means we have to protect the king's land from little groups of bandits such as yourselves and ya fucking friends there hanging by the tree. Now, if you don't want to end up like that fellow in the dirt, I'd suggest you drop your weapons and come along with us."

"And why would I come with you," asked the knight, and he could tell the captain wasn't exactly sure how to respond.

"For professional questioning, of course."

"So you say. My name is Sir Hadrian Blackwood, and in your hands, you hold your future king, Prince Cassius Helladawn. If you have any respect for the crest upon your armour you will hand him over."

"Like fucking hell you are, and like fucking hell I will," said the captain, laughing with his comrades.

There must have been over a dozen of them and that was too many for Sir Hadrian at his age, but then he saw him. In the distance, by Taku, stood Mitsunari with Kazemaru in hand. The wind blew in strength, and Mitsunari's robes fluttered in the wind. He knelt by Taku and whispered something in his ear before standing again and taking three slow steps forward towards the enemy.

"That your friend there, yellow face?" laughed one of the soldiers. "I raped his fucking wife. And then . . . then I raped his little girl. She screamed. Oh, she screamed, all right. Gets me hard just thinking about them." Mitsunari said nothing. His eyes spoke for him. They spoke of death. They spoke of suffering, and they spoke of deep, patiently-waiting malice. He unsheathed Kazemaru. The blade whistled with the wind, and if it had a face it would surely be smiling. Sir Hadrian saw this and unsheathed his blade as well. They stood a chance now. He knew it. Mitsunari knew it. And the fuckers in red sure knew it.

Cassius went for the hunting knife at the side of the captain and drove it into his heart without thinking and without feeling. He turned, gripping the thin air for something to throttle, and his dead body fell on top of Cassius. Mitsunari dashed towards three of the men and was met with two bolts. He ducked under one and split the other in two before slicing through all three of them. Blood sprang into the air and painted the nearby bushes. Sir Hadrian stood his ground, waiting for them to come to him . . . They fell into his trap. Countering his enemy's attacks, he pierced his lungs and then quickly moved onto the next, slaying one more, spilling his heart onto the floor. Sir Hadrian lifted the body of the captain and checked on the prince. He was safe.

Ivan, who had cut his bonds with one of the soldiers' knives, unsheathed his sabre from his scabbard and joined in the fight, cutting the wrists off one of his foes and watching him scream in agony and disbelief, the same disbelief that he'd seen on Taku's face. With the company's three best swords in full swing, they made quick work of their enemy. Mitsunari had the pleasure of killing the last of them.

"Please! Please! Spare me! I have a daughter too. I didn't take part in any of this, I only watched in horror," said one of the soldiers, lost in his tears. But with one swoop of Kazemaru, his head fell from his shoulders and toppled to the ground. Mitsunari cleaned his blade, wiping the foul blood off, and put it back in the sheath. Sir Hadrian ripped the gag away from Cassius's mouth, and what he saw was not entirely what he had expected. Cassius sat without emotion, and his words were plain and without life.

"I killed him. They're all . . . dead. Dead. No more. Ashes, nothing more, nothing less," said Cassius, looking into the dark void of shock and not into the physical realm in which he sat. Sir Hadrian sat down beside the boy.

"It is never easy taking your first life. And you have begun to see what the world can come to if we are consumed by death and anger. We will honour them, Cassius. We must give them a proper burial."

Cassius sat up, but he was still far from himself. There had been so much death and so much fear. He could not shake away the sound of their screams, of Callum trying helplessly to fight off the soldiers only to have a knife put through his gut and be forced to watch as his mother and little sister were raped and defiled. And as this occurred, Cassius had cowered away, hiding. Maybe he could have saved them . . . and maybe not. But death by failure is better than living with it. And the prince would be forced to sleep at night, knowing what could have been and resenting what was. Their lifeless bodies smelled similar to last night's supper: nothing but meat, seared and flavoured with sorrow. He looked down into his hands, which held Astrid's silly little gift. The flowers had withered and so had Cassius.

And So It Begins

T he night sky was outstretched like a sea of shadow, with a clustered archipelago of midnight diamonds glittering across the
dark canvas. Stars clustered together to look like steam drifting to
worlds and places unknown. Cassius found that he could not blink,
not even if he wanted to. He *needed* to look out towards the sky and
the jewels of wonder that it held, he *needed* to be distracted. It had
been a week since they buried Taku and his family, and a week since
Cassius had killed that man, a man that held the banner of House
Helladawn to his chest and wore it with pride. Yes, that man tried
to kill Cassius, and without thought, the prince returned the favour
and was successful. There was blood on his hands now, and it could
not, nor would it ever, be washed away. He had done the right thing,
and still, Cassius felt like he had done some sort of crime against
humanity and himself. Each time he thought about that day and
how those dogs butchered that innocent family and raped and burnt
them until they were satisfied, he felt feverish, hot and yet cold. It
made him want a drink, just a drop and maybe more. It didn't matter

what type of alcohol, simply anything that could distract him and rid him of the horror from within him. He began to notice the effects of the absence of liquor in his life. At times he would awaken, vomiting, in the night, along with uncontrollable shaking that he tried his hardest to hide from the others, but they all knew. *He* knew now that he had arrived at the state in which he would gladly take a drink if it were offered to him . . . he was losing his control.

Sir Hadrian was fast asleep and snoring, but the others still sat around the fire. They had come across several lost horses, likely fleeing from their destroyed farms and pastures, but according to the others, Cassius's horse was a warhorse, one that had wandered away from the battlefield. He could tell there was something different about it, a degree and standard of focus that was not met by the others and an aura of shock and restlessness. It was a stallion, that much was sure, and his coat was as black as the night that sprawled out before the prince. He had not decided on a name as of yet. Still, of course, they had not gained their mounts' trust, and Cassius least of all, but Ivan said that they were young enough to adjust to their new owners.

Cassius sat up and pulled his blanket over his shoulders. He stared out over the woods in the valley below and wondered just how many more days until they would arrive on the eastern shore.

"Can't sleep?" asked Ivan, glaring over at the prince, and the light of the fire masked his face and flickered in his eyes.

"Haven't tried yet," said Cassius.

"You can sit with us if you'd like," said Ivan.

"I wouldn't mind. You know, the wind and the eeriness of the woods below aren't as good companions as you may think," said Cassius, and he stood up and grabbed an apple from his pack, ate half of it, and gave the other to his horse, before sitting down on a fallen log; it was somewhat wet still, and he was soaked the moment he sat down. He looked at the others and was not surprised to see that Mitsunari was absent. He had changed. Something had flipped in his mind, and they all knew that the death of Taku had triggered it. He was even colder than he had been before. He drank rice wine now in solitude and played a small flute that had belonged to Taku, but it was a poignant tune, full of loneliness, a tune that seemed to reflect his current mood. Each morning he would write poetry as he watched the sunrise spill its light over the valley, and at night he unsheathed Kazemaru and sharpened it on a whetstone, but the chilling sound of wet steel in the dead of the night kept the hairs of the prince erected and on edge. He was still very much benevolent and kind, but there was an indubitable unpredictability about him now that filled Cassius with a small drop of fear.

"That was tough to watch, for anyone, Cassius. You don't need to be ashamed if you're feeling shaken up," said Azrad.

"Thanks, but I feel fine," said Cassius.

"No. You don't need to be fine," said Ivan. "If you were fine after seeing a mother and her children raped and murdered, *then* I'd be worried."

". . . It's sick. Sick how someone could feel good about doing those things. She cried. She wailed so very loud for—fuck! I can't." Cassius went silent, peering off into the night, and gathering himself before going on. "And when she cried for help . . . I could see that her own mother's blood stained her little cheeks, and her own mother died as she watched her children—her *fucking* children—be murdered. I never wanted to see this shit, and I never want to see it again."

Ivan stirred the fire and felt its breath on his face. "You know, I've seen many things that still haunt me to this day, and I have the scars on my body to make me remember them. I've seen my friends, who I thought of as my family, burn to death, and also call out for their parents to cradle them once more. It's fucked, it is. The elves, Cassius, enjoyed what they did to us because they never forgot what we did to them. We raped, killed, and enslaved them and we forgot our history, and that is why we continue to make the same mistakes."

"Then is humanity bad?" asked Cassius.

"No. But we are not good either. I don't think there is such a thing, not really. Do you believe that I am evil?"

"No."

"But what if I told you that I would take joy in killing those who made me suffer? The more we are hurt, Cassius, the more we grow numb. *Numb* to horror. This is what the world can do to you, it can make you numb to doing horrific things. Those soldiers are the same thing; they have seen horror and had it inflicted on them, and that is why it is easier for them to take part in horror. We live in a circle of vengeance. I wish for vengeance, Mitsunari longs for it as well, and so do many other souls. We grow numb, and that is just a symptom of life, kid. Now you know what the world is capable of, and you are lucky because there are many kings and royal cunts who never get the chance to know the world in which they rule. But you, Cassius, you've seen it, and you will see a lot more of it before this is all over."

"I know," said Cassius. They halted their speech for a while and let the night drag on until the prince finally spoke again. "Hey, Ivan."

"Yeah?"

"What's Medearia really like?"

"It's beautiful," said Ivan, and he could tell that his words shocked Cassius. "Beautiful, but with a pinch of horror."

When Cassius had fallen asleep, it was only Ivan, Connell, and Azrad that were awake, breathing in the heat of the fire before them. There was something on Ivan's mind, something that could not be shaken off or ignored. He had to ask them. He had to tell them. "Have you two ever thought of . . . having more?"

"What do you mean?" asked Azrad as he lay back on the log and stared up above at the stars.

"I'm talking about power."

"What about it?"

". . . I don't know," said Ivan as he stared into the dying flames that cooked the air around them. "Have you ever thought of . . . *being a king?*" Ivan's eyes immediately shifted forwards and stared at the others, and they were surprised to see that he was being serious.

"Not really," said Connell.

"Me neither," said Azrad. "I always felt bad for kings and queens. Just seems like it'd be boring as shit. Why?"

"Because I've wondered . . . just what the world would be like if there were people like us ruling it; people that knew what the world was really like, that's all."

"Well, it seems like Cassius is getting a good taste of the world, don't you think?" But Ivan didn't respond. He only sat there, letting his thoughts carry his mind into places it would never dare go before. And still the question in his mind reigned supreme, *how could someone like me ever get the power to be a king?*

✳

The water flooded out of the earth and its arteries of stone and down towards the river below. Cassius steered his horse to the right of the path, looking down into the ravine and up towards where the waterfall began. He saw where the rock face opened up to vomit its liquid innards into the beautiful and everlasting green veil of the woods. At the bottom of the fall what was once a solid wall of water was stagnated and broken down into vapours that gave birth to rainbows, and next to these shy little rainbows, sparrows bathed and gossiped about faraway mountains and the beauty of the world that was hidden from the eyes of Cassius, and any other human for that matter. After mere moments that felt like an eternity of being lost inside the arms of the wilderness, he continued to follow the others.

Since the death of Taku and his family, Cassius had wanted to approach Mitsunari; it was easy to see that he was still grieving. But consoling people was never something he was rather good at, and he put it off for some time, hesitating to approach him. To his surprise, it was Mitsunari that approached him instead. The Sarakotan rode up beside the prince until their pace was equal. ". . . Cassius . . . I . . . I am sorry you had to see those things, back at the farm," he said, and Cassius could tell that Mitsunari too found it difficult to talk of such emotional things, as if the right words were always difficult to find.

"No! There's no need for you to be sorry. I'm just . . . well, I can't help but feel terrible for you after what happened . . . Are you all right?" A pleasant piece of surprise was found on Mitsunari's face, for few ever genuinely asked him how he was feeling, and he *did* feel terrible.

"I . . . miss him . . . I feel like my last friend has finally been put to rest," said Mitsunari.

"Not your last," said Cassius. "You've got us, right?"

". . . Yes. Yes, you're right. I *do* have you." A smile then crept its way onto Mitsunari's face, one that Cassius had rarely seen before, and it naturally brought joy to him, and Cassius smiled as well. It seemed that, for the first time, he had finally found the right words to say, and in the process, he made a friend.

For three days they rode together, heading east and through a vast number of places and environments that were new to Cassius, through seas and storms of red birch trees and meadows that were illuminated by the early sun rays and livened by the sounds of crickets and grouse.

They had passed the front lines of the war and into the heart of Sacadia, where there were few to no signs of the violence that ensued to the west. Villages and towns lived in harmony, and they appeared to be just the same as the ones in Hellandor and the other western provinces. This surprised Cassius, although he could not place why. He had always had the preconceived notion that anyone who wasn't sided with his father was an enemy to be punished and made an example of, but how could someone punish folks such as these? They had done nothing wrong, and yet Cassius knew that it would not be long until the Casthedian armies would ride through this land and rip and tear the roots of its beauty from the earth.

The woods around them began to lighten and fade into an open stretch of grassland, and it was then that Cassius saw it: there was a gull in the air, watching the newcomers before they greeted his sea.

"Do you smell it?" asked Azrad.

"I do," said Cassius. "I smell the ocean."

"Who would think that after what we went through before we would be happy at the sight of water," said Azrad, and Cassius could hear his snickering laugh from behind him. Ivan kicked his horse with the back of his boots and quickened his pace. He was eager, and as if a language were conveyed that did not need the primitive techniques of speech and word. They all began to follow him into a trot.

The town of Yorkfall was rougher than what Cassius was used to. It reminded him of Hartshire, however this town was far larger. The voices of sailors and merchants blended to form a dull sound that rang in Cassius's ears. So many things were happening all around the prince the very moment he and the company arrived through the town's gates. He simply needed to follow Ivan, but even that was easier said than done. The dense concentration of human bodies formed almost a homogenous being of flesh and thoughts that brushed up against Cassius and his horse, cutting him off, and all the while he received malevolent glares from eyes of all colours. They peered and then spat. Somehow, they knew. They knew he was not one of them.

"Stay close!" said Ivan. The others followed their guide until the sign of the Oak and Fire Inn suddenly hung above their heads. When there was room, the company hitched their horses and entered the inn. "You four find yourself seats—no fights. Follow my lead, Blackwood; we're gonna get ourselves a boat," said Ivan. The two of them walked over and sat at the bar. They could feel the glares of the mangled men at their sides. They had twisted beards that hung to their chests, with faces that were darkened and wrinkled either through the misfortunes of life or simply the marks of the mines.

"What now?" asked Sir Hadrian.

"You wait. And as for me? Well, I'm hoping my contact has done what my letter instructed him to do. Once he arrives, which shouldn't take long, I'll go and talk to him and then I'll introduce him to you."

"Why me?"

"Don't worry, you'll find out. Just promise me that you'll follow the act."

"What act am I putting—"

"Shit, there he is," said Ivan, and he left the knight where he sat. After a few minutes of awkward waiting, Ivan returned with a man by his side; he was young, either that or time had been gentle on him. He wore a cap that was too large for his head and a tunic that was ripped and stained at the waist.

"Sam, I'd like to introduce you to my father. Oh, and by the way, you'll have to speak pretty loud; his ears aren't what they used to be, and the same goes for his eyes. Ain't that right, Pa?" Sir Hadrian knew his role exactly. He did not like it, but he knew what he had to do, and he would do it, even if it meant shaming himself.

"What're you saying, boy?" shouted Sir Hadrian, looking out into somewhere far away from where his audience stood.

"Told you he's old. Alas, dotage takes us all, right? Now the reason I was wanting to talk to you is that, well, you see, I know your father owns a fleet of ships of his own, and the thing is that two peasants such as ourselves can't afford a ship. And it's my father's birthday as of right now, and his wish is to be at sea with his boy as we once did long ago. So, if it isn't a bother, we'd like to set sail for the afternoon, and of course, we'd return it before sundown," said Ivan.

"Yes, I've read the letter, you don't have to explain yourselves anymore. Look, I'd love to help you two out, but the only reason I came here is to tell you no to your face. My father needs all the ships he can take right now, with the war and everything. I'm deeply sorry, I am, but I can't go lending out ships to just anyone nowadays," said the boy. Ivan bit his lip in frustration. He had not planned on the boy saying no (which was quite unlike him, to not plan for a potential thread of events). But before he could conjure any rebuttal, Sir Hadrian was already moving his lips.

Blackwood you sly, sly fox, you, thought Ivan.

"You're a fine young lad either way, and no feelings have been damaged in the process, have no fear. But please, you came a long way, allow me to pay you for the trouble," said Sir Hadrian.

"No. You mustn't, it is fine," said the boy.

"I won't hear another peep out of you until I get you your money, now," said Sir Hadrian, and he searched through his satchel, or at least he made it *seem* that way. "You know what, I think I may have dropped my purse down by the back entrance. Would you guide me there, boy? My son is as useful as a sack of shit for a Sunday breakfast."

The boy hesitated but finally gave in by social obligation, for it would be rather rude to decline any elder that was in need. "Yes. Yes, of course!"

Sir Hadrian stood up from his chair with assistance from Sam, and as soon as he rose, the knight arched his back and made his best effort to truly appear as if dotage *had* crippled his body and his senses.

"Which way is it?" yelled Sir Hadrian.

"Just this way. I'll lead you, don't worry," said Sam. As the two approached the back door, Sir Hadrian knew that this was the perfect place. There were no eyes to watch him. His posture straightened, and his face seemed to almost grow younger as he turned and looked at the boy; he towered him, and the boy swallowed down his saliva, but his throat was too dry to do so. "Um, well, so do you remember where you dropped it?" asked Sam nervously.

"Dropped what?"

"Your purse."

"Purse? What about it, I've got it right here." And the knight pulled his coin purse out from his satchel and shook it.

"You gonna pay me or what?"

"Pay you? No. In fact, you're going to be paying me with some facts about where your father keeps his largest ships."

"What are you talking about, old man?" The boy laughed, and he turned his back to walk away, but his shoulder was caught by the talons of Sir Hadrian.

"I wasn't asking."

When Sir Hadrian had wiped the blood away from his hands, he took the boy's keys and the paperwork that belonged to his personal vessel. They had a ship, just not a crew. The boy groaned in pain as Sir Hadrian walked away, but before he did so, he flicked a coin over to him. "How's that for your troubles?"

Ivan now sat with the rest of the company, and Sir Hadrian sat down to join them.

"Got us a boat," said the knight.

"Well shit, that was easier than I expected, but still we're technically about to steal a ship," said Azrad. "Don't get me wrong, I'm all for that, but a voyage like this will take some time to prepare for, and I don't want that boy waking up and telling his pops what you did to him."

"That's what rope is for, Azrad," said Connell, and an uproar of laughter circled around the table.

"You want to kidnap him?" asked Azrad.

"Listen, we'll rent a room upstairs and he'll be our guest until we've prepared," said Ivan.

They had a ship.

Now all that was left was the preparation. What was once a dream was a reality. It was happening. When the mere thought of leaving on this journey had taken hold of Cassius in its enthralling hands, he had not exactly expected it to work out. After all, few things ever went his way. He was Cassius now. Not just a prince, not a title, but his own person, defined by actions and experiences that forged a new personality—his own.

✳

The men and women of Yorkfall were sound asleep; the moon kept them that way.

"Is everything ready?"

"Not yet."

"Get it ready then. There's no more fucking around. I don't want the guard called on us."

Cassius walked down the silent streets, and he could hear the rest of the company speaking from their rooms in the inn. It was his job to scout for guards. There was nothing. Not yet, that is.

He ran to the docks. Nothing.

He checked the alleyway. Again, nothing.

Their path was clear, and it had better be, for everyone's sake, but Cassius was far more concerned with failing Ivan's orders rather than being caught by the town guard. Suddenly, a whistle came from the second-floor window of the inn—it was Ivan, who waved him inside.

Cassius entered the inn with a frantic quickness in his step. This all reminded him of the times when he and Vidicus would try to escape from the palace walls, however, each attempt was an utter failure and ended with Sir Hadrian catching them by the ears. Cassius was older now. And now, ironic as it was, he had the old knight at his side, ready to draw blood to protect him. Cassius rushed up the stairs, turned the corner, and entered the room, where he saw an unconscious Sam tied to one of the beds with a gag in his mouth. The others were in the room next door around the dinner table with a map displayed for everyone to see. Cassius recognized it immediately as the one from the tower. The palaver halted once the prince arrived at the table.

"Clear?" asked Ivan.

"Clear," replied Cassius.

"Good. We will be at sea for thirty-four days if we're lucky, and once we're out there . . . there's no turning back. Once we hit those shores, we are in enemy territory. We move only at night and during the day we sleep. Have we all gathered enough food?" asked Ivan, and a yes came from the others. "I pray you all packed light, but not too light. There will be things to eat and gather there, but only to a point. The deeper we go, the more the land will change—you will see things that travel far from your comprehension." Those words put a chill down Cassius's spine. "So, if there is anyone who does not wish to go or is having any second thoughts, there is no shame in staying." And at this, there was nothing more than silence . . . They were all ready. However, Cassius was not, regardless of what his words would tell the others. His heart knew his voice was hollow, and it betrayed him. "Well then, we have gathered our supplies. Now for the ship."

Ivan and the others turned from the table, but Sir Hadrian stayed, and he grabbed the prince's attention before it was too late.

"Cassius. If you have a moment, I have a gift for you, something—well, I hope you'll never need it, but I think it'll be foolish to think that you won't," said Sir Hadrian.

"Oh, you should not have. I'm sure I could have bought it myself," replied Cassius.

"No. I promised to work with you on your sword hand, but alas, as you can see there is little time for practise when we are on the road."

"Let's see then." Sir Hadrian led Cassius over to the corner where a blanket was draped over some sort of unidentifiable object. Sir Hadrian unveiled the object to reveal a cuirass over a layer of chainmail. Cassius could only smile, a twisted and childish smile that reminded the old knight of when the prince was young. "I—I don't know how to thank you!"

Sir Hadrian grinned. "Do you like it?"

"I love it!"

"I had one of the local blacksmiths forge it. Now I know it's far from what your father would have gotten you, but it'll protect you, and I had the smith put your initials on it for you." Suddenly, Cassius felt his throat burn and his eyes water. He was crying. It was unexpected, like the first flakes of winter snow embracing the autumn leaves. Sir Hadrian put his hand on the boy's shoulder. "Shall I adorn you, my prince?"

"It would be my honour." Cassius laughed.

"You'll have to be quick then," said Azrad. "Fuck! We've got company."

"Thugs?"

"Guards," said Azrad, walking past the knight to gather his weapons, and the others took up arms. They would set sail that night, but only if its sails blew bloody. The hinges to the door snapped and the bending and breaking of wood clapped and ran up the stairs. The city guard spilled into the darkness of the room, and torches in hand, they searched the lower premise and then halted at the beginning of the stairs.

"Whoever is up there, you'd better come down peacefully, or we'll be coming up not so peacefully!" said one of the guardsmen. He was young and still with a pimply and oily face from his early teens, and his voice cracked at the tail of his warning.

"The fuck are we doing here, Rory?" asked another. "There's not a chance in Ederia we'll find the quartermaster's son here." But Rory ignored his friend and continued to shout upstairs.

"We're in search of a missing person! Just so happens we've also got reports of suspicious activity coming from this very inn."

"No need to shout," said a voice from the far corner. Rory raised his torch to illuminate the owner of the voice, but all he could see was a thick body of smoke and darkness.

"Y-you'll be showing yourself now if you know what's good for you!" shouted the other guard, stepping closer and closer to the corner from where the ominous voice originated.

"Colder. Colder," said the voice. The guard turned and walked in the other direction. "Ah, warmer! Warmer." The voice was so close now that they could nearly feel the moistness of its breath on their cheeks and the humidity that was emanating off their silver tongues. Rory lifted his torch to see the cold eyes of Mitsunari, and the guard fell back on his hands and feet, wiggling away from the threat like a worm writhing in the dirt, but his escape was halted by a firm hand on his neck that was as coarse and rough as oak.

Rory was lifted, and when he expected to see a face, he was disappointed as his ascent continued until finally the wild face of Connell was illuminated. Rory dropped whatever he had in his hands.

"P-please," he whispered, "let me live, I begs ya."

"Sure," replied Connell.

"Thank you, sir, you won't hear a peep out of my mouth, not me. I thank—" The boy's gratitude was cut off by a deep cough of blood that sprinkled the face of Connell. Rory looked down to see a knife in his gut. He looked back to the face of Connell, and his last feelings of life were that of betrayal, and his last image was the grin of a giant holding him, telling him that everything would be fine. Nothing ever was. The other guard ran to the door only to have his feet swiped from under him by the leg of Mitsunari, and as the boy hit the hardwood floor, he dropped his broadsword.

"Pick it up."

"W-what?"

"Please, pick it up," said Mitsunari, and he lunged closer to whisper, "I have no need to kill you—" But the boy was already dead, and Mitsunari could see that Azrad had thrown a small knife into his neck. "You should not have done that," said Mitsunari.

"No time for honour, we got a boat to catch," said Azrad, and he smiled as he wiped his knife clean of the boy's blood. He was right, time *was* of the essence, and thus he swallowed his words.

"Let's move," said Ivan. The company escaped from the inn and into the sleeping city of Yorkfall and moved with haste towards the docks. Dogs barked and howled in the night like maidens gossiping about the latest town drama that was occurring. Even at a jog, Cassius was still behind, being weighed down by his armour.

The streets were quiet apart from the hounds behind them and the bickering of married couples, but it was a silence more relatable to the tension of an object before it finally snaps, releasing a tumultuous roar that sings in contrast to the earlier silence. The only thing Cassius could hear was his wheezing breath that, with each exhale, he could feel scratch the inner linings of his throat. An arrow adorned in fire whistled through the sky and rained down on the shoulder of Cassius, penetrating his mail slightly, but enough to make the prince drop in agony.

"Cassius!" yelled Sir Hadrian, spinning around and flying back towards the prince, and before him, he saw the town guard close in from the alleyways. At the centre stood a knight on horseback with a bow in his hand. He was nocking for another shot. Sir Hadrian pulled the arrow from Cassius. The young boy screamed in pain, and the knight then stepped over the prince to protect him from any attack that would come their way. Azrad and Connell hesitated in their escape and turned back towards the fallen prince.

"There's no time!" Ivan said. They looked back at their leader. They knew it was foolish to halt, but they did so nonetheless. Ivan kept on. The knight had drawn back his bow to its full extent, but through his visor, he saw Azrad launch a bolt towards him that seared the air around it, causing him to duck and let loose his arrow poorly. His horse reared up on its hind legs as the guardsman around him stepped forward and into formation for a volley of flaming arrows.

There was no fighting this battle, that much was certain to Sir Hadrian, and so Connell lifted the prince onto his shoulder and the three rushed away towards the docks, weaving through the labyrinth of fire that was being conjured around them. When the company arrived at the gate, they saw Ivan there waiting for them. Sir Hadrian quickly withdrew the keys and gave them to Ivan before looking back to see the coming storm of soldiers rushing towards them. There were too many. Far too many—nearly three dozen.

"Down!" roared Connell and the company braced against the vertical wall that ran along the side of the docks. Fire pierced and crawled through the thin wooden wall, peering through, getting a look at the company. As soon as the volley was over, they stormed through the gate and shut the door on their pursuers, only to find that they were being expected; guards stood waiting for them before the ship. Mitsunari approached the enemy and swiped for his throat. He did so with expert precision. Blood sprayed into the salt water of the sea. The attack of the next soldier was quickly blocked by Sir Hadrian and their two swords worked with each other, spilling death onto the floor. A guard approached Connell, only to be kicked into the water (Connell could feel his chest cavity crumble under the weight of his foot). Blades flew out of the fingers of Azrad and into the skulls of his foes, but Ivan was eager to secure the ship and leaped over to the bridge and onto the deck. While the company made quick work of the guards on the dock, they saw that the gate was being torn down . . . and quickly.

Another volley.

Fire. Fire and blood.

An arrow sliced and burned the flesh behind Azrad's knee, and he too dropped, biting his tongue—he was too proud to show pain. Connell hoisted him on his shoulder, but with the help of Mitsunari. They leaped aboard their vessel and cut the ropes as fast as they could. The boat escaped from the tight grip of the dock, tearing off bits of barnacle and seaweed that had tied the two together, and slowly it began to drift away as three men of the company that could push with oars released them from the port.

They escaped the guards but not their arrows. Again, there was another desperate volley, but it was still a threat to be feared and so the company rushed inside for cover. They made it through the first door, but the second was locked, and it dawned on them that Ivan was not among them, and the only place that seemed likely for him to be was behind that second door.

"Did you lock it?" asked Trevor.

"Yeah, she's locked, all right," said Colton, and the two crept forward, cornering Ivan.

"So, I see all this commotion is your doing," said Ivan, keeping his composure. He did not know what to expect from these two, but he would treat them as worthy adversaries. Unknown to him . . . they were. Trevor and Colton uncloaked themselves, revealing elvish attire that triggered painful memories. They then touched the backs of their necks, and their Marks of Medearia were revealed, but furthermore, their skin and very faces changed to that of elves. Ivan recognized their faces. He would always remember those eyes; how could he forget? He could not and would never. "You were there! You were there at the Pools," said Ivan.

"Yes. Yes, we were," said the one who had once appeared to be Colton. "And now we are here to kill the rat that should have squealed long ago."

"Well, if we're gonna do this, let's do it properly, shall we?" The two elves backed off, ready for what the human had in store. Ivan threw his cloak to his side, revealing his rather elegantly crafted leather armour. He unsheathed his sabre, and it was a sword that the elves knew was not made by any man; it had been crafted in Medearia. "Draw," said Ivan. The elves drew their swords and took to their unusual stances that seemed to almost replicate a viper, slowly moving back and forth, poised and ready to lunge with its fangs destined to poison. Ivan took to his own that he himself had created through a mix of traditional Ederian techniques and that of Medearia.

They each feinted.

Ivan did not flinch.

He feinted back, but they too did not move. There was nothing for a time, only calculated reads of movements, predictions based on inductive research of their enemy's motion. One elf lunged forward, thrusting his blade towards Ivan, while the other swung down on the skull. There was only one survivable option, and Ivan took it. He sidestepped to the left, ducking under the vertical swing, and making a slash of his own that was parried. Sparks scattered in the air. The elf who had parried feinted to the leg and instead went high towards the neck as the other did the same on the opposite side. They were good. Each attack was simultaneous to the other's, making it far more difficult for Ivan to make his usual calculations. Again, he was left with only one option, and he ducked under each of their blows and swung his sword down on theirs, trapping their blades against the floor momentarily before the two elves, realizing the danger, leaped backwards to safety. But Ivan gave the two little time to refocus, and he lunged towards them with a series of swings, like cat swiping in the air at the birds above, but these swings were blocked as the other made his attack, cutting Ivan below his ribs. The elves drew back again with smiles on their faces.

"That was all we needed," said one. "One taste. One lick of your blood and that would be enough for the poison to stop your heart."

"You think I'm a fool? I know your kind better then you have guessed, and that'll be your final error," said Ivan.

"Is that so?"

"It is. I have kept antidotes for your poisons ever since my last journey to the hell you call home. But which poison would it be, I wonder?" asked Ivan, but the tone of his voice was sarcastic. He knew which poison they'd used; he could tell by the effects it was already taking on his body. "Mamba, isn't it? Yes. You know it is. Black as mambas get." Ivan laughed.

The elves bit their lips in anger, and they watched him as he drank his antidote from a distance. But they were not about to let him breathe for much longer, and they attacked now with their full strength and ire from within. But Ivan was not someone who one approached without a care in their step. Ivan caught the elf by his wrist as he came forward and spun him around, putting a knife at his throat while pointing his sword towards the other foe. "Step and he dies," said Ivan. The elf watched the human with deep malice in his heartbeat and fury in his sword hand.

The elf moved.

Ivan threw the knife that was pointed toward the elf's throat towards the other, but this attack was blocked easily, for it was not meant to kill—it was only a distraction. Ivan sank his teeth into the neck of the elf and threw him to the side, and the other elf was struck in awe by what he had seen. So much so that he hesitated, and that was a mistake paid for only in blood. The elf was quick, but not quick enough. Ivan's sabre was wet with the thick black blood of an artery, and the liquid spilt in strings from the tip of the sabre and onto the floor. But the elf was not dead, for Ivan wanted his demise to be slow as he left this world into his sacred land of the Ecaval. Ivan bared his teeth like a wolf snarling at its enemy. "I hope that was a good enough introduction to my personal poison," laughed Ivan. The elf watched his friend fall into the endless slumber of death, and the veins of his skin appeared black with an alien fluid coursing through them, sickening his body.

Before the elf below Ivan could curse him in his own tongue, he ended his life with one last thrust of his blade. He cleaned his sabre and then wiped the sweat from his brow. He had taken both antidotes, but they had a toll on his body, and he would need to rest and wait for the fever to release him. It was then that he could finally hear the banging on the door, and after he had found the key off of the bodies, he opened it to see the wary faces of his friends leaning up against the walls. They had all been through hell. They had all suffered, but they would make it. The Company of Ekmere seemed to prevail if only by a thread and a drop of serendipity that came from no cloud.

"Let the wounded rest," said Ivan. "Those who are able, I recommend you prepare yourselves . . . for the road is still long."

Long Live the King

The shadow crawled forward, overtaking Vidicus as he roamed the arid wasteland of his dreams. He had no goal in this realm. No aim. No drive. He simply walked under a shadow that cloaked him, hiding him from any eyes who wished to watch. This was the third night in a row of dreams, and he had arrived at the state in which he could tell when he was and wasn't dreaming. He looked up to see the object that produced such a shadow over him, but he saw nothing, and so the unexplainable darkness around continued to encircle him but without any clear meaning . . . not yet. The wind roared overhead, chilling him until his eyes watered, and he hunched forward, decreasing his size in order to hide from the wrath of the pernicious gales. His skin felt loose and withered, but even that paled in comparison to the pain he felt inside; it was strange and difficult to articulate, but he supposed he felt empty, or freshly hollowed, as if someone had come along and scraped out every feeling of joy he had felt and replaced it with numbness. Those who took from him did not even do the decency of replacing his happiness with sorrow, instead, there was nothing; he was a shell with an idea of an issue but no compass that led him to its roots.

"If I speak, will you listen?" said a voice from inside his head. It was the voice of a woman, and he knew immediately who it belonged to—it was her. It was always she that came to him at night. When that *woman* had first begun to visit him, he remembered little of their moments together, but the more he listened to her, the more he began to remember, and so he now had a recollection of ideas and moments that he wished so dearly he could forget. Alas, they were too appetizing to leave behind. She had spoken the truth the last she visited Vidicus, she was indeed a part of him. And so Vidicus thought he could tame these thoughts of power and murder that she planted in his mind, but they too were just too appetizing to ignore. Had he gone insane? Yes, driven to madness by the prolonged suppression of surreptitious thoughts and aspirations, and so said aspirations took the form of *her*.

"I am listening," said Vidicus.

"Good," said the voice. "Are you really going to continue to call me 'woman,' or 'her'?" asked the voice.

"Why? Would you like a name?"

"Yes. Yes, I would like a name."

"How about Malka?"

"It's rather nice; deadly but seductive."

"I knew you'd like it."

"You know me all too well, my little prince, but do you trust me?"

"Of course."

"Good, now do as I say and follow my lead," said Malka, and her body seemed to blow in with the sand. She turned around and smiled at him, and the pale skin of her naked body contrasted beautifully against the sand of the desert. Vidicus followed her. He did so until his lungs burned and there was a searing pain in the arches of his feet, as if he wore hot coals as shoes. The ground of the desert then began to climb more aggressively until he was forced to crawl upwards on his hands and knees. Somehow, he knew this was her doing; she wanted to see him on his knees, crawling through the loose sand in desperation to do as he was told. After a lifetime of crawling had gone by, he lost his feeling in his limbs, but they were still able to move. He was nothing more than a brainless head moving through an ocean of stones. And then he saw it, but he second-guessed himself at first, thinking it was some sort of awkwardly erected stature or stone. But it was not. The throne of Ekmere stood before him on the flatter section of the desert, and beside it sat Malka. "Why so slow, little boy? I've been watching it for you. Are you not going to thank me by at least sitting down?"

Vidicus opened his mouth, gasping for air, biting into nothing to try and sip any sort of liquid he could find even though he knew his attempt would be unsuccessful. The shadow was still around him, but it almost seemed to decrease as he moved closer and closer towards the throne. He stood up and began to walk towards his goal. And then he was there. Right before him, the throne smiled—it knew what it was doing, it knew how desirable it was. "Go ahead, sit down," said Malka. Vidicus caressed the armrest with his finger, and the shadow around him shrivelled up, but the instantaneousness of it startled Vidicus, and he drew back his finger only to see that the shadow grew back to its normal size. He touched it again and then withdrew his finger once more to see the same thing occur. "Give in to it," she said with fire in her eyes, and it was only then that Vidicus was able to notice she wore the face of his mother. "You deserve more than to walk in someone else's shadow. You know it to be true. You deserve to cast a shadow that engulfs all Ederia. Do it. Sit down."

Vidicus could resist her words no more, and finally, he did what she commanded. He sat down, and it felt just right. Suddenly the desert was no more, and it was replaced with rolling green hills, crystalline rivers and apple orchards. The shadow was gone, and so was Malka. Vidicus smiled. There was a crown on his head now, and he stood up to survey his newfound kingdom of green. It was beautiful. It was perfect. It was exactly how he had envisioned it. But then he noticed something amiss, a minor imperfection in his world. The grass did not sit even. He crouched down to investigate and found that the grass underneath his feet was rather loose, as if something was freshly buried below its green facade, and so Vidicus, with his hands, pulled the layer of grass to reveal the decomposing head of his father. He expected himself to be horrified, but for some reason, and one he could not explain, he felt nothing.

He knew what it really was.

He knew that that was the price he would have to pay to find his treasured kingdom.

The currency of death.

Vidicus awoke in a layer of his own sweat; he was being engulfed by a fever. His breathing was deep and rapid. He needed to calm down. This time he remembered it all. Every word, every hidden notion and desire that was inside of him was plainly visible. It was as if the sun had finally risen after all this time, and what it illuminated was not worrisome anymore—it was ambitious, but it could be done. He *could* kill him. Of course, he would have to be smart about it, calculated and all. But it could be done, and if anyone could pull it off without suspicion it was him, his very own son.

✻

Cornelius wondered if any of his sons had received his letter by now, and if they did, what would they think. It had been two weeks since the letters went out. Surely Vidicus had received his, and it wasn't like him to leave it unread for very long, but Cassius on the other hand—well, Ekmere was far away, and so it was more likely that he hadn't received it yet.

The king sighed, rubbing his forehead to ward off the headache. It was late, probably one or two in the morning, and for some reason, the thought of these silly little letters kept him, the king, awake at night, like they were some sort of love letter to his beloved, and he was too anxious to sleep for the possibility of his letters not being worded well enough, or if something, even a single phrase, was not conveyed properly. Cornelius brooded over the candlelit tabletop, fighting off sleep as long as he could until he heard a commotion outside of his tent that drove away any thought of sleep. There was shouting, followed by greetings and the cries of soldiers on horseback. Someone had arrived. But who?

Cornelius stood up from his seat, but before he could exit his tent, a guest was already staring at him, eye to eye. It was Vidicus.

The king let out a sigh of relief; this meant Vidicus had read his letter, and furthermore, he had likely enjoyed its contents.

"Vidicus, it is good to see you. Although I must say the timing is peculiar," said the king.

"Is it? My apologies, father," replied Vidicus.

"Would you like to sit and have some tea with your father? The kettle has cooled, but I'm sure it is still warm enough." Vidicus did not reply. He instead sat himself down, and Cornelius did so as well. "So, how do you fare? Are you enjoying your new position?" asked the king, pouring his son some tea and a glass for himself.

"I am well, father."

"That is good," replied Cornelius, but he could tell that his son had not seen sleep in days. His eyes were dark, but his skin was as white as a ghost. Vidicus's facial expression did not move, and the king could see that he was in no hurry to progress the conversation. "Any word from your brother?" asked Cornelius, clearing his throat and then sipping his tea.

"No."

"I see. I hope Sir Hadrian or Julias has been able to keep his . . . habits in check while you and I are away." The king laughed;

he was trying to show his gentler side, a side less cold and blunt, but this time, it was Vidicus who was being cold, and he did not chuckle in the slightest. "Did you read my letter?"

"I did."

"Listen . . . you have every right to be angry with me. I have forgotten my duties as a father, I will admit to this." Still, there was nothing from Vidicus, nothing at all. "I can see you are upset."

"Upset? Whatever for? I have never felt better," said Vidicus with an eerie grin on his lips that let his teeth peer through. "Are *you* feeling all right, father?"

"I suppose I could do with some rest."

"Here, let me ease you. I have brought you a gift."

"You have?"

"Yes. But you must close your eyes," said Vidicus, and his father laughed in disbelief.

"I find it rather hard to believe that that is necessary," said Cornelius.

"I see it is your wish to upset me, father—"

"Fine!" interrupted the king. "Fine, they are closed."

"Good. Now, only open them when I say so, and no peeking. I'll know if you peek, father." The king did as his son said, and Vidicus circled around his father's back. In his hands he held a box that he then placed before his father. "You may open now."

"What is it?" asked the king.

"Go ahead. Open it."

Cornelius unlocked the small wooden box, and what he found inside rather surprised him, but also filled him with poignancy. It was the metal rose.

"Did you take this from me?"

"Correct! I took it before I left for Bruxstan. Sometimes, father, I look at it to remember what a ruler should be, and I try my hardest to model myself after it," said Vidicus, now holding the rose before his father's eyes. It was at this moment, and for the first time ever, that Cornelius felt unsafe around his son. It was something in his eyes, his skin, and the tone of his voice that frightened him; he was poisoned by malice, and it was easy to perceive.

"Vidicus, I think you should get some rest; I can see you are not well."

"I don't look well?" asked Vidicus, tilting his head and smiling in a way that was almost unnatural. "Let me tell you a story, father. Would you like to hear?"

"No, I would like you to sit back down in your seat."

"It's about a boy. He lived in a house with his family and older brother," said Vidicus, and his voice almost seemed childish now as he smiled. His left hand gripped his father's shoulder, squeezing tighter and tighter as his story progressed. "And every night at dinner, he was always forced to eat after the eldest son, and thus our poor protagonist was always left with the scraps—"

"Vidicus!" roared the king, standing up to face his son's insanity and imposing his wrath upon him. But this time it did not work. Vidicus felt nothing, and his madness would not cease.

"Scraps on Monday! Scraps on Tuesday! And on and on and on it goes. I want you to say it, father."

"Say what?"

"Tell me just why Cassius, the perpetual fuck-up, is to be king instead of me, your most loyal and ever endearing son?" he asked, throwing his hands in the air.

"This is the way things are, Vidicus. I will speak no more of it," said Cornelius, and at this, Vidicus smiled again, but this grin was dubious. His skin wrinkled and curled, his eyes sank into his skull, and his teeth now appeared more like fangs. He let out a boisterous laugh of pain. He was sick, and some sort of evil had corrupted him, teaching his mind to conjure malevolent thoughts. The king turned away from his son, but little did he know that he had just turned away from a man with murder in his eyes. This was a mistake.

"Damn you!" said Vidicus, and he grabbed the metal rose in his hand and in the other . . . he held a knife. Vidicus crept behind his father and slid the sharpened edge of the knife around the king's throat. Blood and shock spilled from the king. But it was not over, not yet. Vidicus pulled the king down onto the ground. His father tried to scream, but his cries were replaced with gurgling blood. Vidicus looked into his father's eyes, and he saw hate in them, fury, and shame. It was those eyes that cut just as deep as any knife, and so, with the rose, Vidicus plunged its metal stem into each eyeball. It was a sight too unbearable to see, and so he covered the face of his father with a pillow, but it did not take long for the blood to seep through. Again, and again, he plunged the rose's silver stem into the skull of his father, holding back his own screams of fury and terror, and watching the pillow be painted more and more red with each vicious attack. It was odd, his father's skull was softer than he'd imagined, and with each blow, he could feel the king's face soften and fold to the shape of his hand, likely the result of a shattered skull and the moulding nature of the brain giving way to his fist.

It was done.

Cornelius Helladawn, his father, was no more than a lifeless body with only tremors of movement left. Vidicus stood, panting and grunting in his paroxysm of malice. He backed away, avoiding any thought of regret and slipping through the tent's exit.

Vidicus was now one step closer to being king. All that was needed now was the death of Cassius, and all of Ederia would be able to fit in his palm.

The plan was going well.

The Fall

For forty days they sailed east.

For forty days they suffered, balancing between starvation and survival, and teetering between madness and sanity.

For forty days and forty nights they wondered if they would ever see solid land again. Fights broke out each week between the company's members and each conflict usually pertained either to who received each ration that day and who did not. It was either that or someone would doubt if they were taking the right course.

For forty nights they had lost their senses and misplaced their intuition and reverted to madness in its stead. Even Sir Hadrian began to doubt their voyage, and so it was up to Ivan to keep the company together. On the forty-first day of their voyage across the open sea, they once again awoke to nothing, nothing but a clear glass surface of grey that wrapped itself around them. Those who slept that night awoke to rain. Cassius climbed down from his bunk and crept down the hallway towards the restroom, which consisted of a cracked mirror that was leaned up against the wall and a tin bucket that they would toss overboard once it was full. However, even considering the miasmic vapours that drained out of each of their stools, Cassius had grown used to the smell of his own shit and piss that greeted him each morning. He looked into the mirror—he had changed. His skin was tightly wrapped around his bones, and his face was more angular. Cassius smiled.

If only father could see that I've managed to grow a bit of facial hair, thought the prince. But truth be told, it wasn't much of a beard. Rather, it was what would be expected of a young man: long and spaced-out strands of wiry hair that oiled his skin, causing him to break out.

His stomach growled at him, demanding food, yet it would get none; it wasn't Cassius's day to eat. A week ago, their rationing strategy had changed, becoming more and more conservative as the voyage went on. However, water was what they really needed. *Was it a day? No, longer,* thought Cassius, pondering the last time in which he had had the gracious privilege of sipping away at his waterskin. His mouth was as dry as the summer soil on a farmstead that was busy baking under the sun, and the corners of his mouth had split open and had begun to bleed. His body was weaker and getting weaker by each gruelling day that consisted of a constant fight for survival. He wanted to sleep away, but not here, no. His bed at Ekmere was calling for him, and so was the bottle, but now he knew that any form of alcohol would simply dehydrate him even further. Cassius, however, did not care; he did not *want* to drink again—he needed to. At the moment, it was the one thing that promised salvation to him, but it would betray him, and Cassius knew that well.

Again, as the prince looked into the mirror, he could see the shakes coming back . . . and then he felt it: the burning sensation of stomach acid rising upwards through the inner linings of his esophagus. It was acidic bile, ready to pour out of his body. Cassius came to his knees and leaned over the bucket, breathing in the fumes of human waste that encouraged him to vomit even more. The bile then poured out of his mouth, like a poison that broke down his innards and withered away his gums and teeth. He was sick. He needed a drop, just a drop of liquor to soothe his pain, and he knew where he would find it.

"What's the matter?" asked Ivan from the doorway.

"Nothing. I'm fine," replied Cassius, coughing a bit at the thick concentration of saliva that gathered at the back of his throat.

"Like hell you are. Could be scurvy," said Ivan.

"No. I mean, it could be, but—" Cassius trailed off, leaning over the bucket and vomiting once more, curling his body around the bucket now like a snake strangling its prey.

Ivan then understood, piecing the shards of clues together: Sir Hadrian had said to ignore the prince's calls for any alcohol. And now this: shaking, vomiting—he was an addict, all right. "How long has it been?" asked Ivan. Cassius looked up at Ivan in confusion with his own spit dangling from his jawline, but he then realized what the man was alluding to, and there was no hiding his pain from that man.

"Over a month," said Cassius. "Over a month without a drop. Not a single fucking *drop!* Please, give me at least some good news and tell me that we haven't drank all of the rum and vodka yet."

"We have not," said Ivan. "But you'll not get a single bottle. I'm sorry, but I can see you've changed from your former self. You're not the same boy that you were back at Ekmere, and I'm not about to walk you back the way you came." Ivan then knelt next to the prince and held his hair back and patted the boy on his shoulder. "Here, have some of my water, but take care not to drink too fast or you'll vomit it all back up."

Cassius wanted to thank him, but before he knew it, he was already starting to gulp down as much as he could of Ivan's water-skin. "When you are feeling up to it, meet me up top. You have questions, I can tell, and I shall now answer them."

Once he had vomited all he could, Cassius took his leave of the loo and stumbled his way up the stairs. He was weak. His body felt empty, as if the life within him had been quickly sucked away and thrown to the sea, and he could still taste the bitterness of the stomach acid on his tongue, burning away at his insides and the roots of his teeth. Cassius unlocked the hatch, and before opening it, he threw his cloak that he had found on the ship over his head and readied his body for the fall of rain and the monotonous rocking of the sea.

Azrad manned the wheel of the boat as Ivan sat beneath the deck of the captain's quarters with Mitsunari at his side.

"Sit down," said Ivan. Cassius did as was commanded and sat beside the two of them. The rain was rather calming now, and the three of them huddled away, hiding from the tears of the sky. Ivan smoked his pipe, pondering something that would likely appear strange to the prince. "Here," he said, passing over his pipe to Cassius. "I wished to speak with you two, of course, to answer any questions you may have about where we are going, but also to warn you of it. The elves of Medearia, Cassius, are ruthless." Ivan then leaned closer to the prince to reveal the weight of his words as Mitsunari had a better idea of what would be awaiting them than Cassius did. "I allowed you to come solely based on what I know, and I know that if you stayed in Ekmere you would likely meet a similar fate as your grandfather. But I also know that you possess not a single idea of what truly lies in that land. You do not know the horrors that will come for us." Cassius could now feel the hairs on his skin point upwards. "If they manage to capture us, promise me that you will not hesitate in taking your life. Promise me, Cassius! It would be a kinder fate than what they would have planned for you."

"But that's not gonna happen, is it?"

"It may. But it also may not. If we are smart and stay disciplined, we might just survive."

"So," said Cassius, "what truly is the reason for our journey east?"

Ivan smiled—it was good that the boy was catching onto their lies. It meant that there was some magnitude of intelligence in that head of his. "I see you were not fooled by my words at the council. You are right, we are *not* travelling all this way for resources."

"You're trying to kill someone, aren't you?" asked Cassius, and the prince's words were sly, as if he already knew the answer to his question. Ivan looked at the boy, and he could see how he had grown; there was a degree of sharpness to him now that was bred purely from their days in the wild.

"I see there can be no more fooling you. Yes, we are here to take one's life, a life that could prove to be quite a threat if it is left alive."

"Who?"

"Their leader, King Estideel."

"I see, so you believe that this King Estideel could prove to be a threat to Ederia," said Cassius.

"Yes."

"What makes you think so?"

"As I've said, I have made this journey before, Cassius, and the last time I was here I spent most of my days locked away in their castles. In my imprisonment, I could do very little, but what I could do— and do quite well—was listen. And so, I listened, and I watched. I heard talk of war and of a coming storm. That, my prince, was years ago, and so their preparations have been made; each action has been calculated to the fullest extent. They are prepared for war."

"And so, we have made this journey to assassinate a king. Well, why lie to me then?"

"Have you not listened at all? From what I have gathered, Medearia has held our land in its palm for hundreds of years without us even knowing, and that is by the grip of its spies watching us. If I told the wrong person about the existence of such a land—I would have died. If I tell the wrong person about the true intentions of this journey—we die. Do you see?"

"I see," said Cassius.

"You say this King Estideel has been preparing for war, but why?" asked Mitsunari.

"Hatred, that's why. After the dragons hatched from the earth, it was not only humanity that fought them off. No. The elves and the other races of Medearia came to our aid and then years of peace ensued . . . But peace has its limits, it seems. Like I've said before, our great saviours became our slaves, and a genocide followed, all because we cannot learn to love what appears different to us."

"How do you know this?" asked Mitsunari.

"*Almost* every record of that part of history was erased, but I don't know why, or even how something of that magnitude could have been done. And even then, I would think that the knowledge of what had happened would be passed down, but it's as if people simply forgot. Unlikely, I think. It's as if something or *someone* made the men and women of Ederia lose that part of history, possibly so that Medearia would be left in peace."

"Almost?" asked the Sarakotan.

"Have you heard of the Massacre of Folka Island?"

"Of course."

"Then you know that on Folka Island, off the shores of Vuldhear, the scholars from the local school discovered a shipwreck in the seas. But what if I told you that this ship was not, in fact, made by any man, and instead, it was actually elvish. Everything on it was lost . . . except for a chest that was kept untouched in a pocket of air within the ship. Inside were tomes and letters written by Medearia's spies. Inside this chest was where I discovered King Henselt's diary entries but also something else—a talisman. The scholars brought the chest back to the island, but it was then that they noticed that the talisman behaved quite strangely. They did their tests, and the material was unrecognizable. Everything they did there was catalogued very carefully and thoroughly, and on the third night of having the talisman in their possession, it began to speak to them." It was then that they noticed that Ivan grew pale and almost fearful, and he held out his hand to the falling rain, allowing himself to be distracted from the moment.

"And then what happened? How'd they die?" asked Cassius, and even he was quite familiar with this infamous part of history.

"... Then ... I touched it."

"What?"

"I ... was one of those scholars. It spoke to us and told us all of the horrors inflicted by mankind, and at night, when the others were asleep, it spoke to me and me only."

"What did it say?" asked the prince, and he grew a little startled now, as if he was a child listening to his mother tell him a frightening story by the fire.

"It said that I must rediscover its homeland . . . but the others ... the others were not meant to keep this information."

"And so, you killed them?"

"No . . . *It* did. After it spoke to me, I must have fainted, and I awoke to see the school in flames . . . and my brothers and sisters were dead but not by the fire. Something else killed them, and that *something* allowed me to flee."

The three of them then grew silent, waiting for the other to break said silence. "Tell me, have you had any more of these dreams?" asked Ivan, and they could tell that his story had taken a great deal of courage for him to tell.

"No," the prince lied, and Ivan was quick to see it but decided to pretend that he had fallen for it. "But who exactly is the grey-haired elf?"

"... I wish I knew, truly. But I don't ... However, I do know that he is dangerous and to be feared."

"So how do we intend on doing it? How will he die?" asked the prince.

"This," replied Ivan as he took out a capsule filled with a small sample of a violet-coloured flower. "It is wolfsbane, and it is quite poisonous."

"Will it be enough?"

"Oh, it will," said Ivan. "I'll make sure that it is."

Sir Hadrian then took a turn steering the boat, and a few hours had passed when Ivan went down below to speak with Azrad and Connell. Again, *something* was on his mind. When he walked inside their room, the two of them were lying down on their bunk beds. Of course, Connell was on the bottom as always. Ivan closed the door . . . and locked it. "Do you trust me?" he asked.

"What? Of course."

"Can I trust you?"

"Always," replied Connell as he sat up.

"Good . . . good." Ivan paced the room, gathering his thoughts, for he was about to say something he had wanted to say for some time but was uncertain of the reaction he'd receive. "What if I told you that I am planning something that goes beyond killing the elvish king?"

"I'd ask you what you're planning, of course," said Azrad.

Ivan took a deep breath . . . and exhaled slowly. "Estideel has an army, yes? I've begun to see that army as a tool, one that can be used to our benefit if wielded carefully. *Very carefully.* What I am about to propose does not leave this room, are we clear? It stays between us, and if I choose to, I might tell Mitsunari."

"What are you getting at?"

"What if we wielded such an army? What if we somehow gained control of it? The three of us could conquer just about any-thing . . . even Ekmere."

"You're fucking crazy." Azrad laughed, but he could not hide it, his curiosity had been ignited.

"I don't know how we'd be able to control such an army, to use such a tool, but after the death of Estideel, I believe it'd be somehow possible."

"What about Cassius? What about the kid?"

"It pains me, it does. But if he does not submit to me . . . we'll have to deal with him . . . and Blackwood." The three of them then fell into silent thoughts, and Ivan prayed that they would agree to help him. "Think about it, what wouldn't we be able to do? We could have all the power we ever dreamed of."

"All the power *you* ever dreamed of," said Azrad as he leaped from his bed.

"If I had power, if I had the throne of Ekmere, I would use it for your benefit; you'd have all the gold you could ever wish for. Trust me, brothers, as you always have. I'm not saying that we are about to stab them in the back, but I need to know that if we found a way, you'd help me sit on that throne . . . Maybe Cassius would comply?"

"I doubt it," said Azrad bluntly. He then looked over to Connell and then back to Ivan, and he pondered it all very thoroughly. He liked the boy and the knight, he did, but he also liked the idea of power. *Power* was something that every man longed for, regardless of how much they denied it . . . And he would not deny it any longer. "I'm in," he said finally.

"Me too," said Connell.

"But if we can, I'd rather have no harm come to Cassius," said Azrad. "But then again, we're still assuming that this is even possible."

"The impossible is rather interesting, wouldn't you agree?"

❈

Ivan saw Sir Hadrian standing at the bow, looking eastward for any sign of land. He approached him from behind, and the knight turned to him as he did so.

"We should have been there by now," said Sir Hadrian.

"The wind has not been kind," said Ivan.

Azrad sailed the ship slowly now. The rain had settled down, and the sky was taken by a ruthless layer of fog that hid their path from them. The ocean was easy that day, and the smell of salt water was an evil tease to their unsatisfied desire for hydration.

"Something tells me that you are leading us into certain death," said the knight.

"You're wise to be wary. If not, then Medearia will make you pay, trust me." And then Ivan turned towards the knight and stepped closer. "I will not be responsible for his death," he whispered and then looked over towards where Cassius sat.

"I understand. The boy will be my responsibility."

"Good. How do you feel?" asked Ivan, and the knight appeared rather surprised at the hearing of this question, so surprised, in fact, that he immediately assumed there was some hidden gibe in his words.

"Fine. Why?"

"You don't seem fine. You've kept it hidden well, I'll give you that, but I have better eyes than the rest of them."

"I don't follow you, Ivan."

"I can see your sickness. At night you writhe in pain—chest pain if I am not mistaken. And your breathing has slowed. In short, you are old, and your age is catching up with you." Sir Hadrian's face was expressionless, but he grimaced underneath his mask of composure. He was right. Sir Hadrian had kept it hidden well until now, but as their journey progressed, his heart was failing him. He needed to be more careful from here on out, or else—regardless of how hard he fought against it—his body would collapse under his own ego and drive to serve and uphold his standard of honour. He could die. After decades of preparing for a warrior's death, he'd learned how to not fear such a death long ago, but death by his own body failing him frightened him and chilled his fearless soul. It was a thought that felt inevitable and utterly wild and uncontrollable.

"Do me a favour, Ivan," said Sir Hadrian, and his voice finally seemed to waver in courage, although only slightly.

"Sure."

"Don't tell the others. Please," said the knight, and those words from a man like him carried an unmeasurable weight. He had finally admitted to his dotage.

"You have my word," said Ivan, and he now turned to Sir Hadrian. "Look behind you."

Sir Hadrian turned around to see a seagull perched on the edge of the ship. They had made it. Land was upon them. Sir Hadrian could not move.

It was true: there was land beyond Ederia, and this simultaneously proved every word that Ivan spoke of about the elves of Medearia. "So," said Sir Hadrian with hollow laughter seeping through his voice, "I have been fed lies my entire life. There is no edge to the world, and we are far from alone."

"Come! Gather the others inside! You remember the plan, yes?"

"Yes."

Once the company was inside, there was a spell of disbelief that fluttered across the room, and silent whispers of, "Did we really find it?" poured out from Cassius's mouth. They had, indeed, found it. The prince was nervous. It felt like every day of his journey had led to this very moment, a moment not a soul in Ederia could prepare for. *Deep breaths, Cassius. You've got this. We've been over the plan a hundred times. You've got this,* thought Cassius.

Ivan arrived and joined the others at the table.

"The anchor's down. Now, we all know what is about to happen? We all know the plan?"

"Yes," said the others.

"Well then, let's get to work," said Ivan, and the others sprinted to their duties. Their arrival had to go unnoticed, meaning all had to be silent, and a ship as large as this would surely give them away, and thus the company took to finding each lifeboat they possessed and readied themselves to row into a small cove. It was difficult, however, to see anything through the mist, and to their disliking, they were left guessing as to what or even who waited for them on that ominous shoreline.

The boats were in the water, and they had their things; every last provision that had to be saved for the journey was stored in their bags. Cassius put on his armour and was with Sir Hadrian and Connell, and not a soul would test the air with their voice. No word was uttered.

They had one goal and that was the beach. Any minor stray from the plan could prove disastrous, even now. Connell rowed slowly through the water, and the mist knelt beside them, hiding their path, and blowing tension into the air. Cassius looked down into the water. It seemed normal, but still, he assumed that what waited below could shatter his mind with the abnormality of its nature. He dipped his finger beneath the surface; it was quite warm, as if the breath of some gargantuan monstrosity of a serpent boiled the abyss beneath them.

They had lost sight of the others now. They would have to trust their ability to navigate the labyrinth of mist that blinded them. Connell could not see just how far away the shore was, that is until he broke through the mist like some warrior taken by the teachings of war and breaking through the enemy line.

They then saw it.

There it was, before their eyes.

The boat rode up onto the stony shoreline. Connell was the first to get out, and he was followed by a hesitant Sir Hadrian, and Cassius too took his time. The prince stepped out and onto the land that his mind had once pondered repeatedly. He felt the wet stones beneath his feet and wiggled his boots deeper until they nearly sank beneath the ocean of rocks. He took in the air: it felt clean, and each breath seemed to cleanse his body. He was finally there, they all were.

Medearia was upon them.

The forest began abruptly, just a dozen yards from the sea, and its dark face watched them with lively eyes. Cassius stared back into the woods, and it felt alive, living, breathing, and always watching with composed wrath. It sent shivers to his skin. Cassius was wary of what stood before him, and Medearia smiled back with its fangs open to see. This place was surely different from Ederia; it felt wild and untamed, as if the very land was bold and nearly egotistical, and Ederia was broken, tamed by the lashes of humanity.

The three of them knew that waiting too long on the beach was a risky idea, and so they took cover at the entrance to the woods, but even that felt ultimately deadly. They could feel the breath of the wild on their backs. Soon enough, they saw the others arrive on the shore to meet them, and without words (for sound was their enemy) they greeted each other with congratulatory eyes. However, they also knew that the quest was far from over. They readied themselves, checking if everything was in order, for once inside the soul of the woods, all order would be lost and replaced with a beautiful hysteria that would surely arouse the joy of the forest and amuse it. And so, the Company of Ekmere looked upon the opening of the dark woods, and they felt the walls close in. Elsibard was nigh, and Estideel, the king of the high elves, was their next target.

※

When Ivan had first escaped from the Pools, he never imagined he would ever come back to Medearia, and as night slowly crept upon them, they were camped quite close to where he and Baldwyn had once slept. The same trees loomed above, singing melodiously as they bent, creating crackling arches, just as they once had, long ago, and they were likely to continue doing so for the rest of their days.

After filling up their waterskins from a nearby stream, the company was silent. Even Azrad did not dare speak a word out of fear of unwanted ears listening to his voice from the shadows. The fire burnt low, and Cassius studied the never-ending dance of it and its instant cries and pops. Meanwhile, Mitsunari sharpened his blade, and thus an awkward veil of silence struck those around the flame. No words were needed. Their goal was absolute. No more useless palaver. They longed for dusk, and alas, that was a way off. The hours of dusk meant the next evening of travel, and the next coming of shadow, meant they would be closer to the end of their journey and ridding themselves of the eerie feeling of this place. Even in the sunlight, the woods sent out foreboding calls of unknown animals that Cassius never wished to look upon, and every now and then he found himself caught by the calls of the forest, like soft whispers that carried out malevolent songs to tender ears. Cassius rolled over and threw his blanket over himself. It was time to rest.

"I think we could all use a little rest," said Ivan. "We make our way north at dusk. There we shall make way for the Pass of Mordthand. We should save our energy for then." Ivan's tone was dull and emotionless; the journey was taking its toll on everyone, even him.

＊

Again, the whispers of the woods poured into the ears of the prince as he slept. Night had fallen upon them all, but the others were still yet to wake, and in the powerful darkness of it all, Cassius thought he saw a light flicker in the distance. He rubbed his eyes, thinking it could have been some hallucination at the result of his exhaustion, but it was not. No, this light was real, it had to be. The prince sat up in his bed and squinted his eyes to focus on what had caught his attention. Yes, the light was blue, and it illuminated and fought back the darkness, keeping the shadow at bay.

Then there was the sound of crushed leaves and snorting, and it seemed close to Cassius's ears. He looked around again. Still, not a soul was awake.

Strange, he thought, but not as unexplainable as the light that roamed the moonlit shadow and spread its holy illumination like veins. There was something about it, Cassius could not understand why, that felt benign and peaceful, and that contradicted every feeling of this land he had felt so far. Again, there was the sound of whispers in his mind, but Cassius could not understand the language.

Still, he could tell by the tone that something was not quite right. Cassius stood up. Although his mind said not to, his heart pulled him towards the meandering blue light. It was a light that warmed his insides, made him feel that he was safe, made him feel at home. The prince roamed freely, but almost in an unconscious state that was a blend between the volition of his heart and the feeling that this light gave him.

As Cassius drew closer to the origins of the light, the sound of feet slapping against leaves, crushing and twisting them against the soil, became louder and louder and were joined by snorting and deep, bestial breaths. Two black eyes then protruded from the darkness, and so Ruedenhiem, the Great Stag of the North, looked upon the prince, towering over him, and his proud antlers filled Cassius's eyes with a light he did not know until now; it was a light of heavenly hues that bewitched him. His snout leaned forward, smelling Cassius as the prince gave out his hand for the stag to smell it. Ruedenhiem sniffed the fingers of Cassius and drew back slightly—a new smell, a scent that he had never known before. It was strange, alien-like, and yet still somewhat familiar. He was the one. He was the one the Sage spoke of. He was the boy that could unite the continents and shatter the coming storm of war between Ederia and Medearia. The Sage had found Ruedenhiem long ago and had spoken to him about what the future held and how this *boy* would trigger the events that could fix everything.

What was burning could be fixed, and the Sage had prophesied that this *human* would be the one to fix it all, or so the Sage hoped. But the future was unpredictable and so was the balance between hate and harmony, for that balance could lean towards war, and it soon would have if Ruedenhiem had not found the boy. But he had. Cassius was right in front of him, and it was time for the true journey to begin. Cassius placed his palm on the forehead of Ruedenhiem, and somehow, words filled Cassius's mind, and this time he could understand them.

The word "follow" rang in Cassius's ear. He didn't understand what was occurring, nor did he understand just how this word was transferred to him. But he needed to obey. Still, his mind was foggy, but not from sleep. No. He felt controlled by fate, and the prince gave in to its arms and let himself be taken by it.

The prince followed.

Ruedenhiem was quick, and so Cassius would have to be quicker, and that meant he'd have to shake off the effects of sleep and sharpen his mind. He was in the wild now. The prince followed the stag through the forest, climbing over rock, squeezing through a thicket, and then bolting through the level plains of the woods, following the light. What seemed like scattered images of a dream that passed in seconds was, in actuality, hours of running through the shadows and into vast meadows where the moonlight found him and gave him hope of brighter days. Cassius followed until his lungs gave out, crying for mercy from the constant sprint. Ruedenhiem stood beside him. They were there.

Cassius could smell it and did not wish to look. The terrifying snarls and sounds of beasts pierced his ears like handfuls of cutlery squeezing through his canal and sinking into his eardrum. The sight sent blood-thinning chills in his body.

The swamps were before him.

Ruedenhiem walked onwards into the swamp, but Cassius, hesitant to follow, stayed put only to have Ruedenhiem look back at him. Cassius knew to follow him now for that look was one that could not be ignored. Onwards they went.

"W-where are you taking me?" asked Cassius.

No answer. Instead, he received silence and the pale eye of the moon upon him. His senses were coming back to him. The allure of the creature had put some spell-like veil over his senses and intuition, but once they entered the boundaries of the bog, that spell began to diminish. He turned to see which way he had come, but the woods were shadowed, and the blue light was gone. Cassius looked back to find the light, but the stag was nowhere to be seen. Had it been a dream, a hallucination conjured by the dark arts of this land?

Suddenly, a hand touched Cassius's shoulder, and he knew it well. His father crouched beside him.

"Look! He's got your smile," said Cornelius.

Iris laughed. "Well, Viddy definitely has your eyes."

Cassius was no longer in the swamps. He was now at Ekmere, in his parents' quarters, and from a third-person perspective he watched his parents hold both him and his brother, but he and Vidicus were no more than infants. His parents held each of them, cradling them and smiling at their beautiful creations. Tears flooded Cassius's eyes. "Just wait, my love, one day he'll be as big as you, and he'll be king just as you are now," said Iris with a grin.

"I'm sure he will, dear. He will be a good king; I will make sure of that. But I doubt he'll have a queen as beautiful as I do!" said Cornelius, turning to his wife and kissing her on her forehead before placing his son down onto his bed. But Cassius, as he was now, was a ghost in the room, watching it all happen, and he wished he could speak. He wanted to scream to get their attention, to speak to and hug his mother once again as he once did long ago. But his voice was gone. He could not speak, and as hard as he tried, he could make no sound, for each word was drowned. Murdered by the dream.

And then it was gone. He was back in the swamps. Alone. No father. No mother. Not even a brother to bring him comfort.

He took a step forward, but his foot felt no solid ground beneath it, and Cassius fell through a cloud of thickets and thorns. He felt his skin rip and blood poured down from his cheeks.

He fell.

And when he landed, his head smacked against the stone floor, and the last image he saw was a woman beside him. She was in a deep slumber and had been for years.

It was her.

It was Sathelia.

The Prisoners

There was a crack in the inner gem of the necklace. *She always was a wild girl. That crack represents her perfectly: too busy to attend to her own internal issues and far more focused on fixing other's imperfections. Or maybe it shows how she had come to terms with her own imperfections and realized that flaws are only natural, and no matter how perfect you might appear, you still are infected by flaws. Or maybe it is just a necklace that she dropped on the ground. Nothing more, nothing less,* thought Estideel.

The elvish king reached out to touch the necklace that was once worn by his dear Sathelia, but he retracted his fingers before touching it. He was afraid—afraid that his touch would somehow rob it of its value. It was the last thing that reminded him both of her and her mother, for Aurora, his queen, had passed it down to Sathelia when she was but a little girl. But then again, Sathelia always was his little girl. One that loved to disobey and flee from her royal expectations, but a part of Estideel always admired that about her. She was brave, so very brave. However, her bravery betrayed her that day eight years ago when she fled to the swamps. Her body was never found, but they didn't need a body if they knew someone was heading there. Instead, they accepted that they were gone, and did their best not to think about the common fact that their loved one had struggled in their brutal death, likely crying for help in their woeful desperation. This necklace was a haunting reminder of that night, yet he could not rid himself of it; it represented her but also the night he lost her—a cruel dichotomy.

Meanwhile, Gwallin marched behind Wraithenor. They were heading for the king's personal quarters. They had news from the sea elves, and their message was for the king's eyes only, but Gwallin wanted to be there, for he, after all, had been the one present when the raven had arrived, and that had to give him some right to be there, some magnitude of significance. It did not, no matter how hard he wished. He knew it meant nothing to anyone but himself.

"Hurry, Gwallin, we are already late," said Wraithenor, who despised being late, especially for a meeting with the king himself.

The two opened the doors that led to a crossroad in the palace. They headed left and up into the tower where the king would surely be. They arrived, but he was not there.

"Looking for someone?" said Estideel from behind them, walking out of his daughter's empty room.

"My lord!" said Wraithenor, and the two of them bowed and stood back up once the king had signalled them to do so. "We have an important message from the sea elves, they say—"

"I can read it myself, thank you," said Estideel, and his tone was forlorn and distant, as if his words were false echoes that came from afar. Wraithenor handed over the letter, and let the king read it to himself. "And so it begins," he said, handing back the letter and walking through his subordinates into his room.

"What does it say?" asked Gwallin, and the others halted, looking back at the young and foolish elf with eyes of disdain; he had spoken out of turn, and their disapproval killed his dreams from within him, dreams of companionship with powerful figures, aspirations of being someone who was somewhat important. But these fairy tales were murdered with just two glances.

"A ship was spotted sailing towards the mainland; a ship not of elvish make," said the king, and just like that, the dreams were revived, and Gwallin could breathe once more.

"Not of elvish make? But then who could it be? What other race would be bold enough to land on our shores without notifying you, my king?" asked Wraithenor.

"That is what I intend on having you find out, and quickly," said Estideel. "There will be a changing of the moons, and I can have nothing interfere with the invasion, and even this lonesome ship and the fluttering of its sails could create the storm that breathes life into the fires of our demise. Go. Gather your best hunters and see to this matter yourself."

Wraithenor and Gwallin then left their king, seeing to their orders, but as soon as they were gone, Estideel wandered back to his daughter's room. Even still, there were dolls and other trinkets that she had once played with long ago in her youngest days. Estideel sat on her bed, stroking the soft fabrics of her sheets, and holding a doll; he remembered the day he had had that made for her, which was strange. Elves lived for centuries, and so it was rare for them to hold onto insignificant memories. But he remembered the way she smiled that day, the way she twirled in her dress and fell back onto her bed, giggling and laughing as the spells of summer took her away, and then, with but a snap of time, she really was *taken* from him.

Estideel dropped the doll onto the floor and let loose his tears.

✳

There was something strange in the woods that night, Wraithenor could feel it. There was something in the air, a taste of something unfamiliar; his scouts had not lied, although he had never doubted them. When the king read the letter that morning, speaking of a non-elvish ship sailing towards Medearia, he could not believe it. It had to be a mistake. But he trusted his king's intuition with his life, and so he would see to this matter himself. But now that he had arrived at the beach, it was undeniable that a foreign stench plagued the air.

"No sign of the ship, only footprints," Gwallin said.

"Which means they must have rowed to shore," said Wraithenor, almost whispering to himself as he knelt, studying the prints. The moonlight spilled its beauty upon the black canvas of the ocean, and the evening chill had arrived just as Wraithenor and his scouts had. There were a dozen of them, and they had spread out over the tree-tops for surveillance of the land and would return once Wraithenor gave them the signal. A high-pitched whistle rang through the night, and it came from Wraithenor, yet it sounded far more like a morning bird that had awakened too early than any sound that an elf could make. His men came quickly, dancing over the treetops to meet him at the beach.

"Tell me, what did you find?" asked Wraithenor. His men hesitated to answer; they themselves were surprised at their failure. "Well? Answer me."

"Nothing. We found nothing, sir," said Urvath.

"Nothing?"

"Could it not be the sea elves?"

"No. No, I do not think so. They are the ones who gave us news of a ship sailing towards Medearia."

"They were," said Gwallin.

"Then certainly it could not be," said Wraithenor.

"Then who?" asked Urvath, but Wraithenor made no response, for he was lost in thought, strolling across the moonlit beach, pondering, and brewing up predictions.

It can't be them, could it? No ... But also, I'd be a fool to not prepare, not to make sure it isn't them, that there are no ... humans *that have come. After all, it's happened before, and so it could happen again,* thought Wraithenor. Then suddenly, he turned back to his men.

"Bring me my bow and my blade . . . tonight, we hunt for men," he said, and his followers could not believe the words of their general.

"But it cannot be—"

"But it *is*!" said Wraithenor, and he unveiled his grey hood that hid his charcoal-black hair, and he took his bow and sword from Gwallin. "Have any of you hunted humans before?" There was silence. They were far too young to remember the days of old, but even he was a young elf then, barely anything more than a child. "Well then," said Wraithenor, now striding to and fro in front of his hunters like a war hero about to rally the hearts of his army. "They are slow-minded but unpredictable, and if they are capable of making this journey, they are surely greater than any average human. Thus, we must be on our guard, no matter who we hunt, no matter what we kill. Go! Take to the trees and make your way east. We shall find whatever prowls our woods, and we shall rid the forest of their disease. May starlight stalk your steps, brothers."

His men flooded away into the darkness of the woods, and they were gone in an instant. But Wraithenor took his time to study the prints. *Five? No. There are six of them, and each print is well spaced— they were in a hurry. One set of prints is deeper than the others, meaning there is a larger human among them,* thought Wraithenor, and he stood back up and approached the treeline, and then he sprang up into the air, balancing on each bough and branch of the tree, leaping higher and higher until he was high enough. Thus, the pursuit began.

He could smell them, but only faintly. They must have arrived in the morning. It was then that the thought crossed his mind, like a sour dream coming to spoil the joy of a perfect slumber. *Could it be Ivan?* thought Wraithenor. *No. There was no way that he had lived. I saw that arrow pierce his heart. I saw him die before my eyes.*

But even then, it *could* have been *him*. It was unlikely, but still, it was possible. And if Ivan had survived that arrow, and if it was him that they pursued, even Wraithenor would have to be on his guard.

✳

Ivan released his ear from the tree only to once again put it back, feeling the vibrations of the forest. Something was coming and quick, likely more of them. Connell strangled Gwallin with his iron fists, shutting away any useless squeal for help. They had their hostage, and now all that was needed was for them to catch the bait. The company encircled the camp, ready for battle.

"Where is Cassius?" yelled Sir Hadrian.

"I don't know. They might have taken him," said Ivan.

"Those fuckers!" shouted Azrad.

"As much as that rat may squirm, don't gut him," said Ivan. "We need him if we are going to parley for Cassius's life."

"Are they getting closer?" asked Sir Hadrian, and rage smouldered from within him, and sparks of fire flew from his tongue as if his ire had poisoned his speech. His sword was ready, ready to taste the blood of any elf that was foolish enough to touch the Prince of Ederia.

"Yes! They are coming, and there are many of them. Connell, make sure they know we have one of them! It is the only way we'll have a chance of surviving," said Ivan.

The full force of the company would be unleashed as soon as the enemy was in sight. They were all ready for death to breed like wildfire in that forest. They were all ready to die. The enemy was nigh, and the infinite waiting for battle was as nearly brutal as the physicality of it.

"How close?" asked Azrad, but there was silence from Ivan. "How close, dammit?"

Still, nothing, but then Ivan turned and unsheathed his sword.

"They are here."

Azrad was quickly pulled from the ground by the strength of a rope around his neck, and he was suddenly in the trees, surrounded by the enemy.

Wraithenor walked out on a branch of a tree for all to see him, and Azrad struggled as the rope tightened around his neck.

"So, I see you survived, Ivan."

"Don't be foolish now, Wraithenor, we have one of yours as well."

"You do not surprise me, Ivan. You'll have to pardon me, my common tongue has grown rusty over the years, but let me make things clear to you humans. I have all of you. An arrow for each of your hearts. Don't bother looking for my men, you won't find them, not if they don't want you to."

"Where's the boy?" asked Sir Hadrian, growing impatient.

"Boy?"

"Don't deny it, you creature. I know you have him."

Wraithenor paid no attention to the old knight. This conversation had gone on long enough for his liking. He whistled, and his men appeared out of the shadows with their bows drawn back and aimed at each member of the company.

"Tie them," said Wraithenor, and his men did as their general commanded. Each member of the company fell to their knees, save for Sir Hadrian. The knight was too proud to bend his knee to these *things*. Too proud and too worried. He wanted to hide it, but the absence of Cassius drained his composure. However, nothing could be done. They had lost, and the yellow eyes of the elves mocked their defeat, intensifying the flames of failure.

Wraithenor let himself fall to the ground. He landed silently on his feet but did not break eye contact with the old man. He could tell there was something different about him, a rare strength that one was only born with. Ivan had that strength as well, that stubborn will to not only live but thrive. The elf unsheathed his blade and held it to Sir Hadrian's throat, but he was unwavering, and to

Wraithenor's surprise, something as simple as this gave him a small amount of respect for this man. He sheathed his sword. The elf had only been testing Sir Hadrian, and he knew that well, but there were few men in Ederia who had had the privilege of being tested and living to tell the tale. But they'd have to live this time, and Urvath touched the knight with the cold head of his arrow before breaking his stance and kicking him into the dirt. Each strike was done with rage, and the company watched as Sir Hadrian, the Pride of Ederia, was beaten into submission as if he was nothing more than a stray dog who was bold enough to wander too far from home.

"Shall we bring them to the Pools?" asked Urvath.

"No," said Wraithenor. "Bring them to the Pits. I want to see them die with my own eyes."

It was then, at these words, that Ivan found hope, and even struggled to hide the grin that was growing on his lips. If they were heading to the fighting pits, that meant they were heading for Elsibard. They were prisoners, for now, but that may be exactly what they needed to make it into the capital. There was hope, but it would have to be silenced until it was ready to be unleashed.

Strangers in The Dark

S he was beautiful, Cassius could not help but admire. The blood
running down from the side of his head mattered little now, not
to him. His body ached, and a debilitating pain ran down from his
tailbone into his legs, shutting his movement down momentarily,
but the prince carried on and sat up. He looked above to where he
had fallen through. It was day now, and small crumbs of rubble and
rock sifted through the briars and down onto his forehead, but the
woman beside him was not fazed. She didn't even move . . . as if she
was dead. However, it was an unnatural beauty, one that Cassius had
not seen before, and of course, she was one of *them*. An elf. She was
one the enemy. And yet, Cassius struggled to summon any bitter
feelings for her; he could not even build the foundations for hatred,
only wonder. Her hair was white with traces of black at the ends,
and he was overwhelmed with the idea that he was breaking some
unwritten law of attraction. One that stated that man and elf could
not fall in love, and yet he did so anyway. He *was* in love. It felt wrong,
but the nefariousness of his thoughts excited him furthermore like

he was a child again, staying up past his bedtime, waiting for his parents to come and scold him for being a bad boy. It was only then that Cassius caught himself staring, and he lightly slapped himself on the side of the head at the realization of his rude behaviour. This was no whore. This was a *woman,* one to be respected and not treated as an object. Her clothes were ripped and torn; she had been through a lot, and she had obviously received the worse fall out of the two of them.

She stirred.

Cassius fell back, surprised by what he had seen. She appeared to be trapped in the throes of a terrible dream. The woman then tossed and turned, fighting away at the nightmares that stung her mind like a nest of scorpions.

"Hello?" There was no response, and the prince let his back slide down against the wet stone, and it was then that his head began to throb as if his skull was being besieged by an army of pain. "Hello?" he asked once again, this time a little louder, but still the elf made no response. Cassius knelt by her side and gently shook her. He was closer to her now, and he could smell her beautiful fragrance that filled his stomach with a hurricane of butterflies. Her eyes would not open.

However, Cassius then noticed something, a sudden and violent change in the lighting. The walls were now an emerald green, as if he had had his head plunged down into a lush and vibrant lagoon. How could he have forgotten—it was the necklace given to him by Sir Hadrian. Cassius looked down at the stone and clutched it in his hand. Its light was pure and vibrant in the dark depths of the cave, and its touch filled him with hope. He thought of the company and what could be happening to them.

"Now where did you find a stone like that?" asked a voice from the darkness. Cassius turned around, blood and adrenaline pumping through his body.

"Who said that?" asked Cassius, backing away from where the mysterious voice had come from. But even that was unclear. Darkness encircled the prince, blinding his vision from what the cave held secret. A flame from a torch then unfurled like a whip, illuminating a hooded figure that walked slowly towards Cassius.

"So, we finally meet," said the hooded elf.

"Get away from me!" said Cassius, cowering against the opposite wall of the cave. The ominous elf's face was hidden in darkness but was revealed as he withdrew his hood, letting loose his long grey hair.

It was him, the one from the dreams. "I-it's you!" said Cassius, but the wonder in his voice was quickly replaced with fear, and he unsheathed his weapon, pointing it towards the elf.

"Strange. How did Prince Cassius of Ederia come to find the stone of *En Estar* in his possession? You continue to intrigue me," said the elf.

"Back off, I'm warning you!" said Cassius with feigned bravery from within. The elf looked at the boy's sword as if it was a mere primitive tool that he himself was far too proud to use, and so, the flame from his torch suddenly grew into a tornado of fire that enveloped them both in a forest of heat. But as quickly as the tornado had erupted, its walls were torn down, and the fire retracted back into the torch.

Cassius was speechless. He had seen magicians before, but they were all clowns who fooled you into giving you their money. This was no clown, no magician. No, *he* was something else entirely.

"Put that thing down before you hurt yourself, and be silent for a moment," said the elf, and he knelt beside the girl and whispered ancient words into her ear; it was a language far too old for Cassius to even comprehend the depth of it. Sathelia stirred slightly and then a little more. She was awake, and her eyes were like burning violet rings that were fresh out of the forge. Cassius saw them, and remarkably they reminded him of his mother's eyes. "Sathelia? Whisper if you can hear me?" said the Sage, but there was no answer, and the seconds that passed after his questions were like days in the burning wastelands of uncertainty.

"M-mother," whispered Sathelia, yet she trailed off into a string of unidentifiable slurring, and her voice was dangerously faint, as if it would fade into nothing.

"She is very weak. We cannot leave, not yet. We must wait for her to come to her senses," said the Sage.

Cassius stood up, readying himself for his grand monologue, but as quickly as he had stood up, the prince fainted out of shock, and Vandulin, the Sage of Western Medearia, now found himself caring for the both of them.

✳

When Cassius awoke, it was the afternoon, or so his instincts told him. The sun was kept hidden away by the rain clouds above. The grey-haired elf rested against the wall next to him, or so it appeared. He looked to be sleeping, yet his eyelids were open, and his eyeballs had rolled back into his head. Cassius came to. "Who are you?" he asked.

"Me? I have been called many titles. Vandulin is what you may call me."

"I've seen you before, in my dreams."

"Yes," said Vandulin, and he stood up before Cassius, who only now was able to get a good look at the elf. His robes were grey but alluring: his right shoulder was adorned in a pauldron of exotic green and blue feathers. But his eyes were what *really* frightened Cassius: they were dark and bottomless, as if they were the definition of nothing, nothing but a sublime wasteland that has been destroyed through thousands of years of anguish. They spilled sorrow into his heart, and Cassius was given an idea of the true pain those eyes had seen and endured. "I have waited for our meeting, and I have sculpted fate so that we may see eye to eye as we do so now." Cassius did not follow completely but chose to make it seem as if he did.

"Who is she?" asked Cassius.

"Her? She is Sathelia Litherius, daughter to King Estideel Litherius, and she has been gone for quite some time."

"What do you mean?"

"Her father thinks she is dead—all of Medearia thinks she is dead," said Vandulin, and Cassius fell silent for a moment. "So, what will you do now?"

"Me? Nothing! I'm going to get the fuck out of here and forget any of this nightmare ever happened. I mean, I don't even know where I am—and I *barely* know how I even got here! I need to get back. I want to go home." But the prince began to trail off as he hyperventilated in his panic. He needed air. He needed answers for everything around him!

And then Cassius realized that the princess was awake, and she rose up from where she once had lain. She too looked to be in a panic.

"W-where am I?" asked Sathelia, closing her eyes and holding the palm of her hand to her forehead. But as soon as she opened them, she saw the Sage, and instincts took her, and without thought, she bowed, kneeling, and scraping her knee on the wet rocks beneath her.

"Stand, Sathelia. There is no need for such manners at this moment. Listen to me carefully. What was your last memory?"

"I . . . I think . . . I remember swamps. Darkness and fear, and . . . my mother. I saw my mother."

"That is impossible, Sathelia."

"It was not her. I remember seeing wraiths and fiends of the night, and then I fell. Yes . . . I fell," said the princess, and Cassius could see her delicate hands trembling.

"Sathelia, you have been touched by evil spirits, and they have left their mark on you," said Vandulin as his eyes pointed to her hair. Hair that was once black had now been dyed with the blood of a ghost—white as a cold moon. "You have been stuck here for eight years."

"What?" Sathelia fell back down to her knees. "But—no! No, just yesterday I walked amongst the trees of Cassemor under the sweetness of the sun." Her eyes began to water, but she was able to keep them at bay, so much so, in fact, that her shock was replaced with wonder. "Who is he? What is he?" she asked, looking over at Cassius as if he was some new animal she had not seen before.

"His name is Cassius, and he is the one who found you, albeit he had much help from hidden hands."

"It is not an elf. What is it?"

"*That* would be a human," said Vandulin, and Sathelia stood up immediately and pressed her back to the wall, fearing even the very word "human."

"It cannot be! What is it doing here?"

"He has his own goals that I am not aware of, but he himself is not aware of what fate has in store for him, not yet. But fate will find him, and I have spent many years dictating it so that we may meet here."

Cassius did not understand them. They spoke in their native language, but it did not take a scholar to figure out that she possessed some form of interest in him.

"What of my father? What has happened?"

"He prepares for war with Ederia."

"Then what is this human doing here?" asked Sathelia, and Cassius could sense a small amount of disdain in her tone that was mixed with wonder.

"We need him, Sathelia. He is the one, the one to unite Ederia and Medearia once again and stop the gears of war from turning, but it must be done quickly."

"Good luck convincing our people that that is what is best for us."

"We shall see."

"Hey! What the fuck is going on?" cried Cassius.

"How is your common speech?"

"I can get by."

"Good. Try to be nice, he's been through a lot as well," said Vandulin, and the two then turned towards Cassius. "There will be time for questions on the road to Elsibard, but first you must both follow me."

Both Cassius and Sathelia choked on their words, and Vandulin turned before they could spit them out, and thus they were forced to follow him into the darkness.

It did not take them long to reach the other side of the caves, but the journey was done in silence, and it was damp and cold in the darkness of the cave. It felt refreshing to finally see light and exit through the curtains of vines and back into the bogs. This region, however, appeared inhabited: small clusters of raised huts spread out across the swamps like reminders of hope and civilization in land as wild as this. The smell made Cassius's stomach writhe at first, but he soon grew comfortable with the stench. Vandulin led them both down a small dirt path that sank downwards into the bogs, and it was there that a wooden bridge snaked through the algae-infested water and down towards what appeared to be a small village.

"Are you going to kill me?" asked Cassius, and there was silence followed by the rolling of eyes.

"Cassius, if we truly wished to, you would have been long dead by now," said Vandulin without bothering to look back towards the prince.

"What is our business with the moon elves?" asked Sathelia.

"We need to reach Elsibard soon, and I'm sure you are eager to as well, thus we need transportation. Why, does it bother you?"

"*It does.* They are unruly folk."

"And so are you, I have heard."

"Excuse me?"

"You pride yourself, princess, on your couth, but seem to forget it. These will be your people one day, just the same as the other races of elves shall be." Sathelia was beaten. She could not outwit someone like him, and deep down she knew he was right.

The village of Lunus was small, barely a village to Cassius's eyes, and poor, fitting for the land they inhabited. Cassius made sure to cloak himself before entering and kept his head low. Vandulin and Sathelia may have seemed to tolerate him, maybe even consider him important, although, for what reason, he still could not tell. But these elves would surely find a way to kill him if they could, likely drown him in the mires—quick and bloodless. The moon elves of Lunus were something out of books to the eyes of Cassius and they even frightened him. They looked and behaved nothing like Sathelia and the Sage; their skin was thin, nearly translucent at times. Their bodies were just as amphibian as they were humanoid. Cassius looked at one but only with his peripheral vision; direct eye contact was far too risky, but from what he gathered, they were large and hunched over, with some having bluish to greenish skin, dyed by the environment around them, and they were hairless and wet. Cassius shuttered. His hands trembled and not from any symptoms of addiction. No, this was fear.

"Keep close to me," whispered the Sage, and he quickened his step. The prince could feel the touch of their aquatic eyes burning his skin like an elderly man touching him where he did not wish to be touched, and he felt raped by anxiety. One deep breath at a time, that was how Cassius carried on, and that was all he could do as he watched the Sage approach one of them.

They halted. Vandulin appeared to be speaking to one. Now every eye in that village was on Cassius, or so it seemed. From the left, he could make out one whittling away at the end of a stick, sharpening it to a point before getting up and walking behind him—eyes still fixated on the newcomer. They could smell it—the scent of something new. And then they were off again after an exchange of coins.

Good, they have a currency, meaning there is still something to latch onto that reminds me of home, thought Cassius. And even something as simple as that lit a candle from within him that gave him hope of ever actually *coming* home, and he latched onto it like an abandoned child choosing to never forget the last memory he possessed of his parents before they were gone. One of the moon elves led them down a path that shot out of the village back into the bogs, and the only things that kept them away from the water were thin wooden planks. Each step felt like stepping on wet and mouldy bread. Cassius would be surprised if it held for much longer. At the end of the bridge, four enormous boulders stood there, towering over the four of them, and just how four boulders had landed so close together and at a place without any mountains amazed the prince, but this was Medearia after all.

A series of small stairs were carved into the side of each boulder, and before Cassius knew it, Vandulin and Sathelia were already making the climb up them. He hesitated for a moment and couldn't afford any longer or else he would seem even more out of place; thus, he took part. The nearly vertical stairs were slippery and wet, with moist patches of moss slipping away as he held onto them, losing his grip and having to move quickly to regain it. A boulder was designated for each of them: Vandulin took the largest, while Cassius and Sathelia's were not much larger than a carriage. *Ok. So, what the fuck now?* thought Cassius. The moon elf waved them goodbye, and suddenly the boulders rose from the ground, and four legs and a head rose with each one and broke through the water's surface. This was no boulder.

It was a turtle, but far different from the ones that inhabited the ponds of Ekmere's palace.

"WHAT IS HAPPENING!"

"Calm down, would you! It's just a Tiethedon," said Sathelia. She looked back to make sure they were alone. "Do they not have those where you're from?"

"Not like this," said Cassius, trying to make his voice not sound shaky when talking to her.

"Speed up. We can't have you lagging behind," said Sathelia, and her tone was that of royalty; she had the same bodacious whip in her tongue and an identical haughty aura.

"Well, that's easier said than done, if you don't mind me saying."

"Give it a pat on its left side for it to go left, a pat on the right to go right, and one in the center to speed up—it's not hard!"

Cassius would have responded, and every instinct inside of him told him to return with a rude reply, but he was far too busy fearing the beast that carried him. Soon enough he got the hang of it—not all of it, but enough to get him beside the others. The Tiethedon moved quicker than Cassius thought it would, striding through the shallow waters like a stallion galloping through the meadows of dawn.

There he was, bound to another journey, separated completely and torn away from everyone he loved. Cassius would not know yet, but he had just crossed the border into something greater than himself, a pivotal fate that was meant for him, but one that he himself was not ready for.

The Tree was all around them.

It was the essence of their world, and it tied everything together with a perfect balance between light and dark, benevolence and malice, peace and war. Vandulin had read the signs. He knew the balance was breaking, and somehow the stars pointed towards that boy, a boy who was born into greatness but was only discovering it now.

The Tree was burning.

Life was aflame.

The Heart of the Enemy

From Lunus, it seemed as if the swamps would go on forever, that is until the stench faltered in its perniciousness, and Cassius knew somehow that the end was near. It was silent now. There was nothing, save for the odd and prosaic line of questions and answers between the three of them, and so they travelled the vast lonely land that stretched out for miles upon miles as if they were ants crossing the sea of a giant's stomach. As darkness defeated the grey sky, the fog rolled in from above and slept across the green blanket of the bog. Cassius could tell that Vandulin was something powerful, but even he seemed to be wary of what came once darkness fell, and he did not wish to be here when it did. Sathelia had seen what the shadows possessed and feared it too, but also respected the dangers of this land, for there were many, and Cassius had still yet to taste what Medearia really held in its heart. However, Cassius, sooner or later, would have to sink his teeth into its heart, whether he liked it or not; the choice was no longer up to him.

They veered their mounts northeast, hugging the region where Vandulin knew the forest would once again appear. Cassius doubted that. Everywhere he looked, he could see nothing but a flat and lifeless world that was sick with the grotesque life forms of the bog's ecosystem. Larvae from insects squirmed, hatched, and swam through the murky water like schools of fish but would often get caught in webs of algae or other sickly subjects of this ailing part of the world. It was the scab of Medearia, seemingly ruled by some god who dictated the seasons of plagues and plight.

"So how did you find me? asked Cassius.

Vandulin slowed his Tiethedon so that he rode at the pace of the boy. "I did not find you. I simply knew that you would be coming to this land, and I spoke to a friend of mine."

"Oh yeah? Which friend?"

"You have already meant him, although you have yet to be formally introduced."

"Who?"

"He is Ruedenhiem, lord of the woods of Cassemor, and he has been my closest friend for a lifetime and more."

"Ruedenhiem? Where is he? How foolish could I have been! Is he all right?" roared Sathelia, suddenly piecing together more fragments of her memory of the night she fell.

"He is fine. He knows how to take care of himself, Sathelia," said Vandulin.

"Trust me, I know."

"So that light . . . that was . . . your friend? A deer?" The two elves stopped immediately. Cassius could smell the disdain and horror coming from them.

"He is no deer! Have some respect, human!"

"Sathelia, that is enough!" said Vandulin, and his words were calm and yet terrifying, as if each word was soaked in fire. They were all motionless now, stopping to let the night creep up on them. "You will show more respect to him from here on out. I will hear no more

debate." And Cassius could see flares of anger in the Sage's expression, and to his amazement, his once melancholic grey eyes now sparked and were ignited to the colour of fire. A drop of his power. Cassius knew not to piss him off now.

"I'm sorry, Sage of the West. I have left the path of starlight, but I shall journey back to it," said Sathelia, and her eyes were not brave enough to meet the likes of his, and her voice stooped low and sounded sullen yet also obedient. However, her obedience was the work of tradition; it was the words of her people, it was their way. The path of the stars could not be left, and those who did would be forced east, into the lands where the stars dared not wander.

"Good. Now, as difficult as this may be for you to understand, Cassius, I am not your enemy," said Vandulin, stirring his mount and continuing the journey. "Do you know what it is I do?" asked Vandulin, but he knew what the prince's answer would be.

Cassius was stuck. He did not know what to feel: whether to be scared or inspired, whether to run back and find the company and surely die in the process or follow the path that was rolled out before him. He would listen, and he would try to understand. Listening to Cassius's silence told the Sage enough, and simply solidified what he already knew. "I cannot tell you all, for human life is sadly short. But I can tell you that the stars speak to those who can read them, and it is my sole purpose to read and glimpse what fate lets me see of it. Do you remember what I showed you up north?" Cassius thought hard for a moment, but then the dream slowly began to tumble into the forefront of his mind.

"Yes. You showed me . . . fire and blood. Despair and hate," said Cassius, trembling slightly at even the thought of what he had seen that night.

"That is what the stars have shown me as well. That is what the stars say is to come, and it is my purpose to keep that from happening."

"And how do you intend on doing that?" asked Cassius.

"You."

"Me?"

"Yes. The details of star reading are complex, and my vision of the future is limited by what I am allowed to see, but once I have seen it, I, and only I, can change it, and it starts with you, Cassius. You were destined to come here. It was the work of the stars that you fell into that pit, and thus a future king of Ederia was faced with the one who is to be queen of Medearia. Two halves can be reunited, and it starts with you two."

"But why me?" asked Cassius.

"That is something you will have to show me," said Vandulin, and suddenly Cassius saw the face of his father in something so alien and strange. He saw friendship, and even love in those he had been taught to call enemies.

"I do not doubt you, but *if* you are right, what is the next move, and how will my father ever tolerate a human in his presence?" asked Sathelia.

"He will have to. Even the kings and queens of Medearia must honour the words of the sages, for my words are the thoughts of the stars, and the stars are the children of the Ecaval."

The trees of the neighbouring woods slid further into view. They were shy and short in appearance at first, but as their path leaned further north, the sludgy mess of the mires became scarcer; mud and water turned into dirt and pines. The Tiethedons would go no further. Their land had ended at the borders of the woods, and thus the three travellers were forced to dismount. The hard, pine-covered floors of the woods felt strange to Cassius; he had grown used to the gut-wrenching soft textures of the bogs, but change greeted him kindly. Sathelia stepped out into the rain of the falling pine needles, catching them as they fell.

She was alive. She was coming home now, and she danced under the forest's eyes with glee in her smile and eagerness in her feet. She was *eager* to be home, to see the loved ones of her life once more, a life she stupidly threw away and paid the price for it. She let out a long whistle that sprinted through the forest floor, weaving through the underbrush in a solemn pursuit to find what the princess sought—her companion.

There was a long stillness, and then Vandulin was eager to move—they could not camp here, not this close to the swamps. Then he came. Strutting through the forest with the walk of a king came Ruedenhiem. His eyes sparkled with joy as he saw the princess, and Sathelia's did just the same. The two embraced, and Sathelia once again mounted her loyal steed, one that was lost without her.

"Do we get one of those?" asked Cassius.

"No," said Vandulin plainly. "You shall ride with Sathelia. I have my own." And the Sage walked over to a tree and placed his palm on its scaly hide, whispering something to it. There was silence. Then, there was a faint tremor, like a distant whisper from below the earth. A roar came from the deep depths of the forest, one that tore Cassius open from his ribs and into his lungs, taking his breath away. Movement could be heard. Bushes and branches cracked.

She had arrived.

Cassius heard the blood-bending snarls and growls of a predator from behind him, ready to kill. He could not move. His body failed him. And then there was nothing. Cassius turned around to see the Sage riding atop a panther. She was as large and as black as the night sky

"Zora can bear only one, for she will only grant the privilege of riding her *to* one, and it is a bond for life," said Vandulin, and so Cassius approached the stag instead. Sathelia did not give a glance to the human below her. It felt wrong, keeping company and being friendly to something that was the enemy. But if she was being honest with herself, she felt more genuine intrigue toward the boy than hatred. Afterall, the majority of elvish hostility towards humans was the result of history books and stories. Most elves were simply too young to have lived through the genocide of their people. She had no personal reason to have disdain for him; no human had ever wronged her. But her father, *that* was different. Humanity *had* wronged him. Although Sathelia always believed that people are defined by the present and not by the past. Her father always told stories of the days before the genocide, when humans and elves lived together. But those stories were followed by ones of blood and suffering, so the idea of conversing with a human seemed to break every social law she knew. However, the Sage's words were like a king's. Whatever he said, it had to go, and they lived by this law. It was the way, regardless of whether one felt it to be the wrong one.

To Cassius, this was a royal chariot. He could have been at the rear end of a donkey for all he cared. It didn't matter, as long as he was close to her. He felt some sort of attraction. It was unexplainable and a feeling that was quite absent when he was around any other woman but her. The three of them rode the path that would lead them back to Elsibard, and they did so even as night was upon them, but soon after, they halted and left the trail to set up camp. Cassius was silent and kept to himself once their camp was assembled. He would try to escape once the two of them were asleep. He still couldn't trust them, no matter what they spoke of and what delusions they sickened his mind with. He had to get back to the company. And so, he leaned up against a cozy pine tree, watching and waiting for the right moment to run.

Cassius tensed his muscles, ready for movement, yet still, he feigned his sleep. His eyes were closed, however he was sure that the two elves were asleep, and if there was to be a time in which he could flee, it was now or never. Slowly he turned to his side and curled his legs up before rolling onto his knees, and he could hear the leaves below him crack and pop where his legs were pinning them to the ground. The silence was broken, and Cassius froze. He listened for a moment, waiting for one of them to wake, to hear the sounds of footsteps coming from behind. There was nothing. And so, Cassius resumed his surreptitious crawl to his gear that he had packed before he slept, but his movement was halted by the instant touch of a naked blade on his throat, something he was growing far too used to.

"Going somewhere?" asked Sathelia from behind, holding a knife to the boy's throat. She was quick, and Cassius hadn't heard a thing, not even the crackling pops of dead holly on the forest floor. Before Cassius could reply, Sathelia flicked the blade away, sheathed it, and then sat down beside the prince.

"So, am I your prisoner?" asked Cassius.

"No. The opposite. It's not wise to wander these woods in the darkness, so consider yourself lucky that I stopped you," she said.

"Well, I'm absolutely overwhelmed with gratitude!"

"Spare me from your sarcasm, human."

"I *have* a name," said Cassius, staring out into the woods, wondering just where the company was and how they were faring in their journey.

"Fine then. Let me be clear, Cassius, if the Sage has contacted you, you cannot ignore it, or else."

"Or else what?"

"Misfortunes find us. But for some reason, and one that I cannot see, Vandulin believes you are the missing piece that is needed."

"What do you mean, 'missing piece'?"

"I mean that you are of value to him."

"Why?"

"That is a question for him, not me."

"What is he, really?"

"Only the sages could give the answer in full, for I do not know everything. However, *I do know* that there were once many, and now there are only two—no one knows what happened to the others. Each sage has some form of connection to the earth and to the stars, and they assist this world along the path of peace, with doom below us on each side. They can peer into all possibilities of our future by reading the stars above, and they manipulate events or forge them so that our future stays bright. Think of it like this: the world is fueled by the constant balance of good and evil, and it is the sage's duty to maintain that balance."

"I see. Will I be able to see my friends again?"

"That depends. It is odd for the enemy to be landing on our shores right before my father plans to kill you off. So, what are you doing here, Prince Cassius?" she asked with a playful nod of fictitious respect. Cassius thought for a moment. He could certainly not tell the elf of his purpose here, but he doubted his capability to lie to someone as sharp as this, and so the words climbed off of his tongue on their own and without waiting for logic to touch them.

"Do you really think that while Medearia has watched us from afar that we have not kept a close eye on you?"

"Impossible. We would have known," said Sathelia, leaning back on her hands as if she was struck by the boy's words.

"But . . . you didn't," said Cassius, and he could not hide the smirk on his lips. That was good. He was learning to lie. "We come with peace offerings from my father and all of Ederia."

"Well, Cassius, you seem to have grown a little more interesting. You should speak to my father then. But you shall have to be masked. Vandulin will not be there to protect you from my people, and especially my father. It'll only be me."

"What? Where is he?"

"Gone. He is a sage. They do as they must, and it is not our place to ask. Get some sleep, and do me a favour: do not die tomorrow."

"No promises," said Cassius, and he leaned back against the sleeping pine tree and slept deeply for the first time since Ekmere, something that felt like a century ago by now, memories of memories. He dreamed of home and of his former self—a prince who looked to be no more than a stranger to Cassius now. He was different, and he was beginning to grasp the answer to his father's question: Why should he be king?

It would take a lifetime to find the answer to that question if he remained at Ekmere, and he would be crippled by age before he became the man he could be. But fate chose differently for Cassius. He could now touch the answer, even hold it, but not look inside.

※

When the sun sprinkled its light atop the forest, Cassius and Sathelia rode with it, and it wasn't until the sun began its descent that Elsibard was nearby. They travelled across a plateau of deep woodlands and numerous lazy rivers that would lead them down into the valley of Utherious where Elsibard awaited them.

Cassius ran his hand through the inside of his satchel, looking for any snacks to satisfy his hunger. He found an apple; part of it was bruised and so he spun it to reveal the shiny red face, one that was torn off and destroyed by his teeth.

"What is that?" asked Sathelia.

"What?" replied Cassius with pieces of half-eaten fruit dancing around his gums.

"That, right there. The thing you're holding in your hand."

"An apple?"

"Apple," said Sathelia to herself. "I'm not familiar with it."

"Are you serious? You don't have things like this here?"

"No," replied the princess.

"Oranges?"

"No."

"Pears?"

"No."

"Do you people even eat food here?"

"We do," said Sathelia, not picking up on the obvious sarcasm in Cassius's voice, "but I doubt there are words for them in your tongue. Look, we shall pick from this tree here." Sathelia said no words of direction, nor did she steer Ruedenhiem by any form of reins; he understood them and what their desires were. They approached the tree, one that looked somewhat familiar to Cassius, however the fruit it bore he had not seen. They rode under a hanging branch that spied on them from above, and Sathelia picked a fruit that appeared the ripest. "Here, I'll take the first bite, and then you can try."

"There's no way I'm even touching that thing!"

"Oh please, don't be craven," said Sathelia, rolling her eyes. "If you act this way in front of my father, I doubt he'll settle for any form of peace. You must have confidence."

"Fine! I'll try it!" said Cassius, grabbing the strange fruit and sinking his teeth into its purple hide.

He let the taste sink in. He savoured it. And soon his taste buds kicked in and scolded him for so being hesitant in trying something this amazing. "Holy shit . . . remind me to never mistrust your taste in food."

"Do you like it?"

"I love it," said Cassius, and he caught the elf shedding a smile in her mirth, one that glimmered in the sunlight.

Ruedenhiem rode back to the tree, and the two harvested all that they could. "What are these called?"

"In our tongue, the word is '*Hists.*' It is said that they can cleanse the soul and return it back to the path of the stars."

"Well, I'm not feeling too cleansed, but if I feel anything, I'll let you know," said Cassius.

They rode in rather comfortable silence from then on, and they watched the sun climb down, reluctant to deprive the world of its light, but just before it hid away behind Mount Mordthand, it shone upon the city of Elsibard, and Cassius—one who believed he knew what large and beautifully crafted cities looked like—was introduced to a new kind of architectural beauty and innovation. Even from the plateau on which they stood, he could see the diversity of cultures in its streets. It seemed endless. Even its poorest of areas were still encased by towering stone walls and smooth parapets that glided along the city's borders.

Sathelia caught the boy in his state of shock and decided to pick up the pace, breaking his ataraxy and amazement as their mount climbed down the crag and down onto the path that would lead them into the valley.

＊

Ivan's shirt beneath his leather jerkin was nothing more than shredded pieces of cloth, hanging by stubborn threads of fabric. His skin was scarred already, and so when the whip came down, it bled easily, and thick red streams ran down the muscular arches of his back. They were all in this state.

The company was breaking.

None could speak, for a whip on their already opened flesh would be their punishment. Wraithenor led them up the mountain pass, but they were yet to begin the real climb. Their captors had chained their human prisoners and forced them into a single-file line with each man chained to the other, and thus this made for slow progress, and the touch of a whip was the cure for anything in the eyes of the elves.

"Blackwood?" whispered Ivan, and as he spoke, his gums ached, and blood trickled down from his molars. "Blackwood?" said Ivan once more, but again, there was no answer from the knight, and instead the tail end of a whip gave its reply. Ivan winced. He knew pain and what it could truly amount to and how much despair it was capable of summoning within a man, thus he knew he could endure, but, strangely, he thought of Cassius and where he could be. At first, the prince was nothing more than a weight on his shoulders, one that he had expected he'd be forced to hold up on his own, but he found himself actually caring for the boy, and this sudden emotion and worry sparked in his heart the gears of hope.

The ground began to slant, and small pieces of rubble ran down the mountainside as the wind howled through the pass. Ivan's wrists had already begun to bleed where the shackles were, and each twist, writhe, and turn burned at his flesh, tearing at any vestige of leftover skin.

The elves spoke their own language, but Ivan was capable of grasping a few words, and so he listened to everything and anything. "The Pits" was something that came up a lot, and he knew just what that meant: they would be forced to fight in the Pits of Utherious. The chance was small of them making it out alive, but death was something that had followed them ever since they'd left Ekmere. He knew that each of them was capable in a fight, but these were trained elvish pit fighters, and in the state they were in now, Ivan wondered if he could even ponder the thought of grasping a sword hilt. The style was different than the Ederian knight, the stances, the grips; if any member of the company aside from Ivan stepped into that arena, it'd be like fighting blind. He'd taught himself the basics of the Medearian techniques, but he was still a novice.

If fate were feeling merciful, they'd have time to rest before the fighting began, but that was something only a fool could count on. And then the question froze his thoughts and gripped them like a vice—*where was Cassius?*

He had built some sense since they found him up north, but common sense would not be enough for a single night alone here.

Ivan felt the first kisses of snowflakes on his cheek as they travelled up the rocky slope that hugged against the sheer cliff. Small clusters of juniper berries were scattered below his knees, and they made him think of home, of the days he wandered as a free man, studying the world as he rode upon its wave. These were good times, but they were gone now. Instead, they walked under a grey dome: sunless and deprived of life, and each sweet juniper was bathed in the trickling strings of his blood.

A storm was coming. However, this storm was without clouds, without thunder, and without rain. This was a storm of war, and the drums rumbled in the roots of the mountain. Ivan closed his eyes and thought of *his* plan. It was one that he had not shared with anyone aside from Connell and Azrad, but when the time came for the gears to turn, he only hoped that the others would follow, and if the knight resisted—even though he did not wish for this to happen—he was prepared to do what was necessary.

All the nights of preparation would pay off if he kept his cards close . . . very close. The boy could not know until it was too late, although he too might prove to be . . . problematic.

Cards were close.

Eyes darting to each foe.

Ivan's plans looked to be unfolding, and the Pits were all that was left before the second to final stage of the plan—the death of a king.

The King of Medearia

B alls of sweat hung by the strings of hair above Cassius's lips, and
he could feel the culmination of sweat begin to allow his mask
to slide up and down his face. His heart thumped obnoxiously, not
allowing any calming thought to take control.

Lub. Lub, dub. The drums of his heart continued in their song,
and Cassius fiddled with his leather pants, tugging at them and
forcing them into folds and stretching them until he realized how
abnormal he looked. He was not nervous, he was terrified.

Sathelia walked with him, and both of them were cloaked in
black, keeping their identities hidden in the streets of Elsibard.
Just as the moon elves had, the high elves of this city could smell
Cassius's human stench, one that curdled their blood in disgust,
and he had caught many of them avoiding his path out of respect
for their own sense of smell. He would not have made it a foot into
these walls without the mask that Vandulin had left behind before
he left, but even then, he kept his sword arm ready for anything.

However, Sathelia seemed confident, yet also eager to see her father. If only Cassius could say the same.

As of now, the doors stood before them. To her, they were home, a pillar of safety and a sign of her place in this world. Cassius could not have felt any different: to him, it was more than just a door, it was an eye. An eye that knew something, knew every secret Cassius had ever kept. It stripped him naked and forced him under its cleansing light. But it was also something else, it was proof. Proof that he, as a man, was capable, and once he entered those doors, he would deal with whatever awaited him as a *man*.

If only father could see me now, thought Cassius.

"Come, you'll be fine," whispered Sathelia. "Just stay close and keep your tongue still; if they hear you speak, they'll *know*."

Cassius gulped and let Sathelia approach the guards at the door. One of the guardsmen raised their arm to signal the two travellers to halt, but Sathelia was born with boldness and temerity in her, and so she ignored the guard's warning, and her eyes were fixated on the door. Swords were drawn. Cassius gripped the pommel of his sword, but Sathelia's hand shot across him like a streak of a spider's silk, blocking any attempt of a draw.

"*State your business and show your face, stranger!*" Sathelia looked up at the two guards, striking them down with her burning eyes that impaled each of them with a spike of sublime beauty. She then lifted her cloak, revealing the unnatural allure of her hair, but the face was undeniable. But still, the sight was unbelievable. Cassius was too busy looking at his companion to notice the guards dropping their swords.

"It—it cannot be . . ."

"But it *is*, and you both stand in my way. I'm sure my father would not wish to hear that two of his most treasured protectors tried to protect him from his own daughter." Fear throttled the guardsmen's throats like an eagle's talons around its prey, and the guards leaped to attention and turned to the door to open it for their princess.

"With respect, your highness, who might your companion be?"

"*A companion,* and that is already more than you deserve to know."

"Yes! Yes, of course, your highness, my apologies."

The door opened, and the halls of Elsibard posed glamorously before Cassius. A long blue carpet ran down the main hall, and it hugged against the calm and serene ebony marble floors that were broken up with veins of silver and gold. The air was cool and soaked with elvish pride and arrogance, and a chandelier loomed above in an arch of starlike diamonds that danced in their flight. Halfway down the hall, the ground met a small staircase that climbed upwards. Cassius's eyes followed the staircase until he saw *him.* Down at the end, he saw him, the king; he did not sit at his throne, but the blinding sparkles of his crown shot out in every direction, and Cassius could feel it and see it in him: the walk, the stances, and the unchanging look of superiority on his face—they were those of a king. Cassius supposed he recognized these traits purely from being his father's son. As Sathelia walked, the crowds divided and split away from her as if her presence was a thread of lightning splitting up the night sky. Most did not recognize her, and those who thought they did quickly shunned the thought of it truly being her. Rich and haughty aristocrats stagnated their long and drawn-out palaver and eyed up the newcomers. Cassius eyed them also, studying each face, taking in what he could. The palace reminded him of home, and he could see himself and Vidicus playing by the feet of the throne and mother and father watching them in delight. Even here he received crooked glances of disdain and annoyance.

It became all too much so suddenly. The glacier feel of the air, the catlike eyes of those around him, and most of all, there was *him*—Estideel.

He was a target.

He was a calculated threat that hid from view, ready to pounce on his prey, and he was the instrument of Cassius's journey, and in some ways, his vindication of his soul. Spiders began to weave their webs of hysteria in the prince's mind, clouding judgment and distorting the room.

Lub. Lub, dub. Again, Cassius's heart pumped, telling him he needed to leave, that he needed to go home, and he needed to see his family again. The lights. The dresses. And the all-consuming notion of the unknown and questions left unanswered swung around the plains of his sanity like children resisting the call for sleep. For the first time, he felt a burning sensation on his neck that formed in an ideogramic shape, as if he was branded by the iron of an artist. His hand grabbed the back of his neck, but it was no use . . . the heat grew and grew until he winced under his mask. Visions of Vandulin fluttered in the back of his mind, and the word "mutiny" rang like bells under his skull. His jaw clenched and locked together, and Cassius felt his feet catch on a dress, and before his body could even land, he knew it would be over, his journey was at an end, and the foreboding moments before it were mockery from the foul mouth of fate.

He landed. There was silence, but nothing that appeared scornful or malicious. The prince stood up, brushing himself off and peering across the room for any insulting outbursts of mirth and laughter. He blushed, but then noticed that Sathelia's hand was tight around his left wrist and that each elf was now speechless upon seeing what stood before them. Cassius looked down towards his knees and saw the scattered remnants of his mask.

Cassius turned only to see the observing crowd leap back in fear. "What is it?" said some.

"It's—I can't believe it," said another with disgust.

"But *I can*," said a voice from behind the prince; it was soft and melancholic but deep and harmonious. Cassius turned to meet the owner of such a voice, and within inches of him stood the king. Cassius's heart jumped into his throat, blocking any whisper of a fright. "I see a lost boy who seems to be quite far from home," said Estideel, and the crowd fell silent. "So, how do you wish to die? With honour, or without pain?" Still, the prince's words were stubborn and would not spill out. "Well then, I see no reason why this cannot be painful—"

"Because you'll have to deal with *me* after." Estideel shifted his gaze from the boy to the woman behind him, and what once was a cold and hardened evil in his intentions was thawed. Estideel's eyes flooded. It was her.

"What illusions jest before me?"

Sathelia smiled, tilted her head, and let her happiness take her. "No illusions, father, it is me." Estideel bothered not with words and instead embraced his daughter, feeling the euphoria inside her and quenching the evil that blackened his heart.

"I . . . I thought I lost you, but my heart never forgot its love for what I held dearest, and holding it now in my arms—" Estideel's voice was strangled by the hands of tears and fell into hushed whispers. "Get out," commanded the king, regaining his power in his voice, and those around them fled to where they belonged. Estideel held Sathelia's hands in his and kissed them briefly. "I have something for you. Come!" said Estideel, and the two of them, overtaken by the reigns of their joy, left Cassius behind. The hall was empty. The prince was alone.

"It is almost time," said Vandulin from the shadows.

Cassius turned, frightened but also intrigued. "Time for what?"

"Your training," said the Sage, leaning away from the dark corner and walking towards the back of the prince. "How is your mark progressing?"

"What mark?"

"Your neck."

"There is no mark on my neck."

"Oh, but there is. I'm looking at it as we speak."

"The burning," said Cassius to himself.

"Yes, the burning. It is the Mark of the Sage."

"Start making sense, and what fucking training are you talking about?"

"The training to be a sage, of course. You cannot avoid fate, Cassius."

"Here you are again, talking about *fate! Fuck fate!* What is it, huh? What do you want from me?"

"I want you to end what is coming," Vandulin said, and his expression grew cold momentarily. "It is your purpose to cure a world that is sick, sick with blood and violence; you have seen these things!"

"But I do not understand how or even why something like that falls to me." Vandulin stepped closer to the boy.

"You want to know why your purpose is such? You expect a simple and complete answer, but in this search for self-reassurance, you have already found it—it lies in your actions."

"My actions?"

"Cassius, I read the stars, I do not command them, and so I cannot tell you why you must carry this weight, but I *can* tell you that great actions are a symptom of great aspirations. You have already proven yourself capable of being a king, just look at what you have accomplished trying to find that out. Keep faith in yourself, Prince Cassius. Keep faith and may starlight stalk your steps."

The elf turned into the shadow . . . and he was gone, as if he was nothing more than a mirage or a gust of wind on a calm autumn morning.

"Cassius," said Sathelia, and she wore a necklace around her neck, one that the prince had not seen before. "My father wishes to speak with you. I do not *think* he will kill you. I have told him about the Sage and your purpose here." Yes, the *purpose*, one that was becoming more and more difficult to see.

✳

"You think I did not know that there were . . . *humans* crawling around my shores?" asked Estideel. His expression was plain, and the light of the fire painted his face in shadow and the deep red hues of the flames magnified the deep lines in his face. His hair was long, but it was a shade between white and blonde, one that Cassius could not place in his mind just now. "Well?"

"Of course not," said Cassius, trying to hide his obvious gulp and lack of confidence.

"Your father is bold sending his first son for—what was it you said? Peace treaties?" asked Estideel, and he laughed to himself.

"He is bold, my liege. In fact, he is quite similar to you."

"So, you have come here to insult me?"

"Never," Cassius said, wishing Sathelia were there with him to guide him through the series of her father's threatening inquiries. "Ederia is the strongest it has ever been, and it is led by a cunning man. My father knows that there shall be a needless slaughter, and, if I may presume, I think you know that as well; any conflict that you pursue will result in the death of thousands of men and elves."

"All wars require blood."

"And there have been many wars that could have been avoided."

"Not this one. This is inevitable."

"I know you have grown a hatred for my kind, and I know the things that we have done—"

"*YOU KNOW NOTHING OF WHAT YOUR KIND HAS DONE!*" roared the king, standing up and rushing the prince, towering over him and allowing his face to wrinkle and curl like a viper ready to strike. He was old, not as old as Vandulin, but old enough to know the pain of the past, that much was certain. Cassius held his courage. He was poised now, months older but with years' worth of wisdom. Estideel soon settled down, and his lifeless expression returned as he sat back down in his chair. "There are more of you. As we speak, they are on their way to Elsibard."

"They are?"

"Yes. I assume they came with you on this journey?"

"They share my goals, yes."

"Unfortunately for you, I believe you shall fail in your goals, although they are brave."

"We shall see."

"But I have already seen," said Estideel, and the glimmer of his eyes sent a shiver down Cassius's spine. "So, Sathelia tells me that you carry some significance to the Sage."

"From what he tells me, yes."

"I'd be wary of him if I were you."

"I am wary of everything in this land."

"I see you have your father's wit." The king laughed. "Follow the Sage's words. They are what keep our people alive, *but* . . . he will do anything to assure that we remain so."

The room fell quiet for a moment, and the two let the fire choke and spit out shards of wasted embers in the melodious agony of its death. Shadows folded and jumped sporadically in the background, and the king attempted to speak, but his thoughts were carried to Sathelia as she walked through the door, adorned by new and clean clothes that were without rips. Cassius turned to look; it was impossible not to blush. Her dress matched her eyes, and as she entered the room she spun and pinched out a small smile and a laugh. Again, all the bitterness and malice that Cassius saw in her father was immediately gone now, and his face went soft like a cold meadow warming to the rise of the sun.

"Father?"

"Yes?"

"Can Cassius accompany us on our walk? I'd love for him to see the gardens and the flowers in bloom."

"Sathelia, you have only just arrived, do you not wish to rest first? *And*," said Estideel, turning towards Cassius, "he might be our guest, but he is not a welcomed one."

"Father, he has travelled much further than I have, if anyone is due with some rest, it is him," said Sathelia, turning to him, and

Cassius now noticed no disdain or disgust in her eyes when she looked at him.

"No. No, I'm fine. I'd like to see the gardens, if that's all right?" Estideel gave a reluctant nod, and he let his daughter take the lead, but as Cassius passed the king, he grabbed the boy's wrist and pulled him close.

"Just because you have won her trust does not mean you will ever win mine. For all I know, you could be quite the threat," whispered Estideel.

"Why would he send his son to get his hands dirty?"

"I seem to recall you having a brother, and from what I have heard, he is far more capable of being a king than yourself, is he not?"

"Guess we'll never know."

"It appears not, but appearances are often deceiving."

The dark sky above felt like an ocean with stars creating ripples of light. The three walked with each other down into the courtyard that stood in the center of the palace. Exotic leaves and flowers leaned over to watch those who passed, and there were large insects that seemed like fireflies at first to Cassius, but as he drew closer to where they flew, he saw that they had bodies more similar to those of small lizards, with bioluminescent wings that spun in circles, creating a dance that consisted of spins and twirls until they reached high enough. Cassius approached three that took refuge near a fountain, and as he reached out to touch one, they sprang open their wings and twirled into the sky, and flashes of pink and yellow pulsed through the darkness above. Sathelia looked over at the boy and smiled at the sight of his innocent wonder.

"To be forward, my daughter, I have many questions," said Estideel.

"I'm sure you do." Sathelia laughed. "Although I was not sure of what had happened to me until the Sage explained it, he said that I encountered a wraith, one that took a part of my vitality."

"A wight . . ."

"You think?"

"There are few creatures in those swamps that could have done such a thing—it was a wight. But tell me more of Vandulin"

"You still do not trust him, do you?"

"If you knew what I knew, you'd not trust him either."

"He was there when I awoke, and from what I can tell, he had followed Cassius into the cave in which I fell."

"How did the boy end up in such a place and so far from his own kind?"

"Ruedenhiem led him," said Sathelia.

"I would like to speak with Vandulin . . . alone."

"About what?"

"About *him*," said Estideel, looking over towards where Cassius walked alone.

The prince was far too busy looking at the world around him, studying each branch and leaf, feeling the texture of it all and the smells they gave off. By the end, his hands were covered in layers of what he thought was sap, and he washed it off in one of the garden pools, but as his hands sank into the water, the colour changed: clouds of bright blue light seeped away from where his hands were until the entire pool was one singular body of bioluminescence. He laughed in shock, then drew his hands out and was surprised to see that they were still there and fully intact.

"I could show you so much more," said Sathelia. Cassius turned to see her and felt his stomach simultaneously twist like a fragile thread of string. "There is a place that I always used to visit before when . . . well . . . when I felt overwhelmed, which is something I bet you might be feeling. Would you like to go there in the morning?"

Cassius peered deep into her eyes, and he could feel the tenderness of her soul touching his. Her eyes did the same. Sathelia looked deep into Cassius's sky-blue eyes and no longer was able to feel any hate towards him, and if she tried, it simply felt unnatural. "Yeah. Yeah, I'd love to see this place," said Cassius.

Sathelia smiled briefly before waving her hands through the bushes to the right of the fountain, and more flocks and colonies of insects and animals sprang into life, conjuring their colourful coats before the two of them. Estideel watched his daughter stand side-by-side with the enemy; he hoped her ignorance of human nature would not break her, but he knew hope was a fool's talisman and that one day she would be forced to know first-hand the atrocities that humanity was capable of.

He will only fail you, my daughter. He will only fail you.

The Pits of Utherious

The company looked up in horror at the nearly lifeless body of Sir Hadrian. His hands were tied to two posts, and the rest of his body hung with his feet barely touching the ground. Beneath was an aged pool of dried blood, piss, and shit, and the fetid smells of their misery strangled them as they awoke. The sun had risen now, and even Mitsunari would not attend his usual meditation. They were convinced. Today was the day they died. They hardly had the strength to fight, and if Sir Hadrian was forced to walk, he might never walk again. The company hardly spoke, and when they did, it was never things of joy and hope—*hope* died on the beach. The five of them had been split into three cages that lay underneath the city, and they could feel the thumping heart of it above; it was alive and knowingly let them suffer in this poisoned realm they called home. Victims of the most recent pit fights would be dragged along the circular prison halls, leaving trails of blood behind them that served as a warning for the other prisoners . . . and then came the *screaming*. When a pit fighter survived, they were killed elsewhere. No one knew where this place was, but based on the sickening cries that they would hear they knew it was further below them. Ivan had once thought that they could escape this way. Maybe by himself, but not with the others, although he could not leave them behind. He had known Azrad and Connell before this, but they hadn't yet been like family, thus what had once been a collection of strangers sharing an unfocused goal was now a band of brothers. But now they saw only death . . . *and it saw them too.*

Azrad shuffled along the stone floor, scraping his ass and legs, and breaking the scabs that were already there. He signalled Mitsunari for water by putting his hands out and pretending to drink. Mitsunari found himself stuck for a moment, stuck in a field of thought. He thought of home. He thought of rich cherry fields that sprawled onward as far as the eye can see, and when the wind ran through, the holy smells of spring and summer became living things that solely existed in his own solitary senses.

"Hey," said Azrad, and his voice was strained, as if the linings of his throat were coated with barnacles that bit out and chipped away at him from inside. Mitsunari fell away from his happy place and back to the world. He checked for water. There was none, and he could see that Azrad's face sharpened with anger.

Oh, he's lying, all right, that much I know. That dirty fucking Sarakotan! After this is all over, I'll drain him clean of whatever blood he's got left and see how much water he's got stored up for real, thought Azrad, although he meant none of it . . . Hunger and thirst could change the way a man thought and perceived the world around him. Anyone not a friend was an enemy. If he does not carry food, he *becomes* the food. Lo, misery could make a man do things he only dreamt of, but once he has done the unspeakable, he realizes that he has followed the teachings of a nightmare.

Azrad felt the touch of a hand on his shoulder, and he quickly turned around to see Connell. In his hand he held a bowl that had been collecting rainwater that trickled down the stone walls of the area. There were likely three days' worth of rainwater in there, but even that was no more than a few sips.

"Thank you," said Azrad, and he quickly gulped down what he could, leaving the last sip for any who needed it, however, in truth, he still needed it, but these were his brothers. If one suffered, the rest would suffer with him. "How is he? Is he okay?" asked Azrad with droplets of water hanging from his lower lip.

"Blackwood?"

"Yeah."

"How good could he be?" replied Connell.

Azrad thought of a response but was too spent to even manage to hold a conversation. The mountain had been their foe for two days, and once they had conquered it, Sir Hadrian took a turn for the worse. He could still speak but only the basics. Water and food were the only words he needed desperately now. Anything more would be too much for a soul as crippled as his, but it was not broken completely, not yet.

For a moment, they all gathered close to the bars of the cell that circled around the area and let the sun touch their skin in the glorious moments of its ascension. Ivan's hands gripped the rusted iron necks of the bars, twisting with rage and a desire to be free. More sunlight spilt down over the outer lip of the colosseum and into their cells, and it was then that Sir Hadrian opened his eyes, and he too took refuge at this moment, and it felt as if a god had dropped a shard of beauty in a land of pain; it wasn't supposed to be there, but it was. The arena was coated in an ocean of crimson light. Its beauty was unquestioned and so was its undeniable aura of dread. It was the perfect morning for death.

The guards were coming. Ivan could not see them yet, but the soft thumps of their metal boots on the stone floors gave their entrance away. They would not torture them today. No. Today was their day. It was their day to fight and die as the elves of Elsibard looked down upon them without an iota of pity in their screams. The guards needed them strong in order to put on a good show and give the crowd what they came for. As they came into view, Ivan now knew it was the end of the road. He had had hope of their survival before, even flirted with the idea of escaping, but now they walked down the final road with their destination in sight. Death.

One of the guards withdrew a key and unlocked the door while the other pointed a spear towards the prisoners, keeping them at bay and under control. Ivan had seen one of the inmates charge the guards during this process only to see him gutted before them. They left his body there for days, likely as a message, and it was a message that was well understood. Ivan retreated to the opposite side of the cell where he'd be furthest from the guards, but they followed him and cussed and spat at him like he was no more than a stray dog. His hands were shackled, along with his neck, and the two guards ripped him from his cell and led him down the hall. Mitsunari was next. It would be their time soon, their time to be tested.

✳

It had been three days since Cassius had arrived at Elsibard. His identity to most was kept hidden by the mask, and he was only permitted to take it off when he slept or when he and Sathelia would roam the wilderness of the valley. Sometimes, they would go further, but today she would show him the woods of Cassemor. They packed nothing. "The forest will provide," she had said. "But we must go in the evening. I know a place to spend the night, and you may see the full beauty that this land holds."

Cassius did what she said, he packed nothing. They left in the afternoon atop Ruedenhiem, and they did so until dusk was upon them. Ruedenhiem slowed his pace as they began to approach the black border of Cassemor that rose above them, washing away the lingering light of the day. Cassius gulped. "C'mon!" said Sathelia, dismounting in a hurry and trotting over to the edge of the forest where the meadow's grasses stood tall, hiding the lower half of her body.

"Quit panicking, I'm right behind you," said Cassius. She looked up towards the sky and spotted the faint glow of the early stars.

"Actually, we should wait here until the light is fully gone."

"You're joking, right?"

"Have some faith in me, would you?"

"Fine."

They waited in silence, but it was a sort of comfortable silence where their emotions and thoughts were tangible enough so that speaking wasn't necessary. Cassius was in love. *She* may not have been, but *he* certainly was, and it was enough to wipe out every other thought he had until every ponderous moment he had was aimed at her. The throne was forgotten. His addiction was a distant memory. His goal, well, he began to question it entirely. And the company was ancient. *But never forgotten.* When the sky reached its icy black hue, Sathelia stood up from the meadow and looked deep into the woods where the tree branches formed arches to invite them in. They entered. Nothing abnormal happened, and Cassius watched out for anything irregular but hoped he'd see it soon. It was a forest. Nothing special. Cassius opened his mouth to speak, but Sathelia raised a finger to keep him quiet.

"Hush," said Sathelia. She closed her eyes and tilted her head into the gentle breeze that ran through the woods like the breath of a cave. She began to sing, but the words were an ancient form of elvish taught to her by her father. Cassius couldn't help but feel as if she was speaking to someone, and the tone of her voice told him stories of loss and pain. Her voice was the rain that came with the misty dawn, beautiful but without joy. After a minute she stopped, and tears hugged the arches of her cheek as her eyes were left looking like drowned flowers after a storm.

"What's wrong?" asked Cassius.

"Something isn't right," she said, and her voice was faint.

"What is it?"

"I have spoken to the woods. I can hear her calling to me, but her voice is muffled. She is weak."

"She?"

"It doesn't matter, not yet. Let us keep walking. There is a boat we may take."

The breeze from before strengthened and whirled through the forest floor for a moment before leaving them. Cassius took a step forward . . . and the woods of Cassemor came to life. The floor gleamed, flashing exotic greens that the prince had never seen nor comprehended before, and the veins of light ran like rivers. He took two more steps, and with every step came the light.

"Come. Follow me," said Sathelia, and she turned to smile at the boy. The two ran through the forest, and it lit up with every step. Trees and moss shivered with life and entire ecosystems marched through and up in each direction. Flowers sprayed pink dusk that lit up under the moon, and Cassius ran through it all. As they ran together, each worry that weighed them down was left behind. They did not have to have any care for royal expectations, nor of how anyone thought of them. They were free.

Koi fish swam slowly up the sleeping river with jellyfish and turtles who carried marine flowers on their backs. Sathelia found the paddle next to the boat and let Cassius step in first before pushing them off the bank and into the river. When the water was disturbed, it lit up with a series of bright aquatic hues that shot up through the water and touched the world around them. Life was a painter, and Cassius was only being introduced.

"My harp!" said Sathelia, and she pulled her treasure out from under the seat. Her fingers strummed it gently to regain their memory.

Cassius laughed gently to himself. "Of course you can play the harp," muttered the prince.

"What's that mean?"

"Well, it just seems like there's so much you can do . . . and then there's *me*. Only thing I've ever been good at is screwing things up or embarrassing the people around me. In fact, oftentimes both."

Sathelia put the harp down and scooted to the seat nearest to Cassius. "I think there's more to you then you let on," she said.

"Trust me, if there was, you wouldn't be able to get me to shut up about it."

"Maybe there's more to you than even *you* know of."

"I hope so," said Cassius, losing his humorous tone and resting on a cold place in his heart.

"Here, let me teach you," said Sathelia with a smile that cheered Cassius up instantly. She turned and grabbed the harp, presented it to him, and then let him take it. She looked at his grip, sensing how awkward the feel of it was for him. "Just relax! Let it lean on your shoulder, and try strumming," she said. Cassius did just so, and although he was still stiff, he relaxed his shoulders just a little. She leaned forward and touched his fingers, slowly guiding them to the correct strings. A shiver of fear and pure love ran through his body and whipped him to attention. Butterflies flew into a storm of dance in his stomach. She was so close, and he felt almost honoured to be in her presence, to smell her sweet perfume and to feel the warmth of her breath on his skin. Her eyes frightened him with their unexplainable aura that seemed to almost see through him. He gulped, but his anxiety held his throat in its grip. "Just. Like. This," said Sathelia, and as she spoke, his fingers plucked at the strings to play a simple melody. Cassius smiled and practised the tune thrice before handing the harp back over,

"Never played an instrument before—thank you," said Cassius, looking down at his feet awkwardly. But while he looked away, Sathelia's cheeks turned red, and *her* nerves got the better of her, and so she turned away to hide and began to row towards an island that stood at the widest point in the river. A large tree took up most of the island's diameter, and its twisted, hollow body rose up and curled over them with a green aura emanating from its boughs like chandeliers. The current of the river was slow but swift enough so that little rowing was needed for them to reach the shore, and once they did, Sathelia was the first to get out, and she sank her bare feet down into the smooth pebbles like she had done a hundred times before, but this was different. She was not alone now. She came here to break free from the world and be left alone, but now, she supposed, she came to break free with Cassius. There was certainly more to him than he knew—traits of bravery and perseverance that he was only just discovering. Sathelia liked that about him; he wasn't overly arrogant like the other men she had met before, he was humble. But there was a mysterious melancholy within him, a sadness that dictated every thought and action he had. Sathelia had seen this in her father before but couldn't see why someone like Cassius would possess it.

"Where to now?"

"Follow me," Sathelia said. Cassius followed her lead, and they entered through an opening in the tree. It was hollowed out, and Cassius expected for it to be earthy and wild, but it was . . . a bedroom, and a large one at that.

"This is where I used to go when I felt overwhelmed with every-thing," she said.

"Everything?"

"All the responsibilities, you know. And that constant foreboding knowledge of royal expectations. And that haughty mask that I'm forced to wear wherever I go can drain the soul."

"I hear you. I do, really," said Cassius. "You're lucky, though. I never had a place like this where I could just unwind. That's what the bottle was for."

"The bottle?"

"Drinking. That's the friend I always turned to, and it wasn't long ago when I thought that I could depend on such a friend, but such a friend only proved to be a debt." Sathelia looked at him with wonder, and the answer to her question came to her. She tried to hide it, but her look said it all.

So that is where your sadness comes from, thought Sathelia. *But not all of it.* "Would you like to sit?" she asked.

"That'd be nice."

Without a command, the roots of the tree reached out and formed the shape of a chair for Cassius to sit.

"H-how did you do that?"

"The Sage spoke to you about the Tree, yes?"

"He did."

"It is what gives this world life, but it also can grant us abilities. Areas that are closest to its roots hold power, and we elves can harness this power, but only momentarily. However, the sages are the wardens of the Tree, and they may harness this power when they please."

"It's insane to think Ederia has lived for so long without any knowledge of what goes on here."

"It's insane to think that a human is not as evil as I was told you'd be."

"Can I ask you something?"

"You may."

"How did you end up in that cave?"

Sathelia hesitated, lost in the events of the night she fell and what she had seen. And then finally, with reluctance, she spoke. "I was looking for my mother. You see, she had died not long before, but we did not know why. My father thinks it was suicide, but a part of me wanted to believe that she was still out there, and that is when I made my way to the swamps, and *that* is when I fell. Foolish, I know."

"Sometimes foolery can make us do things we never thought we were capable of. It was a foolish thing for me to come here, but I did."

"And why did you? I know you have come here to suggest peace, but why did you really choose to come?" asked Sathelia, and the question almost startled him. She was quick. His thoughts seemed to almost belong to her as well. And she too had lost her mother. *She seems to know my pain*, thought Cassius.

"To prove something. To prove something to my father, to my brother, to my people, and to my mother. But also to myself."

"What are you trying to prove?"

"That . . . that I am good enough for the path destiny has given me."

"If you were not enough, you would not walk down such a path. The hardest climbs often have the greatest rewards waiting for you at the summit. My father once told me that your life is a mountain. You climb and climb. Sometimes things get tough, but with each step, you grow stronger. And once you have reached the top, you may look at the valley below and be grateful for the hard road you faced," said Sathelia, and she stood up from her bed and took Cassius's hands in hers. "I can tell your road has been hard, but I can see the starlight that stalks you. Your mountain is steep, but at your summit lies in greatness." She smiled. Cassius trembled, blushed, and then smiled back. "Would you take my necklace off?"

"Um . . . of course."

"Thank you."

She turned towards the mirror and let Cassius unhook her necklace. She did not like the touch of his hands on her body. No. *She loved it.* Cassius let out a yawn. It was getting late.

"Where am I to sleep?" he asked.

"How many beds do you see?" replied Sathelia with a grin on her lips.

"One."

"Then you're with me," she said and blushed, and this time Cassius caught it clearly. It was wrong to be with a human, to be with the *enemy*, but it felt right. Cassius unhooked *En Estar* from his neck and placed it beside where she kept her necklace; the two looked quite similar. As they slipped underneath the covers, the magical light of the tree dimmed. Sathelia rolled over and faced away from Cassius but pressed her body on his. The heat, the overwhelming tangible lust, it could be felt in the very air they breathed. They shut their eyes, and *En Estar*—the elvish necklace of fate, gifted to Sir Hadrian by an Eye of Medearia and then to Cassius—shone brightly next to its partner, *En Eseer*. Two stones, a man and an elf, Ederian and Medearian, all interlocked by fate. They were the ingredients for a fate of peace, and such a path was woven by Vandulin, but the path was hidden from their eyes, and they could not see the blood that was to come.

✹

The world was nothing more than a black void with the smells of blood and fear as their guide. Ivan and Mitsunari were blindfolded and left in separate cells to hold them before their fights. Just exactly where they were they could not tell, but likely close to the armoury. It must have been getting close to midday by now from what Ivan's senses told him, but his sense of time was hindered by the lightless realm that they inhabited. Footsteps. Keys clinking on iron bars. Ivan and Mitsunari heard it all, and they were not surprised when they felt a shove on their backs and they were led out of their cells, and without realizing it, the two reunited in the hall and circled around the circumference of the arena until they took a right into the armoury. Wraithenor awaited them inside.

"You have one hour," said Wraithenor, and hearing his voice filled Ivan's body with one last surge of hate at the thought that he'd been beaten. The elf approached the two human prisoners and untied their blindfolds.

"One hour for what? So you can watch the final moments of our lives and laugh as we cling to the thought of survival?" said Ivan.

"Oh no. Not now. Almost all of Elsibard will be doing that the moment you two enter the arena. We'll be returning your weapons, and furthermore, you may practise your . . . *human* tendency to pray to your gods for forgiveness."

"Noted," said Ivan.

"The others will join you soon enough."

"And I thought you were cold-hearted."

Wraithenor did not reply, nor did he look back as he left to gather the others. First it was Connell and Azrad, and then finally Sir Hadrian was dragged through the door, and the elves dropped him like a bale of hay before he could gather the strength to walk. It took him time, but he eventually gathered the strength from somewhere to join the company in one last sit. The knight exhaled, and it seemed his soul seeped out with every breath he took. The dark thought of failure sat with the company in Cassius's stead. All that was missing was a fire to keep them warm and a dome of darkness and starlight overhead for them to read and ponder over.

"I have failed," said Sir Hadrian, and his voice was as lifeless as the grave. "I thought I'd be able to keep him safe . . . but now . . . he likely sits alone in death, far away from where he should be. I loved that boy. I loved him like he was my own."

Not even the witty charisma of Azrad could break through the blockade of bleakness that held them all in its wrath. There was nothing. No last sprint for life. No strand of hope. Only acceptance.

Suddenly, Ivan stood up. "Look at us," he said. "I did not bring you all on this journey for us to die like slaves and leave this world in self-pity. No. This is not us, and this is not our day to delve into the hands of death. *That boy is strong! And something tells me that somewhere his heart still pumps with the tenacity of a king and all the kings before him!* And we, my brothers, we are carriers of a new time, and our quest is not complete. Consider me fey with insanity, but I will die before I see Ederia bleed out by the blade of its enemy.

"Why do we sit? If we are to die today, then let us die in the way we deserve—*by fire and blood!* A warrior's fall shall be the only way the scholars shall depict our story, and we will have it no other way," said Ivan, and the company saw in him the leader he had always been. They felt it. *All of them did.* Death or life did not matter anymore, and such a thing was eradicated from their minds; there was only the mission, and the thought of seeing Cassius, their king, alive filled them all with a life force they did not know before. Ivan's hand reached out for Sir Hadrian. "If he has fallen, then we owe it to him to stay alive."

Sir Hadrian's face rose from the catacombs of failure, and the remnants of his soul returned to him again. He rose, and the company rose with him.

Ivan looked over towards where Wraithenor watched them. "*Ready your warriors! They shall have their metal tested by the finest Ederia has to offer them,*" yelled Ivan, and his spirit was wild and free, and he spoke up to the guards who watched them from behind a parapet that stood on a floor above them. The door opened, and Wraithenor met Ivan's untamed ire with a fury of his own.

"*If it is death you wish to meet, then that can be arranged.* The crowd always loves it when the prisoners have a bit of fight in them," he said.

They were armoured and unshackled, and their weapons were given back to them. Mitsunari felt good having Kazemaru back in his hands. They took up arms, ready to fight, and even Sir Hadrian returned to life and quickly took to practising with the sword. All of this was overseen by guards who grew wary of possible retaliation. The arena had mocked the company for days, but they now invited the feeling of battle.

※

"Wake up! Both of you wake up!" Sathelia opened her eyes only slightly, and the light of her pupils shone through the slits of her eyelids. Cassius sat up in the bed, eyes still closed, and he was oblivious to the man that stood next to the bed. He yawned, then stretched his back by arching his body, and then finally he opened his eyes and saw Vandulin standing there. Cassius was startled, and his hands dragged him away from the elf. "Come on! Get dressed," said Vandulin.

"What on earth could it be, Vandulin?" asked Cassius, rubbing his eyes; he was still groggy from sleep.

"Your friends need your help."

"*My friends? The company? The—*"

"There is no time! Such a thing is not on their side."

Cassius shot up and grabbed his things, and Sathelia did the same.

"Where is Ruedenhiem? We must take him," said Sathelia.

"He is too far," said Vandulin.

The Sage was wild with worry, as if he was weighed down by the gravity of the situation, and his eyes flickered from their usual grey into a smouldering orange that signified the fire inside of him. Cassius was lit by a similar flame. "Outside, now!" Cassius and Sathelia followed him to the shore of the island, where they watched a great cloud of smoke be conjured in front of them, hiding Vandulin as it twisted like a tornado of ash and smoke. When the smoke was settled, it slipped back into the earth, and the Sage had morphed into an eagle. Its feathers were a light grey with streaks of black that ran down from its eyes, and the feathers on the crown of its head were bent upwards, creating a powerful crest. Vandulin could not speak in this form, but he could communicate through thought, and his will spoke to the two of them with a dictating power. "*Get on!*" said the voice in their head, and Cassius and Sathelia mounted the eagle, and without warning, Vandulin's great wings pounded the ground with a hurricane that caused the entire forest to bend its knee to the Sage's power. They rose above the towering trees and quickly wished Cassemor farewell as they were carried off with haste never seen before by each of them. Cassius sat behind Sathelia and clutched a handful of feathers as he tried to stay on.

*

The constant booming of the crowd rumbled in the deep. *"Ve Caleythre! Ve Caleythre! Ve Caleythre!"* Each chant shook the bones of every man in the arena. The company waited in the darkness. No light was allowed to touch them, and from the darkness, they were meant to be cleansed by the light, and thus death would be their mercy; this was an elvish tradition but was also the calm before the storm, the silence before the music of death. Mitsunari knelt at the end of the tunnel while the rest of them sat on the wooden benches with heads bent down towards their knees. Their spirits were not broken, but this was a time of meditation, a time for serenity and to poise the soul. The armour was cumbersome, and the corners were jagged and would slice into their skin each time they twisted their bodies, but it was enough. It could save their lives, and that was all that mattered.

"Ve Caleythre! Ve Caleythre! Ve Caleythre!" The crowd now roared even louder, knowing that it was almost time. "Death by light" was what it roughly translated to in the common tongue. And they heard it. The grinding of stone on stone. The door was opening, and the light of the world shined through, blinding them all. They walked out to see thousands of elves all sitting in attendance. The sound bit at their eardrums like two nails sinking in slowly. A dozen or so guards made sure they walked to the center by pointing spears at each of them, and when one lagged, they would receive a slap on the calf. Connell was slowest and fell victim. His calf was cut but only slightly and not enough to limit his mobility. Each of them found themselves paralyzed by what surrounded them at all angles. Hate and a lust for violence were what they felt, and the air was thick and polluted with it. Again, there was the grinding of stone on stone, and the crowd cheered even louder as they saw their very own warriors walk out as if they were royalty. Some, in fact, were royalty. These were some of the best Medearia had to offer, and the thought of death in the Pits was almost nonexistent for them, however their competition never strayed far from being low-life criminals that had

only wielded makeshift knives a few times. The Company of Ekmere was different, far different. Each Medearian warrior walked out slowly but never looked away from their prey. Some wielded spears and others had scimitars, but most held curved swords that were decorated in rubies or diamonds. The Ederians took to their defensive position, ready to fight and ready for *death*. It all would start once the king had arrived, but he was not there, and his absence was the thread that held the chaos at bay.

As Estideel walked, Freya walked by his side, and their pace was quick as they began the short journey to the colosseum. "

"Who is fighting today?" asked the king.

"I am not certain . . . but I have heard rumours," said Freya.

"Rumours? What *rumours* have you heard that I, *the king,* have not?"

"They say they are humans. Talk has gotten out about the one that appeared in court, and thus, fear grows of an attack."

Estideel stopped. "Humans?"

"Yes, well, as far as the rumours go, my king."

The king took a moment to gather his thoughts and brew up ideas.

If the rumours are true, *then these are without question the companions to that Cassius boy. What is keeping me from letting them die? Nothing. I am not open to the idea of peace, nor do I believe that that is their purpose. However, if I listen and agree, my hands stay clean and without blood. If I let them die, I make an enemy of my daughter.*

"Come, Freya. I would like to see these *humans* for myself." The two continued and took a shortcut through the gardens and down a staircase where a patrol of guards was already stationed, and they led them two furlongs down the roads of the city until they were joined by another patrol. Behind a door that was solely meant for the king and his suspects were stairs, and they followed them upwards towards the highest balcony of the colosseum, where only a select group was allowed access. The chants of "death by light" shook the walls around them. Spiders tumbled down from their homes and were followed by crumbs of stone and dust that had stood in its place for hundreds of years. This was tradition, and the presence of the king and his family was expected.

Once at the top, servants prepared Estideel's seats with cushions, and at the table there were various fruits and fragrances. Nude dancers spun in the corners and approached the king with smiles and lustful looks about them, but Estideel waved them off. He was not an elf that took pleasure in such things. He had been with no other aside from his wife, Aurora, but he was no fool either. He saw Freya's advances on him, and they were focused and calculated moves for more power in the court. He let it happen. She was no threat to his power, but to show her any love back, that would be dangerous. Estideel sat down, and he was quickly cooled by the wind of a fan that one of the servants held. It was hot. The culmination of bodies and sweat changed the very climate.

Before them all was the arena's floor: a pit of hard and dehydrated soil with sand and rocks; it was harsh terrain. And then there they were. Five humans standing before thousands of elves. He could almost see the faces of those in attendance that were close enough to see that these prisoners were no elves . . . these were harsh examples of *things* that they were all taught from birth to hate. Humans. Some even left, but not out of disappointment, it was out of fear. Estideel smiled out of disbelief and amusement. *So, Cornelius, what type of men did you send to do your bidding?* thought the king.

Suddenly, the crowd went silent as more and more realized that the king had arrived. Waves of hushed whispers ran around the colosseum like a frantic plague of rumours that spread to all.

It was time.

The games could begin.

"Where is Sathelia?" asked Estideel.

"She is still out. I believe she is in Cassemor," said one of the guards. This disturbed Estideel. He did not like it when she left without telling him. It reflected poorly on himself, especially by missing an event such as this.

Each Ederian knew the time for battle was upon them, and each eyed up their opponents. It was to be five versus five. Then came the drums.

BOOM. BOOM. BOOM.

With each thump of the drums, the Medearians stepped closer, raising their hands in the air to get the crowds riled up even more.

BOOM. BOOM. BOOM.

Ivan looked over at his foe. He was dressed in full ebony armour. The companions of Ederia looked at each other. If they fell, it would not be easy, and to the crowd's surprise, the humans leaped forth towards their enemies, charging them with some sudden burst of glory. They did not fear their death, and that would be their greatest weapon.

The fighting began.

Connell eased his pace once he closed in on his foe, and he studied the spearmen, examining his strange and swift movements. The elf was far smaller than Connell, but he was *far* quicker than him. The elf feinted, stepping forward with his lead leg to see if the giant before him would react. There was nothing. He did so again, and still, the human was calm and unfazed. Seeing that this was ineffective, the Medearian charged, thrusting his spear twice with a blinding speed and accuracy that took Connell by surprise, and he was lucky to have deflected the first and side-stepped the other. Connell wouldn't give the elf time to recover; he had to finish this quick because he had little hope of outlasting him. Connell's blade thrust forward, missing the target, and then whirling upwards and down for a vertical strike. This was parried perfectly, drawing the Ederian's sword further downwards, and the elf spun, knocking Connell aside the helm with the steel end of the spear. Connell's teeth clashed together, and the taste of smoke filled his mouth. He heaved his sword across, aiming for the elf's torso, but this time he met no resistance. The elf rolled under, distancing himself from the human.

Each member of the company fought against their own foe, and so far, there was no clear victor. The elves had not expected to meet this much resistance, and they fought with a hunger to satisfy the audience with a clean kill. But it was not given. The feeling of controlled and tamed horror filled Sir Hadrian. He felt young, and he moved like it too. He was now the aggressor, forcing his opponent farther and farther back as if he was possessed by the thought of his former self, when he rode atop proud and beautiful mares into battle, duelled worthy knights, and embraced the grinding insanity of war. He was a tamer of hate and an artist of the colour red. Suddenly, the pace of the fight changed, and it was now Sir Hadrian that was on the backfoot, being forced to defend against two dancing scimitars that were wielded behind a worthy advisory that was gilded by the rich ink of malice. Every warrior was born this way, and the only way to tell was to fight one another, and thus you knew not only what your opponent was made of but what they had been through, their struggles in life and their grand achievements. All this was said with one glance. Sir Hadrian and his foe spoke novels to each other with each blow. Alas, such a genuine conversation of wills ceased as the elf looked down to see his flaw . . . *his one mistake*. He had fallen into a trap that had been laid several movements ago; he was an inch, a fraction too far forward, and the old man made him pay, thrusting his broadsword into his enemy's breastplate and smiting him where he stood. Sir Hadrian saw the look of disbelief, and the life that his foe had lived was reflected in his eyes. It was a good life. Its final stages were now, and they were painful and full of regret.

The crowd went silent.

Their champion had fallen.

Sir Hadrian looked around the towering ring that encased him in a choking hold of hostility, and he smiled. *But then it came.* It came like a bitter reminder that the final stages of his life were not so far off as well. Quickly, he was torn from his sudden dream of days long past by the piercing feeling in his heart. His feet went numb, and his neck tensed. He fell to the ground, splashing his knee in the pool of blood that had spilled out from the elf. His breathing was slow and drawn out, and the roof of his mouth was dry, as if it was filled with dust. He clenched his jaw and rocked it back and forth as his body writhed in pain. His heart was dying. Some *disease* that was born for the sole purpose of cruelty watched over him, guiding him towards a painful end.

But then . . . then the pain was gone. And in its stead was warmth. It was a warmth much like the feeling of a mother keeping him safe, reading to him under the watchful eye of candlelight in the dark. It was a lover's whisper in his ear, telling him of things that aroused his happiness, or the first embrace of the sun on his skin after the darkest of winters.

A certain *peace* was found. Sir Hadrian did not see the waves of battle around him, nor did he feel the sickly touch of another's blood on his. No.

He saw a creek with small grey stones rising through it like teeth, and sunlight basked and slept on its morning facade. It was Ederia. Home. Trees surrounded him, and they too watched the sunrise before them, ridding themselves of the last vestiges of winter on their leaves. If he was to die, he could do it now, and there would be no regrets. No self-pity. Nothing. Nothing but the constant understanding of the beauty of the world. Age was killing him.

Azrad was the first to fall victim to his foe's abilities, and the Medearian's sword shattered his guard, and he then kicked the Ederian onto the dirt. Azrad felt the taste of sand in his mouth. He spat, and droplets of blood had mixed with the dirt. To his surprise, it reminded him of home. It reminded him of Ruzadia. Back then, his brother was still alive, and they would head out into the desert where their mother had always told them not to go. They did this because, if they were lucky, they'd get a glimpse of an old ruin that the wind would dig up when the storms flew in. Only the top half would be visible, but at its pinnacle was a ruby the size of their hands. Again and again they would wander off into the desert, where they'd look in awe of the beauty of the jewel. With each visit, their wonder grew, and so did their yearning for it. Until one day, Azrad set out with his brother, Radin, and when they happened upon the jewel, they fought for it. It started off playful and no different from their usual scraps, but as their emotions boiled to a simmer, each shove, each push grew a little harder.

Radin caught his brother with a fist to the tooth, and Radin watched as his little baby brother yelped in pain, and tears flooded his eyes to their brim. With one last spell of blind hatred, Azrad shot up, pushing Radin with what force he still possessed all in one final effort to win over the stone and call himself the victor of yet another brotherly scrap. This was not just any other scrap. Radin fell, and he did not get back up then, nor did he ever. When Azrad knelt to investigate, he was greeted by the deep red hue of blood that glimmered over the spoiled pink of his brother's brains. That hue of red was haunting. It was eternal. It was merciless in its rage against his mind. *That*, that right there was the colour of red that Azrad spat out as he crawled desperately away from the elf. Instead of focusing on the moment, Azrad wanted to be there with Radin, wandering the desert, chasing unknown stars, and reading the constellations that guided them. He longed for those sleepless nights under the desert's moon, where things were silent, and the creatures of the dark were peaceful through the touch of the wind. This was it. This was where he thought it was going to end, with a sword through his back . . . *But it never came.* Before the elf could thrust his blade down towards his wounded enemy, Ivan was upon him. Azrad looked up to see a sword slowly slide across the throat of the attacker, and blood sprayed into the air as if it could not wait to be unleashed. The body went limp and fell to its knees, and eventually the elf fell flat while his muscles were still convulsing, pumping more and more blood like a sporadic seizure. The dead had no knowledge that the fight had ended, nor would they consider such a thing. But it was true. Another champion lay lifeless.

"*Get up! Come on!*" yelled Ivan, but his friend was stuck looking up at the ebony warrior before them, and slowly Ivan joined him. There he stood, calm as a glacier under a moonlit evening. The warrior took off his helm, revealing his pale face, and his long, dark hair. His face put a smile on Ivan's. It was Wraithenor.

Finally, Ivan would find vengeance on the one responsible for his pain. *It was him.* His mind wandered back to that day, that gruesome day in the mountains where men were diminished into bones, and those who lived like himself lived a life of solitude and an unexplainable and unquenchable thirst for revenge. Robert. Baldwyn. These were Wraithenor's trophies, his famed achievements that he used to mock Ivan's mind, and it worked. It had worked for years. Those *eyes . . .* they were the eyes that watched him always, and they watched him now. But things were different. Ivan had a sword in his hand, and it had tasted elvish blood already.

The rest of the world was blocked out. It was only them. Wraithenor pointed his sword towards Ivan, and the two drew closer, making small reads of each other's movements, habits, and behaviour. They had *both* looked forward to this. Ivan charged with speed and made a horizontal cut. Such a blow was blocked, and sparks flew into the air like embers of the sun. Ivan turned, stepped back, and waited. Wraithenor feinted. Nothing. He stepped forward again but this time it was no bluff. With one hand he wielded his sword with grace and elegance, and he made each movement look effortless. Ivan did his best to parry; the movements of the Medearian were strange and organic . . . almost . . . artistic. Ivan's hand reached for a blade he kept at his waist and threw it, slicing the cheek of Wraithenor. A fine red line was brought to life on the elf's cheek, and blood crawled out of the crack like hands stretching outwards, wanting to be let free. Wraithenor touched his wound and licked the blood off his fingertip. Finally, things were getting interesting.

Then they heard it: a faint whistle in the wind that grew louder in pitch and in volume, savagely cutting away at their hearing. The world was there, and then, in a matter of seconds, *it was gone*. The world was nothing but a shapeless void of smoke and ash. Ivan coughed and gagged as the clouds hit him in a wave, knocking everyone to their knees.

In the darkness, Wraithenor saw his opportunity. He could likely beat Ivan, but he was in no mood to test this theory and would not leave such a thing to chance. Thus, he went for Sir Hadrian. He could hear the old man's broken breath, and he pursued it like a phantom. There he was, fresh for death, and the kill was inviting yet almost too easy. Nevertheless, he went for him and was there in seconds. Before Sir Hadrian could stand and fight, the sword was already in motion. Another wave came, but there was no powerful blast, only the swiftness of a winged beast gliding through the mist. Wraithenor felt his blade stop and thought he'd likely hit a bone. But his cut had been perfect. No bone would have resisted it. The smoke settled. Vandulin's hand gripped Wraithenor's blade. Their eyes met, and the Sage saw the fear in his eyes. Vandulin flexed his hand and shattered the sword into pieces. Wraithenor stepped back, and he was stuck between shame and shock. The Sage's face was malevolent and cloaked with the heat of his own power. His robes fluttered in the wind, and he threw the shards of steel in his hand at the feet of Wraithenor and then looked away, as if he had grown bored of their encounter.

Cassius and Sathelia were there as well. As soon as he could see, Cassius drew his sword. What had come upon him he could not tell, but it was some obligation to protect those he loved. First, he ran to Sir Hadrian, and the old man's eyes were overtaken by joy. He had not failed, and he drifted into sleep as Cassius came to him. He dreamt of the times long ago when he would train the sons of Cornelius. He had never wedded nor had children, but these two boys were the closest he'd ever get. Maybe one day, in a different life, he would know the feeling of true fatherhood . . . one day.

Estideel rose at once. His skin was hot with outrage, and he looked upon the Sage with disdain. It was time to bring an end to this, to these humans, these viruses of the earth. If they were not dealt with soon, his people would begin to doubt him and see weakness, and questioning his leadership over the invasion, if only slightly, could prove disastrous. But that *Sage* kept them protected for reasons unknown, cocooning them in a web of foolish prophecies, and Estideel's very own daughter, who had just returned after so long, was slipping away from him. He could feel it. One day, and it would not be far, she would have to choose between her own people and the enemy. It made him sick. So easily had he lost his control of his own kingdom, simply by allowing what seemed impossible to unfold in front of his own eyes, but what was certain was that his love for his daughter was blinding him to the proper decisions he must make as a king.

"Bring the guards . . . *I WANT THEM ALL IN CHAINS!*"

"But, my king, what of the Sage?"

"WHAT? WHAT OF HIM? CHAIN HIM. HE FORGETS HIS PLACE, AND I'LL HAVE TO SHOW IT TO HIM, IT SEEMS!"

The guards knew such a thing was wrong; to go against the wisdom of the sages was already blasphemous, but to chain one as if he was some drunk outside a brothel? Well, it was unthinkable. But the king's words were absolute. Unquestioned. Thus the signal went out, and guards stormed the arena. The company readied themselves for another battle, but Vandulin looked around and appeared to be whispering something to himself. His eyes rolled back. As the wind rolled in, it took the Sage and the company with them, and their bodies crumbled like dust until they were ash floating in the air, yet still very much alive. Sathelia was left behind, and she looked up to see the wind fly over her head and away to Cassemor. There they'd be safe from the wrath of her father, but a confrontation was inevitable.

The Throne

The wind carried harsh reminders of that day long ago when Vidicus had seen his mother buried here. It was the same cool morning breeze, and the leaves on the trees shivered. The breath of the mountain was unforgiving, and Vidicus climbed it. Beside him was his father. It was a closed casket; the face had been too torn apart to be shown. Distant family members walked along behind Vidicus, and behind them were the council members of Ekmere. They wept, and the sky did so as well. The air smelled of rain and alpine grass, and the clouds above were soft and wet and were the colour of sleepless eyes. But Vidicus did not join in the sickness of melancholy. Nay, *he rejoiced*. This was his doing after all, and he had not come so far down the path of mutiny to stop at the nearest touches of regret. He might have felt some form of sorrow *once*, but not now, not anymore. Years of neglect had all led to this moment, and they had created the man he had become. An evil was upon him, and its grip was blinding, choking away at the man he once was. *Envy can be the gears for hatred.*

When they took the final bend down onto the shoulder of the mountain that overlooked Ekmere, he saw his mother's grave, and it dawned on him like a merciless surprise—he had never been up here since *that day*. That day when he saw his mother's face as lifeless as the first sheet of snow on a winter's morning, and he had seen that same look on his father as he died.

There was little time to spend in the palace, no time to speak to Cassius. Although he was not surprised to see his brother's face absent. In fact, Cassius likely hadn't realized that father was even dead. Vidicus pitied him no longer. It was not his time anymore, and it never was.

Vidicus stopped. The ancient oak tree stared deep into him. It was relentless . . . *it knew*. Somehow, it saw through Vidicus's thick facade of sadness, and it could feel the sick happiness that slept in his heart. The oak was his mother's guardian in death, and Vidicus's presence was nothing more than a threat to his mother's slumber. The others stopped as well and took to their positions for the burial. Most said little, for not much could be said. The death of their king was so unexpected and swift. Rumours of sickness or even enemy assassins spread about, but only *one* knew the truth. Julias stepped forward from the crowd, looking back at Aaron Froy before speaking his words of respect. The rain grew heavier and besieged the earth with the strength of the heavens, but the men and women of Ederia stood solemnly in respect.

"Ederia might be divided, but in this time of division, we have been brought together by a tragedy. It was something none could have foreseen, not even the wisest of us. I knew Cornelius well, and I knew his father, and thus I know that his father looks through the pall above us with a smile on his lips. But during such a tragedy, it seems that we might find some form of unification, and we may see that we all shared a similar love for a man that safeguarded this empire to its pinnacle. Blessed are we—"

"That is quite enough," said Vidicus with an almost amicable grin. Julias halted, mumbling to himself in his confusion.

"As you wish, Lord Vidicus. It is only normal that—"

"*Stand in your place, old man,*" hissed Vidicus, and the old man obeyed. Vidicus paced back and forth, pondering like a conductor of thoughts before finally standing still. "Our great King Cornelius Helladawn, alas, is dead," said Vidicus bluntly, and the silver hue of deceit was heavy on his tongue. "I feel . . . so sorry for you all! This is such a poor and—well, a rather uncivilized place for final moments." Those in attendance noticed their prince's strange behaviour. It was almost humorous, as if he had adopted traits of his brother. Luxtheilian guards stood behind the crowd, ready for any order given to them by their lord. "I might pity you, but let it be known that I also thank you! You are the worthy sacrifices that shall bring forth an era of . . . *peace.*"

Confusion rolled over the mourning audience, but it was not their place to speak out against a grieving prince who was clearly sick with sorrow. Vidicus turned and walked towards his father. His lip snarled in disdain, but his coldness was thawed by the presence of his mother. He could feel her. She was there. "Who bestows themselves with the honour of being the arbiter of my fate? I choose such things. *This is for the greater good of the people. They need a king with kingly attributes,*" whispered Vidicus, and he opened the casket to see the limp body of Cornelius, and then he leaned in closer, as if to tease any lingering shard of his father's soul. "Cassius cannot give these things . . . you know this, father; you know this, mother. *So how dare you judge me for transcending heights that require decisions you could not even fathom!*" spat Vidicus, and these cruel words truly did put to rest the soul of his father, and he was put to rest in a bed of thorns.

Vidicus then raised his arm.

There it was.

The signal.

Vidicus took one deep breath in, and with it, he imagined the feeling, the smell, the texture of the throne and the magical aura that words were too primitive to convey. He could not look, not yet. He wished to see the face on his father's lifeless body as those who followed him joined him in the grave. The Luxtheilian guards drew their weapons. Those who saw ran, but were quickly preyed upon. Most were oblivious, and as punishment they received the image of their own blood dripping down their throats. Hysteria erupted suddenly. Screaming. Crying. Fear and dread. They were all butchered. Aaron Froy was the first to fall, and he bled out slowly, crying, revealing what type of man he really was. This was something that Vidicus knew was necessary for his ascendancy to power—it could be unquestioned, and fear was his tool for peace. They were all slaughtered and eradicated like a disease, and Vidicus stood, listening to the near orgasmic sounds of terror that symbolized the beginning of a new era. Julias grimaced. His wounds had not been done cleanly, and he soaked the grass beneath him with his own fluids. He crawled, but his hopeless flight was stopped by a foot on his neck, pinning his head to the blood-soaked soil, and it stank of the metallic odour of death.

"Where is Cassius? *WHERE IS MY BROTHER?*"

"*CURSE YOU!*" said Julias, spitting out blood and choking. "*YOU SHALL MEET A FATE WORSE THAN DEATH, AND WE SHALL ALL LOOK DOWN UPON YOU AS YOU LIE IN AN ETERNITY OF PAIN!*"

"I'll say it once more," said Vidicus politely. "Where is Cassius?"

"*We do not know. He has vanished. The people of Ederia will know the truth—it always comes to the light, and you shall be judged accordingly for your actions.*"

Vidicus had no words left in him to spare. Instead, he watched the man he'd once called his mentor die . . . and he did so slowly, but Vidicus made sure to watch every second of his downfall. He wanted to see *it*: the beautiful look on his face and the shimmer in his eyes when he realized that there was no getting out of this and that he would die in a matter of moments. That look finally came, and it put a smile on Vidicus's face. The prince's blue lips curled into a dubious grin.

It was done, and if Cassius was out of the equation that meant that he could climb those steps alone and untouched. There was no one now, not a soul that could tell him otherwise. The throne was his. Throughout his whole life, it had always called to him.

He was meant for this.

He was born to be king.

✳

Ekmere was alive below and smothered by the rainfall like an abandoned fire that was more ash than flames, sizzling in pain as the droplets of water splashed down upon it. Vidicus let the natural air rub his body as he stood out on the balcony where he would once watch his father do the same. He let himself soak, feeling the fingers of the water drip down his brow and fall down onto the stone. Each inhale was wet and cleansing and summoned all the happiness it could and funnelled it down into his heart.

Sometimes in order to create a world of peace, you must first burn what you love most, as they are what bind you to your personal burdens, thought Vidicus, and this notion, this betraying idea is what he kept in his mind. In a way, it helped justify what he had done, but he knew there was nothing that could wash out the blood on his hands. It was eternal, and he would take such pain to the grave. It was a king's responsibility to carry the weight of emotions in silence. If he was weak, his people were. Countless days of thinking about this moment rushed through him like a thrust of wind that chills one to the bones. Even when he was a child, thoughts of being king were harmless ideas that flew into the deep regions of his mind, and he could not yet predict what they would create, but as he grew older, such thoughts were not so harmless. They were powerful.

They were dictating.

They were maddening.

He walked inside with the wind in his feet. The table where he and his family would eat stared back at him, appalled by the man it saw. He ignored it. Any acknowledgement of any flaw would birth the opening stages of self-loathing, and so he walked on, listening to echoes of the past. They haunted him; spat at him, preyed upon him like a pack of scorpions bred for torture. Insanity is what it was, and as much as Vidicus tried, he could not ignore the crystalized pictures of his childhood, one that he had betrayed so violently. And yet he kept on. Down the stairs he went, and into the throne room that rose like a galaxy of memory. And yet he kept on. Crossing the timeless realm alone like a parasite wiggling through guts. On and on he went, but then he stopped. He could not step forward, not yet. There it was—*the throne,* calling to him with the hum of the universe that was very much alive in its existence. Its teeth were visible only through the instrument of the mind, and it too was alive and created by the strings of power. It was an altogether unscrupulous thing that would twist one's very morality until it liked what sat in it. And yet he kept on.

One step.

Two.

Three.

His feet slapped against the marble floor like paddles on the flat face of water. His finger traced the armrest, and the spirit of sin touched him back, raping him until Vidicus bent to its will. The crown was only the object that led the people, but this—the throne—was the puppeteer of dynasties, and it watched its puppets fall and rise as naturally as the sun and the moon. Vidicus could not breathe. He sat and was taken by the arms of a beast. Displayed before his eyes were not the glorious halls of the Casthedian people. No. A layer conjured by something he could never know wrapped itself around his eyes, and he saw Cassius. But he was far from any brothel or inn; he was in the woods. He looked older and more grown . . . he looked as if the Cassius he'd once know was finally pulled out of the abyss of self-pity and forlornness. It was his brother—*his real brother.* The vision faded. Vidicus fought it, clenching the image with his eyes, wanting to see Cassius for a second longer. Alas, it was gone. *Everyone* was gone. He was alone, and he felt the cold touch of something well needed on his skin. Vidicus looked down at his hands that were curled up like claws, and he saw tears.

Before the Storm

V andulin was late. He despised being late. He strutted down the hallway as he eyed the guards positioned outside the courtroom's doors, and they could not bear any elongated stare-downs with such an elf. The hue of the walls was dark and cold, and it reflected the taste of the air, which was affected by the breath of the palace. The guards lowered their heads as a sign of respect as he passed them by and into the court where Estideel and the other members stood waiting. Each member had a designated seat that was carved into the circular walls. He was surrounded by them all but was far from fazed. Estideel stood up. He had made sure to dress in the finest white robes he could find. This was to be a battle between himself and the Sage, he knew it, and he was prepared for anything.

"So," said Estideel, "The Grey Wolf of Medearia has returned. I see you are not as wise as you think yourself to be." Vandulin knew immediately just how poorly the king had taken his arrival in the arena, and his presence here filled the king with a predatory instinct to berate and gibe. This would not be so easy, but Vandulin always

knew approaching a den of vipers would be undoubtedly dangerous, at least for the vipers, that is.

"You will see no lack of wisdom from me, my king. I remain just
as I always have. Rather, you might see the symptoms of bravery
in me; volunteering to be the victim of a room so hostile has never
been my preferred environment."

Estideel licked his lips. He was excited about this. Finally, he'd
have the chance to prove himself the true power of this land. "Sit,"
said Estideel. Vandulin took his seat beside Bulldior, an elf that he
himself respected, and contrary to some others of the high council,
he could be trusted. The high council was made up of the oldest elves
in Medearia, and with age came power. Vandulin had seen each one
be birthed into this world. Such a thing irritated them, he supposed.
He could feel each gyrating eye stop on him and stay there for too
long for his liking. "I, King Estideel Litherius, Warden of the Lands
of Life, hereby bring this council to a beginning. I think we may
all have come to the same conclusion that there is much we must
discuss, especially about our *places* and where our presence *belongs*,"
said Estideel, looking over at the Sage, who returned a glance of his
own. Before I bring our core subject to life, is there anything you feel
you might need to say?" There was nothing; they knew what they'd
come here for.

"I would," said Vandulin, and the room choked on its own silence.

"Do you now?" growled the king.

"I see no reason to dance around my proposition, so here I must
say that it is time that you swallow your pride and hate, and you
listen to the words of Cassius. We must make peace."

Estideel stood up and hunched over the podium like an animal
sickened by its hunger to kill, and his face wrinkled in annoyance.
*"How dare you bring up that thing's name in this court. I have tolerated
it only by the thought of my daughter's wishes."*

"If you remain blind to the fact that this will not be a war so easily
won, you will find yourself on the losing side."

"And just who told you this? The stars?"

"They have guided our people since the beginning. Trust me, my friend, do not abandon them now; I have seen the horrors that await us if you follow through with this."

"You do not scare me with your fictitious theories of the future. Your way is old and forgotten, and it seems you aim to spread fear into my people. Is that your goal? To weaken my power by making me question my own perception?"

"*It never has been.* You know this. Once you and I called each other friends, and as your friend, I know that you are wise, but even the wisest sometimes get fooled by their own emotion. Please, listen to me. Hear the humans out."

Estideel would not break eye contact with the Sage. If he did, he'd lose the ground he'd gained by the wit of his words. The other council members looked around, vexed and fearful at hearing that some unknown horrors awaited them if they were to go to war. It may not have been his goal, but Vandulin's words *did* frighten them, and it was true that no king ever strayed far from the teachings of the stars.

"I cannot fold on my plans, *Vandulin.* The wheels of war are already in motion: ships are being built; armies have been gathered, and our vengeance becomes more and more clear by each growing day. I can almost see it, that horrid land that we once called home. I shall release it into its beauty once again and bring forth a cleansing."

Vandulin rose from his seat and took to the centre of the room, freeing his ire only a little. The grey eyes of the Sage sparked and turned into fire, and when he spoke, his voice was as deep and boisterous as the rolling of thunder up above. "*Will you all simply allow your king to lead you into a needless death? And do you truly wish to walk into the trenches of an ocean of blood and let it be your coffin? If so, you bring shame to your resting kin!*" said Vandulin, aiming his words towards each council member, and thus sewing his power into the room.

"My king, if I may," whispered Bulldior.

"Go ahead, teach the jester that stands before me," said Estideel.

"He is right."

Estideel whipped his gaze over. "Is that so?"

"It is what I believe. If there is no doom that awaits us, and we listen to the Sage, we shall be fine. But to ignore him when he could be right is dangerous, and we have nothing but time on our hands."

"That we do, Bulldior, that we do," said the king, calming himself and sitting back down in his chair and resting his chin on the tips of his fingers.

"This would be putting not only our king's life at stake but our people's. I do not like the idea of letting vermin walk amongst us, let alone our king," said Freya.

"You forget, Freya, daughter of Lithay, that it is also my duty to protect the king. You will be safe if I have something to say about it," said Vandulin. Estideel was now poised and deep into thought, and he took the time he needed to come to a decision. It was impossible to make one without Sathelia's heart on his mind. She loved Cassius, he could see it in her, and her love grew bolder in expression as it became more and more obvious. He sighed and let out a long and desperate exhale.

"Fine. It is more than my pride that is at risk for my potential actions, it is my people. I will . . . listen and open myself up to the idea of peace," said Estideel, and the Sage nodded in respect. He knew it was not easy for any king to have his decisions second-guessed and doubted. The council came to an accord, and briefly, the king and the Sage shared words that were safe from disdain. When all had spoken their mind, they returned to where they belonged.

Vandulin listened for the wind while he sat on the garden benches, and when it came, he went with it, returning to ash and making his way to Cassemor where the company still waited.

✳

Ivan let his back curl, and he leaned forward, as did the rest of the company while they listened to Cassius's story. He began from the very first night they spent there all the way until now. He was surprised at just how much his tale gripped their attention, binding them to his words. Cassius left out most of the details with Sathelia, knowing that his companions would be unable to look at him the same for the things he felt for her, and he said little of the Sage and the hidden mark on his neck. But as he told his tale, he couldn't help but notice the sudden gauntness in the face of Sir Hadrian: his skin was more tightly wrapped around his cheekbones, and it was pale and uneven in complexion. He was sick. But the presence of Cassius and the knowledge of his survival were all that he needed right now to carry on, and so he did. He carried on through it all with a smile on his face. When Cassius arrived at the moment where he had met the king, everyone, even Connell, stared at him with their jaws open and their eyes enthralled by the power of Cassius's story. Every now and then, he would hear an, "And then what happened?" followed by either approval or disbelief; no one, no human at least, had done these things since a time that was long forgotten.

They were all circled aside a narrow vein of icy water that walked down from the mountain, and they rested upon a layer of dew and moss that stank of morning perfumes. The hard air that embraced the inside of their lungs with a cool thrust flowed through the trees of Cassemor, and the company took refuge from the wind behind the hide of a tree. Ivan tried to guess which type, but to his disbelief, he had never seen this species. This forest, he had never been to, but somehow it was described to him by the feeling in the atmosphere that these woods were old. Very old. Full of untainted life and a natural magic culled from the depths of the earth. It was in the dampness of its hide, the wheezing of its breath, and as the others were listening to the end of Cassius's tale, Ivan roamed down the creek in awe of what he saw and then returned shortly after.

"You should see it at night," said Cassius.

"Yeah? I worry about the *other* things that will prowl these woods when that comes," said Ivan, turning almost frantically towards the others and returning back to the circle. "It's good to have you back, Cassius," said Ivan with a smile that was genuine and pure.

"Sure is, kid," said Azrad, patting Cassius on his shoulder, and Connell, still licking his wounds, limped over and flicked a smile out from nowhere and patted him on his shoulder as well—which was significant coming from him. Mitsunari showed his respect and started finding the ingredients for a fire. This was the first time Cassius had ever received this kind of genuine respect that was earned and not bought by his title. It separated him from the world and helped illuminate his worth to himself. He *was* worth it. He *did* deserve this respect, and the feeling brought a warming euphoria to him that burnt away all self-doubt. Mitsunari came back with a bundle of boughs in his arms, and he and Ivan started on the fire, whittling away at the strange material to make enough kindling. When the fire began, it was noon, and once again, they sat around the flame, pondering the journey, and conversing like they used to. The laughter was ritualistic to them, and *all* found a sense of brotherhood to the man next to them. Such a gift could fill every hole in Cassius's heart. He could be healed. And then it came to him, it was sudden and swift, and the thought rang tumultuously inside of him, screaming so loud it could not be ignored. *This* was what being a king was about—to extend your love to your people regardless of social class; it was to acknowledge the power granted to you but resist its control over you. It was about forming a connection with your people, as you are only as strong as they are. You are one. *He,* as king, was tasked with speaking for those too quiet to be heard. It would be an honour to wear that crown again, and he'd treat it as such . . . He'd have to.

"So," said Mitsunari, poking at the red guts of the fire. "What will you do after this, Cassius?" The prince took his time, dancing with his ideas and letting his thoughts course through his body.

"I'll rule," he said, looking up to his brothers with the face of a king, *of a man*. "But not like any other. My father once told me that a son's only obligation is to correct his father's wrongdoings and learn from them. He also once said—and it might sound foolish to you all but—well—he told me a good king is like a rose. The thorns are his power, and each petal is a sample of his grace, and a *good* king will have both; a good king knows when to spill blood, but he also knows the bravery that comes with mercy and forgiveness."

Sir Hadrian looked at the young prince, perplexed but also overtaken with joy at the sight of the man before him. If this was the Cassius that was to sit upon the throne, there would be an era of peace that would surely ensue, and he would be blessed to watch the beginnings of it. They then let the fire do the talking, listening to the crackle of it shred the space around them as the darkness of the woods seemed to consume the light of day.

"It's almost time, my friends," said Ivan suddenly, breaking the wave of silence. "We have come here for *one* reason, for *him*. And he is close, so very close. We alone have the chance to save our people, but it must be done now, and we must begin to plan. Estideel needs to be dealt with and soon"

"I agree. The more we wait, the more his suspicion shall grow, and he'll hunt us, I'm sure," said Sir Hadrian.

"How are you feeling?" asked Mitsunari, looking over to the old knight. "Are you strong enough yet?"

"I'll have to be."

"Good. Something tells me that we'll be needing that sword arm of yours before this is all over," said Connell.

"That much I am certain of. But we must keep the amount of blood spilled to a minimum. The more deaths, the less likely our chances are of leaving this place alive," said Ivan. He then took the poison from his satchel once more and presented it to the others. "*This*, this right here is how I intend on killing him, but we need a way to get into that palace."

"Cassius, out of all of us, you alone have spent time with the king. Is there anything, *anything* about him that could aid us in this task?" asked Sir Hadrian, and Cassius felt the eyes of his brothers fixate upon him with questions ready to be drawn.

"Well," he said, trying to put together his words into coherent sentences, "he is cold-hearted and not so easily swayed, and I have told him that we have come here to discuss peace, although I doubt he believes me . . . but . . . there is something else."

"What is it?"

Cassius didn't want to answer. It felt wrong to betray her like this, and he loved her, he did, with all his essence. But he could not let his emotions misguide him, not here, not now; the stakes were simply too high. "His daughter, Sathelia, she . . ."

"C'mon! What is it?" shouted Azrad.

"He cares about her," Cassius finally said, and he let out a deep and thorough exhale. "His feelings for her could be used . . . I don't know, maybe as a tool."

"I like your thinking, Cassius. Love can be a deadly thing," said Ivan, standing up and strolling to the stream again to tame his ideas.

"Where are you going?" asked Mitsunari.

"For a stroll, Mitsunari, for a stroll. Would you care to join me?" Ivan crossed the stream, soaking his leather boots in the cool wrath of the water, and he skipped over it and into the belly of the underbrush of Cassemor. Mitsunari followed. The two walked across green woodlands together until Ivan knew that they were far enough away from the camp. "Well, it wouldn't hurt to gather some more firewood."

"Agreed." Mitsunari gathered what he could, but something told him that this was not the true reason for their journey away from the others. "So, why'd you *really* ask me to come along?"

"I knew you'd see through it, so I may as well just say it," said Ivan, and Mitsunari turned towards him, and the look on his face was full of dread, something Mitsunari had never seen before in him. "There is something—something that I have not told you or anyone aside from Connell and Azrad." Mitsunari took a step closer, crossing the stream until he was nearly close enough to feel the heat of Ivan's breath on his cheek. The Sarakotan did not speak, but his eyes told a tale of their own, forcing him to speak and capturing even the likes of Ivan under a spell of obedience, although only momentarily. "I embarked on this journey to bring an end to Ederia's greatest enemy, one that would have the world soak in blood if it meant humanity would suffer . . . but that is not the only reason I have come all this way.

"You see, Elsibard is now the heart of Medearia, and it seems whoever controls Elsibard holds an unfathomable amount of power, and with that power comes *armies*. You might not see it, but I do— Ederia is weak while the power is shifting, and with an open rebellion, it's the weakest it's been in decades."

"What are you saying, Ivan?"

"I'm saying that if we find a way to control Elsibard, we now have an army, and with the army that Estideel has assembled, *we can take Ekmere. We can take Ederia, or whatever we want.*"

"*What you are saying is nothing short of madness,*" said Mitsunari, baring his teeth in a hushed paroxysm of anger. "Just who would take the throne of Ekmere? And how do you intend on convincing all of Medearia to serve *you*?"

"They don't have to serve me . . . they only need to serve *her*. You heard Cassius; the king's daughter can be used. People will do and say just about anything if you put a knife to their throats, and once Estideel is dead, naturally, his daughter would ascend the throne, but every word, every action she does could be dictated by us if we never fail to keep a knife near her gut. If we control her through fear, we can control the people of Medearia."

"You have a problem."

"I have many," said Ivan.

"Are you forgetting about Cassius? If you later decide to invade Ederia and besiege Ekmere, I doubt he or Sir Hadrian would allow you to do so."

"That is why I need your support, my friend! I wish it were not so, but if it is needed, we will have to . . . bring an end to them both."

Mitsunari took a step back, as if the words of Ivan had attacked him. He laughed. He had not foreseen this, and he thought himself a fool for it. "You're going to offer me something, aren't you?"

Ivan withdrew a hefty sack of gold from his satchel, and he threw it up in the air a few times before passing it over. Mitsunari looked inside and was more than satisfied by the amount. "That's half. You'd get the other when I sit on that throne, and when that happens, the world would be yours. I could give you anything. All I need from you is your sword. I need to know that if it is needed, you will not hesitate to draw blood for me—to kill the prince and any who would stand with him."

Mitsunari looked over to where the others were, and the warm glow of the fire drifted throughout the forest. He heard their laughs, and the mirth of it all reminded him that he too had found love with his companions, a new sense of friendship that he had not felt in years. He looked at the gold and then back at them. He closed the purse and put it in his satchel. "Fine, you have my word."

When the two came back to the camp, they came with a dark secret. They sat back down and fed the fire with the wood they had gathered. It was time to plan. Time that they figured out just how they would bring death to King Estideel. "So, you have told the king that we come with good intentions?" asked Ivan.

"Yes," said Cassius.

"That's good. It is something. For now, I should at least tell you all how I plan to use the poison. If I can apply it to a pair of gloves, all I'll need is to touch him—a shake of the hand would work."

"But that's just it, we need to get in that palace and gain an audience with him," said Azrad.

"Indeed . . ." Ivan was stuck. But they had all come too far to fail, and so their success felt nearly inevitable to them. When the fire was reduced to embers, Mitsunari wandered off to search for more wood. It was too early for sleep, and yet Cassius cocooned himself inside his ripped sheets and warmed his face by the fire, letting its waves crash against his skin.

The wind then pulled through again, and with it came ashes that clustered together, forming a humanoid figure. A face was formed along with its details—it was Vandulin. Cassius stood up immediately, and the Sage felt Kazemaru tickle his throat. He turned to see Mitsunari hidden in the shadows, but his heart did not skip a beat. Instead, he gave the Sarakotan a pompous smirk.

"Sorry to intrude," said the Sage. The company stood at the ready, looking over at the elf to spot any threatening motions.

"Easy, my friends. This is Vandulin, the elf who saved me from the swamps and you from the arena," said Cassius.

"And just what is he doing here?" asked Ivan.

"Maybe if your friend puts that piece of metal down, I may tell you," said Vandulin. Mitsunari looked over at Ivan, and he read his face and sheathed his blade. "Well then, the king asks for your presence, peacemakers, for that is what you are, aren't you?"

"Yes," said Cassius, pulling himself ahead of Ivan and speaking to the elf directly. "We are."

"Then he would like to hear your proposition. Now, will you come with me? There are beds in the palace already awaiting you."

Cassius looked back at the others, asking for their opinions with just a look. He approached Ivan and leaned into him.

"I don't like this, Cassius, and we are not prepared," said Ivan.

"Time is not with us though. We can trust him . . . he needs me. But just why is still unclear."

"Needs you?"

"More on that later. For now, I say we go with him. Something tells me he needs me alive."

Ivan thought for a moment, acknowledging the others in his decisions. "Fine. Mitsunari, kill the fire. Let's see what Estideel has to say to us."

Vandulin waited by the creek while the others gathered their things and readied themselves. After a moment of peace, he stood back up and looked towards the rising smoke of the humans' camp.

It didn't take them long to get ready; they were used to being on the road, and travellers like this knew how to move with efficiency. When the Sage returned to them all, Ivan was still preparing, organizing something that couldn't yet be seen. When he was finished, he turned and slipped something into his pocket. Vandulin recognized it immediately. The purple hood of the plant was distinct and obvious to him; it was poison, wolfsbane, to be exact. He required only a glance to see what the man's intentions were, and to say the least, the Sage was more than intrigued. Few could trigger his curiosity, but it was now in full spirits, and it blazed like a wildfire that knew no boundaries.

✳

They did not travel by wind this time. The night was in full swing when they reached the towering pale walls of Elsibard that grew abruptly out from the earth. Each man had a mask to hide his face, and their hoods sank low over their brows as they huddled together under the rain, shuffling along behind the Sage towards the palace. They were guided by the light of a lantern that illuminated quite little, but Cassius, every now and then, was able to catch faces watching over them, hiding inside their homes. The city was surely plagued by curiosity, and what had happened in the arena was likely the talk of all of Medearia by now. Cassius shivered. It was near midnight, and he did not have the courage to look up towards the moon out of fear of the falling rain crashing against his eyes like plummeting drops of iron. He writhed, pulling his shoulders up and down—it was his neck.

What had the Sage meant when he spoke of training? Am I gonna be . . . like him? A sage? The mark was hidden most of the time. In fact, he had not seen it since it first appeared, but it still burned beneath his skin, and he feared the thought of Ivan ever seeing it. Also, the more he thought about it, the more he feared and loathed the idea of what would happen to Sathelia after—well—after the *deed* was done. After her father was . . . *dead*. It was rather unbelievable to him. So many days travelling, enduring the pernicious places of the world, from freezing in the north to sleeping in an elvish palace that, only months ago, Cassius would never have thought to even exist. He supposed he was rather interested. There was so much he did not know about this land: the people, the places, the religions, and this business of being a sage. Never before did Cassius believe in things like destiny; he did not know whether to fear it or welcome it. All he knew was that, as of now, his entire way of life had changed. It was moving all too fast, as if he was drowning in a river that perpetually led him to the unknown. Even now Cassius made feeble attempts to latch onto any stones that stood in the swift river of life, trying desperately to steady himself and prepare for whatever lay ahead, but destiny was relentless in its grip on him; the more he tried to move against it, the stronger it became.

By now some elves had left their homes and watched the company migrate through the streets. Some were merely curious, while others had nothing but disdain and disgust in their eyes, and they spat in their direction, for they guessed who was beneath the masks. Ivan and the others kept their heads down as their pride was demolished. The cold had soaked them to their bones by now, and there was nothing they could do to fight it. Darkness swallowed them all as they walked underneath a bridge, but as they resurfaced from the tunnel, it seemed as if stars had fallen onto the city streets to pay respect to the travellers. But these were no stars, they were lanterns. They floated hither and thither, being supported by the magic that birthed this city. Upwards the street slanted until they approached a gate where several guards stood half asleep. Vandulin spoke only one word in the elvish tongue, and it zapped the sleeping soldiers into attention. A paper was in the Sage's hands, one with the signature of the king, likely to give permission for the company to enter the higher districts of the city, and this piece of paper, along with Vandulin's reputation, could carry them all into the warm halls of the king's quarters—right where they wanted to be.

The journey through the guts of Elsibard took nearly an hour, and it was spent in constant paranoia. Even Mitsunari could feel his heart pumping beneath his chest. Rooftops hung over them, and strings of water batted their hoods from the eaves. Azrad stopped momentarily, peering into one of the houses; he could only see a pale scalp with loose threads of hair, and then it turned to him, revealing two golden eyes that caused him to jolt backwards and return to the company's march. The elf from inside smiled and cackled at him and allowed the blood in his gums to bleed and the greyness in his teeth to show for the mysterious masked man outside his home. Azrad shivered. He did not like this place, and while the world of Medearia was certainly startling, he could not help but feel that there was much that was hidden from him, *much* that was not being displayed, *much* that was happening that the eye could not detect. He did not know this, nor would he ever, but an unnatural malice was crawling back into the world, an evil that could eradicate all forms of peace and harmony, and it was all due to a brewing poison—the poison of war.

They crossed through four more districts of the city, and with the passing of each border, the buildings and the people seemed to grow in quality and wealth; they were reaching the higher classes now. Then, through the shadows of night, the palace of Elsibard loomed overhead, becoming visible, then quickly invisible through the flashing of lightning. Connell looked up, halted, and then gulped. Of them all, he found it hardest to fight against the fear of the moment. And yet he kept on, pushed his head down, and moved forward, just like he always did in life. He held strong and kept his doubts and anxieties at bay beneath his rough exterior. This act was killing him each day, and he knew it, but he would never have the courage to let go of his pride. Never.

When they had climbed up the stairs, the palace walls and door stood before them, barely visible beneath the wall of water before their eyes, and it was harshly illuminated with each streak of lighting. The door smiled at them all, teeth soaked with cruel intentions.

"Is it you, Vandulin, that leads these strangers through the night?" shouted one of the guards, raising his lantern to get an idea of who approached. The wind whirled about, pulling violently at them all, making them eager to enter into the warmth of the palace.

"It is. Hurry, our guests' appetite for the rain has all but diminished," said Vandulin.

"I'll keep my eyes on them—*both eyes*," said the other guard, who kept his distance from the humans out of fear of contracting some sort of disease. To him, they were animals, and wet dogs didn't belong inside the city's walls, especially not the palace!

The doors crept open, and suddenly, as if it had little significance, *they were in*. All of them. And thus, the plan began, and hysteria sat at the ready, waiting to strike. When the doors were shut, the downfall of rain and the booming claps of thunder were silenced. The company stood awkwardly, scanning their environment, looking up and down the obsidian-coloured interior. All that was heard was the moaning of cold air travelling through each crack and opening within the palace walls. Three elves then entered through a doorway on the left, and they greeted Vandulin with a slight but respectful nod, and they laid their hands out towards the soaked travellers.

"Your weapons, of course," said Vandulin. Cassius was the first to give up his sword, one that he had hardly used, but even then, he still felt unprotected without it; he'd rather have it and never have to use it than not have it when he needed it most. Sir Hadrian followed the prince, and then, although understanding the importance of it, the others handed over their steel with reluctance. Ivan guessed that it was now time to be searched. Of course, this was expected . . . but it was also the moment that Ivan loathed the most. The capsule containing the poison . . . was in his mouth. He could feel the smooth glass rubbing against the inside of his cheek, and he could only pray that the poison would stay inside the bottle. And as if the trap of dread that they had been kept in was not brutal enough, a familiar face entered through the door. Wraithenor walked in smiling. He approached Ivan specifically and then halted when he knew he was close enough to kill. Even through the mask, the hatred in Ivan's eyes was tangible. Wraithenor looked over at the servants and commanded something in their strange speech, and the servants quickly went to work with brutality in their touch. Vandulin was gone . . . and so were their weapons. Cassius was the only one to notice this as the others had their clothes and masks stripped from them and searched thoroughly. Their apparel had been ripped and abused during their time as prisoners, and trinkets and prized possessions that had been picked up along their journey fell out from their pockets and were thrown to the side. They retrieved a hefty sack of coins from Mitsunari, one that Sir Hadrian immediately took note of.

"Had that the whole time?" asked the knight. Shame drew its shadow over Mitsunari, and he couldn't find the courage to reply. Taking a bribe went against everything he had ever stood for. If his sister saw him now, she'd spit on him, and so would each of his ancestors for bringing shame to all who carried the title of Saranorn. The elves gave the purse back to him, and as he held the gold in his hands, he almost felt like throwing it away. *Almost.*

Then, it was Cassius's turn. Their pale and cold hands invaded his body; his armour and hood were torn and ripped from him. Finally, the circle of humiliation had come around, and in a way, this shame was able to provide the final piece of understanding to Cassius. Now he was able to grasp what it truly felt like to be *nobody*, someone without importance or any significance in the world around them. And Cassius could not help but feel that if he dropped dead at this very moment, the world, the universe, would not even blink, for in the grand perspective of it all . . . none of it *really* mattered. The silk robes, the rich foods, the lavish lifestyle, and the title of prince or king mattered little without any purposeful self-creation. In that cold and humiliating space where the breath of the wind touched his naked body, shaming him and his very existence, he figured that the answer to his question of why he deserved to be king was not something words could ever answer—it was only actions that would ever do so, and he was happy with the answer that they provided. He doubted his brother would ever set off on the journey that he currently was taken by. He laughed to himself and smiled. Cassius thought of the moment when he'd return and see the look on his father's and brother's faces. Of course, he'd have to deal with quite an earful and quite possibly a smack across the face, but he'd have no regrets. In the end, he'd have shown them all, and without a doubt, his father and brother would be proud of the Cassius that stood before them.

Suddenly, he was smacked across the back of his head, freeing him from his sudden dream and pulling him back to reality. *We still have much to do,* thought the prince. The elf behind him shouted and nudged him forwards.

"You will follow me," said Wraithenor. "The king will await you in the afternoon of tomorrow. For now, you'll have time to plan out any pitiful proposition you aim to make to us. In my opinion, it is useless, but we elves have always known your kind to be . . . well, inferior as far as intelligence goes, so it wouldn't be fair of me to judge you for it. So, come. You will be shown to your *separate* rooms."

"What of our clothes?" asked Cassius, and the elves turned to him. They had not expected to hear a word from him, and if anything, they were amused.

"Your fabrics shall be burned, and your armour will be melted down," said Wraithenor. "They smell of feces and dirt, you did not really think that you would be allowed in the presence of the king in some rags you found in the streets? No. There will be appropriate attire waiting for you."

"Come, come. All of you," said another elf. He was far skinnier than the rest, and next to Wraithenor his body cowered underneath him. His name was Cibile, an older elf but with the tenacity of a young spring leaf looking into the face of summer with excitement. His thinning grey hair was combed back, and he wore a pair of glasses that no Ederian had ever seen. The glasses had a gold chain that wrapped around his neck, and the frame of them was made of pure silver. They seemed years beyond any pair of glasses Cassius had ever seen, even amongst the scholars and aristocrats in the cities of Ekmere, Aaronor, and Vuldhear. It began to appear more and more obvious that the inhabitants of Medearia possessed a plethora of knowledge and advanced technology that surpassed anything that was possessed back home, and if Estideel was to get the war he wanted, Cassius doubted even someone like his father could be victorious.

Cibile led them through the palace. He spoke little, only saying something when he felt it necessary to show off the architecture or statues that were found in the west wing, surely a tactic to prove the elvish superiority. At times he delved into brief history lessons regarding the city. It reminded Cassius of when his father used to do the same, leading him and Vidicus around Ekmere, telling them tales of the first Casthedians to sail to Ederia and how the Casthedians— which the Helladawns were descendants of—helped save the people of Ederia from the dragons. Cassius loved tales like that, especially ones that happened so long ago and yet captured someone within them, letting them see a world that has long since been lost.

"What was your name? I don't believe I've asked," said Cassius.

"My name? It is Cibile," said the elf without turning towards the prince.

"Do you know anything of Ederian history? Anything of the dragons?"

"I do."

"Well, were there ever any dragons here, in Medearia?"

"Once, yes. From what Vandulin has told us, they were once creatures of unfathomable beauty and allure! But ever seen since the Great Breaching and the War of Fire, their kind has grown few in numbers, and it is said that they sleep in the heart of the earth, letting hate consume them."

"Wait! So, you're saying that they are still alive?"

"You humans do not know very much of common history, do you? Of course, they are alive! The Great Breaching? The War of Fire? Do you know nothing of them as well?"

"I know only what my father has taught me: that my people, the Casthedians, sailed over as their home sank into the sea, and once they arrived, they hunted down each and every last dragon there was."

Cibile stopped. Turned. And looked at Cassius as if the prince was jesting. As soon as he realized the boy was being honest with him, he erupted into violent laughter. Tears wetted his eyes, and he was forced to wipe down the insides of his glasses. "Okay . . . whatever jest you are trying to attempt . . . please . . . stop," said Cibile, but his words were difficult to make out through the constant laughter. "Wait, you're being serious? By the stars . . . you are!" He put his glasses back on and returned to leading them to their rooms. "When your ancestors came to Ederia, they were nearly wiped out. In fact, your entire species was nearly killed off. Vandulin, who at the time was king of Medearia, gathered our armies and sailed west.

"Thus, the War of Fire began, and for years the grasslands and prairies of your land were wet with blood, and mountain tops were burnt and coated in ash. It only ended when Vandulin challenged their king, Vulldarkhan, *and he defeated him*. When the war was over, humans and the many races of Medearia lived in peace . . . I only wish it could have lasted."

"What happened then? Why did the peace not last?" asked Cassius, too enthralled by the elf's stories to remember his place, and that he also was without clothes.

"Nothing good, Prince Cassius. Nothing good." They were silent again. Cassius could tell that he had struck quite the nerve in Cibile, and he actually felt bad for him. The clear sense of sadness in his eyes was easy to spot, but it made his question even more dire and not having the answer to it felt like a painful burden that he now was forced to carry. In the hallway that they were in, ten doors were on the right, and to the left were a number of paintings: one was of Sathelia and her father, but the other one next to it was someone else. Below it read, *Aurora Litherius*. It did not take long for the prince to put the simplistic puzzle together in his head: it was Sathelia's mother. Apart from the black hair, she looked almost exactly like her. Already Cassius began to miss Sathelia, and he hoped that she'd be at the meeting tomorrow just so that he could see her again, for after tomorrow, he likely would not.

"On the right, you will find your rooms. Cassius, your room is the first," said Cibile. The company gave each other one last long look before they entered their rooms.

This was it.

The final stretch of their journey was now in sight.

When the door behind him closed, Ivan could breathe again, and he spat out the capsule onto the bed where the elves had neatly placed his attire. He picked up the robes and looked at them before trying them on; they were the colour of deep blue, one that could only be found in the purest of seas. He was relieved to not be forced into a tight doublet in which he could barely move, or even breathe, for that matter. A poncho was also to be worn over top, and it was a far lighter blue; these two pieces made up the common apparel for any elf that lived under the palace roof. He quickly adorned himself. Already something had gone awry; Ivan hadn't predicted that they'd go so far as to burn their clothes, and without the gloves, the poison could not be handled. They had not exactly had much time to form any *real* plan, and improvisation was always a deadly idea, especially in moments like this, but it was now their only option. The rest of the company knew that any form of a plan had already been lost the very moment the gloves were taken, yet they could not voice their distress. *Everything* had to appear perfectly fine. They *needed* to stay calm.

Ivan paced to and fro from each opposite wall of his room before sitting down. He then grabbed the glass capsule and looked upon the poison.

Well, Ivan, just what do you have planned this time? he asked himself while twirling the poison between his fingers. *A plan that cannot be adapted is no plan at all. So, think, you fucking scoundrel, think!*

Then, suddenly, a knock on the door broke his concentration. His eyes darted towards the origins of the sound, and he was quick to hide the poison underneath his sheets.

Knock.

Knock.

Knock.

"Who is it?"

"A friend," said a feminine voice from behind the door.

"Odd, I don't recall having many friends here. And just what exactly does this friend of mine intend on doing?"

"To pass on a treasured gift. But to do that, you must let me in."

Ivan looked around for a weapon. He knew better than to blindly let strangers inside. He armed himself with the candlestick that was kept by his bedside, and he waited by the door. "You may come in." The door was opened ever so politely. It was Freya.

"*Well*, I must say it is a first for me, to see a human so close up."

"I've seen your kind in the flesh before, but I've yet to see one that calls itself a friend."

"Oh, but I am, and you have more than you think you do." Freya closed the door behind her. She looked at the candlestick in his hand and grinned, and then sat down at the foot of the bed. "You have nothing to fear from me. In fact, I would say that you have something to *gain* from me, something you might *need*."

"Cut to the chase."

"You have a friend in high places, one that is more than capable of pulling the strings behind the king's back. One that wishes to see you succeed in your . . . plan."

"Can't say I follow you," said Ivan

"Oh, but you do. I know more than you think."

"And what exactly do you *think* you know?"

"I know that you are not here for some useless peace treaty; I know that you come here with murder on your mind; I *know* that you intend on killing the king. But I also *know* that there are many in Medearia that wish for you to succeed. This foolish war that Estideel is so keen on pursuing is as personal as it is unnecessary. If you ask me, it's the result of a petty disdain, and he'll have his own people suffer if it means getting what he wants."

"And just what does he want?"

"For there to be blood on his hands."

"So, just what exactly can I *gain* from you? We don't have all the time in the world to get this done." In her hand, Freya held a silk purse, one that she handed over to Ivan.

"Go ahead, open it."

Ivan did just so, and inside were two pairs of gloves and two vials. He looked up at the elf, astonished. "How . . . ?"

"No room for talk, I am running out of time. They'll notice soon enough that I am gone from the council meeting. One vial contains a poison, but be careful, it is far deadlier than the one you already possess, and it should be easier to apply to the gloves. In the other vial is the antidote in case you don't know what you're doing. Now, I must leave before any greater suspicion begins to grow." Freya stood up from the bed and went for the door.

"Wait! Just how do you know so much?"

She turned to him and smiled, baring her teeth, which were like white needles. "As I said, you have a powerful friend, and he and his wolves watch us all, you and your companions especially," she said, and that was all. She was gone. Lost to the unknown world that lived beyond the door to his room. He sat down, perplexed by it all. There was so much that moved in the shadows, and its next movement was hard to predict, even for him. Yet still, he believed that this "friend" of his had not caught onto his *other* plan, but he'd have to be far more careful now. He had now entered the deadly game of politics, played only by the rich and thus never before by him.

Once Estideel lies choking on his own blood, we are to make it back to the safety of Cassemor. Yes. Yes, that's when the kid dies, and if the old knight tries anything, we'll gut him too. After some time, we'll make it back into the city, and we'll find that daughter of his and make her squeal. She'll be nothing more than an instrument of my will once I'm done with her.

My time will come.

My time will come.

Ivan found himself staring into the void, pondering his own desires. He thought of a time that had long passed, a day that had been born into this world long before he had ever sailed east. A time before the pain, when suffering was something he simply did not know. He remembered the days when he was a boy like all others, with a loving family that knew how to raise him well. He would go hunting with father in the day and come back home in the evenings to help mother with supper. Then, as Ivan sat back in his bed and prepared for sleep, his eyes began to water as more and more memories flooded his mind, like the precious rains that bring the desert back from death. He remembered when his father went off to war, leaving him and his mother to tend to the farm. He wished he had the memory of his father coming home, but that was something that never happened. It didn't take long for the war to reach them, and when it did, the Casthedian flag flew on the horizon, signalling the dread that was nigh. When the king's armies came through, rape and anger came with them. Ivan recalled the moment as if it had just happened, when the soldiers broke down the door, robbed them, and then raped his mother. She talked less and less after that. A week later Ivan found her in the fields, glass stuck in her wrists. Her body's lips were as blue as ice. All of it, every drop of pain Ivan felt after that day he knew was the result of that flag dancing on the horizon, the dragon banners flying high, mocking the peasants below. On that day, when his mother's body had been drained of its blood, and the dirt was frozen on her skin by the grace of the morning frost, he knew he wanted to stop this kind of sorrow from touching anyone else, and he didn't care what it would take or what it would cost.

But now, he knew just how. How he'd stop the butchering. But it was only possible if he sat on that throne in Ekmere. Only then would he be at peace.

My time will come.

My time will come.

❋

The candlelight was slowly dying. Mitsunari lay restlessly as the rest of the world was deeply hidden away in slumber. Too many things were on his mind that night, and he couldn't bring himself to blow away the candles and fall asleep. He sat up. Under the sheets, it was far too hot, and he let himself cool down by sitting at his bedside. He picked up the sack of coins from the floor and withdrew a single piece, and the light from the candles danced off its golden surface. What was he doing? He had tried so hard for so many years to bring back the honour he had lost, but by betraying Cassius like this at the first sight of gold would be throwing it all away, burning the last remnants of self-respect he had. He dropped the sack to the floor, and his head sank to his knees as his hair came untied and fell loose. He then ran his hands through the portion of his hair that was white—a constant reminder of why he did not deserve the title of Saranorn; a reminder as to why he did not deserve to live.

"What has gotten into you, brother?"

"Who said that?" asked Mitsunari, raising his head to see for himself. There, illuminated in the dying flames of the candles, stood the spirit of his sister, Yuikiri. "H-how can this be? I saw you die!"

"Lifeless is my body, but my soul could not be more free." She sat down, put her arm around him, and embraced her brother. Mitsunari had not felt this form of love since the day of her death, and he began to weep, letting go of all the emotions that he had kept hidden for so long. Mitsunari tried to speak but found that he could not. Yuikiri touched a tear from her brother's face as it fell, then she stood up before her brother, looking down at him as he fell apart in front of her.

"I—I'm sorry," said Mitsunari, too ashamed and broken to look at his sister in her eyes.

"There is a lot in you, brother, a lot in you that should have been released long ago. I am glad to see it finally come out. You don't know just how happy it makes me to see you shed a tear. Know that it is not too late to make things right, it's not too late to begin to heal your wounds."

Mitsunari shouted and threw the coin purse across the room, and the gold flew hither and thither, bouncing off the walls. "I am lost, sister. I don't know the path that lies before me, but I do know that it is home to many hidden dangers. But avoid them? It seems I cannot. If I stay loyal to Ivan, I am betraying those I love, but if I do not, I would still be doing the same."

"Sometimes, it is hard to see which path is best for us in life. At times, it is clear. However in others, our sight of what is evil and good is blurred, and we are left to decide for ourselves, and sometimes we are wrong. But we are only ever wrong when we betray our heart's desire. So, what does your heart say to you?"

"It rarely speaks to me. It has been cold ever since I failed to save Lord Shinzu . . . and allowed mother to die. But at times, I can hear its desperate whispers, yet its words are weak."

"You failed Lord Shinzu, yes. But no one has punished you more for that than your own self. As your sister, I too can hear the whispers of your heart, and sense that it would grow even colder if you were to let Cassius die. Bringing joy and protection to people has always brought you the purest form of happiness."

"You're right! I cannot stand by and let a boy, the future for all of Ederia, die. It's funny, you've always been able to understand me better than I understand myself."

"Of course, I do! It's my job as your sister, after all." Mitsunari laughed, and his tears fell to the floor beneath him, forming a pool that created a reflection. And as he looked at his own face, he felt only the desire to pull himself together again, to reclaim the honour, the self-respect, and the natural ability to feel, to truly *feel* what he felt on the inside. No longer would he be a mere cold shell of a man. No. No more.

"I will always miss you, Yuikiri," he said looking up and choking on his own words and tears. But no one was there. No sister. Nothing by the dying light of the candles. But she had heard his words, he knew it. And although he was the only one in the room, he was not alone at all, and he never had been.

As of now, the gold was worthless. He would pledge his sword one last time. To Cassius. And if he were to fail, he would die trying to protect his prince, his king, and even then, he'd find a way to keep him safe. Mitsunari then lay back down in his bed, blew out the candles, and shut his eyes. Never before had he slept so soundly.

What Is Dead Is
Never Lost

C assius seemed incapable of stopping the constant trembling. In the mirror he fixed his elvish apparel. It was far more comfortable and natural than any doublet he'd ever worn. But in the mirror, it was impossible not to notice it—he was afraid. Terrified. Part of him wished he had Sir Hadrian here to calm him down; something about his presence always made him feel like everything was going to be all right. However, another side of him was determined to conquer this fear himself, and this was the side that was ultimately victorious. He touched the tip of his beard and played with his hair, then he took a deep breath. Inhale. Exhale. Inhale. Exhale—*knock, knock, knock.* Someone was at the door. It took a few seconds for Cassius to notice he wasn't breathing, and therefore he could feel the thunderous thumping of his heart in his chest.

"Cassius?" said the voice, and he was able to relax, it was Sathelia.

"Come in," he said. Quickly, Cassius fixed his hair once more and rubbed the circles under his eyes, but it was too late, she was already inside.

Fuck, I look terrible. If only I'd slept more last night, thought the prince.

"Morning," said Sathelia, and in her hand was a tray with a teapot and two small glasses on it. "Tea?"

"Yes. Yes, of course! I'd love some tea, thank you. Would you like a chair?"

"I'll be fine on the bed."

"Okay," said Cassius, sitting down beside her and taking his tea.

"Careful, it's hot," she said. Cassius blew on it, but simultaneously got a look at her: perpetually beautiful, of course, but also, she was nervous, unable to keep still. "So, today is the day."

"Today is the day, yes. Does your father still hate me?"

"Well, I wouldn't take it personally; he isn't fond of many humans."

"Oh, he'll warm up to me, I'm sure."

"Are you now?"

"Course, how could he not be swayed by my impeccable good looks and my way with words?" It wasn't really a question, only an attempt to make her laugh, and she did, in the polite and discreet way that all who have been taught a life of courtesy did. Each time she laughed, her eyes would squint in her mirth. It was cute, and Cassius looked for it each time.

"A good point. But I'm sure he'll be more concerned with what you have to say rather than the way you appear."

"Well . . . dammit. I was depending on my looks because I haven't a clue what to say to him."

"Tell him the truth," she said, and she looked at him now with concern and care that was as clear as sunrise. "So, what is the truth?"

The sense of comfortability was now all but lost. He couldn't tell her the truth, but lying to her face felt almost as bad, and he felt the sweat on his hands begin to grow. "I'd tell him that I'm sorry. I'm sorry for the atrocities of my ancestors, and they should never be forgotten. But sometimes, the hardest thing in life is forgiveness, and I will ask him to call upon his strength to attempt such a task—to forgive. There is no time like the present to rekindle the fires of an alliance. I'm asking a lot, I know, but I would not have come all this way if I didn't think it was worth it."

For a moment, what he had said *did* feel like the truth. Sathelia leaned in as Cassius's attention was elsewhere and kissed him on the cheek. "Thank you, Cassius," she said, and she saw the red in his cheeks, and both of them shone under rays of love.

"So . . . see you at the meeting, yes?"

"I will see you then, my prince. And may starlight stalk your steps," she said, and again, she smiled, and her eyes squinted just the way Cassius loved. She left him there. He was alone, alone to contemplate her kiss. His hand touched the place where her lips had been, and the presence of magic was undeniable. It was in the air. It was inside of him. Now, nothing mattered, for it could not be seen: the only thing on the horizon was her, and he was blind to anything else.

※

Two hours had passed when Cassius heard another knock on the door. He jumped to his feet, hoping it'd be her. "Sathelia?" He opened the door to disappointment.

"I am afraid not," said Cibile.

"Oh."

"The king awaits you all now. Are you ready?"

"Now?" Cassius looked back into the room and back at the elf. He'd forgotten all about the king, thus when reality crashed upon him like a wave from the Mortem Sea, his mind *nearly* crumbled under the pressure. "Yes," he said plainly, and with those words, there was now no turning back. He'd stepped into the fire, and he'd have to accept that getting burned was inexorable.

"Good. Follow me," said Cibile, and as Cassius followed him out the door, he saw the rest of the company. Their eyes met, and they gave each other one last nod of trust before they walked through the gates of the storm. In their silence, the sinister understanding of it all came to them: it was possible that they'd all die here and now, but if death called their names, they'd do their best to make the journey's end a glorious one.

Ivan had applied the poison given to him to the gloves, and they were hidden away inside his robes, and to protect himself from them, they were kept away inside the sack they had come in. He had also only applied the poison to the top third of the glove, making them safer to work with. After all, this would all be worthless if he ended up poisoning himself.

They passed by the paintings on the left, and on the right was a hallway that led to a series of stairs that ran to the throne, but that was not their path. To their left was a large door whose arch frowned over them all. It was opened as they approached it, and Cibile then stood aside to let the guests enter first.

There he was.

Estideel.

Waiting in a dubious silence, and one look into his eyes was like peering into those of an animal—one that was eager to meet its prey. To his left sat Sathelia and behind was him Vandulin, standing with his arms crossed, watching the scene unfold as if he knew what would happen. Other members of the elvish court sat around a long rectangular table, but Ivan noticed Freya immediately, letting their eyes meet for just a moment before moving on. The door shut behind them, and it shattered the silent space around them, echoing in the far corners.

". . . Have a seat," said the king as he pointed towards six empty chairs to his left. Cassius made sure he sat down beside Sathelia. The two made a quick greeting, and by then they had all sat down.

Silence.

For Cassius, it felt strange, but it wasn't his first time being under the hospitality of the elves, but for the others . . . they did not know exactly how to feel. Connell and Azrad looked around the room, unsure of what to say, and Mitsunari found himself rudely staring at the hosts. "So? Go ahead. Introduce me to your friends, Prince Cassius," said Estideel.

". . . .Well . . ."

"They do have names, don't they?"

"They do. This, to my left is—"

"Ivan, I am called Ivan."

"Yes. Wraithenor has told me of you. And?"

The rest of the Company of Ekmere introduced themselves one by one, each standing when they did so. But now it was the king's turn to stand, and he did just so and then began to slowly walk around the room, looking down towards the rim of the wine glass in his hand. "Bulldior?"

"Yes, my lord?"

"What is the year?"

"1298, my lord."

"Incredible. Time really can pass in a series of moments that are soon to become mere memories. It was the year 762. That was when I learned the feeling of shackles, the touch of rusted iron on my skin, and I learned what it was like to be a slave, to be someone's *pet*. Vandulin knows this feeling as well, as does Bulldior. We know what it is like to see the ones we love be butchered . . . like cattle. Eradicated, like a disease. I was . . . twelve . . . yes . . . twelve when I saw my mother's blood drain from her body and soak the ground beneath my feet. One does not forget such a thing." Estideel was now directly behind Cassius, and he stood still, towering over the prince, and he then leaned in towards him to whisper in his ear, yet still making no effort to make eye contact.

"Nigh sixty years we waited, rotting and waiting for the day to return home. I became numb to the touch of shackles. The smell of blood on my wrists and the rotting of my own flesh was a companion, and the perpetual feeling of hopelessness became nothing more than a familiarity," said the king, now seemingly growling in Cassius's ears, and the prince was frozen under the cool breath of fear. Estideel then backed away and returned to where his seat was, but he did not sit, and the fury inside him was clawing through so that it was now visible in his face. "*And so, you have travelled all this way to tell me, to tell my people that we do not deserve justice for the atrocities of your kind? YOU COME TO TELL ME THAT MY HATRED IS NO MORE THAN A FOOL'S PETTY DISDAIN?*"

The king's voice sang back to him echoes of his own rage, and none dared speak out of turn, all except for one. "That is not what we ask of you, my lord," said Cassius, standing up in front of them all. "I cannot ask you to forget, for wounds as deep as yours are eternal, but their pain does not need to be. Sometimes the easiest option is to hate, and there is no shame in that. I only ask of you to travel along the harder road—that of forgiveness, because at times, it can be the bravest act of all, but also the greatest cure for scars that run as deep as your people's."

"Do not take me for a fool, boy. You cannot swindle one such as me with the wit of your tongue. You are begging for mercy, that is all that I see in you."

"And when did mercy become a sign of weakness?" asked Cassius, and he now grew confident, but as to where this confidence came from, he did not know.

"This is not about power; I have that already. This is about order! Malevolence *must* be meted with equal force, *that* is how order is kept in a world as wild as the one we live in."

"The thought of revenge promises us internal harmony, but that promise is no more than a lie, and sometimes that lie is only realized when it is too late. Please, my king, I implore you—"

"You implore me? Who are you to 'implore' me? You are nothing more than a drop of rain in a storm, a grain of sand in the desert, a single leaf in the forest."

"There are those in your land that bear no ill intentions to my kind, for they have only known a world without us. So why drag your people into a war they do not want, and one they do not need?"

"I speak for the people."

"No, you speak for yourself."

"How . . . *DARE YOU!*"

Estideel was now hunched over the table, fueled by nothing more than thoughtless anger and blind and tumultuous hostility. Cassius looked over at the Sage and saw the smirk on his face, he was evidently enjoying the show. Then, he felt Ivan's elbow lightly jab his shoulder, reminding him to check his manners.

"My king," said Ivan, "I am sorry if my companion has offended you. What he means to say is—"

"Silence," said Estideel, locking eyes with Cassius and Cassius only. "You know, I admire you. You have courage to stand before me and pontificate. You are much like your father."

"You have met my father?"

"No. But my vision is wide, and my eyes see everything, and just recently, they have heard rumours of something interesting," said the king, and he had reclaimed his calmness now and replaced it with arrogance.

"What do you mean?"

"Well, it is not my place to tell you, but I will say that Ederia has changed since your absence. Some say for the better. Such a shame, yet also how poetic. The last time you saw your father, you were no son to him, and it would seem that it shall remain so. You likely wish to return home and prove how much you have changed for the better, but that will never be."

"I don't understand. What do you mean Ederia has changed?"

"We are done here. There will be no more talks of peace. Only war."

Ivan then stood up.

It was time.

The gloves were on.

The poison was ready.

"A shame. Really. It seems this journey was for nothing," said Ivan.

"It would seem as such, yes," said Estideel.

"In Ederia it is a custom that, regardless of the result, both parties are to finish with a simple shake of the hand. Will you indulge me?" Ivan's hand was outstretched and ready to pass on the touch of death. Estideel approached him and stopped when he was close enough to shake the man's hand. He paused, looking over the leather hand before him.

"However, in Medearia, it is no custom of ours, and you will respect our customs when I allow you to sleep under my roof."

"Of course, my king." Ivan's heart stopped. He couldn't be desperate, not now, or else it would seem even stranger, and the king would surely see what was afoot. Maybe he already did? Ivan could kill him right now if he wanted to, but that would only end in each of their deaths, and he wanted to avoid that outcome at all costs. He abandoned the plan and sat back down, switching the gloves under the table. A universal notion of failure grew inside each member of the company, and it was impossible to hide, but as Cassius grappled with the thought of their failure, he noticed that Vandulin was gone, and he thought it odd for him to be absent, after all, it was a part of his duty to protect the king. He kept his mouth shut . . . but he could not help but wonder where the Sage had gone.

"I will give you one week," said Estideel. "By then I wish for you to leave this land, and if you do not, I will have each of you executed and your bodies paraded around the city. Are we clear?"

Cassius was speechless. He sat up from the table and didn't even give Sathelia a glance before turning his back to her. She wanted to say something, but the wrath of her father was too formidable right now to go against. Thus her spirits fell too, and it seemed to her that she'd never again see Cassius and that—as insane as the idea had seemed—a life with him was never meant to be.

*

The hall was empty. It did not matter, it wasn't like Ivan was in any mood to speak to anyone. He leaned against the door to his room with his hands braced up against it. He brooded there for what seemed like an eternity; stars could have been born and died in the time that he stood there, hating himself, *hating* their misfortune. All of it, everything would be for nothing if he didn't find a way, but the way was dark now, and this was a darkness that Ivan didn't know how to tread upon. A burst of sudden anger ran through his body, and in a blink his knuckles were red with blood—he had punched the door. He did it again. And again. And again. Until with each punch he screamed, and the more he screamed the more he hated, and the more hated the more of his own blood was shed, and by then he was no more than a mess, knuckles wet with a fresh coat of red.

I am sorry, mother. I cannot see myself ever gaining the power to change this world. It appears the drums of chaos will play forever, and someone with a fool's dream for change can never silence them. War will infect us again, and this time, it'll bring an end to us all. Maybe that's mercy?

No answer came, and none would come from his mother. She had not even been buried. That day, when Ivan found her, he did one thing and that was run. He ran away and hoped the claws of grief would never catch him; he hoped he'd forget. But he never did, and thus began a life of regret.

Ivan opened the door to his room and entered . . . but something was there . . . something that he *truly* had never expected to see—his sword, along with the arsenal of weapons he'd taken with him on the journey. In each room, every man of the company found their weapon placed on their bed. Just who had placed it didn't matter, all they saw now was a chance, a chance to accomplish what they had set off to do.

There was no knock on Mitsunari's door, instead, it swung open instantly, and Mitsunari drew Kazemaru without a thought.

"Fast as ever, I see," said Azrad, and behind him stood Connell. "Seems we've all been given a little gift."

"Are you insane? If they see you in here, we're all dead," said Mitsunari.

"Not a guard in sight, no need to worry," said Connell.

"Strange though, isn't it? First our weapons, then the palace seems pretty much abandoned. It's all too perfect," said Azrad.

"Agreed. Something isn't right," said Mitsunari.

"Anyways, that isn't why we risked coming here, actually. Ivan has told us that he's let you in on his plan. Look, I'd rather not have to kill the kid too, or Blackwood either, I get it, decent folk they are. But we need to know that when the time comes, you'll have our back."

"Ivan's already paid me, what brings your doubts?"

"Fuck the gold. If we get out of here alive, I'm not trusting someone whose word is as good as the coin he's given. We need to know."

"Then know this," said Mitsunari. "My word is one you can trust . . . and when the time comes, you will have me and my sword at your side."

"Well then, let's find Ivan while we have the chance, see if we can pull this all together," said Connell, but when they entered Ivan's room, there was no one there.

Ivan stalked down the princess from afar, sword in hand. He kept hidden around a corner, watching her, stalking her . . . and following her. The number of guards had grown few in numbers, and he took his chances now to take things into his own hands . . . to improvise. When she moved, he moved, but carefully. He slowed down his breathing, and his mind shifted into that of a hunter's, sticking to the shadows where he couldn't be seen. She went up the stairs with slight haste now. Either she had reason to be in a hurry, or she had begun to feel the sensation of eyes watching each move she made. Ivan considered it the latter, so he held back for a moment and let her exit the throne room. When she did, he checked for guards—no one. It was unusually quiet, and although he didn't like it one bit, it was now or never, and actions had to be taken before they were forced to leave. He sprang into the open and ran past the throne and up the stairs that the princess had taken earlier. She was out of sight. Ivan smelled the air and was guided by the aroma of her perfume. He blindly followed it, rushing his way up the spiral staircase as fast as he could to catch up to her, and thankfully, his sense of hearing saved him from himself. He heard her. She was crying. Creeping slowly towards the sound of her sadness, he found the door and opened it.

Sathelia wiped her eyes and sat up in her bed to see her pillows wet with tears.

Such a fool I am, I should have said something in the meeting, something that would change father's mind, thought Sathelia as she clutched the stone around her neck and rocked back and forth to soothe herself and wipe away her distress. It was odd, her affection for Cassius had crept up on her so swiftly that she hadn't even realized how much she cared for him before it was too late. And now it was. *A halfwit you are, Sathelia! A stupid girl with stupid dreams that never seem to amount to anything beyond fantasies.*

She felt like hitting herself. She regretted not telling Cassius how she felt about him. He was different. He didn't try too hard like the others to impress her, and he was far from perfect, but—to her—it was his flaws that made him appealing, made him relatable. And the fact that he had the courage to change a part of himself for the better, well . . . it gave her hope.

The door made no sound, and no floorboard creaked under the feet of Ivan, and when Sathelia felt his blade gently touch the skin on her throat, there was nothing she could do. She attempted to turn to see who it was, but Ivan quickly took control of her body with ease and drowned her screams with his hand. But even being out-matched, she twisted and writhed as violently as she could, rocking Ivan back and forth, and breaking anything she could to make noise. It was then that Ivan took the blade away from her throat and pinned her on her stomach to the bed. "Move, you die. Scream, you die. Understand?" whispered Ivan, and Sathelia went to open her mouth but soon found a knife ready to slit her open, and so she kept quiet. "You're gonna bring your father to me."

※

When Cassius had come back from the meeting to find his sword lying on his bed, it didn't take long for Sir Hadrian to knock on the door, and he knew it was him right away; he had a special way of knocking that wasn't easily replicated so that Cassius would always know it was him.

"Hey," said Cassius, but his voice was one from the grave. Sir Hadrian rested his hand on the boy's shoulder. He wanted to speak, but something told him to keep silent; sometimes silence is the best medicine. Right now, all Cassius needed was company, someone to be with, and he'd be happy to help with such a thing. "We failed. Terribly, I'd say."

"No."

"No? You heard him, didn't you? He'll sail west, and he'll burn everything that lives along the way."

"Yes, I heard him. But *you* didn't fail. You set off on this journey to find some kind of self-worth, and I think you found it, don't you?"

Cassius turned towards him, and that smile of his was like a warm oak-made fire in the dead of winter, thawing the brutality that surrounded him.

"... You're right . . . I did."

"You know, to me, it was always clear as day."

"What was?"

"You! Who you are, who you *truly* are."

"Just who do you think that is?"

". . . You are my king," said Sir Hadrian, and Cassius caught the old man by surprise and gave his friend a hug. The two then laughed and then reminisced and told each other stories. From Hadrian's tales of jousting tournaments gone wrong to Cassius's experiences from the gutters of Ekmere, they enjoyed each other's company, truly. All that was missing was a cold mug of beer and a plate of food resting in their bellies.

Then, the knight's laughter wavered, and something perked his curiosity. "Strange, I've never seen it do that before," he said, pointing towards Cassius's necklace, *En Estar*. When he turned to see what was happening, he saw that the necklace, which usually was the colour green, was flashing red—a dark and chilling hue, that of blood.

The hair on Cassius's skin then rose.

The room grew colder as if all the light in the world had been put out.

Something was wrong. He knew it.

"It's—*she's in danger!*" Before Sir Hadrian could question it, the prince was running out of the room and into the hall with his sword clutched tightly in his hand. Sir Hadrian followed, and he was quick to do so as well.

Mitsunari and the others were in the hallway when they caught the fleeing sight of Sir Hadrian just before he turned out of view. They looked at each other and ran after them, desperate to find answers to just what was going on.

Estideel was in his study when he heard the voice of Sathelia calling to him. Although reluctant to halt his work, he got up and made his way to his daughter's room.

"What is it, Sathelia? I am quite busy, so if it is your wish to walk the gardens, I will not be able to join you. Tomorrow though, I will," said Estideel as he walked through the doorway and into the mess that was his daughter's room; something had certainly happened here, some sort of struggle. Her mirror was cracked, and her plates were shattered in pieces across the floor while her sheets were ripped and torn. "*Sathelia! Daughter!*" But there was no answer, and the king was thrown into a spell of panic as he searched the room, looking for her.

"F-f-father," whispered Sathelia. Estideel turned to see her in tears and shaking with fear, for the man he knew as Ivan stood behind her with a knife by her throat.

"Not a fucking word," said Ivan, and he'd grown fey and sick with hatred. He did indeed take joy in something like this. It could be seen in him with ease—the insanity, it was growing inside of his body like a sickness that knew no boundaries. "Those gardens won't be there for you tomorrow . . . nothing will."

"Please! Don't hurt her!"

"What did I say? *Not a fucking word,*" said Ivan, and he began to dig the teeth of the blade in her throat, cutting very shallowly, without any intention to kill.

"What do you want? I'll give it! I'll call off my armies, I'll burn down my boats! I will forget Ederia entirely if it means you letting her go," said Estideel, and Ivan fed off of the king's desperation . . . and he enjoyed the taste of it.

"Power," said Ivan, and with one hand he covered Sathelia's mouth, and with the other, he threw his knife . . . and his aim was true. It pierced Estideel's heart, and the air in his lungs seeped out and was followed by blood. A single tear dropped from his eyes, and with that, the last drop of life was gone.

The king was dead.

Sathelia screamed her lungs out until she felt as if they'd begin to bleed, and she cried until she thought it impossible to weep anymore. Ivan threw her on the bed. With the butt of his knife, he cracked the side of her temple, and she was unconscious. Alive. But unconscious. It was then that Ivan heard footsteps, and he drew his sword from its scabbard, readying himself for guards, but what came was something else—it was Cassius, followed by Sir Hadrian. The prince saw immediately a man he viewed as a friend atop the woman he loved, and without thought, he too drew his sword.

"*WHAT ARE YOU DOING?*" shouted Cassius, and there was a deadly malice pulsing through him that no one had ever seen before.

"What the fuck do you think I'm doing? Keep it down, too. You want company? Get looking for the closest way out—*and quick!*"

"Get away from her!"

"*What do you mean? We! Have! To! Leave!* What makes you care about some elvish whore?"

"*Don't call her that!*"

"*Call her what? Call her what she is? An elvish whore?*"

Something then took the prince. Every thought was now dictated by the newborn ire that burned within him, and he rushed Ivan, sword thrusting towards him, but Ivan was far too quick, and he deflected the prince's attack. Then, with the back of his fist, he struck Cassius, knocking him to the floor . . . and the prince's vision of the world around him grew dark . . . until the darkness consumed it all, and he too was unconscious.

Sir Hadrian stepped into the room now, and slowly unsheathed his blade, sizing up Ivan as he had done long ago at Ekmere.

"Well, here we are, old man. I must say, a part of me has looked forward to this," said Ivan, but Sir Hadrian made no response, he was too focused now, and he could not afford to have such a focus broken in a time like this. He knew Ivan was dangerous, but he also knew that there was much about him that he was still uncertain of, and this made him even deadlier. It was then that the rest of the company ran into the room, and finally . . . sides were taken.

"Good," said Ivan. "I'm sorry, old man, but this journey for you is at its end. Mitsunari . . . *kill him.*"

Immediately, Sir Hadrian shifted positions so that he now faced all four of them. Kazemaru was unleashed from its sheath . . . but Mitsunari . . . *hesitated.* The Sarakotan then threw the sack of gold coins towards Ivan and stepped away from Azrad and Connell.

"You may keep your gold; my loyalty cannot be bought," said Mitsunari, and he readied himself for whatever was to come. Azrad and Connell then drew their weapons, and all five looked at each other, waiting for someone to make a move. Ivan was the first to make a move, and he lunged forward to grab the prince, and with such a movement, all five of them shot into action like a whip of lightning capable of breaking the sky in two. When Sir Hadrian attacked, it was aimed at Ivan, thus forcing him to abandon the prince and defend himself. As this occurred, Connell made his attack as well, heaving his sword down towards the knight, but Mitsunari was there to defend him, raising Kazemaru against the brute force that fell from above, and the clash and ringing of metal filled the room for all but a second before they once again stood still. The knight and the Sarakotan stood back-to-back, facing down men who they once thought to be their brethren.

No one moved.

There was complete and utter stillness that could only be accomplished through years of training and discipline. But the silence was vanquished when each of them began to hear the guards rushing towards the scene, and within moments of hearing this, Ivan swung and pushed Sir Hadrian out of his way and ran for the door. There was a tumultuous burst of slaughter in the hallway, and when Sir Hadrian followed him, the only thing that remained were the bodies of two guardsmen, but more were on their way. Cassius then awoke, and at first sight he saw Azrad and Connell at the ready to face the Saranorn, and they knew that although they had the advantage in numbers, they could easily be faced with the penalty of death if they were not careful.

When Mitsunari saw that Cassius had awakened, he was quick to move in front of him in order to protect him. "*GO! GET OUT OF HERE!*" shouted Mitsunari, and Cassius had no time to thank him. Instead, he did as he was told and ran to Sir Hadrian. Azrad went after him . . . but he was stopped and forced to defend himself from the blinding speed of Kazemaru . . . If they wanted to leave, they'd have to kill the Sarakotan, and such a task could not be done without their own blood being spilled in the process. Cassius looked back at Mitsunari and then to Sathelia . . . and he was torn. He couldn't leave her here . . . but he'd have to. "*GO! I WILL DEFEND HER!*"

Cassius's heart was defeated then, outmatched by his instinct to live, and thus he was forced to trust that Mitsunari would indeed keep her safe, and he felt that there was nothing he could ever do to repay the sacrifice that Mitsunari was about to make.

"*Cassius! We must leave,*" said Sir Hadrian, tugging on the arm of the prince, and the two were forced to flee and leave Mitsunari behind.

When they were gone, living mattered little to Mitsunari, and if he was to die here, he would do so in peace, for he'd die knowing that he had followed his heart and that he'd made the right decision.

"So, your word means fuck all," said Azrad

"When we're done with you, we'll go for the boy and break the old shit that stands by his side. And maybe after that, we'll come back here to pay the girl a visit," said Connell, and his laugh was vile, and made Mitsunari even more desperate to succeed now, for he didn't wish to think what they'd do to the prince and the girl if he was to let them leave this room alive. He could not. And if he was destined to die at this very moment, he'd take them with him.

Cassius and Sir Hadrian ran out into the darkness of night with a trail of bodies and blood behind them. They stood on a bridge that ran over a river and led them to an area behind the palace, and the furious sound of the water below was joined by the laughter of thunder in the sky. It began to rain. As the two fled across the bridge, the rain dug into their eyes, blinding them as the wind battered their bones, and in the veil of shadow that had swallowed the world, Cassius felt something blunt drive into his gut. He fell back and smashed his head on the stone parapet. Thick streams of blood ran through his hair, and the last image he saw was the figure of Ivan standing atop the opposite parapet and looking down at the two of them. And then there was nothing but darkness . . . as if the night had swallowed him.

Ivan wasted no time talking and instead, he rushed forward towards Sir Hadrian, and his speed was something borne through the notions of panic—he wanted to end this fight quickly. Even in the blinding rain, Sir Hadrian followed his attacks and parried each of them before drawing the hilt of his sword back and returning a thrust to the chest of Ivan and then chaining his first attack with three others. But the sabre of Ivan was quicker than the normal broadsword that Sir Hadrian was trained in fighting against, and so Ivan's counter attacks were swift and deadly. A single blow touched the forearm of Sir Hadrian, not enough to truly injure him, but it was enough to make the knight doubt himself. However, the footwork of the knight would not be beaten. Such an ability was the result of decades of experience, something that Ivan could not match, nor would he ever.

The duel was not only a test of skill, but it was also one of endurance, and Sir Hadrian's health crippled his ability to prolong the fight . . . and it was only getting worse with each minute. He could feel it: the tightness in his chest as if his ribs were about to snap open, the cruel dizziness, it was all catching up to him now. He knew that he didn't have long until he'd be forced to suffer the true symptoms of his condition, and so he too wished for this to end quickly. Sir Hadrian looked over towards Cassius and knelt by his side, checking for a pulse—he was alive. And when his doubts had been put to rest, Sir Hadrian unbuckled his sword belt and threw the scabbard to the side, for this . . . this would be his final fight. Ivan did the same, and he ripped away his elvish robes until he stood shirtless, and the burnt and scarred flesh of his body soaked up the rain. In one hand, he carried his sabre, but in the other, he held a whip. Such a weapon was unleashed and was swung as if he had managed to harness the lighting that painted the world above them. Ivan's motions were adjusted to that of the whip, and his body was like water: flowing beautifully, yet sublime, as it was still very much deadly. His hair was soaked, and it hung over his face, covering it partly, and Ivan then bared his teeth, like an animal forced to revert to its instinctual knowledge of killing—the man was ready to deal out death. Yet so was the knight.

When Sathelia awoke, she awoke to the feeling of blood on her cheeks. It was warm; thus, she knew it was still fresh. It covered the walls. It dyed the sheets. Blood was everywhere, and the smell of it all nearly made her vomit. She managed to crawl to her bed where she could see a better view of it all. The bodies of Mitsunari and Connell were propped up against her dresser . . . but Connell's head had been cut clean off by the jaws of Kazemaru. The head had gone nearly purple now as the blood had been drained, and his mouth gaped wide, as if the shock was still very present. Her defender had been defeated. Mitsunari's eyes were closed, and he looked to be at peace. Then, she heard the grunting; someone was still alive. When she sat up, she winced. Her head was still in pain, but she was able to look over the edge of her bed to see Azrad crawling towards her, and he left smeared tracks of his own skin and blood behind him. She screamed and leaped backwards, but by then Azrad was on his feet, yet barely. He toppled onto her bed and crawled over to her, shouting, and spitting.

"ALL OF THIS OVER SOME FUCKING BITCH!"

His hands were wrapped around her throat, and he began to squeeze before throwing her off the bed. She cried and shook as she searched for something to defend herself with. The foot of one of her tables had been broken off in the fight, and she armed herself with it and wielded her weapon, but fear rendered her powerless against her attacker. *"No one is here to come rescue you, you little shit! I'm gonna cut your pretty little throat now, but it's a shame that Cassius won't be here to watch it happen. Oh, how I'd love to see the look on his face!"*

He got down on all fours and crept forwards, grabbing the inside her thighs and forcing her to his will. She swung her wooden weapon, and it smote the side of his head and cracked open, sending splinters into the air. But it didn't stop him, only infuriated him more. *"COME HERE."* He roared in her face, spitting, and snarling like a lion, and his knife pressed against her throat. Sathelia closed her eyes, ready to die, thinking that if she just shut her eyes, she'd realize that it was all a dream and that father would be alive and well, and that she'd be able to express her love for Cassius.

She shut her eyes.

Hoping.

Hoping.

Hoping that it was no more than a bad dream.

But this was no dream, and blood sprayed across her face in red dots. But she was not dead. Azrad's mouth gaped wide open . . . and the blade of Kazemaru protruded through his mouth with thick strings of blood running down it. Then, it disappeared, sliding out the way it had come in. Azrad's body toppled to the ground in a spasm of twitches, and Mitsunari fell to one knee before the princess. Guards flooded in the room. Wraithenor attended to the king first, but when he saw Sathelia alive, he rushed to her side, wiping away the blood from her cheeks while the other guardsmen saw to their king.

"Wraithenor," she said, but her voice was weak, "you must save this man. He is dying," she said as she pointed towards Mitsunari. The Saranorn collapsed to the ground, and Kazemaru fell from his hands.

Sir Hadrian Blackwood ripped his elvish attire and threw it aside, revealing his gnarled physique that had worn through time but was still strong and athletic. Scars were scattered along his body as well—trophies and mementos of past wars.

"When all light has died, and its ashes have spread to the wind, the seeds of dawn begin to sprout, and with the dawn comes the day, and with the day, thus is brought the light," whispered Sir Hadrian to himself, and he raised his sword into the air, and when it reached its pinnacle, it began to glow. It gave off a powerful illumination that fought back the darkness, as if it had been dipped in an ocean of starlight. He then lowered it, and the light made his face glow, and now the destructive forces within him were more visible, but his malice was contained, it was composed.

"*Come forth! I want to see if the tales about you are true, Blackwood! SHOW ME!*"

Sir Hadrian indulged him and charged him with a surprising agility in his body. Ivan kept him at bay with the swooping motions of his whip that were difficult to see. The whip cracked and split open Hadrian's right cheek, but this did not stop him. Thrice more the crack of the whip was heard and thrice more he was split open. But once more Ivan snapped the end of his whip . . . and it was caught . . . and it was cut. Sir Hadrian's strength could not have been envisioned, and he pulled what was left of the whip away from Ivan but did not give him room for respite, forcing him to go blade against blade.

Steel against steel.

Skill against skill.

Hadrian swung upwards across his body and caught Ivan by surprise with an elbow to the nose, breaking it. Ivan retreated. He touched the blood that came from his nose and licked it, savouring the taste of adrenaline—the taste of life itself. They crossed swords again, and with each strike, Ivan noticed some sort of heat emanating from his foe's weapon. He had never seen something like this before . . . Was it . . . magic? But there was no time to ponder. The pace of the duel only increased, and Hadrian raised his sword and brought it down with every intention of killing, and his attack crashed against Ivan's sabre, clattering the steel, and sending sparks flying through the air. Ivan saw Hadrian's face: a cold and a malicious light flickered in his eyes. One sword pushed against the other, and the two of them were locked together, staring deep into each other's souls, trying to see if they could spot any iota of hidden fear. Ivan brought his knee to his chest and kicked the old knight in the gut, sending him backwards and nearly toppling him. But it wasn't enough. Although, the light on his sword flickered, and his chest then felt as if he had been stabbed and it was folding on itself. The tightness was too much, and his strength began to fail him. He let out a shout of pain. Ivan saw his chance and attacked, lunging forward for the killing blow, but Hadrian brought his sword upwards to block the attack and shattered Ivan's sabre into pieces and cut him open. A long vertical line of red ran down between his pectorals. Ivan was shocked . . . he was *afraid*. He stepped back, thinking of his next move . . . but he didn't have to. Sir Hadrian's hand gripped the left side of his chest, and his breathing became violent and hoarse.

His heart had a disease. He was dying. He knew it, and he fell to his knees, looking over at Cassius, who was now returning to consciousness.

"*Aaargh*! CASSIUS!" said Hadrian, but the power in his voice had gone out and so had the light in his sword . . . so had the light in his heart. He tried desperately to fight it, to fight the pain, but it was too much. He hunched over, clinging to each breath. And then the realization came to him, like a changing of the seasons. This was it. These were his final moments. Ivan stood over him, holding the knight's sword, but Hadrian did not care. No. Rather, he spent his final moments looking over at Cassius, looking over the son he wished he had, and his last thoughts were grateful.

He was grateful to have lived such a life.

He was grateful.

He was at peace.

Ivan brought the blade down, and Sir Hadrian Blackwood, the Dragon of the North, was no more. Blood spread along the stone face of the bridge, and to his surprise, Ivan fell silent. He *could* speak. But he did not. He thought the least he could do was respect such a man, for it had been a good fight, one he'd always remember. The melodious sound of the rain was unbroken and infinite, and in the moments of silence, he listened to the song of the wild water that fell from the sky. The calmness seeped into him, and he allowed himself to soak it all up before turning towards Cassius.

The prince was delirious and ignorant of the surrounding world, but when Ivan's hand clutched the flesh of his throat, he was forced to come back to reality. There he was . . . dead. When he saw the body of Sir Hadrian, he tried to scream, but Ivan silenced the boy's terror and anguish by squeezing harder and harder around Cassius's neck. Then, he lifted him up so that his back was leaning over the edge of the parapet. Cassius's hand reached out to him, forming some feeble claw that could do *nothing* to stop what was coming.

"What is dead is never lost. May Death tell you tales of peace, for there are few of them in a world as cruel as this. Farewell, Cassius. Farewell, *my king*," said Ivan, and he pushed Cassius over the edge, and the prince fell into the darkness.

✴

The morning was grey, and the riverbed was kept asleep under a sheet of mist. Cassius's legs were broken—bent in unnatural ways, but still, he was numb to the pain. In fact, he could not feel anything below his waistline. The jelly-like structure of his eyes soaked in all the rain they could before Cassius made any attempt to move . . . but alas, he could not. Looking to his right, he saw a trail of blood on the rocks from where he had fallen and above him was the bridge. It seemed so close, yet so far away, as if he had been vanquished into a realm of his own and was unable to return. Cassius looked back over and to his legs, and there, standing before him, was Vandulin, cloaked in the morning mist. The Sage relieved himself of his hood and knelt beside the boy and smiled, but there was an eagerness . . . and almost an excitement in that grin.

"Come," said the Sage, "we have much to do."

CPSIA information can be obtained
at www.ICGtesting.com
Printed in the USA
BVHW032119170422
634561BV00004B/25